VALIANT THE FEW

Len Ferraguzzi

For George Valli,

My longest tenured friend.
Thanks for being a lifetime buddy.
All the best,

[signature]

29 September 2016

First Edition: February 2016

Printed in the United States of America

ISBN: 9781939237-42-2

Published by Suncoast Digital Press, Inc.
Sarasota, Florida, USA

Cover art by Allison Daigle

Dedication

My cousin, Pvt. Joe Panciera, USMC; 2nd Battalion,
3rd Marine Regiment, 3rd Marine Division. KIA Bougainville,
Solomon Islands, November 5, 1943.

My brother, Sgt. Dave Ferraguzzi, US Army; 2nd Battalion,
8th Infantry Regiment, 4th US Intantry Division.
WIA Vietnam, 1967-1968.

My son, Captain Lee Ferraguzzi, USMC; 1st Battalion,
1st Marine Regiment, 1st Marine Division.
Desert Storm-Kuwait, 1991.

And to all who have worn the uniform in war and peace, to all
who showed up when their country called.

Acknowledgments

Many thanks to Allison Daigle for designing and creating the artwork for the front cover of *Valiant The Few*.

I am grateful for the attention to detail and guidance from my editor/publishing partner, Barbara Dee with Suncoast Digital Press.

Contents

"Many the brave, valiant the few."

CHAPTER I

GARAND

DATE: FRIDAY 6 MARCH 1942

TIME: 1030 HOURS

LOCATION: KD RANGE #1
US MARINE BASE
QUANTICO, VIRGINIA

"Gentlemen, what you are looking at is the US Rifle Caliber .30 M1, an air-cooled, gas-operated, clip-fed semi-automatic shoulder weapon. In some circles it is referred to as the 'Garand' after its inventor, John Cantius Garand."

The speaker slowly rotated the rifle above his head for the twenty-seven Marine field-grade officers sitting in the bleachers to see. He wore a weathered campaign hat and starched fatigue uniform bearing the chevrons of an Army staff sergeant, three stripes up and a single rocker underneath. Squinting through the midmorning glare, Staff Sergeant Woody Luzak continued his lecture.

"Think of it as a quicker-shooting Springfield. In the hands of a trained rifleman, the M1 will provide the firepower of three!" He stared into the eyes of a front-row Marine Major repositioning his butt on the sagging bench seat. The Major peered back with a distinct "show me" skepticism.

Woody ignored the group and strode closer to the Major, for the moment focusing his comments into the officer's impassive gray eyes. "And its accuracy is equal to, or approaches the Springfield!" Without changing expression, the Major slowly shook his head from side to side. The disbelief and silent challenge was obvious. In Woody's mind, the Marine Corps wouldn't recognize a good idea if it leaped through their trousers and bit them on their collective dick. This was the third group to whom Woody had presented the M1 that year in a frustrating attempt by the War Department to convince the Corps that the Garand, already adopted by the Army, was the single greatest development in small arms since the invention of the percussion cap.

Christ, if the Marine General Staff won't accept this 'Army idea,' then what in the hell is going to break down this Major's resistance, Woody thought. Last summer, he had been temporarily assigned to the Army Ordnance Center headquartered at the Aberdeen Proving Grounds in Maryland, where huge tracts of the base's 72,962 acres were devoted solely to developing and testing experimental weaponry and vehicles. Now he was a virtual one-man road show, spouting the wonders of the very equipment he had helped subject to rigorous field tests.

Backing away from the bleachers, Staff Sergeant Woody Luzak shifted to a crude olive-drab table braced by clumsy two-by-four plank legs. On it were three military rifles of various sorts. At the base of each stock, a bomb-flame insignia stenciled in white was evident with the capital letters "I' and "O"— the symbol represented Ordnance, the letters identified its custodian, the Information Office. V-shaped cuts in two wooden blocks supported each weapon at the lower stock and forearm grip.

He rested the M1 on the remaining pair of blocks and effortlessly snatched another rifle from its berth. Holding it at the balance, he continued to lecture. "The Japanese Arisaka. Bolt-action. Twenty-five caliber, or more specifically, point two five six caliber. Five-shot clip. Nonadjustable sights."

Pointing it skyward, he manipulated the bolt, clicked the trigger, and effected a sour expression. "It's a piece of Jap crap!" For the first time the group showed some sign of being alive as the officers exhaled a muffled laugh. Luzak returned the Arisaka to its cradle and lifted the next rifle.

"The Karbiner 98. Pride of the Wehrmacht. Manual bolt. Thirty-one caliber. Also a five-shot clip and nonadjustable sights. In my opinion, it's not up to the standards of other German weaponry. Let's say it's the Krauts' improved answer to the Arisaka, but still sadly lacking." He dropped it in its blocks.

Stretching their necks like one huge bleacher beast, the Marines were anticipating the description of the next rifle—the revered Springfield, hero of Belleau Wood, Cantigny and the Marne. Hoisting it, Luzak elevated his voice to a higher decibel. "I don't have to tell you what this is. Up until now, it has been the finest, mass-produced military rifle in the world, better than the Enfield, better than 'em all. Bolt-action, five-round clip, thirty caliber—but with adjustable sights!" The emphasis was on *adjustable*.

"It is the current standard shoulder weapon of the Marines and the Navy and has been since 1903, long before this soldier's birth date. Almost FORTY YEARS in service!" He let it sink in. "We're all aware of the high premium the Corps places on accuracy and the old axiom that one should never, ever, sacrifice accuracy for speed. Well, now you can have both. Someone once said you can't have your cake and eat it, too."

Luzak's free hand patted the M1 beside him. "Well, sirs, with the Garand here, it's like getting two pieces of cake." He paused again, scanning the mass of painfully serious uniforms to detect any semblance of acceptance. *Would any of you statues want to concede that maybe, just perhaps, someone might have built a better mousetrap?*

As in the two previous trips to Quantico, Staff Sergeant Luzak, hardware in tow, had arrived with the Army's Ordnance Information officer, Captain T.S. Longley. Instead of conducting the lecture, Longley would introduce Luzak to the group and then melt away. Standing to the right of the bleachers, Longley now made eye contact with Luzak and paternally nodded his understanding and encouragement.

As far as the Captain's superiors in Aberdeen were concerned, Longley was personally making these presentations in a tireless effort to sell the M1 to all non-believers. Woody rubbed his nose and without display of displeasure for Longley's laziness, dutifully returned the nod. Longley had discovered that Staff Sergeant Luzak's take-charge nature and persuasively articulate arguments were more forceful than his own. He rationalized that Luzak's success in proselytizing M1 "converts" would speed up his own promotion. So work the minds of insecure men.

Woodrow Joseph Luzak was born in 1912 in the rugged Lake Michigan steel town of Indiana Harbor, Indiana. His parents were Slovak immigrants who, fourteen years earlier, had departed Bratislava and the smothering Austro-Hungarian Empire for the promise of America. Woody, the youngest of the three Luzak children, was named after Woodrow Wilson, who at that time was the Democratic Party's candidate for the 28th US presidency. Just before his eleventh birthday, the family moved to Pittsburgh where, less than a year later, his mother inexplicably passed away suddenly after church service.

Pop, old beyond his forty-seven years, died of influenza in 1924. So Woody's sister, Stella, willingly washed and ironed his clothes, prepared meals, provided comfort, and saw to it that Woody hit the books to earn his high school diploma. Love, common sense, and good values were Stella's most important gifts to her little brother. Though only nine years older, she was the proverbial rock.

Following graduation in June of 1930, Woody Luzak enlisted in the US Army, seven years after big brother Tony had signed a similar form for the Marine Corps. Not quite six feet tall and a wiry 182 pounds, Woody was now a career non-commissioned officer stationed at Aberdeen.

"Sirs, we have arranged to put on a bit of a demonstration using expert riflemen from the Marine Rifle Team. The purpose is to clearly convince you of the M l's superiority and not, I repeat *not*, to denigrate the trusty 1903 Springfield." *Christ, I'm talking about the Springfield like it's St. Francis of Assisi.*

Off to the left of the stands, Marine Gunnery Sergeant Ned Collins signaled Luzak that he and his six expert riflemen were ready. Woody barely bobbed his head and on cue, Collins snapped to attention, immediately barking his commands in short, sharp inflections. "Detail, ten hut!"

The six men, who had been standing at ease, clicked erect. All, including Collins, sported a traditional broad-brimmed campaign hat with pointed crown, along with a starched and tailored utility uniform. They were the Corps' finest shots, proven members of the crack USMC Rifle Team.

"At a trail, double time—march!" The tiny formation quickly moved out in step. When they arrived directly in front of the bleachers, he ordered "Mark time, march." They slowed their pace and marched precisely in place. "Detail, halt!" Now it was obvious that the first three Marines carried Springfields and the others, Garands. "Staff Sergeant Luzak, the detail is present."

Though Luzak was of lesser rank, Collins treated him with equal respect. "Thank you Gunnery Sergeant Collins," Luzak said. "Please post your Marines."

"Detail, about face." They smartly pivoted 180 degrees in a single smooth reaction. "Post!" At the order, the six broke from ranks, noiselessly trotted to their individual firing points, and began adjusting their rifle slings.

"Staff Sergeant Luzak, the detail is in position and will respond to your commands for the remainder of this exercise." Master Gunny Collins wore a thin smile, perceptible only to Luzak.

Woody liked Ned Collins. He liked him a lot. Nobody, not even Woody himself, knew as much about infantry weaponry as did Ned. It wasn't easy for a twenty-six year veteran warhorse to admit the M l's claim as the preeminent military rifle in the world. But Ned recognized its remarkable firepower, accuracy, and ultimate killing potential. His own endorsement, though, had fallen on deaf ears in the Quantico bureaucracy. Woody felt that even if Ned were Commandant, he still could not ram it through the layers of procurement desk jockeys. One thing for sure, Ned's sharpshooters, proud of their marksmanship, would make the effort to aim straight and not attempt to sway the results in favor of either rifle. Ego guaranteed impartiality. The demo would be fair.

Facing the bleachers again, Woody addressed the crowd. "Sirs, from left to right, posts one, two and three will each fire a standard Springfield five-round clip. Posts four, five and six, an eight-round M1 clip. One hundred yards will be the distance."

He turned around crisply and faced down-range. Six white targets appeared at the "known distance" of 100 yards, hence the name "KD" range.

"Detail, you will fire at the standing position. Lock and load one clip of ball ammunition." The Springfield and Garand shooters inserted the respective clips, the former slamming home their bolts with the heels of their hands while the M l's spring-driven action did it automatically.

"Detail, sight your targets and commence firing on my command…Fire!" Almost simultaneously, six shots exploded the air. Legs spread, right elbows up and parallel to the ground, each of the three Marines firing the Garand rapidly squeezed off eight rounds in under ten seconds, then came to port arms. The Springfield firers were still hand working their bolts, reacquiring the target and shooting. The last Springfield finally assumed the port arms position at the twenty-one second mark.

In the pits, the KD crew was grateful for warm weather this early in the year. They reeled in the perforated targets, spotted the hits, and returned them so they were visible to the up-range audience still buzzing from the fusillade. Master Gunny Collins, peering through a tripod-mounted spotting scope, yelled out the scores. "Post number one, five in the center circle. Post number two, five in the center circle."

As he shouted results, Collins would traverse the scope a few degrees until he locked in on the next target. His tone was matter-of-fact, never attempting to dramatize the moment. "Post number three, five in the center circle. Post number four, eight in the center circle. Post number five, eight in the center circle. Post number six, eight in the center circle."

Spontaneously, two, or perhaps three, spectators applauded and another politely followed. But the anemic ovation hardly cut the morning air. The acrid smell of exploded gunpowder was more in evidence.

"Sirs," Woody bellowed, "each M1 scored eight bullseyes in ten seconds, while the Springfields each registered five bulls within twenty-one seconds. Two things come immediately to mind. First, Marine marksmanship is outstanding! And second, the M1 rifle in the hands of a squad of such marksmen could tear the hell out of a Jap platoon. Speed and accuracy are compatible and available at last." *I wish I hadn't made that last comment. Beginning to sound like a snake oil salesman.*

As the morning progressed through noon, the shooters fired prone at three-hundred yards and again at five-hundred, with virtually the same results. At five-hundred yards, one of the Garands placed a round slightly outside of the inner circle. The overall conclusion though, was predictable. During the subsequent question-and-answer series, every speaker routinely prefaced his query with how impressive the demonstration was before challenging Woody with concerns he had heard before.

Q: "What is the jamming incidence?"

A: "Negligible, sir."

Q: "Will it hold up in the tropics?"

A: "We're confident, sir. Like all firearms, sand is the great enemy. Keep it maintained and free of grit for maximum effectiveness."

Q: "With that quick rate of fire, won't the average rifleman constantly run out of ammo?"

A: "Fire discipline has always been a virtue, sir. The same point could have been raised when muzzleloaders were replaced by the miracle of the breech-loading rifle."

Q: "Isn't it heavier than what we're used to carrying?"

A: "Perhaps I neglected to mention the Springfield is eight point six nine pounds, while the M1 is only nine point zero pounds. One-third of a pound is hardly a back-breaker, sir."

Q: "Won't we be likely to suffer excessive thumb injuries while inserting the clip?"

A: "True, it is tricky at first, but that's why we **train** people. Through rote comes mastery, sir."

And so it went. Should ninety-nine reasons exist to embrace this extraordinary rifle, capable of making its wielder the dominant battlefield warrior, the bleacher beast would probe for the one excuse to delay its inevitable acceptance. If there were any believers, and no doubt there were some, they kept their mouths shut. Did this reluctance stem from service rivalry, stupidity, or the emperor's clothes syndrome? Woody surmised it was simply a question of *don't make waves*. Orthodoxy, by its very definition, resists change, even when change decisively assures achievement of one's fundamental mission…to kill the enemy with speed and efficiency.

Light rain slowed travel during the return trip to Aberdeen later that afternoon. The 1939 brown Ford sedan marked with Army livery continually shifted between second and third gear to accommodate the traffic flow. Sitting cross-legged on the rear seat, Captain T. S. Longley rambled on about his perceptions of the Quantico *indoctrination*, as he privately preferred to call it. He felt this batch of Marines was *more flexible in their attitude to 'our' Garand. Yes, more flexible… that's what I'll suggest in my report to Colonel Wallace.* Straightening his knees, he half-turned to Luzak.

"You can see the difference." Woody peered out of the side window through free-form rivulets of spattered rain inching down the glass. He paid little attention to the captain's self-serving analysis of the day's activity. The dull chatter blended with the hum of rolling tires to form a numbing background for his drifting thoughts.

It had been three months since the murderous Japanese attacks at Pearl Harbor and the Philippines. Roughly 2,400 Americans had been killed, and the mighty battleships of the Pacific Fleet destroyed in a horrid, single, Honolulu morning. But the Philippine onslaught had been an ongoing battle of attrition. Understrength, under-equipped American and Filipino forces were being driven into the narrow cylinder of the Bataan Peninsula by a merciless Japanese piston.

Woody knew his brother Tony, serving with the 4th Marines, was there somewhere…perhaps dead or wounded. Maybe he was hanging on to the very thread of life at this instant.

Tony, my thoughts are with you, big brother. You're too ornery for the Nips to handle. Survive, Tony, survive!

Lately his brother's chiseled face appeared in his mind's eye just as it did now. Sometimes it was more handsome than he remembered, Hollywood handsome. Other days it loomed out of the darkness, unshaven and sweaty with a fixed stare that reached beyond Woody.

In a blink, Tony vanished and was replaced by a flashy five-foot-two-inch strawberry blonde in ebony patent leather high heels, liquid red lipstick, and charcoal-black flared skirt cut above the knees. A soft yellow satin blouse opened at the throat, framing a necklace of shiny onyx beads that matched her earrings. Woody chuckled inside. That's how he liked to think of Swifty, the way she looked the first time they had gone dancing. When she opened the door all decked out in yellow and black, he suggested her likeness to a two-thousand-dollar bumble bee. Her immediate but good natured retort was, "Then don't get too close to the stinger, big boy. I wouldn't want you to suffer on our first date." That was Swifty—witty, brassy, opinionated, the livest of wires.

And, for Woody, Nancy Swift was loving and caring, the person whom he shared the deepest intimacies of his life. She had become more than a girlfriend, more than a Saturday night movie partner. Their mutual feelings had moved beyond passion to a loftier bond. Marriage was not an unreachable prospect, Woody mused, but the uncertainty of war had put lives on hold throughout the world and theirs was no exception. *As soon as I can dump off these rifles at the armory I think I'm gonna make a bee line to the palace of the bumble bee.* Longley continued his rhetorical babble, heard by neither driver nor passenger.

CHAPTER II
SAN LEO BRIDGE

DATE: FRIDAY 6 MARCH 1942

LOCATION: CORREGIDOR ISLAND, PHILIPPINES

Corregidor, a fortress island bulges from the warm sea like a cephalic tadpole. Newspapers and magazine articles portrayed it as *The Rock* and *Gibraltar of the Philippines!* But perhaps in these desperate hours, *Alamo of the Pacific* would have been the more accurate metaphor. Lying off Bataan's southern beaches, it guarded the entrance to historic Manila Bay. The latter's namesake capital city was positioned twenty-five miles to the northeast.

Though only 1,735 acres, Corregidor was an important strategic sliver of real estate due to its situation at the narrowest chokepoint between the big bay and the South China Sea. Nautical traffic, whether commercial, military or pleasure, entering and departing Manila harbor, was compelled to sail within range of its massive guns.

Falling along an east-west axis, Corregidor's most prominent natural feature was located at the western end, known as Topside. Over six hundred feet in elevation, Topside's dominant height commanded a 360-degree sweep of its three fortified sister islands (Caballo, El Fraile, and Carabao), the peninsula of Bataan, and miles of surrounding blue water. To the immediate east of the high ground sat Malinta Hill, whose bowels boasted a cavernous network of man-made reinforced concrete tunnels and vaults including a three-hundred bed hospital.

Over the years, Malinta Tunnel had been skillfully constructed, electrified, and ventilated by the Army Corps of Engineers. The twenty-foot-high central tunnel alone reached over a quarter mile in length, through which rolled the island's electric railroad. Almost fifty lateral corridor rooms branched from either the main tunnel or its subsidiary spines. The Tadpole's skinny upper tail, hardly above sea level, was referred to as Bottomside. It tapered to the slightly more elevated Kindley Field and Monkey Point which, in turn, extended toward a tinier tip of land, Hooker Point, the island's eastern most extremity. From skull to tail, the entire island stretched but three and a half miles.

After months of vicious Japanese bombing, Corregidor's once lush vegetation had all but disappeared and what remained was a pulverized, blackened spermatozoa coughing dust and smoke. Yet at fortified points around the perimeter, vigilant Army cannoneers and machine gunners stood by their guns, ready to repel Lieutenant General Homma's 14th Japanese Army and Lieutenant General Orata's 5th Air Group. The Tadpole's bite, teethed with massive twelve-inch coast artillery pieces and twelve-inch mortars, had the capability to inflict brutal pain on any intruder.

Housed inside the walls of the Malinta labyrinth were the headquarters of General Douglas MacArthur's beleaguered command and the communications nerve center for defense of the Philippines. All messages to and from President Franklin Roosevelt and the Chiefs of Staff in Washington, D.C., and elsewhere for that matter, were dispatched via Malinta. MacArthur, along with his family and staff, had sailed from Manila aboard the steamer *Don Esteban* to Corregidor on Christmas Eve, 1941. Resolute Philippine President Manuel Quezon had arrived earlier that very same day.

Now two-and-a-half months later, under direct order of Roosevelt, a reluctant MacArthur somberly prepared to evacuate Corregidor on March 12 by way of a mini-flotilla of four US Navy patrol torpedo boats. The plan is to race across dangerous open seas to the principal southern island of Mindanao, where they will board Army Air Corps B-17's for Australia—to reorganize, re-fit, and live to fight another day.

Meanwhile, on Bataan, troops of the starving, disease-ridden US Army's Philippine Division continue their valiant struggle to buy time so the American war machine can catch its breath. The remnant Philippine Division is composed primarily of the US 31st Infantry Regiment, with two companion regiments (the 45th and 57th) of Filipino Scouts (PS). The Scouts, though Philippine nationals, were considered part of the U.S. Army.

Division Artillery is made up of the 12th US Field Artillery Brigade's three small-gun PS battalions. Engineers, Ordnance, Quartermaster, Signal, and other divisional combat support units are now fighting as infantry. Another key outfit is the US Army's 26th Cavalry Regiment (PS) which, like other engaged units, fought with great distinction before pulling back from the broader Luzon land mass to the constriction of Bataan. Battered and exhausted, the horse soldiers actually fought a mounted engagement before having to destroy their chargers. Now, but a ghost of what they were, the 26th carries the fight on foot. This unit too is primarily composed of Filipino Scouts.

Standing in support of the soldiers is the USMC's understrength 4th Marine Regiment, the "China Marines." It had arrived from a semi-permanent garrison in Shanghai prior to the *commencement of hostilities*. The Marines safeguarded the peninsula's port of Mariveles, across the strait from The Rock as well as the island itself. And so the 4th Marines had become a vital part of the overall force that christened itself "The Battling Bastards of Bataan." Philippine Army (PA) forces, heroically fighting under command of senior U.S. officers, have also withdrawn approximately nine attrited divisions to the mountainous Bataan redoubt. No one is quite sure of their precise number, but earlier estimates for the combined US/ Philippine Bataan force placed it at 80,000 troops. But that was New Year's Day. Since then, the gruesome mixture of intense combat, malaria, dengue fever, dysentery, beriberi, infection, and starvation has weakened the defenders to a point where resistance has become a physical near-impossibility. The wicked tandem of an unkind environment and privation is destroying even the sanctity of those precious lulls when the shelling subsides.

Back in mid-February, combined U.S. and Filipino troops had stopped the Japs at the Orion-Bagac defensive line, heaping huge losses on the stubborn enemy and capturing tons of equipment. The battered but dogged Allies were full of fight after this last gasp victory, but over the following four weeks, lack of food and malaria (with little quinine to deal with it) reduced effectiveness to a pittance of its original level. The realization that no hope for reinforcement is in the offing and their imminent human sacrifice has pushed troop morale to its lowest ebb.

Standing at the mouth of Malinta's north or "hospital" entrance, bareheaded Marine Gunnery Sergeant Anton "Tony" Luzak shook a humid cigarette from his pack of Chesterfields. He fed it between his lips and snapped a flame from a small inlaid lighter adorned by a ferocious Chinese dragon. A similar dragon crawled up his left calf, the artwork of an ancient, bespectacled tattooist in Nantung, miles up the Yangtze from his old Shanghai duty station.

Tony sucked on the cigarette as he stared skyward. Dull pain still pulsed through his left elbow where a jagged mortar fragment had pierced flesh and bone five days past. Doc Reisman had pieced it back together while a determined Army nurse removed steel splinters from the rest of his arm, now immobilized by a white plaster cast. The night air represented a pleasant change of environment from the stifling confines below. Turning the cigarette lighter in his good hand, Tony examined the engraved image. *Old Dragon Leg*, he thought, recalling what Salty had called him when they caroused Shanghai's plentiful slop chutes.

The Yankee Dollar stretched a long way for China Marines. Beer, whiskey and Chinese women dressed in slinky western dress were the most prevalent vices. But there were other perks concomitant with duty in the Orient. Distinctively tailored uniforms brandishing embroidered stripes and gaudy under-cuffs were of top quality and cheap to be had. Seven years in China had spoiled Tony to the point where he wondered if he could ever reacclimatize himself to stateside duty. It was a pointless consideration now as he and his fellow China Marines savagely battled to exist—both as a unit and as individuals.

Only last Friday, Gunnery Sergeant Luzak, 4th Marines, commanded a provisional machine gun platoon, part of a larger reinforced company "on loan" to the Army's Bataan front. First Lieutenant George Riley, the platoon leader, had developed a malarial fever which almost broke the thermometer. Shivering and screaming unintelligibly, he offered no resistance when a Navy Corpsman placed him on a canvas litter headed for the overloaded field hospital. That left Luzak running the platoon, which on that day existed only on paper. Most of the gun crews had been fed out piecemeal to support an Army infantry battalion farther up the line.

Tony was circling roster names and scribbling notations on a small wirebound pad in a vain attempt to reconfirm where various crews were posted, when a scrawny runner from Headquarters Command half-trotted up the dirt road. Holding one hand on the stock of a Springfield slung from his shoulder, he used the other to steady his pie plate helmet from bouncing.

"Gunnery Sergeant Luzak?" he inquired, slightly out of breath. "That's me."

"Captain Moran says to get a machine gun up on hill five niner four to cover the approach to the San Leo Bridge. He thinks the goddamn Japs might try to sneak in there."

"Christ, I thought the engineers had blown all the bridges!"

"Not yet. I think the brass wants to wait. You know, in case we pull off a counter attack or something."

"Counter attack, my sweet Slovak ass!" Luzak growled.

The runner shrugged. He handed Tony a frayed and filthy map with pencil indications covering the margins. In the right, upper quadrant sat "Hill 594" with an orange grease-penciled "X" marking a contour point near the summit.

"Captain says you're to set your gun up at the X. There's a three-man observation team up there now waiting for you."

"Did he say how much time I've got?"

"Gunny, he said to move out most ricky tick."

Tony gave the runner a hardboiled stare before asking, "What's your name, Marine?"

"Cassidy. Pfc. Cassidy. Galveston, Texas," he added with a smile.

"Well, Pfc. Cassidy-Galveston-fucking-Texas, you tell the captain its uh," Luzak held up his wrist and looked through the condensation collected inside the Benrus' crystal. "Damn humidity's fogged this thing up. Okay, it's zero-nine-four-two hours. Tell him if the Japs don't kill us on the way up, it'll take four hours to make the hump. If that observation team has a radio, let 'em know we'll be there around fourteen hundred, so they should keep their fingers off the trigger. Know what I mean?" He spit to indicate the conversation was complete.

Cassidy nodded. "Aye, aye, Gunny." He wheeled and headed back, his voice trailing off, "And good luck."

Within twenty minutes, seven Marines and a Filipino guide (ahead on the point) were pushing their way through a break in the thick foliage. The scout, a man named Esteban Sota from Manila, kept about three hundred yards to the front, pausing periodically to read the trees. An occasional breeze and cackling birds flitted among leaves of enormous size. Two flat canteens, machete, and a smaller knife hung from the ammo-pouched belt around Sota's waist. A khaki soft cap prohibited insects from seeking rest atop his dank pate. The scout was a small man, and the Springfield he supported diagonally across the back accentuated his diminutive size.

To Sota's rear, the Marines labored in the morning heat, toting a Browning .30 caliber heavy machine gun and ammo chests. Leading the group, Gunny Luzak carried a pair of chests, each holding a 250-round webbed feed belt weighing about twenty-one pounds apiece. This was in addition to the dangling Thomson sub-machine gun and ammo magazines.

Next in line came the three-man gun crew headed by Corporal Lyons, the gunner, muscling a fifty-two pound tripod. Assistant gunner, Lance Corporal Mooney, shouldered the water-cooled gun and pintle, itself a hefty forty-one pounds. The crew's ammo bearer, Private Brower, hauled a chest in each hand with a third strapped to his back. A spare barrel completed the load.

The uphill struggle over the narrow trail demanded both strength and concentration. Low-riding branches, exposed roots, and frequent mud holes had converted the trail into a dangerous obstacle course. The crew exchanged their weapon components each time Luzak called for a break. Weight exchange wasn't that important, but the opportunity to relax strained muscles and substitute rested ones was a welcome respite. Two more Marines, loaded down with extra ammo and a water chest, followed at a tactical interval. Brutal heat coupled with the wet slime that covered their bodies made each step an exhaustive effort. Shoulder straps and belts cut raw welts, agonizing the already painful trek.

At the group's extreme rear trudged forty-five-year-old Sergeant Stanton "Salty" Waters. A veteran of the Great War (now referenced as World War I), Haiti, and the second Nicaraguan campaign (where he first met Tony Luzak), Salty Waters was one of the Old Breed. Twenty-seven years of service had seen him promoted and busted more than the Corps would care to admit. For the last three years, he had settled in at the rank of a three-stripe sergeant. By right of tenure, experience and knowledge, he should have been a Master Gunnery Sergeant by now. But Salty liked the "dollies" as he called them, and bourbon whiskey, or any reasonable substitute.

A Navy Cross winner in 1918, Waters was usually given the benefit of the doubt by superior officers in deference to his award. But he pushed the limits of their benign tolerance. In order to provide him with a "compromised" billet, he had been assigned as Luzak's Assistant Platoon Sergeant. Captain Moran reasoned that Luzak had greater control over Salty than any other Senior Non-com in Headquarters Company. Perspiration drained through his short-cropped graying hair and down the leathery face covered by four days of stubble. Luzak signaled for a break and Waters, grateful for the breather, set his ammo chests down and slumped next to them. The Gunny walked down the line and smiled.

"How they hangin', Salty?"

"I wouldn't refuse a cold beer. Got one?"

"Here, take one of these." Luzak offered the old marine a salt tablet.

Waters washed it down with a canteen swig, then rubbed his blistered palms on the wet-through utility trousers clinging to his thighs. "How far you reckon this trip is?"

Tony unfolded the creased map and studied the terrain for a few seconds. Returning it to his breast pocket he answered, "Well, cowboy, as the crow travels, it's about four miles. But this is Bataan, you know." A tight smile formed. "And with all the up-'n-down hills and meanders in this damned trail, I figure it's about double that."

Salty winced at the news. "Back home in Oklahoma, we ain't got no hills," he winked. "Four miles is four miles."

"How would you know—you haven't been to Okla-fuckin-homa in a hundred years." They both forced a laugh as Tony extended a hand to his comrade. Salty grasped it and pulled himself upright.

At thirteen hundred forty-seven hours, Esteban Sota bellied his body over the summit of Hill 594, careful not to silhouette himself. He stared below at a small gorge spanned by a rough log bridge. Underneath it, a narrow but swift river splashed its way over and around jutting boulders. The scout remained still for a few minutes, then slowly backed off and reported to Gunnery Sergeant Luzak, resting about a quarter mile to his rear.

Twenty minutes later, Luzak returned with Sota to the crest. Waiting for them was another Filipino scout, who evidently had observed Sota during the first trip. He greeted them with a toothy "gotcha" grin. The two small men engaged in rapid conversation, part Tagalog, part Spanish, with a staccato of English slang. "Okay, okay, okay," was evident more than once.

Sota explained that Emilio would lead them to the observation team concealed about 100 yards downslope. Several minutes passed before the remainder of the column linked up. Then they all proceeded on the final leg with Emilio showing the way.

"Gunnery Sergeant Luzak, sir." He offered a soft salute to the emaciated officer holding the funniest looking telescope he could ever remember seeing.

Ignoring the salute, the thin man identified himself as "Captain Howell, and this is my radio man, Corporal MacTavish." The radio operator's week-long growth of scraggly red beard gave his face a look of being well-fed, but his loose-fitting uniform provided testimony to lack of rations and fatigue beyond the norm. Red MacTavish tacitly nodded acknowledgment.

Sergeant Waters ambled over to the group and Luzak made the introductions. The four men moved to a small outcropping perhaps forty feet wide. Foliage directly below the vantage point had been hacked away, leaving a clear line of sight to both ends of the bridge. "Perfect line of fire," Salty confirmed. "I figure about three hundred and seventy-five, maybe four hundred yards at a forty-five degree angle."

"That's how I calculate it, too," Captain Howell agreed. "Corporal MacTavish cut away most of the obstructive growth, but you might want to widen it in case you need to traverse your gun a hair more."

"Aye, aye, sir." Tony responded. He gave Salty a silent *let's get it done* gesture and Waters picked up on it.

Waters craned his neck toward the haggard crew. "Gun to be mounted here." He pointed to a spot near the outcropping's rim. As they had done hundreds of times, the machine gun crew promptly moved to action. The gunner rushed forward, slamming the tripod into the hard-packed dirt. He wiggled the legs to insure the feet bit. They wouldn't slip once the heavy gun was in place. Right on his heels, the assistant gunner mechanically snapped the cumbersome Browning into the tripod cradle. Traversing clamp tight, dial clamped trunnion and elevating pins inserted and turned down. Elevating arc clamped.

The third member of the team, the ammo bearer, brought up his load and hit the deck. Mooney, the assistant, flopped down to the gun's left, popped open a canister and only awaited the signal to feed the first belt into the hungry receiver. Corporal Lyons, kneeling behind the piece, flipped the rear sight and made quick adjustments to the sight leaf and T & E. Yanking back on the bolt, he made a few checks before releasing it. *Headspace okay and so is the barrel locking spring.* He locked in the big gun on the bridge entrance across the gorge. "About four hundred yards, Salty!"

"That's my boy," the sergeant approved. "Lyons, now that the gun is secure, take a short break. Then have the boys scoop out a hole and protect this position as best you can. I don't want to be Jaybird naked if counter-fire comes in."

Later, as the men were digging in, Tony Luzak approached Howell. "Know what I'm thinking, sir?"

The captain rolled his tongue inside a hollow, sour mouth that hadn't tasted hot chow in weeks. "That this is a one-way mission?" he responded.

"Exactly, sir. Once the shooting starts, it's only a matter of time before the Nips wade the river downstream and work their way up here. Why the hell haven't we blown that goddamn bridge anyway?"

Jabbing a finger towards the bridge, Howell explained. "Hell, we didn't even know it was here until daybreak when Emilio showed me. On the map it appears as a ford. All the major bridges have been demolished, the ones that'll support motor vehicles. San Leo is a secondary bridge. However, I'm surprised it's as substantial as it is. If it wasn't there the Japs would clamber down the gorge and slop across the river. My belief is that they'll take what they think is the quickest and driest path of least resistance.

"Initially, I was going to have our howitzers zero in and take the damn bridge out. But we can do that anytime. Maybe we'll make our own luck and turn it into a killing zone, kind of a bonus. Either way we're ahead." Howell extended his lanky arm and squeezed Luzak's shoulder. "Gunny, your job is to keep San Leo Bridge clear of Japs for as long as possible. Slow 'em up. When it gets too hot to hold your position any longer, that means they'll all be stuffed up on the other side of the river, just like a collapsed telescope. I'll be observing from the crest with MacTavish. When we contact Fire Direction Control with the message, 'Grapevine Harvest,' the Army's gonna drop artillery on top of the Japs and blow the crap out of them. The doggy FDC people have had the coordinates locked in since morning. Hopefully, your group will bottleneck the Nips long enough to set the table. Once the arty starts falling, haul your gun out of here and get back to HQ Company. Any questions?"

"Semper Fi, sir." Tony showed a thumbs-up salute.

That evening, the two ammo bearers were settled in a listening post about a hundred yards to the front and downhill from the machine gun. One slept while the other stayed alert. Sleep would come easy after the day's grueling march. Back at the gun pit the crew dozed. Luzak and Waters rested in a second foxhole off to the right. Salty and Esteban had lugged a large log with twisted limbs and placed it in front of the depression. The gun crew had done the same. It provided near invisible concealment to anyone observing ahead, while providing a fair amount of cover. Esteban and Emilio had disappeared, to be in place so they could reconnoiter the bridge at sunrise. Neither would return until after dawn. Jittery listening-post sentinels were liable to shoot any movement while it was dark.

Captain Howell and MacTavish were presumably perched to the rear of them, in readiness to assess and report any impending fireworks. Afraid to noisily swat the countless insects that crawled about their necks and faces, the men casually squeezed them until a snap could be sensed between their vise-like fingertips. Bataan sits less then fifteen degrees north of the equator. *About the same as Nicaragua,* Salty figured. *Insects seem equally as vicious too. Nicaragua, Bataan, Santo Domingo, Haiti, Guantanamo—why is it they always send us to wherever there's heat and bugs? Well at least there's no rain.* Roughly four minutes later, the initial patters of water slapping floppy tropical leaves announced the coming of a greater deluge. Truly, it rained like hell for nearly two hours.

First light arrived slowly, then erupted like an exploding furnace overhead. Shafts of hot sun penetrated the jungle canopy, baking the earlier precipitation to a punishing level of humidity. The returning scouts shared an ugly breakfast of canned beans and crackers. They buried the empty tins lest every crawling creature on Luzon converge at the bivouac. Steamy utilities were barely drier than they had been during the downpour. Lyons bore a swollen red lump on his chin where a nocturnal spider had nipped away. Such are the conditions that men will endure in order to kill each other.

Approaching high noon, Corporal Lyons thought he saw a reflection near the San Leo Bridge's far approach. He nudged the others and silently pointed. Several minutes passed before a crouched soldier in shiny helmet and backpack appeared. Even at this distance the hidden Marines could identify the traditional Japanese puttees wrapping the man's calves. Moving slowly, he pushed his Arisaka out front while examining each side of the bridge. No doubt he was searching for detonating wires. *That Jap's smarter 'n we are,* thought Tony. A second soldier, probably an NCO, came into view and made a more thorough inspection of the bridge's underbelly. Lyons motioned the assistant gunner to be prepared. He glanced at Luzak whose head shook vigorously… not yet. One of the listening-post Marines slithered through the verdant undergrowth to report movement on the bridge. Luzak nodded that they were aware and waved him back to the LP. They were tense beyond anything they had ever experienced, save Salty perhaps.

The Japanese point man stealthily crossed the bridge and knelt at the ready. It was clear he was nervous. His head made rapid movements left and right as though on a swivel before he cautiously slipped up the jungle path. *Esteban and Emilio are down there. I hope they've got that Jap spotted and get rid of him real quiet.* Tony watched Jap number two display a series of hand and arm signals, indicating to those behind him that the bridge was safe.

The hollow clomp of hooves on wood resounded up the gorge to the confused Marines manning the Browning. Their curiosity was quickly answered by the entrance of a skittish mule. Struggling to calm the beast, its khaki-clad handler shortened up the bridle lead while rubbing the animal's taut neck. Waters was able to discern what appeared to be the tube and base plate of a heavy mortar lashed to the beast's back. Another soldier ran to its opposite side to grip a slack section of the bridle. He too acted to steady his rambunctious charge. Gunny Luzak laid his hand at the back of Lyons' sweat-soaked neck. The gunner was tracking the group's progress through the metal sight.

"Wait until they get within fifteen feet of this side. Then open 'em up," Luzak whispered.

"Roger." It came out more as breath than voice.

A second mule and set of handlers appeared, and then a third. Ostensibly their crate packs contained mortar ammunition. Lyons had picked out a firing point in line with a weathered post roughly fifteen feet from the Americans' side of the span. When the mule hit that location, he would fire. His anxious finger barely tickled the trigger.

The first five rounds shattered the mid-day silence like a startling crack of tropical thunder. Wood splinters erupted just below the front mule. Quickly adjusting his fire, Lyons raked the big animal then stitched his bullets across the remaining seventy feet of bridge and into the hidden jungle beyond, where the Japanese caravan had presumably bunched up. The mortar-laden mule, squirting blood from a punctured chest, brayed in pain, kicking out wildly at its unreachable tormentor. Disoriented, it crashed through the flimsy hand railing and plummeted in a slow cartwheel to the swollen river, taking its tangled handler along for the fall. The other two mules were down, one still twitched until the machine gun spit another sweep of death. This time he concentrated on the fallen soldiers pressed against the wet crimson planking before unclenching his fist from the moist trigger grip.

19

Lyons knelt back and exhaled, "Whew." In less than a minute, he had wiped out at least five men and three mules. Until today, he had never killed anything in his twenty-three years except the indifferent dispatch of insects, fish, and a few unlucky reptiles. The destruction below, however, stimulated conflicting reactions as exhilaration and nausea competed for his attention.

On the San Leo Bridge, a wounded Japanese soldier moaned for help. His shielded comrades sympathetically called back and soon one exposed himself in a futile resolve to rescue the disabled man. Lance Corporal Mooney elbowed the gunner, but before he could react a single shot rang out and the would-be rescuer screamed before stumbling to his knees. A second gunshot finished him. Emilio and Esteban were on the job.

An hour ticked by since the ambush, and all was still. On the bridge, an orgy of buzzing flies lapped the sticky ooze splattered over the seven silent carcasses. The wounded man no longer called out. He was either unconscious or dead. If the former were true, the hideous sun would broil what little life remained.

On the perch, Captain Howell magnified the carnage through a captured Japanese Nikko 25X artillery scope, pocked but serviceable. *Should I call in the Arty now or wait a while until the Japs get impatient and push the tail-end of the column up closer to the bridge?* He was still considering his options when a loud boom and concussion shocked his thoughts.

A Japanese soldier, probably the one who had slipped over the bridge, had threaded his way up to the firing position and lobbed a potato masher grenade into the gun pit. The unsuspecting crew took the full brunt of the confined blast. Somehow the two scouts had missed him and, with luck in his kit pack, he had circumvented the L. P. too. Gunny Luzak, huddling with Salty in the other hole, was stunned for the moment. Sensing still present danger, in one quick movement he snatched the Tommy gun and wheeled. Thirty feet away, the Jap was bringing his rifle to bear on possible survivors. Incredibly, he had not seen the second position. Salty's concealing log had probably saved their lives. So Tony let fly a long burst directly into the surprised enemy from abdomen to throat. At ten yards the impact of a dozen .45 caliber slugs doesn't leave much to ship home.

Luzak covered his partner as Waters rolled into the still-smoking depression. Lyons, his chin missing, and Mooney were both dead. *That spider bite means nothing now*, Salty thought. Pvt. Brower was crumpled under the gun which had been blown over. Miraculously, he had survived with minor fragmentary wounds. Bloody but otherwise intact, he kicked the gun aside. Pushing to his feet, he stumbled as though intoxicated, and hollered, "Yahoo!" before sighting his dead buddies. Mouth agape, Brower sat back, wide-eyed. Salty attempted to dust him off, advising the shaken private, "Don't look at 'em son. Get in the other hole with the gunny." He gently pushed him in that direction.

Within minutes the two sergeants had stoically covered the dead Marines with about ten inches of earth after stripping them of near empty canteens and pistols.

"What's keeping Howell from callin' in the big stuff?" Waters inquired.

"Maybe he's going to wait just until sunset, figuring he'll catch more of them bottled up," Luzak answered.

"Bullllshhhit." Salty drawled, dragging out each word.

"Look at it this way—if the Nips are transporting those big-ass mortars, chances are they've got a deadline to be at a specific location. So they'll be forced to bring up more troops to secure the bridge. The more they commit themselves, the more targets for the artillery boys."

"Bullshit, again. The sons-a-bitches probably already got some people infiltrating downstream. In hours they'll be parked on our front porch!" As he talked, Salty consciously watched the San Leo Bridge through the gun sight, cognizant of even the slightest movement.

Suddenly, a challenging high-pitched voice was answered by the roar of many cheers. Again and again, each time progressively more intense. It sounded like a coach exhorting charged-up athletes during a locker room pep talk. For five minutes the strident clamor continued.

"Get ready boys," Luzak warned simultaneously as the action unfolded. They stormed out of the jungle in a frenzied stampede. With fixed bayonets, about a dozen howling Japanese hurdled the bloating corpses. Flies by the thousands scattered in every direction. Salty blazed away, mowing down the enemy in full stride. Those who weren't shot tripped over those who were. The screaming never stopped; neither did the Browning. Sergeant Waters methodically banged away until the heap was motionless.

"Feed the monster," Waters urged. Flattened out beside him, Luzak eased in another belt. The fire team hardly missed a beat. All told, they counted fourteen new bodies. The angry gun spat an additional 500 suppressing rounds into the tangled vegetation from where the suicide charge had originated. Hopefully it would keep the next wave at bay.

The Japanese strategy was fanatically simple. If the troops had made it to the other side without drawing fire, they would have fanned out and secured the high ground, allowing the pack animals to proceed with their lethal cargo. Should the Americans start shooting again, Japanese spotters, having identified the source, would probably drop mortar fire on target until the Browning was junk. As for the fourteen corpses, the sons of Japan were as expendable as the flies who feasted greedily on the new bounty.

"Hot damn, Tony! If we knock off a few more, the weight of all them dead Nips will collapse the whole damn bridge," Salty cackled. Brower slid over a spare ammo chest and reported that the gun seemed to be overheating. Upon examination, the barrel's dented water jacket was found to have an eighth-inch hole.

"Jap grenade must have popped it," Private Brower observed. "Water leaked out." The water chest and condensation hose were also ripped. Without so much of a concern, Sergeant Waters removed the screw top from an empty canteen. Prying out the cork gasket with a GI issue TL29 service folding knife, he fashioned it into a conical plug. Salty squeezed it into the tiny opening until it would go no farther. Next he worked up a wad of saliva and deftly applied it to the protruding plug.

"Swells it up," he grunted. "Anybody got to pee? We're going to need seven pints to fill 'er up. That's over a quart each, the way I figure it." The little drinking water that remained would be needed to rehydrate their depleted bodies on the trip back. Their bladders, though, should be able to produce half the required volume. Moments later Brower had urinated about a pint into a canteen which Salty's steady hand was transferring into the weapon's steaming water jacket. "Nothing stinks worse than hot piss," Brower volunteered.

"An eloquent young man," a chuckling Salty complimented.

Gunnery Sergeant Luzak hadn't said anything for a while. Now he spoke. "Boys, I'm going to chat with Captain Howell, see what's delaying that Arty." Luzak had covered about seventy-five yards when an unmistakable thunk echoed across the gorge. Several seconds passed before the fat mortar round harmlessly slammed into the base of Hill 594. The Japs no doubt had dug in their base plate and fired an adjusting round. The next one would be closer to the mark.

Thunk, thunk, thunk. *Oh God, there's three of them.* Luzak dove into a natural pocket formed by the elongated roots of a mammoth banyan tree. Geysers of wet earth and shattered rock erupted from the ripped hillside. The Japs lobbed five more salvos on ground barely downslope from where Tony hugged the jungle floor. Trees were leveled and boulders gouged from centuries-old resting places. He lay there breathing heavily, his nose pressed into the furrow it had plowed. When he was sure the barrage had ceased, Luzak thrust himself erect only to discover the shock of a shooting pain tearing through his left elbow. Blood saturating his tattered sleeve confirmed the obvious.

Tony Luzak careened headlong through the devastated landscape. Attempting to brake his uncontrolled dash, a boot heel skidded on the green slime that formed the jungle carpet. He fell to a sitting position, looking into what had been the machine gun hole. Wiggling his backside, Tony worked his way down. Brower was dead, shredded. The veteran sergeant wasn't much better, but his face was unscathed and positioned straight up. Luzak's working hand tried to cradle the old China Marine's head. Maybe he could comfort him for a short moment, but Salty blinked once and was gone. A fitting tribute announced his passing as Army 105 mm howitzer shells crashed down on the Japanese side of the San Leo Bridge, "harvesting the grapevine." For twenty-five minutes, the barrage obliterated everything out there except the bridge and its ghastly pile of carrion.

Remarkably, the two listening post Marines had cheated death and now crouched above the scene. Luzak directed an index finger at Salty's breast pocket and motioned the nearest leatherneck to open it. Reaching in, he extracted a small, flat pigskin pouch worn and discolored from a herky-jerky itinerary that had carried it from Caribbean to Orient, port to ship, barracks to whorehouse. This pocket in a pocket embraced the talismans that touched the soul of Sergeant Stanton Waters, USMC. "Like a Cherokee shaman," he once remarked of his belief that articles meaningful in a man's existence stirred memories of crucial turning points and spiritual bonds. This was the mystical jewelry of a man's trip through life and therefore, should be treasured more than "bought trinkets."

The young Marine shook out the contents: an early model dog tag holding the stamped information of Salty's identity; the Navy Cross' simple blue and white ribbon supporting the burnished medal; a folded oversized black patch bearing the white star and Indian head of the US Army's 2nd Infantry Division. During the Great War in France, the 5th Marines, Waters' old outfit, were a permanent part of the 2nd Division and wore the colorful shoulder patch. Several other charms whose meaning could only be interpreted by Salty also spilled from the pouch—a flat, smooth, cloudy maroon stone no larger than a nickel; what appeared to be a human tooth; a short brass key, and a wrinkled sepia photograph depicting a faded young woman barely visible. Captive in this piece of stitched hide slept the spoor of but a solitary man's travel through time, and perhaps his destiny.

"Pin The Cross on his collar," a tearful Tony croaked. The Marines did it with a special gentleness and returned the odd collection to the breast pocket, treating it with a reverence reserved for holy relics.

While one Marine wielded his helmet to scrape dirt on Waters' and Brower's common grave, the second slit open Tony's sleeve and bandaged the mess as best he could. "What are your names, anyway?" They told him but Tony was too occupied to remember or care. He would ask again when he released them back to their parent outfit. "God bless these four Marines."

"Amen… let's get the hell out of here!"

The episode at San Leo Bridge seemed in the far distant past instead of only a few days ago. Cupping the dwindling Chesterfield, Tony Luzak sucked in a last drag before crushing it against the concrete bulkhead entrance to Malinta Tunnel. He pinched the burnt end, making sure it was extinguished as a prelude to returning the precious *clippy* to the half-empty package, to be enjoyed later when the urge moved him. Behind Luzak, another figure slipped out of the open portal and walked in Tony's direction. "Good evening," the shadow softly greeted, but the tone sounded somewhat aristocratic. Instinctively, Tony realized an officer was present. Enlisted men have a sixth sense about such things.

"And to you too, sir," Tony responded.

"It's a placid evening as well, in stark contrast to the suffering north of here," the man said as he studied the pipe in his hand before lifting it back to his mouth.

"Aye, sir."

"Marine or Navy?" the man inquired.

"Oh I'm a jar head, sir. What clued you?"

"When a man says 'aye' he can only be one of three things, and I'm confident there are no Coast Guardsmen on Corregidor!" He blew out a long sweet stream and emitted a short cough. Even in the meager light of night the officer was aware of the plaster cast. "Where'd you pick that up?" He aimed the pipe stem toward the cast.

"Oh, an obscure place no one ever heard of called San Leo Bridge."

"I've heard of it," he emphatically corrected. "Were you with the machine gunners? That was quite a show. The artillery wiped out a mortar company and most of an accompanying communications section. Put a real crimp in Homma's offensive! Combined with our other efforts, it's taken the enemy this long to regroup."

Tony could better distinguish the man's features now. High forehead, strong chin. "Yes sir, I'm Gunnery Sergeant Luzak. I...I was in command," he stammered as he recalled a vision of the hasty grave site. "My guys stacked 'em up like cord wood." Beads of perspiration formed on his forehead.

"I know, I read a brief of the forward observer's post operation report."

"That would be a Captain Howell, sir?"

"Yes, I believe that was the name." He rapped the bowl on the concrete until the embers trickled out. Stomping on a persistent coal, he turned to re-enter the tunnel. The officer paused, "And thank you Gunnery Sergeant Luzak for your personal valor and the gallantry of your men. Their sacrifice and those of our brothers in arms will never be forgotten by me!" He reached out to touch Tony's cast gently spreading his fingers as though to feel the warrior energy sealed inside. Three stars fastened to the man's collar caught what little light existed. Luzak gulped a breath, suddenly realizing with whom he had been sharing the last few tranquil moments.

"Good night, General MacArthur."

CHAPTER III
MALINTA

DATE: 13 MARCH 1942

TIME: 0830 HOURS

LOCATION: MALINTA TUNNEL

A grimy pink rubber ball about the size of a nectarine rolled freely along the soft-lit corridor, only to be trapped under a beat-up boot. From around the corner, its hurrying pursuer came into view, clad in rumpled suntans. Single gold bars adorned each collar point, signifying the grade of Second Lieutenant. The tall officer loped with the fluid smoothness of a track athlete, the only contrary note being an arm which pumped slightly out of sync. Spotting the squashed sphere peeking out under the sole, he slowed to a halt.

"Ah there you are," he smiled, shaking his handsome head as though chastising a mischievous child. "I've been chasing you through half the laterals in Malinta complex."

Lifting his boondocker, Gunnery Sergeant Tony Luzak liberated the ball, permitting its recapture by the stooping lieutenant. First impressions can often fall victim to misleading circumstance. Signals flashing through the gruff sergeant's pissy mind were not the most flattering the lieutenant would have preferred. Fortunately for him, superior rank prescribes a required modicum of respect.

"Here it is, lieutenant." Luzak eased a short kick to help propel it along.

Somewhat embarrassed, the officer snatched the ball with a left-handed swipe. He acted to say something as if to explain, but thought the better. Shifting it to his right hand, he squeezed its sponginess repeatedly. "Thanks gunny." He exuded a boyish grin. "Sometimes my toys escape me."

The humor was lost on a sullen Luzak. "Aye, sir." *The shelling must have really gotten to this beauty.* Before the conversation could disintegrate, the apple-green door before them swung open, and a pale clerk typist wearing the sole stripe and crossed rifles of a lance corporal stuck out his head.

"You can wait in Colonel Howard's office, gunny." Then, spotting the newly arrived officer, "Oh, Lieutenant Delane, I'm certain the Colonel wants you there at the same time. He should be returning from his inspection tour any minute." Luzak couldn't help but raise his eyebrows, contemplating what his future could possibly have in common with this *ball-bouncing butter bar.*

They passed through the clerk typist's cluttered work space. Stacks of crammed yellow file jackets and miscellaneous paperwork surrounded a banged-up Underwood typewriter. A cracked black and white glossy photo of Marine Commandant Thomas Holcomb hung above the Underwood, sternly observing all those summoned and dismissed. Picture-frame glass was not evident, perhaps broken in transit from Shanghai. Wire baskets marked "IN" and "OUT" flanked another faded green door displaying an unpretentious six-inch wide cardboard sign, "Col. S. Howard." Delane's hand gripped the knob when the phone sounded a quick short ring.

"Colonel Howard's headquarters, Lance Corporal Corbin speaking." There was a short pause. "Yes, Colonel, they're both here." A longer pause followed. Corbin touched a balled handkerchief to a wet nose. The wrinkled linen closely matched the color of his tired face. Months of tunnel existence with little or no exposure to sunshine had shrunk his skin pigment to a ghostlike pallor, Malinta white. "Only one message, sir. General Wainwright's aide called. He requests your presence at the command center…1300 hours." Another lapse came. "Yes, sir, I'll confirm it immediately and I'll have them at Kindley chop chop." He listened again. "Yes, sir. Thank you sir."

Lance Corporal Corbin twisted his torso to face the two men.

"There's been a change in plans. You're to meet Colonel Howard at Kindley Field. The Colonel's vehicle will pick you up outside of the east entrance in five minutes."

Less than a mile separated Malinta Hill from Kindley Field, but the zealous wheel man compressed that distance via a hair-raising, foot-to-the-floor trip. The bouncing three-quarter-ton truck was missing its windshield. Rushing wind blew through the three cramped Marines, exaggerating the sensation of speed. Drivers don't relish being out in the open where they might fall easy prey to cruising Zeroes hunting targets of opportunity.

The little truck jarred to a stop below the cratered air strip. Standing outside of the dilapidated Navy Radio Terminal, the Old Man wiped perspiration from within his open-collared shirt. A welcoming breeze worked its way off the blinding glare of open ocean. Colonel Howard removed the pie plate helmet, gratefully permitting cooler air to soothe the dampness surrounding his head. Both men quick-stepped to him, Delane a half-pace in the lead.

"Sir, Lieutenant Delane reporting to the Regimental Commander as ordered." His right hand curled a salute, not the variety one would anticipate delivering to a full-bird colonel.

"Gunnery Sergeant Luzak reports to the Regimental Commander as ordered, sir!" The gunny's salute was razor sharp, textbook perfect, right out of the Corps manual. *Balls, this kid wouldn't know a hand salute from a hand grenade.*

Sam Howard, leader of the 4th Marines, patiently gazed into their pupils before returning the salute. "At ease, gentlemen. Even though I'm enjoying this bit of wind, we'd better move inside."

They squeezed into a room no larger than a one-car garage. Buckled chicken-wire caging suggested that at one time it had served as a supply or spare parts locker for Navy radiomen. Two battered chairs, a high stool, and chipped battleship-gray desk furnished the makeshift office. One half-blown-out wall allowed hot sunlight to flood most of the interior. It was the only illumination available. Japanese bombs had long ago destroyed electrical service.

"Please be seated." Delane and Tony quickly sat, the gunny maneuvering the clumsy cast to one side, trying to minimize the red lip print prominently beckoning all to see. Blinking neon would have had a less conspicuous presence.

"What the hell's that?" Colonel Howard challenged.

The gunny's face displayed a blush of discomfort. Rolling his buttocks on the hard bridge chair he cleared his throat. "Well, it's kind of a good luck charm, sir. Some of the Army nurses were putting lipstick on and kissing all the guys' casts over in sick bay. I guess they thought it was good for morale... or something." Weakly uttered, the final two-word afterthought approached the apologetic.

"Morale," the colonel parroted. A small smile crept over his lips. "The nurses are doing a hell of a job!"

"Yes, sir," the duet of Luzak and Delane answered in unison.

Those who served him knew Sam Howard to be a man used to extracting the most from the least. He demanded efficiency beyond the norm and usually received it. In the pre-war economies imposed by a penny-pinching Congress, the military had been forced to operate with the barest minimum. Men, equipment, transportation, housing—all were in short supply. Training in the States in some cases had reached humiliating proportions. The Army grudgingly utilized drain pipe to simulate mortars, broomstick and box configurations to dummy up machine guns, and two-and-a-half-ton trucks to represent armor. Of course the word "TANK" was painted broadly on the canvas bed cover to everyone's mortification and amazement. "Wow, a tank!" a sarcastic trooper was heard to exclaim in mock wonderment. "I've never seen one before!" It was difficult for servicemen to take a lot of it seriously. Yet it all seemed appropriate to pork-barreling congressmen sipping Jack Daniels in the comfort of a lobby hideaway. Lobby money squeaked loudest, so naturally their wheels were first in line for lubrication.

Issues influencing re-election also took precedence. Post office buildings in the home district dazzled voters. Of course, the generous largess of grateful contractors was part of the game. Sometimes delivered in brown paper bags, tribute filled expectant pockets without ever so much as a mild protest. In a world ablaze, national security suffered the crippling neglect of a pompously naive federal legislature. Because the political establishment left America unprepared, good men were now pushed to perform the near impossible, some perishing in the process.

Perhaps the most debilitating imposition foisted on exasperated commanders was a practice termed "dwindling." Against their judgment, military units were compelled to operate at dramatically reduced levels of their normal manpower complement. Howard's 4th Marine Regiment represented a scornful example of the dwindling principle. Simply explained, replacement troops were withheld. As a consequence, the Fourth had shrunk from three to two battalions in China. Compounding the lunacy, both active battalions were short one rifle company and the surviving companies each were minus a platoon. So a slice here and a pinch there had depleted the regiment to semi-strength by the time it arrived at Olongapo, Philippines, around Thanksgiving, 1941. Only 772 officers and men made the voyage. A regiment? The shell existed, but in truth it was only half-full.

Already stationed across Manila Bay in Cavite, providing anti-aircraft support for the US Naval Base, stood the 1st Separate Marine Battalion, also lacking people. By the end of December, a persuasive Howard had integrated it into the 4th Marines, reconstituted as the 3rd Battalion, 4th Marines—or Three-Four (3/4) in Marine parlance. Though still undermanned, the Fourth had significantly improved its organic strength. For Colonel Sam it was comforting to be approaching TO&E strength (Table of Organization and Equipment). Patience is a virtue unlike any other. Unfortunately the problem now facing the Regiment was inevitable entrapment in the Corregidor womb, like a mature fetus unable to flex its muscles.

"Gentlemen, we've got a bunch of ground to cover with less than a half hour to do it, so let's start with the good news. Lieutenant Delane please stand."

Delane shot to his feet, the sponge ball bulging in his tight trouser pocket as though he had magically sprouted a new organ. Black-haired, blue-eyed Andrew Saber Delane stretched out at roughly six-feet-two inches, so the amusing protuberance was *eye* high to the seated Luzak. The more one tries to ignore the obvious, the more it behaves like a magnet regardless of how reluctant the viewer. The gunny's eyeballs decided to focus undivided on the unaware stone face of Colonel Howard.

"How's that mangled hand?" the commander inquired.

Delane extended his right arm, exposing a scarred ham of a hand. Purple discolorations identified the locations of freshly healed pin holes and stitch marks. The small finger was missing its last digit, new skin covering about a two-inch stump. "It's getting better, thank you, sir. A Navy surgeon removed all the hardware last week. The paw itself seems okay, but the pinky tip is still somewhat sensitive. Right now it's simply a question of getting all the parts moving and building strength. I've started squeezing a sponge ball to work out the kinks." Delane's conversational yet respectful response contained not even a hint of false modesty, his comments most matter-of-fact.

Looks like I've misjudged him, Luzak confided to his conscience, still troubled by memories of the bridge episode. The Colonel came around his desk to Delane's front. Reaching into his pocket, he pulled out a small beige cardboard carton. Howard's thumb covered the cellophane window obscuring its contents.

"Nobody is slower to promote than the Marine Corps, FIRST LIEUTENANT Delane. Many advancements are the result of time in grade. I'm pleased to inform you that yours is for outstanding performance in addition to tenure. Congratulations." Colonel Howard punctured the cellophane and tore out the gleaming silver bars. "Give me a hand here, gunny." The two men removed the young officer's collar insignia and replaced them with the new badge of rank. "I'm sure you'll agree it's long overdue."

"You'll get no argument from me on that account, sir."

"Incidentally, your official date of promotion is 4 February."

Reconsidering his premature assessment, a repentant Luzak took a half-step backwards. "Sir, may I offer your first salute as first lieutenant?"

"You may gunny, you may."

"Remain standing, Gunnery Sergeant Luzak," the Colonel commanded as he reached for a flat box the size of a billfold. His voice took on an air of friendly formality. "For gallantry in action earlier this month at the San Leo Bridge, Gunnery Sergeant Anton Luzak, Fourth Marines, is awarded the Silver Star." Flipping the cover he held it up to Tony's eyes to admire. Dangling from a silky ribbon bearing the national colors flashed a five-pointed star concentrically surrounding a smaller, more brilliant one.

"This is special, gunny," the older Marine muttered softly, pinning it above Luzak's left chest pocket.

Misty tears blurred Tony's eyes and one even dared to streak across his cheek before he blotted it with the back of his rough hand. "Sir, I was just one of seven Marines. We buried four of them and—"

Howard cut him off. "Luzak, you were in command! YOUR action and YOUR men made it happen. YOU drove them up that hill. Fire discipline was patiently maintained until the absolute ideal moment, according to Captain Howell. That's why he recommended you for the Silver Star. He didn't do it lightly. My God man, your position took a killing grenade and still you were able to remount the gun and put effective fire into the bridgehead. Without your leadership, it's doubtful how many Japs the artillery fire mission would have destroyed."

"I'm honored sir, but Sergeant Waters really deserves—"

Howard beat him to the finish line again. Tempering the tone of his brisk retort, he added, "We can't give everyone a medal, gunny. Nevertheless, we've managed to posthumously award Corporal Lyons and Salty Commendation

Medals. I realize you were close buddies. And for what it's worth, there are plenty of officers in this Regiment including this one, who had a soft spot for that old maverick."

"Aye, sir."

"Now let me tell you what this cozy meeting is really about!" The warmth had disappeared.

The Philippine archipelago snakes southward for over 1,150 miles, while covering an east-west expanse of almost 690 miles. Clutched within the vast commonwealth sit 7,100 tropical islands, many so remote that sixty percent are officially nameless. In terms of land mass, the two most dominant islands are Luzon in the north, and Mindanao slinking down to the Celebes Sea. A subordinate strand, Sulu province, ends at the southernmost point—five sweaty degrees above the equator. Sprawling Luzon, the largest island, is roughly the size of Ohio but lacking its compactness. Equally asymmetrical Mindanao is slightly smaller. Numerous other islands lie in between: Mindoro, Samar, Panay, Leyte, Negros, Cebu, Bohol and Palawan, to name the prominent.

The multi-colored projection map covering Colonel Howard's borrowed office wall resembled the type familiar to geography students. Soft yellows, greens, pinks and violets identified political subdivisions against a sea-blue background. Drawing their attention to it, the Colonel placed his finger at the speck of Corregidor. "You are here," he said calmly. "God willing, in a few weeks the two of you should be here." His fingertip slid ten inches down the map and halted at the rose-colored Zamboanga peninsula projecting snout-like from Mindanao's western coast. He tapped it twice for emphasis.

Delane and Luzak reacted identically. Their heads turned to face each other, as though to find an explanation in their mutually quizzing eyes. Delane yanked out the sponge ball and proceeded to manipulate it. Gunny wished he had one too.

Months of interrupted sleep had formed red circles around the eyes of Colonel Sam Howard. Delane couldn't help but reflect on the burden the Old Man must have shouldered these past few horrifying months. The operational and logistical nightmare was problem enough, but to lead Marines, to rally their spirits in a hopeless resistance placed enormous pressure on one's mental being.

"Gentlemen, last evening at 1915 hours, General MacArthur and a small group including President Quezon departed Corregidor in an attempt to re-establish his command elsewhere. I won't go into details because, quite frankly, the less you know about it, the better. But for the record, he's a courageous man who in past wars heroically proved himself under fire. Only a direct order from the Commander-in-Chief could have forced him off The Rock. It would be pointless to sacrifice him here and provide the Japs with a psychological victory as well. His successful escape will gnaw at the Japs. The oriental mind will no doubt drag up an appropriately fatal proverb— something about scorpions and serpents given a second opportunity will grow and sting with even greater venom, etcetera, etcetera. Well, you know what I mean.

"Suffice it to say, the General is a brilliant and tenacious man. Regardless of what happens on Bataan and Corregidor, he will be back… and with a crushing vengeance." Colonel Howard moved a few steps to park his derrière against the desk edge. "Tonight at 1915 hours, twenty-four hours to the minute after General MacArthur's departure, the two of you will unobtrusively board the Philippine fishing boat, *El Corazon Blanco*, and sail the hell out of here for Mindanao. It could very well be the last ship to leave South Dock. General Wainwright is running the show here now and he's granted me the authorization to extricate two people of my choosing with key dispatches and regimental records for the Marine powers to be… somewhere on the great continent of Australia. Those two people are you!"

Slipping the ball into his pocket, an ashen Delane inquired, "May I ask why me, sir, or should I say us?"

"A profoundly logical question," Howard responded. "Well, first of all, you're both walking wounded, but soon to regain your normal strength. In the case of Luzak, his precautionary cast, according to the medical experts, can be shed in about twelve days. Your situation, lieutenant, is as you described it. Time is the great healer but you can accelerate hand strength by exercising it. Soaking the fingertip in brine will toughen the skin. Again, this is the medical staff's opinion. However, in the meanwhile, between both of you, you have but one functional set of hands which restricts physical duty on Corregidor. Additionally, each of you have been exposed to trying circumstances and survived either through skill or good fortune." Drama was not Howard's long suit, but it served him well as he clenched his teeth in a hard grimace. "And for this mission, gentlemen, I need survivors!"

Bending flat over the desk, Howard reached to its underside, jerking up a large cordovan leather satchel, creased with wear. Two metal snap locks secured the protective flap bearing the almost invisible embossed initials, "S. H." A scuffed handle and black looped carrying strap of newly stitched hide, apparently sewn in place for the exclusive purpose of this very mission, completed its odd appearance. "Lieutenant, gunny, the contents of this briefcase are sacred to me and to this regiment. In four weeks or so, we'll probably be overwhelmed. Unless a major miracle prevails, I, Sam Howard, will be the first Marine in history to witness the destruction or surrender of his regiment. No matter how vile the thought, I must consider the reality of burning the regimental colors rather than having them disgraced in Hirohito's trophy case." He choked back a voice cracking with anger, with frustration. "I can only hope, and I'm confident that my hope is well-founded, that at some point the Fourth Marines will be reformed. The precious contents of this satchel will help steep the regiment's tradition and inspire its rebirth."

Recapturing composure that had wandered through an emotional tangent, the Colonel allowed himself a few clearing moments. Stroking his scalp, he continued. "The reason we've conducted our morning meeting in this sorry excuse for a building is not only because there's no interrupting phone, but because I wish no one on Corregidor to know I'm sending some Marines away while others must stay. Negative thoughts fueled by ugly rumor might enter their exhausted minds and cast doubt. Morale and discipline could suffer. Therefore, it's best you don't let anyone know you're leaving Corregidor. Just show up at South Dock before nineteen hundred hours and ask for Antonio Rizal. He's been commissioned to organize guerrilla activity in Zamboanga and Misamis Occidental provinces. Quezon and MacArthur confirmed his authorization yesterday. You two will be hitchhikers on his ride back to Mindanao, aboard the fishing vessel *El Corazon Blanco*. Rizal claims the ability to eventually get you to Australia. In all truth, I don't know how reliable he is or isn't. Your own will and resourcefulness are the keys to making it all happen."

From inside his shirt Howard removed a thick yellow postal envelope bound by doubled elastic bands. "Here, take this. It contains fifty-five twenty-dollar bills requisitioned from the regimental fund. It's not going to do anyone any good in Malinta, Topside, or Mariveles. Use it as you see fit, to buy or bribe your escape to Australia. It must be over seven hundred nautical miles from here to Mindanao... so protect it well. Because I'm not positive if the ship's crew are sailors, pirates, fishermen, guerrillas or all of the above. Boys, just get the satchel through! My thoughts and devout hope sail with you. Good luck."

Lieutenant Delane opened a shirt button and slid in the envelope while Luzak grabbed the satchel, surprising him by its weight. He tore off the key strung through the beefy handle and awkwardly snapped it to his dog tag chain. Howard hand-gestured toward the doorway, indicating the meeting was finished. In the confining space of the small room, the three men jockeyed so as to avoid bumping into one another. Straddling the threshold, Tony Luzak momentarily blocked his two superiors. Solemn eyes reached for the Skipper's. "Colonel Howard, if we make it back and somewhere down the line the Fourth is to be reformed, I pledge to you I'll do everything in my power to gain assignment to the new regiment. And I'll serve in the name of every Marine on Luzon from private to Colonel."

"Gunnery Sergeant Luzak, consider that my last order!"

CHAPTER IV
EL CORAZON BLANCO

DATE: SATURDAY, 28 MARCH 1942

TIME: 1845 HOURS

LOCATION: VISAYAN SEA

Teal blue water shimmered the dappled reflection of a low western sun as a dragging fist cut silvery furrows through the warm Visayan Sea. It caused a rippled prism to spray the length of his bronzed arm. The abstract image took on a surreal perspective distorted through slitted eyes. Yet it afforded his mind a conducive backdrop for self-communion, to ponder his infinitesimal role in the unfolding Pacific war. Suspended above the waterline in a hammock formed from cargo netting, a shirtless Andrew Delane was barely aware of the diesel engine's numbing hum.

Fifteen days out of Corregidor had witnessed his upper torso's graduation from sensitive pink to its present golden brown. Coconut oil provided by a ship's mate had eased that transition. His idle reverie was politely stirred by the slender man offering a crusty fillet of grilled fish. Delane tilted the straw planter's hat from his brow and scaled the latticed nest. Bare feet slapped down on the wide board deck while he stretched the kinks from his neck, stiff with inactivity. He took the fish in a wet hand, the salt water imparting a savory flavor to the flaky meat. "Caviar again!" he exclaimed. "Thank you, Antonio. Or should I say *mucho gracias, compadre?*"

"My word, it appears we have a budding linguist gracing our cruise ship," the handsome Filipino joked. "This evening's schedule calls for cocktails on the Belvedere deck, followed by continental dinner and moonlight dancing to live music by the fabulous Tommy Dorsey Band."

"Will dinner wear be formal or casual, Antonio?"

"Ripped clothing is preferable, and footwear not required, but of course it's the gentleman's choice."

Delane laughed. He spit out a small bone overlooked by the filleter's blade and shucked sea spray from his forearm. *El Corazon Blanco*, vehicle of deliverance, proved to be a ramshackle, creaking 78-footer incapable of purging its eternal stink. Decades of putrid fish and flaming sun had baked a malodorous stench into its very core. Rizal had encouraged the smell, reasoning that any inspecting Japanese would be reluctant to spend much time aboard.

Captain Magsay and his three passengers engaged in a preposterous charade, pretending the rusty vessel to be a magnificent luxury liner worthy of Cunard. Ship's matters were satirically redefined in elegant terms. Drinking water became champagne, a 40-inch galvanized wash tub was christened the "Astor Pool," compartments were staterooms, tin plates translated to china, cups equaled goblets, and so forth. Indeed, the abominably foul odor was designated "aromatic." Zaniness helped placate the tension and drudgery of the cat-and-mouse voyage. The reality of danger temporarily lost itself in farce.

Rizal had employed the first few days at sea to assert his control of the ship and its human freight. Businesslike formality punctuated instructions and conversation alike. Facial expressions failed to accompany either queries or responses. But after a while, he determined that the two Marines were compliant fugitives of no threat to his authority. Familiarity disarms suspicion. Subsequently, he became more engaging and sought out the First Lieutenant for intellectual banter. Within a week, humor had become the common denominator. Even Gunny Luzak participated, once exaggerating the bare bulb ceiling light as a chandelier.

Rizal, himself, was the glowing product of two cultures and an international education. His father had been senior foreman in a hemp processing plant controlled by Abaca Rey Ltd. near Manila. During an extended trip to Davao to assist in installing machinery for the company's Mindinao factory, he courted and ultimately married a Moro woman. Two years later, she gave birth to an infant son, Antonio. Though raised a Manila Catholic, the stigma of a Muslim mother evoked strong prejudices among schoolmates.

But Antonio weathered the snubs and cruelties, perhaps even developing a special resilience from the ordeal. Multiculturalism and a first-class education provided an invaluable asset—impeccable fluency in Tagalog, Spanish, and English, augmented by reasonable skills in the Moro and Samal-Moro dialects. His academic brilliance earned a scholarship to Stanford University, completing an electrical engineering degree in 1933.

An ardent nationalist, Rizal returned to his native land the following March, determined to labor for Philippine independence. Upon stepping from the gangplank, he learned the President of the United States had signed the Tydings-McDuffie Act. The Philippine legislature confirmed it on May 1, commencing a ten-year probationary period at which conclusion the Philippine Commonwealth would assume the status of an independent republic. The young engineer's personal vision as patriot and liberator had been preempted by a stroke of FDR's pen. All that remained was the formation of an acceptable constitution. Antonio Rizal would leave that to lawyers and bureaucrats. During the next four years he prospered as a civilian engineer in the US Army Corps of Engineers, almost exclusively servicing Clark Field.

For some unexplained reason ,Mindanao, island of his mother's youth, became his focus of opportunity. Resigning his comfortable position in 1938, he packed up and moved to Zamboanga where he swiftly gained political influence among both Catholics and Mindanao's approximate half million Mohammedans, known as Moros. Quickly his star rose, a force to be reckoned with, only to have the Japanese invasion stifle his ascension. From afar Manuel Quezon and Douglas MacArthur had recognized his adroit talent for organization and leadership coupled with the political correctness of being half Moro. In the frantic hours before their escape, they tapped Rizal, the hybrid, to lay the groundwork for a resistance movement in Mindanao's two western provinces.

"Andrew, you're soaking that finger into a pickle! Are you making any progress?"

Delane exhibited a fist with the pinky extended for his friend to inspect. Today's three-hour immersion had caused it to shrivel, but the past weeks of cumulative salt water therapy had done just that, pickled it. The new skin had taken on a rubbery toughness. Although improved, he could only sustain a limited amount of pressure to the flat tip.

He inserted the stub into his ear, effecting a comical brain-penetrating illusion. "As a matter of fact, it's made remarkable progress since you allowed me special guest privileges on this splendid galleon." His hand theatrically swept across the ship's rusted breadth.

Antonio munched the last fish morsel and licked his fingers. "You know, you have yet to tell me how it happened."

"Oh, it would bore you to tears," he shrugged.

"You think so, Andrew? Just because I'm an educated man, doesn't make me a patrician."

"I knew that from the way you ate your fish."

Rizal's sudden laugh caused a crumb to jump from his mouth. He kicked it towards the pitted gunwale.

"See what I mean?" the lieutenant added.

"*Si compadre, si*. I did not wish to intrude on your privacy."

"It doesn't bother me to talk about it." He exhaled as if to clear his mind and travel back to Christmas day. "About three months ago, I was assigned to a demolition detail ordered to destroy the Cavite Naval Base, to deny the Japs port facilities and anything else we couldn't move to Mariveles. My outfit was the First Separate Marine Battalion, which is a fancy name for anti-aircraft. We had nothing bigger than three-inch guns.

"One of our batteries shot down a nip dive bomber, so after that they flew above our range and blasted the piss out of Cavite for two solid weeks. Lieutenant Colonel Adams ordered the base's destruction and on December 25, we were dynamiting buildings when the Jap flyboys started a nuisance bombing run. It was crazy, Antonio. We're blowing it up and they're dropping 551-pound bombs on the same targets!

"Anyway, one of our guys got caught in the open and I was yelling for him to hit the deck. He couldn't hear shit in the middle of that mess. A series of detonations erupted near the dry docks and I never got completely into my hole. This hand inadvertently remained on the concrete lip when a fifty-five gallon steel drum that had been blown sky high crashed down, pulverizing most of the bones, and cleanly amputating a piece of finger. Hell, I'm not even sure whose explosion it was, ours or theirs!" He forced a disgusted laugh. "They awarded me a Purple Heart for my trouble... Merry Christmas."

The lazy two-week journey had carried *El Corazon Blanco* through Verde Island Passage along the steamy Mindoro coast. They purposely avoided the open South China and Sulu Seas. Instead, they chugged into the Tablas Strait and serpentined a course through the Jintotolo Channel, gateway to the Visayan Sea. Numerous engine repairs and other tactical stops along the way imposed an agonizingly slow pace. They entered the tapered Tanon Strait splitting Negros and Cebu. So far their luck had held out.

Even though they suffered through intense heat, the relatively calm waters and active breeze made living tolerable. "Baguio," the furious Philippine typhoon, usually strikes July through September, most often in the Eastern provinces, out of their path. Curiously, no Japanese warships had challenged them. Possibly they were too busy strangling Bataan. Today, Monday, March 30, all that would change.

The port of San Carlos lay about four knots due east of their position when Tony Luzak observed a swelling dot in the cloudless sky. It loomed at six o'clock, directly astern of the lumbering fishing boat. Delane and Luzak ducked into an open hatchway where they could see but not be seen. The three deckhands went about their chores ignoring the oncoming aircraft. Antonio took a place among them, his attire and appearance resembling theirs. Roaring in at about 300 feet, the single-engine plane dipped its wing, permitting the rear-seated gunner an open canopied view of the vessel. The maneuver accentuated the bright red balls ominously emblazoned on the fuselage and wings. "Val!" exclaimed Delane as it zoomed by.

"What did you say?" Rizal bellowed through cupped hands.

"Val! It's the name of that Jap plane. They're not all Zeroes, you know. Navy dive-bomber made by Aichi. Probably flying recon."

"You must teach me these things, Andrew."

"When I was transferred to anti-aircraft, the first lessons were in aircraft identification. Fixed wheels, rounded wings, exterior bomb sight, two-seater. Yeah, it's a Val, alright."

Banking east, a mile off their bow, the Jap aviator started a slow looping climb. In minutes he would make another pass, hopefully for just one more look-see. Antonio shouted instructions to the crew as the 1,075 horsepower radial engine screamed in, this time at a deafening 200 feet.

Close enough to smell the fish, thought Luzak. Waving and cheering, the fishermen made jubilant signs of welcome. A short dark man vigorously waved an orange patterned bandanna above his smiling face while no doubt yelling the Tagalog equivalent of *fuck you*. Screeching overhead, the pilot continued his southern flight, waggling wings in response to the excited natives.

Three hours ticked by before a faint spume of smoke rose from the horizon. Captain Leander Magsay, sweat rolling freely from his forehead, studied it through a brass telescope. "Destroyer or destroyer escort, I think." He peered through the tube again. "Too small. Has to be a destroyer escort."

The DE was heading right at them and making haste. Collapsing the scope, Magsay conducted a hurried conference with the guerrilla leader. They spoke in rapid Tagalog; clearly Rizal was in charge. Preplanning for this contingency had occurred four hours out of Corregidor, so the men all knew their stations. Ship's papers disclosed it was returning to the home port of Zamboanga from Batangas, where a new screw had been refitted. The two Marines scrambled below deck to gather foot gear, personal items, and any clues to their existence. Each man strapped on a webbed utility belt with holstered 1911 model Colt .45 semi-automatic.

Flashlight in hand, Antonio took them down another half level, adjacent to a chum locker. Crouching beside it, he removed two finger-tight nuts, then stretched erect to unscrew two more at the upper corners. He wiggled the bulkhead and pulled it free, exposing a tiny space roughly the size of a shower stall or phone booth. Propped on the blanketed floor, the satchel awaited their entrance. The gunny hesitated. "Are we standing face-to-face or toe-to-heel?"

Delane considered the question for a moment. "Well, I'm about three inches taller, so if we're belly to belly, my mouth will be opposite your nostrils… and I haven't brushed my teeth in months. Gunny, I suggest we stand back to back."

"Christ, I never thought of that," Luzak admitted.

"Hurry," Antonio urged.

Each stepped into the stifling compartment, Rizal working the panel into place. They buttressed it while he carefully threaded the nuts, making sure only rust showed. The temperature inside would no doubt hover near 120 degrees Fahrenheit.

On deck, Zorro, the undersized dark man, pried open a sealed bait bucket. A god-awful odor emanated, causing even the conditioned Magsay to gag. Zorro had been concocting the fish guts concentrate for a month. Pridefully, he demonstrated it to his shrinking shipmates before brushing it on various locations, anticipating where the Japanese might investigate. Antonio took the dripping brush below and applied a liberal stroke to the secretive bulkhead.

The DE stood off at about 300 yards with its guns trained at the bobbing *El Corazon Blanco*. Four armed seamen and a chief petty officer accompanied by a junior officer in command motored toward them in a small launch. Wafting breezes had already alerted them of what was to come. One sailor pinched his nose with about 50 yards yet to be closed. Antonio lowered a ladder. It too bore a pungent kiss fresh from the bucket.

First up the ladder climbed a sailor wearing an ammo belt and sheathed bayonet. On deck, he unslung the Arisaka and stood at attention awaiting the boarding party. Close behind, the young white-gloved lieutenant j.g. swung a leg over the rail and held still to survey the ship. The powerful stench overwhelmed his senses. Blinking, he attempted to clear his watery eyes. True to his training, he remained expressionless while nausea squeezed his innards. Another sailor and the equally aghast CPO trailed him on deck. Zorro offered a friendly smile and subservient bow, indifferent to the reeking odor.

"You speak Engrish?" the officer inquired in clipped syllables. He appeared to be breathing through his mouth as if to minimize the smell. *Was he filtering it through his teeth? Why not, the sickening stench was thick enough to strain.*

Magsay approached him. "I speak English, a little bit," he pretended, showing a space between thumb and forefinger. His smile cracked an unshaven puss.

"You have papers, yes?"

"I give papers." The Captain produced them from where he had carried them tucked under his arm.

The Japanese opened the folder and made a show of studying the documents. A full five minutes passed as he examined the stamps. *Obviously he understands very little.* Protocol required him to make a polite bow to the ship's Captain, who should respond with a nod. "You go to Zamboanga, yes?" Evidently he comprehended more than Rizal estimated.

"Yes, we take boat Zamboanga. Catch fish. You like eat fish?" The Captain was playacting to a tee. The thought of fish or anything edible for that matter repulsed the naval officer.

"We want see boat inside," he informed.

Captain Magsay acted impressed, proud to show off his smelly tub. He gestured enthusiastically for the Japanese to follow him. "I have big surprise," he beamed.

What's he up to? Antonio questioned. *Don't overdo it, Leander, or they'll chop us to pieces!*

Speaking in forceful Japanese, the officer ordered the CPO and one sailor to inspect the deck area while he and the other man poked below. In keeping with samurai tradition, the j.g. wore a Kyu-gunto sea military sword, hindering his motion through the hatchway and skinny corridor. Playing the fool, Magsay led the way, periodically calling "come, come" and waving encouragement. Snatching a flashlight from the coughing seaman, the lieutenant unholstered an 8mm semi-automatic pistol, probably a Type 14, and worked the action. Cautious, he wasn't about to be ambushed without a struggle.

The oppressive heat and smell soared to dizzying proportions in the smothering depth of the engine room. Diesel fumes compounded the infernal environment. Magsay jabbed a filthy finger at the idling engine. "Nippon, Nippon," he proudly proclaimed, puffing his chest like a flaunting rooster. The Japanese were confused at first, but soon deduced the vibrating mass of cast iron and steel had been forged and machined in Japan. Freeing a greasy rag draped over a lateral pipe, the Filipino scrubbed the engine housing to reveal raised Japanese characters.

"Hai, hai!" They smiled appreciably, acknowledging Magsay's prideful revelation.

He desperately wanted to show them more: the generator, the fuel pump, maybe the condenser. But their tropical white uniforms were soaked through, bodies almost feverish. They had seen enough. Duty had been served, face saved. The officer carefully avoided touching anything, fearful the odor would indelibly infuse his marrow with a permanence beyond death, beyond ancestral welcome. "Boat okay."

CHAPTER V
FORT DIX

DATE: THURSDAY, 16 APRIL 1942

TIME: 1630 HOURS

LOCATION: 2nd TRAINING REGIMENT
                 FORT DIX, NEW JERSEY

There's something both monotonous and inspiring about running in cadence. Forty-one men grinding out a rugged choreography, each slamming an obedient left foot onto the blacktop in faultless harmony. Forty-one hustling, booted soldiers functioning like one. Sweat trickled through stubby crew-cuts, beading on glistening tanned faces as the platoon's three synchronized squads cantered abreast in column formation. Hoarse voices sang out in echoed response to Platoon Sergeant Starkey's sometimes bawdy, often ridiculous offerings.

"I don't know but I've been told," Starkey called out.

"I don't know but I've been told," the platoon lustily chorused.

"Eskimo pussy's mighty cold."

"Eskimo pussy's mighty cold."

"Sound off."

"One two."

"Sound off."

"Three four."

"Cadence count!"

"One two three four. One two three four!"

Nick enjoyed running with his unit. Regardless, he'd probably bitch about the distance, the pace, or maybe the route, once back in the barracks.

45

Bitching, the unwritten luxury of the soldiering art, is easily mastered. It surfaces the first day one puts on the uniform and is perfected until separation. In his youthful mind, the run, the chant, takes on the status of manly rite, young soldiers double-timing to maintain hard warrior bodies. Strenuous group activity helps form the bond that steels resolve as well as endurance. Cohesive ritual forces rookie and veteran alike to respond instinctively to command. *Oh yeah, let's crank it for another mile.*

"Ain't no use of goin' back." "Ain't no use of goin' back." "Jodie's got your Cadillac." "Jodie's got your Cadillac."

Mythical, ubiquitous Jodie—that draft-dodging son-of-a-bitch civilian slacker who not only avoided military service, but now he's driving your car, working your job and shacking up with your girlfriend or sister!

"Sound off." "One two." "Sound off." "Three four." "Cadence count."

"One two three four. One two three four!"

They were really hauling now. Sergeant Starkey was pushing hard, extending them. Heavy breathing surged through the ranks, but they were in good shape. Seventeen weeks earlier most couldn't do squat…way back when they were PFC's—Poor Fuckin' Civilians. After eight weeks of basic training and an extra two months of advanced infantry training, the company keenly prepared itself for tomorrow's graduation ceremony. "Fuck Jodie!" someone shouted. The platoon panted a collective chuckle. And so it went for another rhythmic mile.

Fort Dix's two-story, wooden shell barracks had all been cloned from the same blueprint, or so it appeared. Each housed one platoon. A series of four were geometrically horseshoed around the neat company street with a smaller single-level building bottoming out the U. It served as Company K's orderly room and HQ, the now busy chow hall positioned rearward. Exiting soldiers dressed in faded field uniforms quickly donned soft billed caps, a conditioned reflex learned day one. Evening mess consisted of franks and beans, boiled potatoes, coleslaw, bread, and green Jell-O containing bits of fruit cocktail. Hardly sumptuous, but Bataan's defenders, who surrendered the prior week, would consider it gourmet. Their tortuous sixty-five mile Death March would see them refused life's barest essentials and subjected to heinous atrocities.

The tang of lime gelatin clinging to his palate, Pvt. Nick Callahan casually strolled across King Company's dusty street. Oblivious to those about him, he re-read the printed orders in diminishing sunlight. That was his name alright, captured in bold capital letters: CALLAHAN, NICHOLAS DANIEL PVT. While his buddies would be swallowed up in the rush to fill out the infantry regiments shipping overseas, he would spend a restorative week on furlough before proceeding to Georgia's Fort Benning. Georgian summers were not exactly balmy. In fact, among experienced old-timers, "sweltering" seemed to be the prevalent adjective. For the anxious candidate, however, weather was a non-issue. He had been accepted to OCS and that's all that mattered.

Provided he met the challenge, in three months' time, second lieutenant's bars would grace his shoulders. Interestingly, Nick was the only GI to receive any orders at all, the remaining company to obtain theirs tomorrow. Hearsay had it that one third of the 160-man company was slated for Pacific-bound units with the balance heading for Europe. But it was only one rampant unverified rumor among many. Refolding the sheet, he unbuttoned his pocket flap and placed it next to his mother's farewell scapular.

Friday's send-off parade would officially confirm King Company's completion of training. Its members would be dismissed, ultimately scattered to battlefields in North Africa, Europe, and the Pacific theater. But all that was momentarily on hold. Tonight's scheduled activity called for Field Day, military jargon for barracks cleaning of the most superior echelon. Everything, repeat everything, had to be scrubbed down, scoured, swept, dusted, disinfected and polished cleaner than a gnat's ass for the incoming cycle. Latrines, bunks, rolled mattresses, rifle racks, windows, floors, doors, brass, butt cans, foot lockers, and metal wall lockers anticipated a double "chickenshit" inspection ninety minutes after reveille. Immaculate weapons were to be signed over to the armorer following the parade.

Butchering the English language came as natural to Sergeant Arthur T. Starkey as breathing God's free air. This evening he huddled the skivvy-clad platoon for what they hoped mercifully would be the closing chapter. They expected it to be the final time third platoon would have to tolerate his webs of verbiage and fractured metaphors. Inasmuch as Nick had graduated college with an English minor, he was acutely aware of Starkey's more subtle malaprops. Callahan viewed it as a form of entertainment in the vein of comic relief. During several lectures, the verbose sergeant unwittingly encouraged amused troops to "get your ducks ironed out." Made no sense but they got the gist.

Sliding an olive-drab foot locker to the center floor, Starkey mounted it, showing off a dazzling pair of spit-shined low quarter shoes. As was his habit, he toted a T-handled steel cleaning rod, utilized as a combination pointer and swagger stick. Out-of-step marchers often felt its prod calling attention to uncoordinated footwork. Drill field aside, its most memorable function was something more startling. The Fort's training reservation encompassed a large sprawling network of sandy ranges, virtually all of which contained open-air classroom bleachers. Seated recruits were expected to remain awake. Sit and learn. Non-coms like Starkey would lurk about, hunting unsuspecting, sleepy prey in the act of nodding off.

Creeping up on such deviates, Starkey's rod would whack their steel helmets with a resounding ping! Metal on metal. Inside the helmet, the sharp reverberation brought all of a man's senses to renewed alertness, save one—his hearing.

"I'm expecting every swingin' dick in third platoon to break his butt gettin' my barracks clean, cleaner than Betty Grable's ass! First Sergeant says no one, I repeat no one, is leavin' here until it's spotless!" He flicked an imaginary piece of lint from his cuff for effect. "Now before you all start drivin' those mops and brushes, I want to make a few quick points." *Here comes the bullshit,* more than one G. I. reacted. Red-faced from an adulthood of NCO Club shots and beers, the stringy-built platoon sergeant thrust the cleaning rod toward clusters of men who feigned intense interest. "Over the last two months of advanced fuckin' infantry training, I've watched you learn things you probably never thought possible. And over that period, it has become obvious to me, Sergeant Arthur T. Starkey, US Army, that a majority of you people have done a damn fine job. But it has also come to my attention that there is another majority that's done a real piss-poor job. And you know who you are!" He swung the rod in a broad arc causing the nearest to flinch.

Callahan kneed the half-grinning G. I. beside him. "How many majorities can you have?" he giggled a whisper.

"Something fucking funny, Callahan?"

"No, sergeant."

"For someone who barely got accepted to OCS, you're pretty damn cocky. I doubt if you could pee and wind your watch at the same time." Spread-legged, he gripped both hands on the rod handle and tapped the locker. "And you want to be an officer? Shit, you won't last one fucking week." Tap tap tap!

"Yes, sergeant." Nick was savvy enough to know he didn't need a confrontation this last night. *Rounding third, heading for home. Don't stumble now, Nicky.*

Humbling point delivered, Starkey broke his intimidating stare from the defenseless private. Playing to the crowd, he let fly one more zing. "Now that we've taken care of smart-ass business, on to the next! There is a persistent latrine rumor circulating around you people that has become a problem. And I don't like problems. Specifically, there's been some crap about two-thirds of you going to Europe and one-third to kill Japs. Where you get these cockeyed numbers from I'll never guess. I know of no, repeat, no orders which support this rumor, and neither does the First Sergeant.

"Some of you people have been annoying the shit out of the company clerk with questions of who's going where. He doesn't know. Repeat, he doesn't know! He hasn't got a clue. As soon as your goddamn orders arrive from Personnel we'll pass them on to you people, probably after the parade. If anyone pesters the clerk tomorrow, he'll end up scrubbing the grease pit in Sergeant Suarez's kitchen, orders or no orders. Is that clear?"

"Yes, sergeant," they mumbled.

"I said, is that clear?"

"YES, SERGEANT."

"That's better." Withdrawing a slip of note paper hidden up his sleeve, Starkey held it to his eyes. "Now, the following thirteen men will fall out in front of the orderly room tomorrow at zero-eight-hundred for yellow fever and cholera shots. The medics will be waiting for you. Acknowledge when your name is called."

Unquestionably, a similar scenario jolted thirty-three percent in King's other three platoons. Had not anyone in Headquarters made the connection between tropical disease and theater of operation? Inexplicably, drill sergeants and the Army in general employ peculiar methods and circuitous signals to disseminate information.

Pearl Harbor shocked the citizens of Chicago into a vengefully patriotic fervor, as it did every other American city and town. The nation had been on the threshold of shaking off the Great Depression when Vice Admiral Chuichi Nagumo's carrier fleet rained destruction on the unsuspecting naval base and Wheeler Field. In *the city of broad shoulders*, strapping young men flooded recruiting stations to pledge the only resource they owned—their lives.

49

Twenty-year-old bakery truck driver, Pat Shanahan, had urged his older cousin with the chiming last name to join up with him. The plan was to serve together, which the cooperative recruiter *guaranteed*. Predictably, Pat was placed on a bus destined for Fort Leonard Wood, Missouri, and cousin Nick Callahan caught the train to Jersey. The best-laid plans of mice and men…

Probably it turned out for the best because it is questionable whether Nick would have applied for the Officers Candidate School option had Pat been with him. The Callahans were a fairly large brood. Three sons and an equal sum of daughters crammed into a five-room brick tenement, a crucifix in every room but the kitchen and toilet. Typical of Irish immigrants, Mr. Callahan steered a bus with the Chicago transit system and mother did housecleaning to earn Catholic school tuition for her half dozen.

Nick, the baby, reaped the studious benefit of privacy when older brothers James and Gerard moved out on their own. That left young Nick the boys' room all to his own at age thirteen. Consequently, grades soared and four solid years of parochial high school prompted the local monsignor to suggest that partial financial aid could be wangled should the teenager attend local DePaul University. So off he went, the first of his clan to seek collegiate excellence. Bus commutation to and from campus rose a step above economical—free! His father's charitable cronies winked their approval anytime Nick hopped aboard, part of the scholarship they rationalized.

Sisters Helen and Maureen pitched in a few helpful dollars whenever possible. They still resided at home, the latter engaged to a recently arrived Kerryman. Patty now devoted her life to prayer and meditation, tending a novitiate at the Convent of St. Vincent. Sandy-haired and blue-eyed with his mother's pleasant looks, conscientious Nicholas D. Callahan worked weekends, vacations, and summers to supplement the small grant. Books and school meals were also his responsibility.

Graduating in June, 1941, Nick exhausted almost six frustrating months pursuing a career commensurate with a degree in commerce. Between interviews, Callahan washed buses, a skill eventually serving him well during field days. Today, in the wake of Japan's sneak attack, Pat's persuasive overture and sixteen weeks in Sergeant Starkey's care, Nick Callahan aspired to OCS and respectability as officer and gentleman by act of the great American Congress.

Author's note: Commencing with the U.S. entry in the war, ten full Army infantry divisions and numerous smaller units would train at Fort Dix prior to deployment abroad.

CHAPTER VI
ABERDEEN

DATE: MONDAY, 20 APRIL 1942

TIME: 0940 HOURS

LOCATION: ABERDEEN, MARYLAND

Two cups of coffee is about twice as long as meetings ought to run. Usually each Monday, Colonel Wallace conducted brief, to-the-point powwows recapping the previous two weeks' progress and laying out the next five days' activity. In attendance this morning sat Captains Boudreau and Longley, Chief Warrant Officer Bradovich, Warrant Officer Junior Grade McCord, and Staff Sergeant Luzak, last in the pecking order. The extra cup poured as a direct result of Longley's laborious queries and conceited ramblings aimed at justifying his own actions. His motives were transparent to all including him. Other than loving thine own face, self-importance is the most incontestable symptom of vanity. But the petulant Captain carried it to a nagging level by chronically inflating his value to the Information Office.

Having experienced the limits of sufferance, Wallace forcefully plunged a half-smoked Lucky Strike into an oversized ashtray already harboring a shallow cemetery of dead butts.

"Captain Longley, your contribution to the Information Office is duly noted and appreciated. But let's not overstate your mission. We are Ordnance's public relations group, only our public is a military and governmental constituency. We inform, we educate, we sell the Army's hardware. Propagandists! Yes, we are purveyors of propaganda amid the apathetic bureaucracy. In some cases we help vindicate past appropriations from Congress and the War Department. When the Secretary of the Army looks good, so does our Ordnance branch. His confidence helps loosen purse strings for future projects. It's that simple! We perform a somewhat passive function… not necessarily critical in the great scheme. Therefore, there is no one in this group who is not expendable. No one!"

The paunchy Wallace fished another cigarette from the waning pack. Snapping his Zippo, he inhaled and allowed the milky fumes to escape through an aquiline nose that ended barely above his upper lip. Pock marked cheeks and raccoon eyes supported the theorem that one needn't be beautiful to be smart.

"That's it," he abruptly declared and slapped a palm to the desk-wide blotter. The men stood to file out, a sheepish Longley hurriedly moved to be first. "One last thing, Sergeant Luzak, would you please remain." Wallace circled a finger motioning him to close the door.

Mild paranoia tingled the recesses of Woody's nape, similar to being called to the principal's office. *What the hell's going on?* Instinctively, he raced through a struggling conscience attempting to recall any rule-bending to which he might have been privy. Chain of command propriety, for the most part, didn't place colonels and sergeants in secluded privacy barring extreme circumstances. *Come to think of it, I did tell that rolly-polly civilian photographer to piss up a rope. Hell, that couldn't be it… not for a full bird to be involved. Maybe it's news of Tony?* Wallace, recognizing the apprehension, attempted to alleviate Luzak's anxiety. "Sit down, Sergeant! It's all good news."

"Yes, sir." He quickly took a chair, but sat erect.

"I've got a situation playing out that only you can help me solve."

"Colonel, I'll do whatever I can." *What the hell is he talking about?*

He dragged slowly before resting the Lucky on the ashtray rim. Leaning back, Wallace interlocked short chubby fingers behind his head, covering a maturing bald spot. "I have to make a choice, or more accurately, you have to make a decision. Two options are open," he mused. Frustrated with himself he began speaking rapidly. "What the deuce am I beating around the bush for? Luzak, at seventeen hundred hours today, I'm going to submit your name for promotion to sergeant first class or… recommend you as an officer candidate!" Thunderstruck, Woody jerked more upright, several conflicting thoughts streaking through his brain.

"Sergeant, either way you win. It's the difference between a little win or one with a capital 'W.' What's your reaction?"

"I'm a bit tongue-tied, sir. This is pretty sudden."

"I know, and maybe a bit unfair." Wallace checked the wall clock. "Nevertheless, you've got seven hours to decide your future."

Woody suppressed a bolt of emotion ranging the gamut from mild shock to confusion. "Sir, may I be frank?"

"Please do."

"What prompted you to consider me officer material?"

"Come on, get off it, Sergeant. This little information circle is made up of lightweights, myself perhaps included. Nine-to-fivers. We might as well be wearing fedoras and three-piece suits. Until you showed up last year, most of us were going through the motions… reacting, not initiating. You've been the only one able to link the guts of our new and experimental weaponry with putting the word out, and know what the hell he's talking about. Your insistence that meaningful, innovative demonstrations at the grassroots level are worth more than articles in some stuffy periodical seems real obvious today. But before you arrived, we never did much of that except for the big-wigs.

"Don't you think I've been aware of Longley's goldbricking while you did everything from liaison work with that Quantico bunch right up to the actual presentations? It's been your idea to get the Marine rifle team involved on that M1 project, to enlist their support. Longley would like us to believe that was his genius, but I know better!"

Wallace pulled a deep stream of smoke into his lungs. He had just admitted his vulnerability to a staff sergeant. Officers aren't supposed to do that.

"Sir, I'm flattered but I, uh, I'm not sure."

"What's there to be sure about? You're probably the most articulate NCO I've come across. I'm not telling you anything you haven't figured out by yourself."

"Sir, I barely scrambled through high school. Officers are college educated… aren't they?"

Colonel Wallace chose to ignore the direct question. "You're bright, have a take-charge attitude, an outstanding record. Self-improvement seems to be a high priority. I see the reading matter on your desk, all that 'how to succeed' stuff. Do I have to go on? Most importantly, people listen to and respect you. And, unlike me, you look terrific in uniform." He paused. "It's okay, you can laugh. It was meant to be a joke."

Woody forced a weak smile, his discomfort yet apparent.

"Look, the Army needs officers, talented officers. That crack about cutting a dashing figure is strictly Hollywood. You know there's more to being an officer than wearing the uniform. Some people, though, put too much of a premium on that thing. Take Longley for instance, he looks splendid at the General's luncheon but… " Wallace fell short of completing the thought. Notwithstanding, the intent was clear. Officers are reluctant to blatantly badmouth their own in the presence of enlisted men, but they've been known to infer conspicuous conclusions. The portly Colonel hesitated, then expounded his philosophy summarizing the essence of military leadership.

"Luzak, let me share a personal piece of wisdom. A rotten military organization is like a goddamn fish, it stinks from the head on down! If you have an outstanding general commanding a division then you have a damn fine division, but if you have a crappy general, you can bet you'll end up with a lousy division. And it's equally true at the regiment, battalion, and company levels, all the way down to the platoon. Have an incompetent platoon leader, end up with an ineffective platoon. In a nutshell, good officers make good units! You will make an excellent lieutenant so it follows that the men you lead will be a crackerjack group. Get my point?" An ash dropped to the fold in his neck tie. He brushed it away, some residue remained trapped.

"I'll do it, sir." The spontaneous leap to acceptance surprised even Woody.

"Marvelous. Take the rest of the week off. Orders were cut back on April fourteenth. You depart for Benning on Friday." An impish light danced in his sunken eyes.

"I appreciate this opportunity, sir. Thank you for your confidence and support."

"You'll be sorely missed."

Havre de Grace lies a few miles north of Aberdeen where the uppermost fingers of the Chesapeake Bay are joined by the Susquehanna River. Wheeling his 1937 black Chevy coupe up the long gravel driveway, Woody slipped it into neutral and eased off the gas, allowing the auto to slow down of its own momentum as he approached the split. The wide left fork led up to the main house, a magnificent three-story colonial showpiece once home to Baltimore elite. In 1940, its twenty-one rooms had been chopped into three spacious apartments for the families of civilian scientists working hush-hush

War Department assignments. Pillared porches and porticoes ringed the perimeter, permitting sweeping views of the sparkling bay.

He pressed the brake pedal, halting to catch a brief glimpse of the late day seascape. A few sailboats enjoyed the final golden half hour of light, tracking trails through the choppy waves. Encouraged by the serenity, he allowed himself a pensive moment. Life was rocketing so quickly with Tony's fate unknown, his relationship with Swifty uncertain, and now his appointment to OCS. The ebb and flow of recent events paralleled the shifting Maryland tide. *How is it all going to shake out?* A gentle beep brought him back. He yanked the gearshift into first and turned into the narrow right-hand car path winding down to Swifty's place. Parking alongside her blue humpbacked Plymouth, he took a few extra seconds before getting out, still in thought.

The former caretaker's cottage had been well maintained, freshly painted clapboard in soft yellow and crisp white window trim made it look larger than its three cozy rooms. The rent was slightly more than Nancy Swift wished to spend, but its location in the tranquil coastal community provided welcome escape from her secretarial demands. Rapping once on the outer screen door, Woody pulled it toward him and pushed open the unlocked inside door. "It's me, honey!" he reassuringly called. The radio crooned an oldie, the melodic strains of Russ Columbo's *Vagabond Lover*. Nancy sang along, emphasizing the lyric, "…in search of a sweetheart, it seems."

"Hi, beautiful."

Smiling, she came out of the open kitchen and stood on bare tiptoes to kiss his mouth. "Something to drink?"

"A cold beer would only add to your dazzling charm."

"You sweet talkin' devil." They walked as one to the kitchen. She fetched a bottle from the Frigidaire while Woody grabbed a church key off a cupboard peg. Snapping off the crown, he took a long draught. "Thirsty boy, huh?"

Woody nodded, the bottle still at his lips. He gulped another mouthful. "Cold and wet, that's how I like 'em"

"How'd it go today, hon?" She moved behind him, rubbing his neck and shoulders.

Draining the bottle, he banged the empty on the counter-top, harder than he wanted. "I'll tell you all about it." He spun around. "God, you're gorgeous," he proclaimed, playing his fingers about her tiny waist and down her hips.

"Aw shucks, I'll bet you tell that to all the girls." She batted her long eyelashes, striking a bashful pose.

"We'd better sit down for this one, baby. I've got a lot to say."

Swifty realized he was serious enough for her to dutifully prance to the living room love seat without uttering a word. Plopping down, she sat cross-legged, her stylish brown, wide-bottomed shorts creeping to expose a solid pair of thighs. Dark hair tumbled shoulder-length as she removed the restraining barrette. She slipped the bulky sweater sleeves elbow high and pursed her lips. She was prepared to hear his expected tale of Aberdeen when a horrid premonition shocked her thoughts. "It's Tony, isn't it?" Although she had never met his brother, she felt the same sickening sensation that plagued Woody these past few nervous weeks.

"No, it has nothing to do with Tony. Although for an instant earlier today, I had an inkling that news of his status was coming my way." He peered into her silent brown eyes and emitted a tense sigh. "It's about me and my life and how you fit into it."

Twenty minutes later, an enlightened Swifty walked to the fridge and plucked out two frosty bottles. She strolled through the portal and handed him one. While she held out the opener, he manipulated the bottle cap under the metal tongue. He steadied it as she twisted the key. It opened with a hiss, the crown falling to his free hand. They repeated the process for hers. She cocked the bottle as if to salute him. "I'm so proud of you, Woody. Here's to—"

"Wait a second," he interrupted. "I believe the toast isn't customary until after the proposal."

"What proposal?" A coy smile trickled across her red lips. *Would he? Was it possible?*

Woody Luzak tabled the beer and groped his pants pocket, producing an unmistakable small blue velvet box. He raised the lid, revealing a platinum ring. The setting embraced a gleaming half-carat diamond. "It was the best the PX had to offer on short notice." Tears welled up as she watched Woody fumble off the price tag yet clinging to the band. She extended her hand in anticipation. "Nancy Ray Swift, will you marry a man about to become the oldest second lieutenant in the United States Army?"

"Oh yes, Woody. Yes, I will." Her voice was hardly audible.

He effortlessly slid it over the knuckle, then kissed the trembling finger. They hugged for a long silent moment, while she sobbed a soft whimper of loving contentment.

"Twenty-nine isn't old," she scoffed, drying her eyes against his already damp shirt.

"For a second looie, it is!"

"You're not old, just experienced." They laughed, then hugged again. "Honey, when do you think we'll have the wedding?"

"I figure in about three months, as soon as I graduate from OCS. You can pin on my bars and we'll tie the knot. Kind of a package deal."

"Why not before OCS," she cooed.

He broke the embrace and thought for a split second. "Why not?" he agreed. The day had been one of unending impulse. "What the hell, we've got a whole three days to get it done." She let out a yip and kissed him. "Now how about that toast!" he shouted.

Some might consider clinking beer bottles a rather déclassé gesture for a matrimonial engagement. From the perspective of wartime lovers though, it was highly romantic. In truth, they clinked twice with pledging kisses in between.

Late that night, Nancy and Woody lay naked in each other's arms, dozing in and out of a blissful sleep. Their energetic lovemaking had exhausted each's biological drive. Sated, he gently stroked her hair. The dark room was comfortably cool, only a sheet covered them. "You awake?" he whispered.

"Yes." Nancy cuddled closer to his smooth chest.

"I'm stretched out here staring at a ceiling I can't see, and I'm thinking, what motivated me to accept Colonel Wallace's offer?"

"Because you want it, and you deserve it." she kissed his nipple.

"For wealthy, educated people, their station in life demands an officer's slot...whether equipped to do the job, or not. Sort of a cultural thing."

"Well honey, that's not you." A tiny giggle escaped her. He chuckled aloud.

"Yeah. We Luzaks never saw the inside of a country club unless we were clearing tables. But seriously, Swifty, I don't think ego-gratification or achieving a new measure of respectability is what's driving me, although I'm sure they carry some weight."

"Then what, Woody?"

"I believe I've developed both an instinct and a desire to lead men. I enjoy the reward of being out in front, making things happen. Hell, I've been preaching to officers, with some success, for a while now. Often I can persuade them to my point of view. Is that cockiness or confidence? I guess what I'm saying is that I feel I belong!"

"Just do the best you can. And don't think too much." She slithered up close to his face and softly kissed chin and lips.

"Uh-oh." They exhausted each other one last time before tumbling into deep, restful sleep.

CHAPTER VII
PLAYERS

DATE: TUESDAY, 26 MAY 1942

TIME: 1415 HOURS

LOCATION: BRISBANE, QUEENSLAND, AUSTRALIA

Semi-tropical Australian climate provided a pleasant respite for two gaunt passengers seated in the gray USN Ford. The tall one rotated the window an extra crank to further invite the invigorating breeze. Flexing his hand, he leaned forward over the front seat to get a better view of North Brisbane, the heart of Brisbane city. Seated to his left a tough-looking man clutched a shabby briefcase with a neat one-inch square missing from the corner flap. They drove along the north bank of the Brisbane River before cornering into a treed side street and then several turns off of that. The navy driver, dressed in smart summer whites, brought the vehicle to a smooth halt, fronting a six-story stone and brick building featuring a brass plaque, "Hotel Fenimore."

"Third floor. Suite three-thirteen, sir. There's a sign on the door that identifies the USMC Mission. Lieutenant Colonel Maxwell should be waiting for you there."

"Thank you, sailor."

"Aye-aye, sir."

Evidently, Maxwell had witnessed their arrival from his office window. He and a Marine captain greeted them at the open gate as Delane and Luzak exited the lift. Both visitors were clad in an odd bag of borrowed military clothing, mostly khaki and rankless. Neckties, or field scarves as the Corps identifies them, were absent. However, their tanned faces were razor-clean and framed with trim regulation haircuts. The colonel spoke first.

"Good afternoon, gentlemen. I'm Lieutenant Colonel Maxwell, and this is Captain Roy Bauer."

"First Lieutenant Delane, sir, and Gunnery Sergeant Luzak."

"Shall we go inside—we're anxious to learn of your escape. All we received was a rather terse signal from HMAS *Hobin* informing that you two were aboard and had somehow engineered your way safely from the Philippines."

Delane smiled. "Well, that's the short version, sir." They stepped through a small parlor which had been converted into a busy typing pool. Four desks, each with a Marine typist pounding away, formed a passage to a pair of smaller offices, presumably once bedrooms. Floral print drapes, militarily incongruous, framed the graceful elongated windows.

As one might expect, the larger room belonged to Maxwell. He settled in behind a fancy mahogany desk with Bauer to his right, facing the seated duo. "Coffee or tea?" the captain offered.

"Not for me, sir" Delane said. "We grabbed some refreshment en- route."

"No thank you, sir," Luzak added, still gripping the satchel. Twenty days earlier they had learned of Corregidor's surrender after a heroic stand. Round-the-clock Japanese artillery had finally pummeled The Rock into humiliating submission. The Army and Marine garrison, low on water, medicine, and ammunition, wearily succumbed to a merciless enemy. Gunnery Sergeant Tony Luzak squeezed his leather charge, unaware his knuckles had turned a ghostly white. With the Fourth Marines gone, its contents took on a more awesome responsibility.

"Let's get started, shall we," Maxwell pleasantly urged. "Smoke 'em if you got 'em. Feel free to use mine." He gestured to a half pack of Camels before him. "Just so you understand our Mission's role, let me inform you that Captain Bauer and I are almost in the intelligence business. That is, we are part of a fact-gathering screen, which assembles worthwhile data ultimately transmitted to official Navy and Marine Intelligence. More than that, I can't tell you." Bauer lifted a lined yellow pad and one of several sharpened pencils, ready to take notes. "Okay," Maxwell directed, "let's start at the beginning."

The lieutenant nudged his chair closer to his awaiting audience. Turning to Luzak, he said, "Gunny, I'm going to retrace our journey, but feel free to interject any comments I omit or you feel are appropriate."

Tony nodded, "Aye, sir."

Delane took them back to Kindley Field and their semi-clandestine meeting with Colonel Sam Howard. He emphasized Howard's orders to pass on the reports and records only to USMC powers which would recognize their intelligence as well as historical value. Recapping their perilous trek via *El Corazon Blanco*, he told them of Rizal and the friendship they formed aboard ship and later in the Zamboangan jungle. Their group had disembarked the fishing vessel and rowed ashore with Antonio on April 2, just after dark. Prearranged, a band of fierce Moros moved from the tree line to usher the landing party to safety.

During the subsequent thirty-two days, Delane and Luzak lived among the small guerrilla group, changing locations on four occasions. Rizal would disappear for two or three days at a time. Ostensibly, he was off enlisting support and asserting command among the fledgling resistance network. A week after their arrival, he showed up with a bearded Royal Australian Navy lieutenant commander, Evan Whitfield. Whitfield, it turned out, was a hydrographer working on loan to the US Navy and Philippine government, charting tide falls and potential anchorages in western Mindanao. When war erupted on December 7, he had been stranded. Patriotic Mindanoans secreted him in their homes at first, but soon he was being bounced around from sugar cane shed to backwater village, and then to their spot in the jungle.

To help pass time, the little band spent the hot afternoons teaching each other lessons which might have future survival benefit. Delane schooled Antonio, Evan, and Tony in aircraft identification. Tony oversaw weapons instructions, mostly in sign language to the avid Moros. The most rudimentary basics in hydrography were explained by Whitfield. Charts reflecting depths and tidal information were spread across a stretched canvas table to illustrate salient points. Evan stored them in a thick bamboo tube plugged at both ends with a cork-like material. In return, Antonio taught a smattering of Tagalog to his struggling students. Harrowing circumstance often engenders close relationships where, in more mundane situations, there would be no common ground for comradeship. Delane and Whitfield hit it off beautifully.

On a moist May 5 morning, Antonio Rizal materialized out of the tangled vegetation and announced that his "three guests will be leaving this evening" by way of an American submarine. Linkup would be on the Moro Gulf coast of the peninsula. Excited, the men made preparations for the overland hike.

At 2340 hours, the USS *Great Requin* stealthily surfaced to a black moonless sky. Almost immediately, three rapid amber blinks flashed toward the quiet surf six hundred yards away. Standing on a rotten stump, Rizal's second-in-command lit a green-glassed lantern and raised it head high for ten seconds. Both lookouts manning the conning tower spotted it simultaneously and alerted the skipper.

On order, the crew inflated two huge black rubber rafts and lashed crates of varying size inside. Sliding them overboard, a pair of four-man teams jumped in and muscled their paddles shoreward. Once near the beach, the guerrillas waded thigh-deep to tow the craft over the packed wet sand. The two Marines and Australian took turns to embrace Antonio farewell and express their gratitude. Rizal wished them good fortune and hurried them through the low dunes. They had already handed over their boots and sidearms to Moros with whom they had struck friendships. Teams of guerrillas quickly offloaded crates containing some weapons and supplies, but the key cargo this inky evening were radios, vital for Rizal's communications net. Splashing into the lazy surf, the three fugitives clambered onto a bobbing raft. "Who the fuck are you?" the petty officer in charge exclaimed.

"We ain't tourists," Luzak said, elevating the satchel above the sea spray.

"Give us a paddle," Delane ordered. "We're Americans—at least two-thirds of us are. Hubba-hubba, let's move it!"

Two-hundred feet below the rolling Celebes Sea, Commander Alan "Buddy" Hamilton entered the compartment where the men had moments before dried themselves and slipped into clothing requisitioned from among the crew. Ragged heaps of discarded apparel lay before them. A seaman scooped up the odorous pile destined for the refuse locker. Introductions were exchanged and information swapped. Hamilton good-naturedly muttered something about being a glorified trolley driver. In return, the threesome merrily toasted him and the *Great Requin* with steaming mugs of black coffee. The underwater voyage went without a hitch, roughly half of it being spent in therapeutic sleep. Twelve days later the sub rendezvoused with an Australian corvette, HMAS *Hobin*, which eventually transported them to the Brisbane docks.

Wide-eyed, Colonel Maxwell slapped his thigh. "Christ, that's some ticklish adventure!" Almost an hour had ticked by since they convened. Standing erect, he ambled to the window and pushed aside the shade, apparently collecting his thoughts. Before he could act though, Bauer spoke.

"My compliments to the both of you for a truly dramatic escape. First rate, it reads like a dime-store novel. Quite a feat!" His face expressed bona-fide admiration. The captain also got to his feet, only to park his lean butt on the desk edge.

"After we arrange for proper uniforms and back pay, I'd like you to stick around here for a few days," he said. "There's a lot of information you can supply which might appear innocent right now, but down the line could be invaluable. We'd like to chat with Lieutenant Commander Whitfield, too."

"Yes, sir, at your service," Delane confirmed.

"We'll get you sleeping quarters upstairs. And I'll inform Command of your presence and temporary transfer to this mission—after which you've got some R&R to look forward to." He winked.

Colonel Maxwell moved back to his desk. "And as for that bag you're clutching, gunny, let me assure you that I served a *ding hao* three-year hitch in the Fourth, and knew Colonel Howard. So I qualify as an old China Marine too. It will be safe with me until I can evaluate it and pass it on to a higher and, yes, equally trustworthy echelon."

"Semper Fi, Colonel." Tony stretched the satchel out to Maxwell. "It's almost part of me. I don't think it's been out of my sight for over two months, except when bolted behind that fishing boat bulkhead." Removing the dog tag chain from his neck, he unsnapped the key and placed it in the colonel's palm.

Noticing the small square missing from the flap, the captain jokingly inquired, "You boys must have been hungrier than you let on?"

"Well, sir," Luzak said, "it's kind of a souvenir for my hope chest. Taught to me by an old buddy we lost in Bataan." Distressed, he looked to Delane for help. *Don't make me explain something I don't understand.*

Andrew Delane broke the mood. "Sirs, we've also placed one-thousand-eighty dollars inside from the regimental fund. I spent twenty bucks in Zamboanga to buy Rizal a sentiment of appreciation that hopefully, will prove to be utilitarian…a silver filigreed pocket compass. Quite handsome. I told him it was a gift from the Fourth Marines for sheltering their hallowed past."

"Surely Sam Howard would approve," Maxwell said.

"I suggest we open the case now and inventory its contents. Then we'll type up a receipt acknowledging its successful disposition." Captain Bauer was an exacting man, leaving zero to chance.

Maxwell twisted the key into the aperture. It took a few jiggles before the lock tumbled. He removed the money envelope, discolored with dank jungle mold, and slid it to Roy Bauer. Searching inside, he extracted three smaller envelopes wrapped in protective oil cloth. Boldly scrawled across the first was the attention-getting phrase FOR THE COMMANDANT'S EYES ONLY, with the second addressed to FUTURE COMMANDING OFFICER, 4TH MARINES. Envelope number three stated USMC COMMAND AUSTRALIA. Comprising the briefcase's bulk contents were two weighty oil cloth sleeves, stitched tight and swathed in medical adhesive tape to create a water resistant seal. The colonel tested their heft and returned them to the bag. Carefully tearing a corner from the third envelope he slit the edge. Maxwell unfolded a single typewritten sheet and briefly studied it in silent concentration. Without a sound he handed it to Bauer and the others to examine.

MEMORANDUM

FROM: COM OFFICER 4TH MAR REGT 1635 12MAR42

SUBJ: DISPOSITION RECORDS/DOCUMENTS

TO: USMC COMMAND AUSTRALIA

CC: COMMANDANT, USMC, WASH DC

SHOULD CONTENTS OF ENCLOSED VALISE BE RECEIVED BY USMC COMMAND AUSTRALIA, PLEASE INSURE SAFE KEEPING OF REGT'S HISTORICAL FILE AND ACTION REPORTS CONTAINED HEREIN. MAPS OF CURRENT MILITARY SITUATION AND ASSESSMENT INCLUDED. IN VIEW OF BLEAK OUTLOOK THOUGHT BEST TO TRANSMIT TO YOU. RECOMMEND FILE BE MADE AVAILABLE TO RECONSTITUTED 4TH MARINES IF AND WHEN DECISION MADE.

SEMPER FIDELIS,

RESPECTFULLY SUBMITTED,

S. HOWARD, COLONEL USMC

ADDENDUM: WITH RECEIPT OF THESE DISPATCHES RECOMMEND PROMOTION OF LUZAK, ANTON J. GUNSGT TO MASTSGT WITH APPROPRIATE COMMENDATION FOR HIM AND 1STLT DELANE, ANDREW S. WHOSE PERSEVERANCE SUCCESSFULLY EFFECTED THIS TRANSFER.

DATE:	FRIDAY 29 MAY 1942
TIME:	1900 HOURS
LOCATION:	PLAYERS CLUB, BRISBANE

Piano music filtered across the dining room and through the bar lounge as the uniformed American serviceman approached a most attractive hostess. Women played an expanding role in the daily life of Brisbane these times. Most of their young men were off fighting Rommel in North Africa, or preparing to stem the Japanese Empire's impending push into Australia while others, usually older, worked in industries key to the war effort. She flashed a warm middle-aged smile. "May I help you?" she said.

He returned the expression. "Yes, I'm to meet a friend for dinner. Lieutenant Commander Evan Whitfield of your fine Royal Australian Navy."

The woman immediately recognized the name without consulting the reservation list. "Right this way please. The Whitfields are waiting for you."

Whitfields? Old Evan is married? The sly dog never told me that.

"You're a Yank soldier?" the hostess inquired.

"Well ma'am, you're half right. I'm a Yank for sure but I'm a Marine, not a soldier."

He followed her swishing gait as she led him past the animated pianist to a smaller wing adjacent to the main dining area. White linen tablecloths with alternating pink and aqua napkins complemented bright crystal and dinnerware. Fresh-cut yellow and white daisy mums decorated the tables and alcoves, adding a convivial touch. "Just ahead, sir. Enjoy your meal and... " she hesitated.

"Yes?" The American pleasantly drew her out, encouraging her to complete the thought.

"Well, I'd like to thank you and your countrymen for your help. Especially that smashing General MacArthur."

They both blushed a bit. "Why thank you, Mrs.— "

"It's 'Miss'—Gwen Cash." She held out her hand.

He took it and gave a gentle shake. "Andrew Delane. I'm pleased to make your acquaintance, Gwen. And next time I confer with Douglas MacArthur I'll be certain to pass on your kind sentiments."

Gwen effected a playful smile. Fortyish, she made up for the years with impeccable grooming and smartly-tailored clothing. Her mild flirtation awakened a long dormant sensation. She surprised herself with what she considered overtly aggressive behavior. *Perfect for Colonel Maxwell,* Andrew thought.

By this point, Evan Whitfield had spied Delane and rose, tumbler in hand, to bellow welcome. "Andy, over here, over here," he gestured emphatically. "My God you look positively bloody magnificent!" His enthusiasm caused his drink to slosh a few drops toward Delane who managed an exaggerated toreador move to avoid getting wet.

"Bravo, bravo," a woman's admiring voice applauded the maneuver.

In the same motion, Andrew grabbed Evan's outstretched hand and turned to the cheering woman seated below him. Her strawberry blonde hair was cut short and swept back along the sides, exposing perfect lobes accentuated by pearl drop earrings. Hazel-green eyes sparkled in the fun of the moment. She lifted her head backwards, revealing full lips and a smooth tanned throat.

"Evan!" he exclaimed. "You never mentioned you were married!" Delane looked into her radiant face. "My lord, I guess if I were wed to anyone this lovely I'd keep it a secret too… afraid someone might steal her."

The Aussie snorted a robust laugh. "You bloody fool. Marla isn't my wife. She's my sister, and she insisted on meeting you!"

"Welcome to Brisbane, Lieutenant. Evan's told me so much about you that I just had to see for myself," Marla said, extending her hand.

Delane seized Marla's fingertips, cool from her iced gin and quinine water. "The pleasure is all mine, I assure you."

"Well, shall we sit or are you two going to gawk at each other like a pair of flaming monkeys?" The two men sat and Evan alerted the venerable waiter looming to his left. "What will you be drinking, Andy?"

"Same as you, I guess. Looks pretty good."

"Gordon's and quinine for my friend please, Winston," he said to the nodding waiter. "Squeeze of lime."

"I'll fetch it straight away, Mr. Whitfield…I mean Commander Whitfield."

"No need to overdo it, Winston. You've known me long enough to dispense with military niceties. Besides, I'm spiffed in civilian clothing."

Evan wore a silver-gray linen sport jacket over a mint-green silk shirt, the collar folded outside of the jacket's wide lapels. Eggshell pleated slacks accompanied by black-and-white saddle shoes completed the ensemble. He looked pretty clubby. "My family has held a membership at Players forever," Whitfield explained. "Old Winston's known me before I could toddle." He snatched a napkin and deftly patted dry his trim mustache, damp with gin.

Andrew was still slightly underweight, although the *Great Requin's* and *Hobin's* ample galleys had helped him recapture some of the poundage lost in the jungle. Roy Bauer's suntan uniform fit him near perfect. His tall athletic figure and dark good looks appeared to have strong appeal for the vivacious Marla Whitfield. Their eyes made repeated contact as the meal progressed. Rack of lamb for three, washed down with liberal quantities of Cabernet Sauvignon, represented the focus of their gabby dinner. Evan pointed out that Australia's promising wine industry anticipated a time when it would compete globally. The evening's libation originated from Coonawarra in South Australia where the Whitfields had been developing vineyards prior to the war. Family wealth though, sprang from an enormous wool-exporting conglomerate with offices in London, Manchester, and San Francisco.

Lieutenant Commander Whitfield's lifelong fascination with the ocean began with boyhood explorations of the Great Barrier Reef, which led to a compatible course of study at the University of Queensland, according to his autobiographical dinner chat.

In 1935, he joined the International Hydrographic Bureau, headquartered in scandalous Monte Carlo, Monaco. The location fit Whitfield's playboy instincts to a tee, as he was able to balance his scientific pursuits with a mildly hedonistic lifestyle. The best of both worlds! Upon his return to Brisbane at age twenty-six, he was contemplating a place in the family business when his father's close friend (who also happened to hold high political office in Canberra) solicited him with a RAN commission to full lieutenant. Parents and both managing brothers blessed the union in hope it would temper the young man's verve. His zest for living had long been a sticky concern.

Now, as the waiter poured more wine for everyone, Evan continued to hold court. Flushed with the vintner's nectar, he related a chain of Zamboangan tales of privation and spellbinding escape. Delane tended to ignore them as he slipped into a blissful rapture completely captivated by Marla.

Oblivious to her brother's proclamation of undying camaraderie with First Lieutenant Delane of "America's bloody Marines," she toyed with a tiny demi-tasse spoon before posing the question. "So tell me about yourself, Andy. Evan's buoyant spirits have centered, as usual, on his abundance of adventurous exploits. What of you? Let's start with your name… is it of French origin?" Evan, having spotted an old school chum, excused himself and teetered after the fellow, conveniently leaving the couple to hit it off.

Andy leaned back, never removing his eyes from hers. He wanted very much to tell her about himself, but without the braggadocio of an impetuous Romeo.

This was a young lady of wealth and culture, yet down to earth; comfortable among elite and servants alike. Marla's bubbly and caring personality endeared her to the Whitfield's household staff since early childhood. Puttering with the gardeners or kitchen help she always gave them a sense of equality by learning from their years of experience. Haughtiness was not a trait indigenous to her character.

"To answer your question, Marla, the Delane name is probably Irish. We have a feeling it must have been 'Delaney' at one point in time, but for whatever reason, or reasons, the first migrant to America, possibly illiterate, dropped the 'y.'" He smiled and turned a thumbs-up gesture. "Probably was a horse thief to boot! My father claims the first Delane showed up in North Carolina in the early eighteenth century as an indentured servant."

"Something like our Botany Bay," Marla said.

"I suppose. Interestingly though, most Irish names starting with 'D-e' originated with French Normans who crossed the Irish Sea—like Delaney, Delancey, Devaney, Delehanty, Devereaux, and so forth. Anyway, for two-hundred-plus years, we Delanes have resided in both Carolinas, although we've always lived near Fayettville on the Cape Fear River."

"And where, pray tell, is that?" Marla asked, leaning forward with interest.

"Oh, I'm sorry. It's in the lower part of North Carolina, inland, in the agricultural country. We're about fifty miles southwest of Raleigh, the state capital. North Carolina is in the southeast portion of the US," he added unsure of her knowledge of American geography.

"So you're a rebel," she laughed.

"Yeah, but over here we're all Yankees, I guess. Evidently, you know something of our history."

"I like to think I'm an educated woman, Andy." The way she said *Andy* caused a bit of him to melt inside.

"My dad went to college at Tulane University. That's in New Orleans, Louisiana. And that's where he met my mother. She was from a fairly well-to-do Cajun family, originally of French Canadian stock. Mom's maiden name was 'Sabre' which is my middle name. Pretty appropriate I think, because I take after her side, physically that is. So apparently there's a lot more French flowing through my veins than anything else."

"Like good Cabernet?" she asked, holding out her empty glass.

They both laughed as he poured her goblet half full. "As for me, I experienced a comfortably secure upbringing with two older sisters and a kid brother. At Duke University, I must confess to being a better cross-country runner than student. In 1938, 'the year of the great hurricane,' as it is referred to by my Rhode Island transplanted sister, I graduated devoid of distinction, and I entered Marine officer school that very same year. For the record, I'm an infantry lieutenant who, during a mad fit of expediency, was shanghaied into temporary duty with an anti- aircraft battalion in the Philippines. End of story."

"Is that where you were wounded?" Her tone switched from playful to one of concern. But she couldn't help glancing at his finger stub. He noticed.

"Yes." *My God, is this love at first sight or am I being swept up in a web of passion abetted by Coonawarra Red?*

"And what does your family do in Fayetteville, North Carolina?"

"My dad's in textiles, manages a large mill."

"Wool?" The mood came to a shattering halt. It was Evan back from his jaunt.

"Cotton, suh! We Delanes are from the South!" He overstated his accent sounding like the fictitious Senator Claghorn of radio fame. They all laughed.

"I'm afraid I've just learned some distressing news," Whitfield apprised. "Remember aboard the *Hobin*, the communications officer indicated there had been a major naval air engagement in the Coral Sea?"

"Yes, I recollect he mentioned it pitted flat top against flat top. What of it?"

"I've just been chatting with a chap in the know about such matters. Reports say your Yank navy lost a carrier, the *Lexington*, and possibly a second, the *Yorktown*. Several smaller vessels went down as well. The Japanese had a small carrier sunk. I think he called her the *Shoho*. Another Jap carrier, the *Shokaku*, was really plastered but apparently survived.

"Evidently the enemy lost a disproportionate sum of aircraft and were forced to withdraw their task force and troop transports supposedly on their way to capture Port Moresby in New Guinea… only a short hop to our Cape York peninsula here in Queensland. Our side is calling it a strategic victory." Whitfield was no longer tipsy. The seriousness of the news had sobered his brain.

"Exactly when did all this happen?" Andrew asked.

"Somewhere around the eighth or ninth of May, I think. I'm not all that certain."

Marla stared at the ashen American. "What is it, Andy? You're not looking well."

"One thing I neglected to mention earlier was that my great ambition was to be an aviator. Three years ago I washed out of flight training at Pensacola. My eyes were good, but not good enough to meet naval aviation's demanding standards. A few of my buddies who made it through were aboard the Lexington. God knows what their fate is."

"I see," she whispered, and reached out to take his hand. "Let's get out of this place, Andy."

"You two are getting on famously," Evan roared, to the amusement of several surrounding tables. Delane stood and moved to assist Marla with her seat. His classical tall, dark and handsome image contrasted her exquisitely fair beauty. Yet they formed a made-for-each-other twosome causing most diners to sit up and admire. An older gentleman puffing a meerschaum impatiently sidled by, escorting a highly attractive and bosomy woman perhaps twenty-five years his junior. "Who is that?" Evan asked Marla.

"Sir Harry Benton and his new bride of less than a year. Harry and Rita are the talk of Brisbane. Used to be his secretary. Recently relocated here from Melbourne. Juicy gossip abounds."

"Really! Well, you know what I've always said."

"What's that, Evan?" Andy played gullible straight man.

"Show me a man who smokes a pipe and I'll poke his wife." He winked a devilish eye and, cocktail in hand, pursued "the talk of Brisbane" into the bar lounge.

"Oh God, he's awful," Marla howled. "Incorrigible, as always."

One hour later, she and Andy sipped intimate sherries at a small pub near the Queensland State government building, where Marla Whitfield worked days as a civilian defense mobilizer. "My part of the war effort," she confessed.

They danced slowly to the unimaginative strains of a lone accordion. But it made no difference. In the reverie of their dreamy trance, it could just as soon have been the Stan Kenton band. Simply holding each other magically reached beyond music to a special plane where sound disappears or merely forms a droning backdrop, like rustling wind or lapping tide. She tenderly separated their embrace and called to the sleepy musician. "*Body and Soul*, please." He blinked a tacit okay. "It's my favorite song and it's American, just like you." A long sensuous breath escaped her.

"Correction…it's *our* favorite song." Andy stooped to kiss her full on the lips, luscious with the sweet taste of cream sherry. Marla stretched to meet his. The kiss was soft and wonderful.

CHAPTER VIII
FORT BENNING

DATE: WEDNESDAY, 26 AUGUST 1942

TIME: 1055 HOURS

LOCATION: FORT BENNING, GEORGIA

At eight hundred feet, the two C-47s leveled off and began their long approach to the drop zone. The Chattahoochee, pushing south and forming the natural border between Georgia and Alabama, loomed as a brown streak against the dry landscape. Columbus and Phoenix City glared at each other from opposite banks, competing for eager GIs and the remnants of their meager pay. From this relatively low altitude, one couldn't help but visualize the tattoo parlors, endless beer joints, and used-car lots down below, and sniff the redneck prostitutes laced with cheap perfume.

Fort Benning, home of the Infantry Officer Candidate School and the Airborne Command, functioned as magnet to the clusters of businesses, legitimate and illegal, which fed off the base's hundred thousand denizens. An unctuous chain of corruption from pimp to law enforcement and up through local and state politicians lubricated the expansive network of dirty machinery all geared to separating moola from soldier… before being shipped toward harm's way.

Not that GIs weren't willing victims to watered booze and clap-infested whores. Pay day weekends witnessed a glut of khakis downtown seeking cold Jax, a shot of Corby's and, if they were lucky, a roll in the hay with someone named Betty Jean or Tammy Dee. If nothing else, the alcohol would encourage behavior of a violating nature and land them in the calaboose, justice implemented in the form of fines which would further oil the big machine. The cycle seemed eternal as fresh supplies of recruits replaced those departed, new meat with skinny billfolds. Soldiers didn't earn much, so volume was the key to the system, and tonnage it welcomed as the sons of America roared through the gate *on pass* to blow off a little steam.

Twin 1200 horsepower Pratt & Whitney engines throttled back to a relaxed whine. Troopers having made a combined total of three jumps on Monday and Tuesday were familiar enough with the routine to recognize the plane's readiness to disgorge its booted cargo. Jump-master Sergeant First Class George Kostos stood by the open door preparing to shout jump commands. Seventeen men comprised the stick. The tension was nothing like it had been for Monday's initial jump, but Second Lieutenant Nick Callahan nervously tightened a secure chinstrap for the fourth time. A high-pitched sound caught his attention. The man seated to his left half-dozed and in so doing whistled through a rugged nose which resembled a prize fighter's. Nick shook his head in amusement at his buddy's indifference to the circumstance and his ability to "sleep in a parade" if it seemed opportune.

After completing OCS and receiving his commission at the end of June, Nick volunteered for airborne training. Idle moments peering skyward at paratroopers floating to earth had captured his fancy and challenged a desire to become one of them. As only one of four officers in his parachute training platoon, he tried to set a disciplined example for the enlisted men. But Nick had only graduated OCS four weeks ago and was yet feeling his way as an officer. That's why he relied on the dozer next to him, First Lieutenant Philip Primo. Cheerful Phil had been an officer for almost three years and knew how to assert rank either via command presence or physical intimidation. One look at Primo in his skivvies immediately signaled those observing that this was a fellow not to be trifled with.

"Stand up and hook up!" Jump-master Kostos' voice boomed through the fuselage instantly after the pilot switched on the red ready light over the cockpit door.

"Let's go, Kid." Primo quickly rose, on his feet before Callahan. Despite the appearance of inattentive sleep, he had been acutely sensitive to his environment.

"Kid" was Phil's pet name for his friend, after Kid Callahan, an old-time welterweight boxer from his home town, Ansonia, Connecticut. All seventeen jumpers faced rearward and snapped their individual static lines to the anchor cable above.

"Check equipment," Kostos ordered. Each man examined his own jump-gear and then that of the trooper before him. The final critical inspection guaranteed against static line foul-ups, especially lines trapped in the chute harness or unwittingly wrapped around an armpit. Nick felt Phil's hand running from his fastener down the static line, making sure all was clear as Callahan performed the identical ritual for the Pfc. standing ahead.

"Sound off for equipment check!"

"Seventeen, okay!" the rear-most paratrooper screamed in a soprano pitch which evoked several nervous giggles from the anxious stick.

"Sixteen, okay!" followed by fifteen, fourteen, and so on, like a string of dominoes trailing its cadence to the exit door. As each jumper shouted his number he tapped or slapped the man's rump to his front, indicating his readiness to leap.

"Stand in the door!" Kostos roared over the combination of wind and engine noise. The men shuffled toward him, guiding static lines along the cable. Up ahead, the Army Air Corps pilot observed their entry into the air space above the lengthy DZ. He yelled "Hit it!" to the co-pilot who thumbed a toggle switch protruding from the busy instrument panel, causing a green light to flash. Reacting to its emerald glow, the jump-master shouted "Go!" and the first trooper, a gritty major, gurgled "Geronimo!" as he tumbled into the bright sunlight.

Numbers nine and ten, Nick and Phil, also hollered the great Apache chieftain's appellation when it came their turn. The prop wash and rushing air shocked that first bottomless step until the jerk of the blossoming chute suspended the plummet.

Drifting slowly, First Lieutenant Phil Primo twisted around to watch the second C empty its load of Army Airborne soldiers. Today represented their fourth jump. At 2130 hours this evening, they would conclude with a night jump. "Like a blind man falling into a mine shaft," an experienced trooper described it. Tomorrow they would receive their silver jump wings, worn above the left breast pocket, symbol of a uniquely modern tribe. Dress trousers bloused over mirror-shined jump boots, and garrison caps emblazoned with the gaudy parachutist's emblem rounded out the elite apparel—part daredevil, all warrior—Airborne, all the way.

The Naugatuck Valley represents the closest thing Connecticut has to the rust belt of western Pennsylvania and Ohio. Valley mill towns like Derby, Shelton, Ansonia, and Naugatuck revolve around small factories and machine shops pumping out brass and copper products, iron castings, and miscellaneous foundry items. New immigrant laborers: Poles, Italians, Irishmen, Swedes, Russians, Ukrainians, and Germans blend with old Yankees constituting the proverbial but veritable blue-collar melting pot.

Autumn is dominated by the frenzy of high school football. Barbers and retailers from rival towns recklessly wager unaffordable sums on the outcome of Saturday's confrontations. Team rosters are packed, for Valley football is a customary rite of passage for area boys. Varsity D or A sewn on a jacket announces the proud wearer has indeed arrived. Residents toot car horns to express pride and support for passing jocks. Even cheerleaders get beeped, sometimes for different reasons. Thanksgiving Day games between traditional opponents exhort feverish beseechments from raucous fans. Landslide wins over bitter foes become reference points in time, "Little Louise was born the week after we trounced so-and-so, 34-14!" Conversation at the mill ignores the poverty of depression, foreign policy, and union elections when the pigskin meets the toe. Monday mornings, the vanquished pony up bets and gear up to endure twelve tortuous months of ribbing until next Turkey Day and a chance for retribution.

The Valley is a place of vegetable gardens and preserves put up for the winter, of boisterous card games at the Vespucci Club or Pilsudski Society, of basement wine presses and jack-lighting deer. Small farms and forests ring the Valley, providing an ample source of food and game. People depend on each other, on family, and friends. The government governed, only. Social services and smothering do-gooders had yet to influence either the simplicity or unfairness of the time. It was pretty much the same in small towns throughout the nation.

For Philip Anthony Primo, growing up in Ansonia had been a joyful experience. Other than his father's premature death from a burst appendix and resultant peritonitis in 1925, things went well for Phil.

His dad, Fausto, as a strapping teenager had journeyed to the land of opportunity from Senigallia on the Adriatic coast of Italy, about midpoint between Ancona and Fano. The greater region is known as "Marche" with the "c-h" pronounced like a "k," its inhabitants referred to as Marchigiani. In America, in the Valley, it was a difficult mouthful to pronounce so the immigrants and their offspring were collectively nicknamed "Markies." Phil liked being a Marky—the food, the subculture, all appealed to his sense of community and belonging. Cleveland Street was more of a dead-end lane which backed up to a small creek. Neat flower, herb, and vegetable gardens framed the simple two-family house with rustic porch where he and his mother, Violet, lived on the second floor. Downstairs, Uncle Ray Romanek and Aunt Rose Marie, mom's twin sister, kept an over-furnished but tidy apartment. Since Fausto's passing, the four of them always ate together as a family with the inseparable sisters cooking up the most wonderful dishes, every meal an event.

Ray and Rose Marie's union had been childless so Phil became the son they never were able to conceive. Romanek's Scrap Yard became the playground of Phil's youth. The locals referred to it as "Ray's Place" and it was here that the boy's body eventually underwent a remarkable muscular transformation. Ray's Place was like a huge weight room with Phil stacking battered auto bumpers and hauling unwieldy scrap iron, weekends and summers. Fifty cents a day swelled to a buck, but hell, Phil loved it. He'd have tossed that junk around just to munch a sausage and pepper grinder with Ray, perched on the pick-up tailgate.

High school football in Ansonia is a religion, and young Primo never missed church. Fullback Phil emerged as the preeminent force in the Valley. Opponents designed defenses solely to prevent Phil's weekly stampede, to no avail. Beaming in the front row, cheering Ray never missed a snap. The Ansonia faithful pounded his broad back each time Romanek's ferocious nephew rumbled across the goal line. College recruiters from the Big Ten and several major independents buzzed around Cleveland Street, but in the end Phil selected Holy Cross in Worcester, Massachusetts.

The speedy Crusader enjoyed a glorious career. At five feet eleven-and-a-half inches, packing one hundred ninety-eight pounds of bone and sinew, he punished the competition with great regularity. Nevertheless, one eventful incident left a mark he would carry the remainder of his life.

November, 1938, his senior season, arch-rival and fellow Jesuit institution, Boston College, was meaner than usual. Late in the contest, The Cross held the ball, third and two at the Eagle twenty-seven yard line. Fullback dive through the three-hole. Phil erupted out of the backfield taking the hand-off in perfect sync. Mud exploded from his churning cleats. The opening was there, narrow but enough to blast through. Phil figured his reckless bulldozing technique would carry him through. Closing the hole, a gargantuan BC tackle stood to deliver a ripping forearm shiver square to the bridge of Phil's onrushing nose. The combined whack and cracking bone split the cool air.

Blood spattered all within spraying distance. Whistles blew three times over before three unconvinced tacklers stopped piling on. "First down!"

Grinning a tooth-absent smile, the red-headed Southie Irish tackle in a respectful yet cocky show of sportsmanship attempted to yank the prostrate ball carrier upright; however, Phil was too woozy to react and would remain so for two blurry days. After the swelling subsided, the school orthopedic surgeon, in conjunction with Worcester's finest Eye, Ear, Nose & Throat physician, attempted to correct the brutal damage. The nose itself was busted in four places, with the septum shattered into a dozen breaks. They reassembled it like a Ravenna mosaic. Though slightly misshapen, it soon worked okay except for one peculiar effect. When Phil slept it whistled shriller than Aunt Rose Marie's favorite tea kettle.

That May, he graduated with a ROTC commission in Uncle Sam's Army. Three months later, he donned the uniform of an infantry officer, ultimately serving at Fort Lewis, Washington, before volunteering for the airborne.

The ground came up quickly. Phil braced himself for impact. Upon sensing the hard-packed clay under his boot sole he relaxed, preventing the jolt from rattling his knees. His body rolled easily with the fall, distributing the collision over his rugged body. Shaking trapped air from the collapsed chute, he admired Nick's near perfect landing about forty feet from where he stood unhooking the webbed harness. Exhilarated jumpers gathered their billowy silks and double-timed to the deuce-and-a-halfs standing by to transport them back to the barracks. Clean up, briefing, and preparation for the night exercise awaited.

DATE: FRIDAY, 28 AUGUST 1942

TIME: 2045 HOURS

LOCATION: OFFICERS CLUB
                  FORT BENNING, GEORGIA

They had grown close these past three short weeks. Deliciously lethal double Manhattans on the rocks offered up by the gentlemanly club bartender were greedily received by Nick and Phil. The drinks represented a celebratory reward for the day's earlier ceremony confirming their ascension into the paratrooper brotherhood. But they also provided fuel for a farewell toast. Primo and Callahan had been assigned to different airborne outfits so it was doubtful their paths would soon cross.

"Phil, I want you to know I feel real lucky to have been big-brothered by you through jump school. Your help meant an awful lot to me. I hope it doesn't end here."

They clinked their tumblers and gulped a healthy snort. "Hell, Kid, I never thought of it in terms of help. More like teammates."

"Yeah, well, thanks anyway." They slurped another inch from the cooling Manhattans. "Remember, I told you about OCS and how fortunate 1 was to have the sharpest guy in our class bunking above me."

"Luzak, wasn't it?"

"Yeah, Woody Luzak. He took it on his own to tuck me under his wing and steer me over the rough spots… like you. Woody graduated number one in our class, head and shoulders over the rest. No contest."

"Good for him, Kid. As my uncle Ray always says, there's only two kinds of people in this world—boosters and knockers—and you have to make up your mind which side of the line you're going to play on. Woody sounds like a genuine booster to me."

"I guess Uncle Ray's been able to distill life down to a pretty simple philosophy." Nick fingered the shiny jump wings pinned to his shirt, letting his nail ripple over the undulations.

Phil laughed. "Yeah, Ray is pretty basic alright. Big-hearted, lovable, and everybody's best friend. Just don't piss off that big Ukrainian though!"

It was Callahan's turn to laugh. "Yeah, just like his pussycat nephew. I think maybe a little of him rubbed off on you."

"I suppose so. I hope so. Ray's pretty special," he added. "Mister bartender, another round please!"

To their left, a cork board carrying bulletins regarding the World War was being updated by an officious captain. Phil wandered over, peeking over the balding information officer's shoulder. Four separate headlines dominated the news: GERMAN SIXTH ARMY TO VOLGA NEAR STALINGRAD. *Where the hell is Stalingrad?* JAPS REINFORCE GUADALCANAL, stated another. Unable to get close enough to read the mimeographed text, he couldn't determine the location of the strange sounding places. DIEPPE RAID DISASTROUS. *Cripes, I'd better invest in a world Atlas.* ENEMY CARRIER FORCE REELING FROM MIDWAY. *Okay, 'Midway' I understand.*

The miracle at Midway had occurred seven weeks earlier, a miracle made possible by unparalleled superior intelligence. An unfailing strategy and attendant tactics executed by the extraordinary guts and sacrifice of Naval aviators and their crews sealed the victory. Four imperial Japanese aircraft carriers and their entire complement of flyers, the irreplaceable cream of Nippon's pilot force, slumbered on the Pacific floor west of Midway Atoll.

Monumental triumphs such as this do more than destroy the enemy at hand. They change the course of history. Japanese leadership now questions its own abilities. Morale suffers the depression of momentum in reverse. Energy which frequently feeds on itself disintegrates into an anemic void. The great battle fleet and its assault troops sworn to stake the pennants of the rising sun in the Midway sand would see them remain furled through war's end. Loss of face, the stigma of unfulfilled declaration, in the ancestral land of shogun and samurai is a shame unquestionably worse than death.

The Code of the Bushido, the warrior's manual of conduct, advises the samurai to, "Win first, fight Later. In other words, win beforehand!" Some call it sneak attack, others a preemptive strike. It had worked brilliantly for Admiral Togo when he annihilated the Czar's Imperial Russian Baltic Fleet in May, 1905. And thirty-six years later history repeated itself, exemplified once more by Isoroku Yamamoto's destruction of formidable Battleship Row and Wheeler Field. Overconfident from the euphoric opium of past success, they arrogantly waltzed into the determined jaws of Admiral Spruance's carrier force and the exacting punishment of his Midway defenders. America was electrified with vengeance of the Pearl Harbor specter. Vicious predator had degenerated to crippled prey. The energized nation now girded to punch the reeling foe into the mortifying abyss of absolute vanquishment.

They banged down the second pair of double Manhattans, caught the barkeep's eye and pointed to the yawning empties. Soon the maracas-like sounds of the busy cocktail shaker rattled news that two fresh ones were en-route. "Hold the cherries this time," Primo called out. "They knock the hell out of us."

"Shit, you'll be whistling like a canary tonight, Phil. The barracks is gonna sound like a goddamn aviary!" Callahan was feeling a bit heady.

"Yeah, Kid, better put a clothespin over my nostrils after I conk off." He merrily pinched a thumb and index finger to demonstrate procedure.

"Perhaps a scoop of bird seed would satisfy your feathery instincts?" Nick was on a roll, milking Phil's strident quirk for all he could.

"Yeah, yeah, yeah." Smiling, he waved off his partner's comedic commentary, dismissing the satire. Nasal concerto, sinus symphony, he had heard it all before.

The bartender strained the whiskey and sweet vermouth concoction over clean ice cubes and set the glasses on dry coasters. Noticing their wings, he asked, "Going or coming?"

"What do you mean?" Nick asked.

"Just making conversation. I'm curious if you're joining a jump outfit here at Benning or elsewhere."

"Both," the fullback answered. "I've been assigned to the five hundred and fifth Parachute Infantry Regiment right here at exciting Fort Benning."

"New outfit, that five-oh-five," the barman said. "The regiment was activated earlier this month. Rumor has it that the eighty-second Infantry Division is going to be re-designated as an airborne division, and the five-oh-five will be part of it." He looked at Nick. "How about you, lieutenant?"

"I clear post on Monday, off to Fort Bragg, North Carolina. First Battalion, five hundred and third Parachute Infantry Regiment. No division affiliation. I guess it's a bastard outfit!"

"Five-O-Trey, they call it," the barkeep knowledgeably informed. Obviously he was retired military—a number of them worked at the huge base and deservedly so. "Used to be stationed here at Benning until last March. A few officers passed through here three weeks ago on their way to Bragg. They really got juiced up. Had to call a courtesy vehicle to haul them out of here. One of 'em kept yelling he wanted to whip King Kong's ass."

"What were those boys drinkin'?" Primo asked.

"Rum shots and beers. Crazy stuff. Makes a man volunteer to sit in the electric chair."

Phil looked incredulous. "Really? Just what I thought, those Five-O-Treys have got no class. Kid, how in the fiddly-dick are you going to survive those crude barbarians at Bragg without Phil Primo to guide your cocktail habits?"

Nick had bottoms-upped the third double and, oblivious of his buddy's stated concern, teetered the stool and crashed onto the checkered linoleum. Casually dropping a ten spot on the polished bar top to cover tab and generous tip, the husky first lieutenant tossed down his drink and lit a long Panatella cigar. He took care to insure the coal glowed uniformly before hefting the semi-conscious Callahan erect. Two Air Corps captains, also feeling no pain, upon entering the club good-naturedly swept aside to permit Primo's and Callahan's dramatic albeit uncouth exit. Slumped over Phil's shoulder in the classic fireman's carry position, glassy-eyed, inebriated Nick saluted the amused officers.

Phil lugged him that way for over half a mile, puffing clouds of white Cuban smoke, disregarding the knobby load as if toting one of Ray's Place's rusted radiators. That night the younger man slept without disturbance even though his lower bunkmate whistled like a ruptured banshee for nine solid hours.

CHAPTER IX
THE CANAL

DATE: THURSDAY, 20 SEPTEMBER 1942

TIME: 0940 HOURS

LOCATION: GUADALCANAL, SOLOMON ISLANDS

The lumbering navy Catalina came in high, the pilot picking out reference points on the big island below: Mount Austen, Cape Esperance, and Savo Island, Lunga Point, and there a tiny geometric strip running along a northeast-southwest axis, Henderson Field. They had departed Espiritu Santo at the top of the New Hebrides strand scarcely 600 miles earlier and flown without fighter escort along the Coral Sea for about four hours, skirting San Cristobal in the process. Five military passengers squeezed among the wedged cartons of medical supplies and other equipment critical to the life of Major General Alexander Vandegrift's 1st Marine Division desperately clinging to the Lunga Perimeter.

Guadalcanal, roughly 2,500 square miles of steamy jungle and malarial swamp, soared from glaring sea level to the Kayo mountain chain and Mount Popomanasiu's commanding altitude of 8,000 feet. Marines occupied only 15 square miles, six tenths of one percent of the entire land mass. But it was, without doubt, the most critical sliver of volcanic earth and mud in contention—for its confines embraced a man-made item of supreme importance. This strategic treasure had forced a brutal test of national wills. The potent assets of vying air, sea, and ground forces were singularly focused on the unimpressive prize, Henderson Field.

Whoever owned the crude airstrip controlled the pivotal upper hand in the broad Pacific sub-theater. With it the Americans held open two crucial ocean arteries pumping troops and supplies to Australia and New Zealand. With it, Japan would slowly strangle New Guinea and range its bombers to wreak destruction on New Caledonia, the lifeline approaches to Australia, and indeed the island continent itself.

Cradling the newly issued steel pot helmet between his thighs, Master Sergeant Tony Luzak folded looping lengths of toilet paper into flat six-by-six squares and inserted them into the liner's webbed suspension. There they would rest, invisible to all but he until nature's requisite summoned their comfort. Genuine civilian toilet paper was a rare and negotiable commodity these days, the military version about as soothing as sharkskin. Army B-17 crews flying out of Espiritu Santo had squirreled away quantities of the store-bought variety, which they would sell or trade to personnel heading toward "The Canal." Entrepreneurship thrives when demand outdistances supply, regardless of environment, and the enterprising airmen had found a pressing need for their luxurious wares.

Tony jammed the remaining shrunken roll into his sea bag and prepared for touchdown. The bump and sudden halt arrived quicker than expected. Crewmen ripped open the squat PBY's hatch, yelling for commuters to deplane "hubba-hubba" and race for cover. Weather permitting, Japanese air strikes from Rabaul were an everyday event, and this morning the sun burned brilliant and hot—ideal for Mitsubishi "Betty" bombers to spill their death.

Unloading details descended on the Catalina like a school of voracious piranha and within minutes had stripped its innards. Sea bag on shoulder, Tony sprinted across the dusty field, sidestepping freshly filled craters. Shattered junks, the skeletal remains of F4F Wildcats, cannibalized of their useful parts, littered the perimeter amid splintered palms. He stumbled in the direction of a side-less tent fly-mounted on wooden pallets wedged inside an earthen revetment. Enjoying its shade, a bare-chested crew chief chewed on the stub of a saliva-drenched stogie, the coal of which had been extinguished days earlier. Clipboard in hand, he half-exited the sandbagged shelter to meet Luzak.

"Help you? I'm Staff Sergeant Williams." Several days of stubble glistened as a rivulet of foul tobacco juice drooled down his cocky chin.

"Luzak… Master Sergeant. Where do I find One-Seven?"

"Christ, the Seventh Marines gettin' replacements already? They just came ashore two days ago, six fuckin' weeks after everybody else." He raised his eyes to emphasize the dig.

"Never mind the horseshit, Williams. Where's the First fuckin' battalion?" Luzak, tutored by Salty Waters and China Marines long-mustered out, could scowl with the best of them. And days of playing airplane tag with oddball connections and unexplained layovers had left him intolerant of even a semblance of ball-busting. Williams got the message, it would have been difficult not to. Tough Tony was as delicate as a freight train, tactfulness never his strength.

"Right." He removed the cigar, if one could yet call it that, and motioned a nearby private. "Rayburn, grab a helmet and weapon ricky-tick and guide Master Sergeant Luzak up to One-Seven's command post. Them Mud-Marines should be right around here." He fingered a position on the perimeter map tacked to a corner tent pole and aimed a sarcastic smile at the antsy master sergeant.

Luzak let the Mud-Marine crack slide. *Fuckin' airdale couldn't find his scrotum with both hands.* Things have a way of evening up.

In a manner of speaking, Williams was accurate, at least the part about the Seventh Marines showing up six weeks after the division's bulk.

The First Marines and Fifth Marines, divisional brother infantry regiments of the Seventh, had splashed ashore back on August 7, followed by their artillery regiment, the Eleventh Marines. The Second Marines, normally an organic regiment of the 2nd Marine Division, was temporarily attached to the Marine 1st Division, filling the vacancy initially caused by the Seventh's absence. The latter had been hung up on Samoa unable to obtain transport until well after the operation had commenced. As a consequence, Seventh Marines had been unavailable for the pre-landing rehearsal in the Fijis as well as the invasion itself. The USMC's First Raider Battalion and First Parachute Battalion had been in the thick of it since the beginning of the Guadalcanal action, along with the 3rd Defense Battalion(anti-aircraft). Attrition among the parachutists had been staggering and it was decided to evacuate them on the ships that carried the Seventh Marines to the island. Even so, the 1st Marine Division at this juncture was a powerful entity, over-strength in terms of its combat components.

At the onset, Marine force elements brutally swept over the Japanese troops across the channel defending Tulagi, and the tiny Siamese-twin isles of Gavutu and Tanambogo, connected by a narrow causeway. Several days of intense fighting had wiped out 1,500 Japanese at a cost of 108 Marine dead.

By August 12, Marines on the Canal had declared the captured airstrip, re-christened Henderson Field fit for air operations by transport planes, Navy SBD dive bombers, Army Airacobras, and mostly Marine Wildcat fighter squadrons affectionately nicknamed the Cactus Air Force. The field was muscled into readiness by Navy Sea Bee Construction Battalions and Marine engineers using captive Japanese bulldozers, steamrollers, and other machinery, fuel and vehicles. Frequently they would labor under perilous conditions, both naval shelling and aerial bombardment. Having been "abandoned" by the USN's battle fleet which had "pulled back," the USMC mobilized to fend for itself.

Several of its combat units still occupied the three diminutive islands across Skylark Channel and nearby Florida Island. Vandergrift, cognizant he had but five infantry battalions on Guadalcanal itself, consolidated a defensive perimeter around Henderson and his artillery support. Aggressive leatherneck combat patrols ventured out, making contact and killing the enemy in small batches; fortuitously, they also located an advancing Japanese column numbering around a thousand troops of the 28th Infantry Regiment. Realizing he had been exposed, the Japanese commander, Colonel Ichiki, determined to penetrate the Marines' position and seize the airstrip.

The morning of August 21 witnessed the Marines' first chilling experience with the notorious banzai charge, a little after 0300. Moonlight and barbed wire combined to illuminate and obstruct two hundred charging Japanese soldiers, while infantrymen of the First Marines shot and grenaded them to pieces. Scores of shouting men got caught up attempting to storm the shallow depths and mucky sandbars of the Ilu River. Lethal American BARs and machine guns ripped through the ranks, aided by selective Springfields picking off random silhouettes. Blood seeping from shredded battle uniforms leaked into the Ilu, alerting the primeval senses of resting crocodiles that an easy menu was available. Screaming, the terrified wounded were dragged off to be silenced by crunching jaws and forceful submersion.

For the handful who pushed their blind charge into the American line, the fighting was truly hand-to-hand with K-Bar trench knives and fists. But they too were slaughtered. Some of the troops attempted a futile end-run, wading through the salt water surf where Ilu meets ocean. The Marines waiting with .30 caliber machine guns and artillery made it no contest. Interestingly, dispatches made reference to the battle of the Tenaru River before someone realized it had been misidentified. Cross-out Tenaru, add Ilu. Upriver, troops stealthily forded the stream and pinched the remaining enemy. With assistance from the Cactus pilots and five tanks firing cannisters, they pursued and annihilated them. In total, the enemy suffered an estimated 800 deaths including Ichiki's suicide. Perhaps more importantly, the Japanese now became painfully appreciative that Guadalcanal would be no pushover. On the contrary, it would become Midway revisited, only this time it was the imperial army's turn to experience smashing defeat.

As the air and naval war spun around them, the Mud-Marines kept their faith. Toward the end of August, the Japanese landed 4,000 more troops, the Kawaguchi Force, and Vandegrift retrieved most of his remaining battalions from the outer isles. September 12 saw a combined force of Raiders and Marine Parachutists holding the heights controlling the defensive perimeter's center with the First and Fifth Marines nailing down the flanks. Lt. Colonel Merritt "Red Mike" Edson commanded the Raider/Paramarine group supported by division artillery.

A ferocious battle erupted up and down the entire line. Exhausted men, weakened by malaria and dehydration, courageously fought and died in their slimy foxholes. Mortars and 105mm howitzers exacted an awesome toll. Six Marine tanks were tossed into the fiery cauldron, five were destroyed. Attack and counter-attack. Positions were stubbornly lost and viciously recaptured. Through daylight and into night the unrelenting enemy surged up Edson's Ridge only to be repulsed. Hold the airfield at any cost! If it fell, First MarDiv would be shoved into the unreceptive tide.

Finally the bankrupt Japanese brigade could no longer rally. Breaking off contact, they retreated across the Matanikau River with merciless Marine Wildcats zooming at treetop level to strafe the demoralized enemy. No written word can capture the precariousness of this action. On several occasions the bloody defenders had come within a whisker of being overrun, only to have repeated acts of individual sacrifice stem the frantic assaults. Edson's Ridge, a.k.a. Bloody Ridge, or to most, simply The Ridge, remained property of the 1st Marine Division, paid for in valor, consecrated in blood.

The Corps had hastily thrown together the 1st Marine Division, a mix of seasoned and new officers, untested boots fresh from the ranges of Parris Island, San Diego, and Camp Elliot. But it was the veteran NCO's gathered from hundreds of postings and remote stations who formed the hard-nosed, never-say-die toughness which calcified the division's stubborn backbone during Guadalcanal's baptism of gore and fire. Later, Samuel B. Griffith II, a blooded participant, would put it: "They were a motley bunch. Hundreds were young recruits only recently out of boot training at Parris Island. Others were older; first sergeants from recruiting duty, gunnery sergeants who had fought in France, perennial privates with disciplinary records a yard long. They were professionals, the "Old Breed" of United States Marines. Many had fought "Cacos" in Haiti, "bandidos" in Nicaragua, and French, English, Italian, and American soldiers and sailors in every bar in Shanghai, Manila, Tsingtao, Tientsin and Peking.

They were inveterate gamblers and accomplished scroungers, who drank hair tonic in preference to post-exchange beer ("horse piss"), cursed with wonderful fluency, and never went to chapel ("the God-box") unless forced to. Many dipped snuff, smoked rank cigars, or chewed tobacco (cigarettes were for women and children). They knew their weapons, and they knew their tactics. They knew they were tough and they knew they were good. There were enough of them to leaven the division and to impart to the thousands of younger men a share both of the unique spirit which they animated and the skills they possessed."

Master Sergeant Anton Luzak fit the mold of the "Old Breed." He and his pugnacious counterparts would impose their unyielding will on the division soul. Their resilience, ornery as it might be, their steely resolve to overcome adversity, to tough it out, would become the hallmark of the 1st Marine Division. Tony Luzak, veteran of the Banana Wars, hero of San Leo Bridge, survivor of Zamboanga, was on Guadalcanal ready and resolute to motivate, lead, and kick ass!

Luzak entered the dugout battalion CP, reinforced with double-wall sandbags and palm log roof. Dropping his sea bag, he arrived at the precise moment a spirited discussion, half tirade, part argument, boomed behind a curtained-off room. One forceful voice dominated.

"I doubt if anyone in this battalion—or regiment, for that matter—has ever seen a Jap on this cruddy island, much less taken a shot at one. That's why it's important for us to gain experience now that there's a lull. It seems to me One-Seven should be aggressively patrolling in force, making contact, keeping 'em on their heels... killing them." The opinionated speaker was obviously the honcho.

Listening intently outside the thin fabric, a young radio operator and a grizzled non-com, presumably the battalion sergeant major, silently signaled Luzak to remain quiet lest he disturb their eavesdropping.

"Sir, I believe Colonel Webb is conferring with General Vandegrift at the division CP. My counterpart at regiment claims they'll be huddling until at least fourteen hundred." The voice spoke confidently, not at all intimidated by the first man.

"Well you should know, you're the S-2! Maybe I'll call on Colonel Frisbie and try to get the ball moving. No sense in sitting around here. I don't want our Marines thinking this is trench warfare and lose their edge. Hell, we did enough jungle training on Samoa to prepare us, all we need now is a little test under fire." The curtain parted, exposing a barrel-chested officer with close-cropped graying hair and rugged facial features lined by the sun. In some respects he resembled a shorter, older version of Luzak. Lewis Puller, Lieutenant Colonel in command of 1/7, took a quizzical look at Tony as if to place him. "Do I know you?" he asked.

"Master Sergeant Luzak, sir. I was in Shanghai when you called the Japs' bluff at the International Settlement."

He laughed warmly. "We really had 'em buffaloed that day, didn't we." It was more of a statement than a question.

"Thirty-cent steaks, and beer at two cents a quart! China duty sure had its perks." It wasn't meant to reflect nostalgia but simply to let Tony know that a special bond existed between Puller and his vets.

"Yes, sir," Tony chirped, "White Russian cabaret girls at Judy Woo's and imperial quarts of scotch whiskey at a dollar a bottle." They all laughed, shaking their heads in wonderment at the events less than a year gone but seemingly like an era in the deep past.

Shifting gears, Puller let them know that the trip down memory lane had concluded. "Well it's all behind us this sweet day. Now we've got to push the Japs off this goddamn island! What brings you here, Luzak?"

"Just flew in, sir, courtesy of a PBY. Been assigned to One-Seven."

"Well, if you managed to get air transport here you must be resourceful. Once you're squared away I'm sure the sergeant major will find you an active billet. Welcome aboard." Then turning to the top sergeant, he added, "As you've probably been listening, I'll most likely be at regiment with the XO. Get hold of me if anything breaks."

"Aye, sir."

Three other officers remained in the rear planning room poring over maps in preparation for what they knew would be a most persuasive appeal by Puller at regiment.

DATE: SUNDAY, 23 SEPTEMBER 1942

TIME: 0630 HOURS

LOCATION: GUADALCANAL

Chesty Puller got his wish. First Battalion, Seventh Marines saddled up and moved out early, a formidable combat force missioned with seeking out the enemy and destroying him. A platoon from Baker Company took the distant lead with point men fanned out toward the west and the Matanikau River. Flank security was maintained throughout the column. Marines loaded down with weapons, ammo, rations, twin canteens, and field gear trudged out of the perimeter passing through positions manned by 2/7 and 3/7. Jungle decay and the stink of unretrieved enemy corpses hung like an invisible cloak in the early morning humidity. Unseen insects raised puffy welts on necks not yet recovered from yesterday's stings.

Until they could determine a proper slot for Luzak, he would function as the battalion's operations chief, reporting to the unit's S-3, operations officer. His duties were somewhat nebulous for the moment, which probably meant he could freelance much of the duration. He liked it that way. They pushed along a treacherous trail. By the time the rearmost men would reach a given point, the footing became soupy, the result of the forward companies churning soil into slop. That night the weary Marines bedded down in the mooned shadow of Mount Austen. Restless and nervous, not too many actually slept.

On the twenty-fourth, a flanker reported a downed aircraft lay among a stand of gigantic tawa trees about 150 to 175 yards south. Tony happened to be in the column where the Marine had reported in, so taking two riflemen along, he melted into the green veil to investigate. No trail existed where they were headed, so the scout did his best to quietly retrace his steps, slipping between bamboo stands and hindering vines. Poor visibility necessitated that they bunch up. The Master sergeant carried his weapon of choice, .45 caliber Tommy gun, perfect for this dense foliage.

The scout, Pfc. T. J. Smith, knew his stuff. Spotting the towering tawas over a hundred feet tall, he signaled a halt. They froze in place for a full seven minutes while he listened for telltale sounds. Nothing stirred. Confident, but not yet totally satisfied, he led them in a wide half-circle so they would approach their destination from the south. The flattened mess of an aircraft turned out to be an Army Air Corps P-40. A demolished but empty cockpit suggested the pilot must have bailed. "No fire or signs of an explosion. Probably ran out of gas," Smitty deduced.

"Hardly any rust or mold either," Luzak observed.

"Probably happened in the last week or so." He made a mental note of the pilot's stenciled name painted below the canopy. Then with scavenging eyes, conditioned by years of "making do," he cast about the ripped wings. The Curtis P-40. Warhawk's firepower was comprised of six .50 caliber machine guns, three housed in each wing. Crumpled into the high rooted base of a tawa, the left wing remained nothing more than a compacted ball of scrap. The other one, though, had possibilities. Poking open the cover Tony released a whispered yip, like someone who's found money in the street. A single machine gun appeared unmarred, surviving impact without a bend or dent. The other gun barrels drooped, unfit for service or salvage. Tony and Smitty extracted the keeper and twisted belts of ammunition. Both of the other Marines took turns positioning the fat ammo belts in criss-cross fashion over shoulders and down chests, like Mexican bandidos in a Hollywood feature film.

Luzak and the scout each grabbed an end of the big air-cooled fifty. "This son-of-a-bitch could come in real handy. We'll have to scrounge for a tripod or some kind of mount." A kid with a new toy couldn't have been more pleased. "Fifties wound only for a moment," someone had said. The woundee generally bleeds to death, the hole is that big.

When Luzak's patrol caught up to the column, the leathernecks were taking ten. Most had removed their helmets in a hopeless attempt to cool down. He moved near the front of the battalion's main body, Baker Company still ahead in the vanguard. The trail had snaked its way near the lower slope of Mount Austen when the sharp crack of small-arms fire echoed through the stifling air. Men moved off the trail and flattened out, awaiting instructions. In the density and smothering closeness of the wet jungle it is difficult to determine the directional origin of sound. A young runner double-timing down the trail reported in gasped words that Company B had walked into an ambush. The CO had been slain and casualties were high. It was that quick.

Before the battalion could react, Baker's Marines had driven the hit-and-run enemy from their position. Thursday, September 27, another boiling, sweat-soaked jaunt in the jungle. One-Seven had been moving in conjunction with Two-Five toward the Matanikau. Yesterday, Puller's group had run into heavy Jap machine gun fire, taking casualties but unable to inflict reciprocal pain of any note. The men were fatigued and jumpy. Prospects of trigger-happiness were strong.

Today, Able and Baker Companies advanced, or so they thought, to a high ridge about one-third of a mile inland. Enemy officers shrewdly counter-moved their troops, blocking the Marines' access route to the beach. Firefights broke out with a deafening racket, only to subside without any apparent orders—they just did.

Overhead, a marine TBF strafed the blockading enemy. He would try to blast 1/7 a path to the beach where Higgins boats awaited to pull them out. A Navy destroyer, *USS Ballard,* moved in to pound away with five-inch guns, pinning the Japanese and widening the Marines' boulevard of escape. Company mortars also swung into action covering the movement. Platoon Sergeant Anthony Malinowski hung behind to cover Able as its infantrymen skedaddled through the growth to the open beach. Firing several magazines from a BAR, he held the anxious Japanese at bay until he was shot and killed. His action, though, had provided timely escort for his escaping company.

Maintaining his composure, Luzak controlled the panicked Marines about him to work a cohesive withdrawal, covering each other as they methodically slipped back. At the beach's fractured tree line where sand met jungle, he plopped the big fifty between a tree crotch, pointing over the gradual rise from which rearguard Marines were descending. Linking webbed utility belts stripped from men around him, he strapped the gun (as best he could) inside the veed trunk. His two puffing ammo bearers unslung the linked cartridges and fed in the first lethal belt.

The exposed beach was taking sporadic fire, dead and wounded were being loaded into the Higgins boats. Pursuing Japanese soldiers, rifles held high, appeared on the ridgeline and Tony thumbed the makeshift trigger, erupting an earsplitting eight-round burst. He missed them by the proverbial country mile. Even so, the Japs recognized they were up against something special and skidded to a halt. A heavyset Marine screamed, "Holy shit!"

and came to Luzak's aid. Crazed by the action, he couldn't stop laughing as he placed both palms flat down on the receiver, pushing his body weight in an attempt to retard the jumbo gun's bouncing vibration. "Shoot the fuckers, shoot the fuckers!" Tony nodded his approval, as he needed no encouragement, and let fly anther short burst.

He was getting the hang of it. In the heat of retreat, several men stopped to marvel at the impromptu .50 caliber gun crew and the helmet-less master sergeant. They cheered him like a heavyweight boxer as officers and NCO's hustled them to the waterline. The cumbersome weapon was difficult to traverse but who cared, the Japs were shying off. Determined, he gritted his jolting teeth and ripped off a long deadly stream. *Just keep firing.*

Another belt was sucked up by the "airplane gun" at the same moment two Jap machine gun crews were attempting to set up their air-cooled, type 1941 Nambus to rake the surf 's helpless targets. The "holy shit" Marine pointed to them. "Shoot the fuckers!" he squealed, an instant before taking a bullet in his throat. Blood squirted onto Tony, saturating his chest as the silenced man fell. A Marine standing by volunteered to take his slot bracing the gun.

The eager Nambu crews were close together, split only about twenty yards apart; that's all their narrow line of sight would permit. Tony hit the trigger and let it cough a lengthy blast. The rounds punched large dusty holes directly in front of the first crew. He had the range and they knew it. The Jap gunner's head disappeared out the rear of his helmet as two rounds caught him flush; the headless body was lifted off the ground, the impact that severe. Both assistants were blown backwards as crimson cavities pocked ragged khaki field shirts.

Meanwhile, the second enemy crew had emplaced its tripod and weapon. A crewman rammed a 7.7 mm ammo strip into the Nambu and it spit a stream of fire pointed at Tony's tree. He retaliated by shooting every remaining bullet as splintered bark and wood fragments danced around his glinted eyes. The Jap gun clanked with a rapid series of dull pings, Luzak's fire pounded the steel piece and its pulverized crew. A split-toed Tabi cartwheeled above their perforated bodies, a foot still inside the canvas rubber boot. For a blink in time the Marine gunner stood paralyzed, frozen in a macabre tableau. Like Leonidas at Thermopylae, Horatio at the bridge, and Roland at Roncesvalles, Anton Luzak, rearguard bulwark, slammed shut the back door.

He searched about. No live Marines defended the beach. They were all aboard shouting and waving to him. "Come on!" The feisty *Ballard* cruised in for another sweep and blasted the ridge with murderous accuracy. He undid the hot fifty and tossed it on a strained shoulder, making a beeline for the revving Higgins boats. A few angry Arisaka rounds harmlessly kicked up sand nearby. Ass-high in salt water, he dumped his treasured fifty over the side and followed it in, assisted by many hands. They howled and pounded his strong back. Dried blood and smudges of burnt cordite caked his exhausted mug. He loved it.

CHAPTER X
LINDEN

DATE: SUNDAY, 11 OCTOBER 1942

TIME: 1500 HOURS

LOCATION: LINDEN, NEW JERSEY

There was nothing dainty about Stella Luzak Romanek as she attacked both oblong loaves of bread, sawing them in half with a serrated bakery knife. Barefoot and comfortably clad in a loose-fitting slip, she waited her husband's return from the Lemko Fraternal Club. Helping other members install a new bar, no doubt they had christened it with a few frosty brews. Humming to the Philco's lively music, she drove the saw-toothed blade through a last resistant brown crust.

Stella rapped the handle butt hard against the rock maple cutting board as if to punctuate completion. Powerful fingers swiftly ripped out the filler, leaving only the stiff shells. *The soft bread will make good stuffing. Maybe I'll roast a fat chicken on Friday night, the way my Vic likes it... if the butcher receives his quota. Take it on the train to Connecticut when we visit Vic's brother over the weekend.*

Stretching out to the pantry shelf, she removed two amber bottles of Coronet Brandy and fitted them into the hollowed crusts, twisting and making adjustments so they nested snugly. Firmly molding the pumpernickel caps over the bottle necks, she paused to admire the ingenious protective cocoons. She continued to hum along as the radio blared the swinging sounds of "In The Mood." Boy, she loved Glenn Miller's music—trombones and saxes blending to a wonderful quality so distinctive anyone could identify it after hearing but a few bars. The brandies cushioned in their doughy canisters would be mailed Monday morning along with homemade apple jelly from Tedelmyer's Farm Stand, Hershey bars, canned pears, pickled pig ears, cigarettes, and her own sugar cookies. Destination: her two brothers in the Pacific.

Stella, the oldest sibling, had no children of her own so she continued to dote on her "baby brothers" whom she adored from the moment mom brought them home from the hospital back in Indiana Harbor. The last she heard was Tony was safely stationed in Australia, and Woodrow on his way to a remote French island she never heard of, New Caledonia. His new wife had recently written her with information of the youngest's whereabouts. Woody and Nancy were fortunate enough to have spent two cherished weeks together on Oahu before he shipped out to the port of Noumea. At least they're both safe, Stella rationalized.

Sister Stella stood tall, a big-boned woman, good-natured, good-hearted, and physically strong. This was no pussycat. She had always worked in a man's blue collar world, having mastered the art of imposing spunky resolve at her various job sites. She could charm or bully, depending on the needs of the situation. Either style was okay as long as results followed. Guys on the job accepted her for what she basically was… one of the boys.

Thirty-nine years old this past March, her more turbulent days were long gone. And even though she could knock back a few bottles of Schaefer beer as quickly and adroitly as any of them, she had reached a point in life where she felt deserving of greater recognition and reward. Plant management had recently concluded that Stella had a sharp mind and good organizational skills, and when those talents were coupled with her demanding presence things had a way of getting done right. Her ability to solve those nagging everyday problems which surfaced "on the line" at the Eastern factory, enhanced her reputation as a take-charge lady.

And so Stella enjoyed her job, her neat little two-bedroom ranch house, and "Big Vic" Romanek, her husband of almost six years. Together they wolfed down thick tasty chunks of fried kielbasa, guzzled cold Schaefer, cuddled to Glenn Miller, and made thunderous love twice a week on the living room carpet. Their old brass bed never would have endured the strain of both their large quaking bodies. Once they had tried it in the bath tub—a couple of jockeying manatees would have been more graceful… and successful. Vic almost drowned so they designated the living room carpet to be the platform of choice for future exercises.

Everything was perfect these days except for Tony and Woody off in the Pacific. She worried like all families, fearing the worst. Food parcels, prayers, and the munitions of war forged with the help of her hands were Stella's contribution to the men in khaki and blue. Eastern Aircraft, right here in Linden, New Jersey, her home away from home, had become her way of climbing into the trenches, of launching off a flight deck. Two blue stars on a silky white field framed in red hung on the front door, proudly announcing that two servicemen were of her household. It seemed everyone working at Eastern had a family member serving in the armed forces.

Eastern, formed January 21, 1942, as an aeronautical division of auto giant General Motors Corporation, was responsible for manufacturing the Navy's Avenger Torpedo Bomber TBF-1 and the Wildcat F4F-4, both under license from Grumman. Later in 1943, Eastern would produce the FM2 souped-up version of the Wildcat, affectionately given a souped-up title as well, "The Wilder Wildcat." Stella had been working on the assembly line before Pearl Harbor when sleek Oldsmobiles, Buicks, and Pontiacs rolled out of Linden to fill showrooms and garages throughout the Northeast. Eastern Aircraft also had plants in Baltimore, Tarrytown, NY, Trenton, NJ, and Bloomfield, NJ, where Big Vic diligently labored as a foreman in charge of producing hydraulic and electric assemblies for the two fighting workhorses of the fleet. Like his wife, Vic Romanek took his wartime effort very seriously and seldom accepted *no* as an answer.

Rivet sorter, inspector, and welder were just a few of the jobs Stella had held at GM and Eastern. For the last seven months, she toiled in the massive hangar-like plant where she had been the number-two person running a gigantic eighteen-foot-high press. The massive hunk of machinery rapidly stamped out precise parts for the Wildcat and Avenger. Four weeks earlier her boss, Don McAdam from nearby West Orange, received one of the dreaded telegrams dispassionately cranked out by the Department of the Navy. His only son, Donnie, a gunners' mate on the destroyer, USS *Blue*, had been killed in action in the Savo Sound near Guadalcanal. A gold-starred banner signifying a military death would sadly decorate the McAdam's porch window. Jean McAdam, Gold Star mother, numbed by grief, would remain secluded at home until long after VJ Day. The Blue had taken a torpedo fired by a Jap destroyer killing eight and wounding twenty two sailors. After being taken in tow the disabled ship was evaluated too severely crippled and, thereby, easy prey to enemy capture. Ordered scuttled she tearfully was sent to the cluttered floor of Iron Bottom Sound. At the Linden factory, Mac McAdam became somewhat of a dysfunctional zombie. His pathetic sobbing and job indifference prompted his removal from overseeing the giant press. Mac's grief threatened to slow down production in a war industry which exacted strict timetables. Schedules had to be met. So he and Jean became simply two more casualties in a war whose cruelty stretched round the globe.

The press required a new commanding general, someone to administer production scheds, change dies, lube and maintain the brute, and, of course, coax it to punch out perfect parts for Admiral King's flying machines. In an era where men ruled supreme, buxom Stella Luzak Romanek, in baggy gray coveralls and work shoes, was promoted to probationary supervisor of the noisy Goliath her fellow workers now referred to as "Stella's Baby."

She had just completed tying a length of waxed twine around the second brown-papered carton when she heard Big Vic's immaculate 1937 Hudson compacting the driveway gravel. Moments later the screen door banged shut and his beefy hand was squeezing her rather generous derrière—the Romanek way of saying "good afternoon." Vic yanked open the yellowed Kelvinator refrigerator and pulled out a bottled beer. "Want one?" he asked, flipping the crown.

"No thanks, honey." Her hair hung down, not pinned up like at the plant. Vic preferred it long and free.

"Wanna hit the carpet?" His grinning face gestured toward the living room. Foreplay be damned, this was a basic couple with no frills needed or offered.

"Sure, why not!" she giggled.

Sunday afternoons in an uncertain 1942 were meant to enjoy life's scant pleasures.

CHAPTER XI

THE RIDGE

DATE: SATURDAY, 24 OCT 1942

TIME: 1830 HOURS

LOCATION: GUADALCANAL

Rain. It fell in blinding sheets, flooding bunkers, undermining structures, washing away tent pegs, collapsing their canvas canopies. Trails turned to muddy pudding and saddled roads to hip-high canals. Men and equipment reached a level of super saturation where they could absorb no more. Cooks surrendered to the elements; all rations, meat, bread, and vegetables had been transformed into a diluted liquid state by the time they passed over one's lips. Engineers witnessed in dismay the product of two laborious months float away. Clothes and boots never dried. Some men shivered in cool agued fever only to experience the hot sweats minutes later. The driving rain exacerbated fatigue, dulling alertness. The only good news was that Hirohito's legions were suffering through the same deluge.

For 2,850 GIs of the US Army's 164th Infantry Regiment, their first week and a half on The Canal had been miserable. Having sailed from New Caledonia aboard the transports *Zeilin* and *McCawley*, they arrived on the thirteenth. An organic part of the Army's American Division, the 164th had been detached and rushed to beef up the Lunga perimeter, temporarily assigned to the 1st Marine Division. Brother regiments, the 72nd and 147th, had remained in New Caledonia along with division artillery (DivArty). Originally a North Dakota National Guard regiment, the 164th had been inducted into federal service twenty months ago and over that time, infused with men and officers from across the U.S. Since early April when they disembarked in New Caledonia, after a spot of tea in Australia, they had trained doggedly in preparation for jungle warfare.

The regiment had expected the air raids, naval bombardment, and 150mm shelling, but no one had told them about the unrelenting equatorial rain pelting the Solomon Islands.

Earlier in the week, the Japanese landed 20,000 men including the premier Sendai Division with only one objective, the same one they had had since August—liquidate the Americans and seize the airfield at any cost. The enemy had maneuvered thousands of troops poised to strike the Lunga defense line's southern position, held primarily by Puller's One-Seven and supported on the left by Second Battalion of the 164th Infantry(2/164). Early in the evening, around 2130 hours, the enemy overpowered a reinforced Marine platoon manning a forward post. The rain had muffled their movement and the Japs were on top of the outpost grenading the defenders in quick fashion. Yelling and heaving their lethal potato mashers, the Japanese directed their principle charge at a point in the barbed wire named Coffin Corner, only this was no football field. Rushing towards it in strength, they were cut down by combined mortar and heavy infantry fire from 1/7 and 2/164.

On some patches of ravaged earth, ammo-less Marines held with the bayonet, meeting scream with curse, thrust ,with parry. The tenacious enemy fell back several times only to regroup, redistribute ammunition, and surge again—four, five, six violent assaults. Sergeant John Basilone, a burly Marine machine gunner, performed heroics so incredible that his subsequent Medal of Honor citation would read like exaggerated comic book fiction.

Puller, in communication with his reserves, 3/164, knew the critical moment was at hand. His position was now in dire jeopardy. Too many Japs, too many Marine casualties. The tenuous line was stretched riskily thin, close to snapping, and if that happened, the Nips would exploit the broken dike by gushing in their spirited warriors in hosts too strong to resist. Victory watched closely, waiting to crown the stalwart. "Put Lieutenant Colonel Hall on the horn," Chesty barked. Hall's 3/164 had been designated the reserve battalion, held back for that urgent moment when they might be required. Ready for action but hindered by blinding rain and a clouded moon, the soldiers could hear but not see the monstrous battle raging ahead.

"Hall here," the Army man responded.

Puller had to make his pitch quickly. There was no time to screw around with long-winded inter-service protocol.

"Colonel Hall, this thing is hanging in the balance. We need your battalion's rifle companies now. We figure there's a reinforced regiment hitting us, maybe more. Division has approved your release from reserve to my sector. A runner from General Vandegrift's Operations Officer, Colonel Twining, should be on your doorstep with written orders authorizing you to commit now."

"I understand and will comply, Colonel Puller. Where do you want us? We're ready to roll!"

Now comes the sticky part, Chesty thought. "In all sincerity, Colonel Hall, I must ask you to voluntarily sacrifice individual direct command of your unit." He waited for a scream of disbelief. It never came.

"Go on. I don't like it but I'm listening." Hall huddled under an ineffective poncho held by a dutiful topkick, while he adjusted the dripping headset.

"It's too dark and rainy to see anything but shadows. My problem is that it would be impossible to laterally maneuver my entire battalion so that your battalion could fill a specific slot in the line. We're under too much pressure. Quite frankly, we don't have the luxury to even debate it, the battle is hanging out there for either side to snatch and—"

Hall cut off the Marine's plea. "And you want to feed my soldiers in among your Marines. So we'd be piecemeal replacements."

"Exactly. I couldn't have said it better. Of course it would only be temporary."

"Colonel Puller, my ego won't get in the way of sound tactics. This flood is impossible. I will move my battalion to a point directly to your rear and have them fan out. I suggest you have some of your Marines come back and guide them once we arrive."

"Good idea, Colonel Hall. And thank you."

"At your service. Roger and out."

For a battalion commander to relinquish battlefield control of a fighting unit he has trained and honed, to see it virtually dismembered into individual riflemen, requires supreme confidence in his own ability not to feel scornfully pick-pocketed. Lieutenant Colonel Hall deserved more than a tip of the hat for releasing his troops.

Turning to the master sergeant who had been taking in the conversation, Puller yelled over the din of incoming mortars. "Luzak, every man we can spare, runners, walking wounded, rich men, poor men, beggar men, thieves. Spread 'em out to our rear and have them guide those doggies to our front positions. Keep it simple, don't dig 'em in. Work on a double strength balance. One soldier in every hole where there's a Marine, two soldiers where there's two Marines, and so on. Got it?"

"Aye, aye, sir."

"And another thing. Keep your fat head down. I want to pin that Navy Cross on you while you're standing."

"I'll do my best, Colonel." Tony spit into the muddy slop and gave the boss man a grateful grin.

"Before you go. Where the hell is that big gun of yours?"

"Weapons platoon, Charlie Company, sir. It's sort of on loan."

Distinct rackety chatter could be heard periodically during the lulls of competing weaponry, comforting frontline leathernecks that *Luzak's Fifty* was on the job.

"Link up. Link up. Squad at a time. Hold hands, form a daisy chain if you have to. Just don't get separated!"

The veteran lieutenant slogged through the ranks of what would soon be his disassembled platoon. Rain slapping off the platoon's helmets competed with his shouted directions.

"Your guides will lead you up the slope. When you get to the ridge-line, belly down and crawl forward. Fan out and pair off with a jar head. Riflemen keep your safeties on until you're settled in place. BAR men should have at least two full magazine belts. Understood?" No response followed. The men were tight. "Okay, lock and load." The solid rattle of bolts sounded as men inserted clips and mags.

"And good luck. You're fine soldiers, you'll conduct yourselves well." Drenched to the bone, the lieutenant grabbed the belt of the guide to his front as another man looped a thumb in his. "Move 'em out!" he hoarsely bellowed. Sloshing and stumbling up the slippery footpath, they passed a Marine 81mm mortar section thunking out fire in speedy succession. Water cascaded down the path's steeper tracts like rapids in a swollen creek. Laden soldiers slid to their knees, dragging down their link-ups, causing each thirteen-man chain to wobble like a drunken python.

Cracking gunfire grew louder approaching the spine as the guide halted the lieutenant's file. An aggressive Marine non-com racing back and forth positioning other Army riflemen clumsily footed his way to them. He instructed the guide to return and lead up another squad, he would take this group the rest of the way. Wearily, the young Marine slogged down the cratered incline. "Good luck, doggies," he wished them as he departed downhill. "Stay real low when you hit the crest."

The lieutenant, loaded down with a burlap sack of "pineapples," as the GIs called their hand grenades, stood at the head of the hunched squad. Darkened by torrential night rain, the obscure Marine who would steer them over the final seventy-five yards, moved closer to the officer. "Password and counter sign. LOLLIPOP and HOLLYWOOD. Pass it on."

The lieutenant was about to relay the codes when he hesitated. Something was eerily familiar about the voice. Incredulously, he asked, "Tony?"

"Woody?"

The reverse slope of an active killing field was hardly the place for a family reunion. Dying men about them were screaming final agonies. Ahead, grenades ripped gaping incisions into chests and abdomens of young combatants, many still in their teens. The two crouched brothers embraced each other in a sandbagged pit being used by corpsmen, and now medics, to hold the severely wounded. After several tearful hugs they agreed to keep apart lest they both die of the same Japanese bullet.

Second Lieutenant Woodrow Luzak, USA, slithered into a slimy hole manned by a Marine gunnery sergeant and a highly agitated youthful soldier. A dead Marine, perhaps the same age, slumped across his ankles. Woody rolled the corpse aside and took a firing position, pushing the nervous GI to the forward lip. Gun flashes and the glare of rumbling detonations reflected off the wall of rain. "Here they come," husky voices boomed from hidden foxholes and narrow trenches to their left and right. A white phosphorous blast illuminated the barbed wire, providing the riflemen with a frame of reference. They adjusted their firing angles accordingly.

"Them mortar gunners are laying down the Willy Pete. Let's get ready," the gunny calmly encouraged. Woody, soaked through with rain and mud, felt a warm sensation flood his crotch and thighs. He had pissed his pants, but this was no time to dwell on an unruly bladder. Readying himself, the lieutenant inserted a finger inside the trigger guard, flicked off the safety and re-assumed his firing position. This was the moment for which Woody had been training since the first day he took the oath as an eighteen-year-old recruit.

A creeping enemy barrage worked its thunderous way up the rise, the blasts rattling bones and teeth. They hunkered down, avoiding the zipping shrapnel. Concussive tremors shocked aching skulls. A few rounds scored direct hits on unlucky foxholes, identified now by only twisted spirals of acrid smoke. Spumes of yellow flame shot skyward, lighting the ugly landscape. Following its destructive wake, the hated foe bolted toward the crest. The frenzied cacophony of screaming Jap soldiers shooting on the run was met with a killing fusillade. Incredibly, the Yanks had taken their knockout punch and survived in force.

Intersecting machine gun fire ripped the enemy troops into shreds. Yet they kept coming, clawing through the withering spray of steel and lead. The gunny methodically worked his Springfield as Luzak and the private leaned forward and pumped out sixteen rapid shots in tandem. They reloaded and continued their lethal fire. "Jap there," shouted the gunny as a ghostly figure wielding a bayoneted Arisaka vaulted the last wire. Before the Marine could reset his bolt, Woody acquired the target and triggered three semi-automatic bullets, dropping him into a sprawling heap.

"What in the name of hell is that?" the gunny marveled.

"What's what?"

"Your Springfield, or whatever it is!"

"This, my Marine friend, is the US Rifle Caliber .30 Ml. But you can call it a Garand!" *Finally, vindication!*

"Jesus, the Army gets all the fuckin' good stuff! How many shots?"

"Eight."

"Damn, that's three more than the Springfield."

The private stopped performing after his opening bursts. Woody checked to see if he'd been hit. He rolled his sagging body, exposing the young face. Above his right eye a small hole trickled a tiny stream of blood. Cleansing rain soon removed the red stain, leaving only a small puncture where the .25 caliber round had entered. He had died without a sound, without a prayer.

Dropping the Springfield, an enlightened Gunnery Sergeant Harry Kalinski snatched the free Garand and uttered, "Show me!" The scene was repeated up and down the line as Marines "requisitioned" the M1s from fallen GIs. There's no laboratory like reality.

Superior firepower, guts, and the open-minded willingness of Lieutenant Colonel Hall to fractionate his command, to disregard interservice paranoia, saved the perimeter and Henderson Field. By dawn, enemy assaults petered out as the combined jar heads and doggies poured killing fire into the last weak attack wave. Japanese corpses littered the putrid battlefield like so many twisted, lifeless rag dolls shot to bits. Sunrise brought vision, despite the dimming rain, and Kalinski, noting a gold bar an Luzak's collar point, realized his hole-mate and M1 instructor had been an officer. In the turmoil of battle, Woody had neglected to remove the reflecting targets of rank. "Sorry if I wasn't all that respectful, sir," he apologized.

"You were just fine."

To their rear, a slithering body wormed through the muck. Unsure, Woody called out. "Care for a LOLLIPOP?"

"Hooray for HOLLYWOOD," came the gruff reply. "HOLLY-FUCKIN-WOOD!"

"Come on in, you crazy Slovak bastard," Woody chuckled. Master Sergeant Tony Luzak's mud splattered head appeared above the rim. He half-slid, half-rolled into the crowded hole filled with over a foot of water, and took care not to step on the two dead Americans. Shell casings and the limp grenade bag cluttered the pit. An empty canteen bobbed above the muddy sump.

"Admiral Anton Luzak of the royal fuckin' Slovak Marines reporting. Looks like you guys had some action," he wryly commented.

"He's an officer," the gunny told him.

"Woody, sir, those fuckin' Garands were everything you wrote about. They really helped carry the action. It's hard to believe that Quantico turned them down." He shook his head, the act causing droplets to spin off his helmet.

Gunny Kalinski plopped back in pissed-off awe. "Tony, you mean some dumb, fuckin' son-of-a-bitch at Quantico rejected the Garand?" This very same reaction repeated itself up and down the line by stupefied Marines at every echelon.

Needless to inform, after Guadalcanal, the USMC would box their obsolete Springfields in cosmoline and commit totally to the Garand. Finger-pointing at Quantico never quite reached the Commandant's chair—but it got close.

Later that morning, October 25, the rain stopped and sun, drying sun, drifted across the perimeter to the cheers of shrivel-skinned men. Unfortunately it served to instigate a seaborne bombardment from Japanese destroyers, several air attacks and crunching salvos delivered by 150mm howitzer batteries hidden deep in the concealing jungle. The Cactus Air Force led by Captain Joe Foss' VMF-121 and its nasty Wildcats exacted a heavy toll in the skies over Savo Sound. Nevertheless, insolent Henderson Field and its surrounding grunts took a vicious pasting. That night saw a duplicate banzai performance by fanatical Japanese infantry. This time though, 2/7 absorbed the brunt of their spearhead.

American casualties were high but the defiant perimeter held. Platoon Sergeant Mitchell Paige, USMC, performed extraordinary heroics equal to those of Basilone. He too was rewarded with the CMH in addition to being granted a battlefield commission to second lieutenant. Many men performed valorous feats that went unnoticed, for they came to be the norm rather than the exception.

Reassembled by Lieutenant Colonel Hall, 3/164 took its place in the defensive line, Puller's battalion shifting and consolidating to make room for the proven dog faces. Wire was strung, positions strengthened, machine guns registered in time to blunt the Sendai Division and its shattered shock troops, never again to seriously threaten Henderson Field.

CHAPTER XII
BROTHERS

DATE: THURSDAY, 24 DECEMBER 1942

TIME: 1045 HOURS

LOCATION: GUADALCANAL

Riding at anchor, the ships lined up in the lagoon-like bay offloading troops and supplies, feeding smaller ferrying vessels. Military vehicles of every sort and their shirtless, sweaty beach parties strained in the late morning sun, hauling cargo to the interior. Viewing the action in the shade of a weathered engineering crate, three hundred yards up the beach a gaunt, barefoot figure puffed a Chesterfield. The sturdy six-foot box had been commandeered from SeaBees a week earlier and crudely fashioned into a hut simply by knocking out both ends to permit flow-through ventilation. Mosquito netting tacked above the exits provided relief from pesky, nocturnal insects. Today the nets were pulled back over the roof and weighted down with Japanese helmets, allowing easy access.

Pulling the nicotine smoke deep into his lungs, Tony Luzak squinted through solar glare and heat waves wobbling off the torrid sand. Three months on The Canal had witnessed the loss of nineteen pounds. His body had suffered a debilitating transformation. Dysentery and jungle rot were now accepted as everyday annoyances, as commonplace as the suppressing humidity. Free-form white ulcers pricked his tender mouth.

Raw lesions remained wherever damp straps and belts had cut into shoulders and waist. Sticky clear fluid oozed from angry crotch pustules. Unseen parasites infested dark crummy recesses wherever sweat and stink collected. Nothing ever healed on Guadalcanal. All one could do was hope for temporary relief until evacuation to a refuge dry and temperate.

Dropping his rumpled sun-bleached trousers, he stepped from their heaped filth and kicked them up to his hand. His cotton undershorts had rotted themselves into oblivion weeks ago. A morning soak in the warm salt water of Savo Sound was the best therapy he could seek. Sliding into lace-less boondockers, he wearily strode the burning sand to the waterline. Booted, nude, and dog tagged, he provided comical relief on an island that manifested the blackest of mankind's urges. His deeply tanned face and neck stood out in parfait-like contrast to a body white and pink.

Tony spit the waning butt into the lazy surf and squatted in a few feet of soothing tide. Sitting back as though in an invisible chaise lounge, he arched a scrawny neck, enjoying the baptism of water dancing through scalp and hair. It filled his ears and washed crud clinging between toes and joints. Sores dilated, yawning open to absorb briny consolation. Armpits welcomed the rush. An anus, scraped and swollen from weeks of involuntary discharge and an absence of humane toilet tissue, pulsed in anticipation of the sea's comforting essence. After scrubbing his stubbled face and throat, he lay in luxuriating stillness, savoring the moment. Ten minutes passed before he grabbed the soaking trousers and brushed them vigorously with fingertips and knuckles. Back at the hut he would spread them atop the roof and summon the sun to finish the job. But for now he would gluttonize skin and pores, hair and membrane, nails and callous, welts and wounds on the tidal Pacific.

After October's great crushing of the Japanese Army, the 1st Marine Division had pursued the enemy and fought many small-scale but brutal actions. Elements of Japan's 38th Infantry Division landed in an attempt to bolster the sagging veterans of Nippon; however, it soon became apparent the issue was no longer in doubt. The Americans would win. CINCPAC and the Joint Chiefs decided to put three fresh divisions ashore—the 2ND Marine Division, the US Army's American and 25TH Infantry Divisions—to guarantee total victory. They would trickle to the big island over the next several weeks. Commanded by Major General Alexander Patch, the overall Guadalcanal force now constituted as the XIV Corps, would hound and hammer the enemy until all resistance disappeared.

At this early part of the US entry in the war, the Army's best-trained, most aggressive troops, in divisional strength, were being shipped to North Africa, but even they had to be tested under fire and fine-tuned. A large number of the initial units rushed to the Pacific theater were drawn from poorly trained National Guard outfits, not given sufficient time to develop disciplined skills and unit cohesion. Many of the officers and enlisted men were ill-prepared, though their bodies and spirits willing. But the pace of the war dictated they be prematurely fed into the grinder. The enemy, well trained and eager to press the issue, wouldn't wait.

Some Pacific Army units, the Americal and 25TH Infantry Divisions among them, excelled thanks to solid leadership and superior conditioning, which quickly forged effective fighting machines. However, others suffered needless casualties as a consequence of poor commanders, unready troops, and a hideous environment. A highly motivated foe took advantage of every weakness. As time wore on though, they became veteran outfits led by seasoned officers and performed magnificently.

Emaciated, malarial and shot up after four months of privation and savage combat, 1ST MarDiv would be pulled back to Australia. There they would heal up, refit, and train for the next conflict. Master Sergeant Anton Luzak was charged with rear-party duty, making sure the Seventh Marine Regiment's gear was properly stowed and shipped. In actuality he had been somewhat of a fifth wheel. But he used the respite to hide out in his "administrative" shack, sleeping and reflecting on the past fourteen weeks. To the south, the rumbling of guns sounded, reminding him that Americans yet slugged it out with a stubborn adversary.

By the time he recrossed the two hundred yards or so to the hut, his sea-drenched body had dried and perspiration already glistened his forehead and sunken eyes. He sprinkled antiseptic powder wherever it would reach and rubbed pungent ointment about his groin.

The infernal sun stood hot and high, no shadow grew from the slender figure trudging up the beach toward Tony. A helmet hung from one of two canteens, a leather-holstered .45 Colt rested against the right hip. Over his shoulder he carried a drawstring laundry sack, sometimes referred to as a barracks bag. As the man drew closer, the master sergeant smiled and stiffly rose to greet him.

"Merry Christmas, ho ho ho!" the guest guffawed. He lowered the olive-drab bundle and placed a free arm over his brother's shoulder.

"And you, Woody, and you," he responded, the voice weak, weary from weeks in hell.

The younger man spread open the bag and withdrew a pair of new khaki shorts. "The brass pulled the 164th out of harm's way for a bit of rest and issued us new skivvies, their way of playing Santa Claus. So I swiped a pair for you, figuring you'd need 'em. And looking at your ugly, naked ass, I guess I was right."

"Gratefully accepted on behalf of every grunt in the fleet." He pressed them against his face, inhaling their freshness, before putting them on. "What else have you in that wonderful bag, socks I hope?"

"Sorry, no socks but… " He flipped the sack, gently coaxing out the contents: three packs of cigarettes, a bottle half full of Coronet Brandy, and a mason jar containing Vic Romanek's homemade pickled pig ears. "Treasures from the sweetest sister in Linden, New Jersey."

"God bless you, Woodrow Luzak, and sister Stella."

The officer tapped a breast pocket causing a letter to rustle inside. "Got mail from Stell' yesterday. Said she received a big promotion at the plant. Those poor bastards working for her are going to have to tow the mark or she'll have their heads."

"I guess so," the Marine chortled. "Hell, I couldn't beat her wrist-wrestling until I was sixteen."

"Really? I never whipped her."

They had always exaggerated stories of Stella's exploits. You do that when someone is special. Sports writers did it with Babe Ruth, columnists with FDR.

"She mentioned Big Vic's brother Ray's nephew is an Army airborne officer."

"Who's that, the college boy football player?"

"Yeah Phil, Phil Primo. Stella says she finally met him in Connecticut at Ray's. He was home on furlough."

"Well, good luck to him and to us." He swigged a belt of Woody's Coronet. His chiseled face had aged considerably since departing China.

An easy wind, holiday gift from the sea, blew in off Savo Sound and the men rotated the hut crate, capturing the breeze in its pine tunnel of posts and planks. Tony broke out his own dwindling brandy bottle, crackers and apple jelly.

Unlacing his boots, Woody pushed them off and slid inside the box enjoying the shade and soft-blowing wind. There they enjoyed as unattractive a feast as ever graced anyone's Christmas table. Pigs' ears, apple jelly, and soggy saltines. What the hell, the brandy made it all palatable!

They gabbed in spurts, more than they had ever, into the early evening. Much of the chat centered on Swifty, the quick marriage and their two tender weeks spent in Honolulu. Tony showed a sensitive side his brother never knew, seeking every bit of information, regardless how picayune, of Nancy Swift Luzak. Background, personality, physical features, childhood diseases, the whole package. He wanted to form a mental picture right down to her favorite clothing, and Woody painted a detailed composite including preferred lipstick and perfume. Unfortunately her photo rested in his duffel bag back at camp. They spoke of children down the line, and retirement in Hawaii someday when they were old and fat.

"You're damn lucky, kid. To your credit, you made your own luck. Worked your butt off. I'm so damn proud of you being an officer I could spit. And you did it the hard way, up from the ranks, a friggen mustang! Kalinski told me you're one hell of a fighting man too. Said you tossed a bunch of pineapples right down their throats, exposing yourself."

Tony playfully changed the mood, grabbing a fist-full of Woody's shirt. Assuming the big brother authority he emoted a mock snarl. "Next time don't be so fuckin' reckless!"

"Thanks, Tony. From what I've heard you're one tough S.O.B. yourself, a living legend. Bataan, Corregidor, boat rides, submarines, Mindanao, Purple Heart, Silver Star, Navy Cross. Kalinski told me all about it." He poured a measure of brandy into their canteen cups. "And here's to old Joe and mom."

"Amen."

They clunked the metal cups and sipped silently for a while. Tony pulled a pack of Chesterfields from his stash and rolled off the condom protecting it from moisture. "We use these scumbags for everything but our dicks. The corpsmen cover battle dressings and medicine with 'em. Goddamn War Department must think we're screwing our asses off... they keep sending them to us by the gross."

"I guess they figure there've been no VD cases on The Canal to date, so they're not about to take any chances. Keep 'em coming!" They laughed. The thought of some faceless bureaucrat conscientiously inventorying Trojans and Rameses, expediting them on their critical way to the Solomons, brought tears to their eyes.

Still guffawing, Tony crawled outside to urinate. "Maybe they ought to send some women with those rubbers," his voice trailed off. Moments later he returned, still shaking his member. "Don't want to soil my gorgeous new skivvies," he chuckled.

Staring into the cup's bottom, Woody sloshed its dregs.

"I'm not sure I should be telling you this, Tony. But that first night on the ridge, I peed my pants. Some hero, huh?"

"Kid, I pissed a quart at San Leo Bridge and again when I won the Cross. It just happens. Tell you what. You don't tell on me, I don't tell on you." He sipped another mouthful, wincing as the alcohol stung a hidden sore.

"It's a deal." They shook hands, gripping real hard.

The lieutenant glanced at his wristwatch. "Whoa, eighteen forty nine. Time for me to go, big brother. I don't want to be gunned down by my own troops after dark."

"Woody?"

"Yeah," he answered softly.

"Is that the same gold bar on your collar that you wore that night we met in the rain?"

"Yeah, it sure is."

"Can I have it?" Tony's voice was soft, almost apologetic. Even the Old Breed have sentimental moments.

"What for?"

"Kind of a keepsake. You know what I mean?"

"Sure, I've got extras." He unfastened the insignia and placed it in Tony's palm. The Marine closed his hand and eyes as if to capture a mystical energy. "And, Tony... "

"Yeah, kid."

"Give the rest of my pig ears to Harry Kalinski. Those Polskas love that stuff too."

"He bought the farm on Thanksgiving Day. Direct mortar."

"Oh."

He stretched out and kissed the old warrior's forehead. "Enjoy Australia and pack some meat on that frame." Their eyes met and in a single instant exchanged more sweetness than the spoken word could ever convey.

"And you keep your head low."

CHAPTER XIII
VICTORIA BRIDGE

DATE: FRIDAY 1 JANUARY 1943

TIME: 0740 HOURS

LOCATION: PINK GARDEN VILLA BRISBANE, AUSTRALIA

Telephones should be instruments of the afternoon or at least the late morning, especially on New Years Day.

Neither of the two naked figures stirred, each anticipating, or hoping, the other would answer the strident ring. Most of Brisbane had been celebrating only a few hours earlier, trying to forget the harsh previous year and welcome the fresh one, guardedly optimistic it would usher an end to the Japanese aggression. For Marla Whitfield, 1942 had seen her countrymen fighting in North Africa and New Guinea, and Australia flooded with American allies preparing to meet the threat. The great commonwealth had assumed status of staging area for huge combat fleets, bomber commands, logistics hubs, communications nucleus, and springboard for tens of thousands of free spending, morale-boosting ground troops.

Submarines silently slipped out of her sheltered waters, providing reconnaissance and a protective screen warding off hostile ships of war. The vicious subs ranged far, striking fat enemy tankers hauling oil from the captured East India Islands, former Dutch and British possessions. Two swarming ports, Brisbane and Sydney, willingly greeted the commerce of battle, soon swallowed by their hungry wharfs and regurgitated inland. Munitions, vehicles, foodstuffs, and personnel were rapidly dispersed to government warehouses, military bases and huge tented bivouacs scattered throughout Queensland, New South Wales and Victoria. Creaking freighters and transports of every configuration originating from San Francisco, Seattle, and San Diego tied up in Australia's bulging harbors, relieved merchant mariners having experienced the anxiety of a trans-Pacific passage.

The swollen docks of America's eastern seaboard and gulf coast had exported their awesome largess via that most strategic of American channels, the Panama Canal. A nervous traverse toward New Zealand and Australia followed. Horizons filled with convoys of hope and victory moved closer each day. Arks of freedom, resolute in their mission, plowed through dangerous seas in an unending chain. The allies were confident they had the will and resources to prevail. All they needed was time, and it would seem Midway and Guadalcanal had provided both breathing room and a sweeping swing of the grand pendulum—momentum.

With all the turmoil about, 1942 had witnessed a momentous personal event for Marla. She had fallen deliciously in love with an American Marine for whom she had risked parental disfavor and social shame. The Whitfields, among their elegant real estate and vast holdings, owned a small six-room Mediterranean-style guest cottage overlooking the ocean near Moreton Bay, about fourteen miles from their Brisbane compound. For the most part, Jock Whitfield had made it available to visiting business associates and dignitaries, finding such people more pliable once he had them on his own turf. Old Jock was rumored to have used the pink stuccoed hide-away for discreet affairs during his more active years. Dubbed "Pink Garden Villa," its colorful flower garden surrounded itself with a graceful arcade and wide, tiled walk suggestive of a Riviera escape. Two airy bedrooms upstairs invited cooling sea breezes through white shuttered windows.

The villa, these days, was the sole province of Marla. She had informed clan Whitfield in 1941 that this "cottage" represented singular liberation, a paramount step in her unfolding life. The young woman would be its exclusive tenant. Her persuasive charm proved irresistible. No one dared refuse her, though there remained a degree of apprehension. After all, mother Cynthia reasoned, independence is as much a state of mind as it is fact. Severing a residentiary umbilical cord is perhaps more symbolic than absolute. At least in this case it was. The point is, Marla dined with the family at the Whitfield compound or Players four nights out of seven.

That is, before she took up with the Yank lieutenant. During the past six months they had been living at "PGV" as he called it, the military having an unquenchable penchant for initialed identity. For a woman of lesser means, co-habitation is simply naughty, but among society's creme-de-la-creme it smacks of scandal.

Her beau, sensitive to Marla's reputation and family situation. maintained separate official quarters at the Fenimore in North Brisbane. But everyone knew it was window dressing; in Marine parlance, a "smokescreen." Andrew remained gentlemanly to the core throughout the relationship, careful to avoid any scenario which might embarrass or divide Cynthia Whitfield and her daughter. She understood the urgency of war had fanned the passion of youth, and was all for it. But passion leads to indiscretion, which can be costly in the long run… reputations sullied, egos damaged, families irreconcilably strained. So mother walked the fine line of confidant and protectoress. Lieutenant Delane proved to be polite, educated, and very handsome. Most importantly, he cared deeply for Marla. The love and respect he displayed was admirable. However, his occupation was a dangerous one and, therefore, fragile. Marriage must be discouraged.

After the fourth ring, Andrew Delane blindly groped for the elusive phone and lifted the receiver. "This had better be important," his hungover throat croaked.

"Andy, that you?"

He recognized the energetic voice. "Yes, Roy. I hope the Japs have thrown in the towel. That *is* the reason you're calling at this hour, yes?"

"Geez, is it that early?" Captain Roy Bauer had a rep for being the consummate early bird but sometimes he didn't realize how his indifference to time affected those around him. He and Delane had become a superb working team and close friends since Andy's arrival in May. "I thought you'd like to know—you're on the list, Captain-select. You should be promoted sometime in February. Now you won't have to call me 'sir' anymore and kiss my ass."

Delane knew Bauer had been on duty all night, unable to attend any of Brisbane's plentiful New Years bashes. Actually he had covered for Delane, it being Andy's turn in the barrel. "Roy, that's great news but it could have held until noon."

"Noon, hell. Consider yourself fortunate! I almost called an hour ago." Now he got around to the true purpose of his call. "How did Maxwell make out? Damn, he was as nervous as a high school prom date. Must have brushed his teeth four times. His gums were turning to tartar steak."

Andy slapped a pillow against the headboard and propped himself to a sitting position. Roy, he knew, would pester him until he gave out with the poop. Marla pushed her pillow against Andy's rib cage and draped a smooth thigh over his knee, content to cuddle up and doze. Overhead, a ceiling fan slowly rotated its noiseless comfort.

New Years Eve, they had agreed, was to have been a cultured evening at the symphony followed by late dinner and romantic cocktails through the midnight hour. Marla reserved four seats at the family's private box, having offered a pair to Andy's Colonel and date. But they would strike off on their own after the concert, leaving Marla and Andy to themselves. Unsuspectingly, a certain brother, one Lieutenant Commander Evan Whitfield, RAN, had made parallel plans, which eventually overwhelmed all of them.

With the family's reputation as patrons of the musical and visual arts came an obligation to fill their balcony box during each performance. It was simple enough, as grateful company employees and guests were provided complimentary access to each concert that the Whitfields cared not to attend. Marla had pocketed four tickets while, unknown to her, Evan procured the other two.

Minutes before the first piece as the musicians were tuning up, the Marine lieutenant and his glamorous partner, clad in shimmering blue, slipped into their seats and held hands tightly. The grand hall buzzed with excitement as concert-goers packed every seat. Tonight, Marla thought, *will be very special.* Moments later, Lieutenant Colonel Gordon Maxwell, looking sheepish and uncomfortable, arrived escorting a stylish Gwen Cash, hostess at Players. Gwen recognized she was out of her element hobnobbing with the elite Whitfields, the very folks she served in her capacity at the club. Regardless, the fact her date was a splendidly uniformed Marine field grade officer helped lubricate the discomfort of any social inferiority. After months of prodding Maxwell, Delane engineered the date between his long-divorced boss and the attractive widow. Everyone needs someone, states the cliché. And vivacious Mrs. Cash seemed the perfect fit for the intense Colonel, or so Andy deduced. Clutching their programs, they all smiled cheerfully and whispered hellos.

Marla went out of her way to dispel any notion of high-born prominence. She and Gwen chatted small talk in hushed tones. Any age or class difference evaporated. As the maestro's baton tapped for attention, a disturbance occurred at the rear of the box. Sweeping aside the burgundy curtain, Evan

Whitfield unnecessarily and loudly said, "Here we are my dear, right on time. Punctuality remains my most redeeming virtue."

Sensing an overpowering presence, the foursome turned to glimpse a stooping Lady Rita Benton, accentuating her plunging decolletage. The latter possessed an enormous brace of perfectly matched tits barely covered by an excessively low-cut, gold evening gown, clinging and glimmering in skin-tight glory. The word *zoftic* promptly leaps from one's vocabulary… with a capital Z! Cut diamonds linked by a sparkling network of platinum settings surrounded Lady Benton's long neck and cascaded into her ample cleavage. The jewelry no doubt was a gift from grateful Sir Harry, currently hospitalized in Sydney with a prostate disorder. The heroic boobs, a genetic gift of the first magnitude, had been hers since age fourteen. She smiled broadly, revealing brilliant white teeth emphasized by wet, rubied lips. Her striking face boldly projected a haughty confidence framed by lustrous raven hair glamorously swept upward. Pear shaped diamond pendant earrings completed the extravagant portrait, bigger than life. Gwen stifled a wide-eyed gasp. Maxwell gulped. Delane ogled. Marla ground a remindful elbow into his indifferent ribs. They all smiled, frozen in an awkward instant of *what's next?* The answer immediately materialized, Evan in black tuxedo pants and pink dinner jacket. He carried a split of champagne and two fluted glasses, something for intermission, no doubt. Delighted to discover his balcony friends, he beamed his pleasure before assisting the statuesque Rita to her seat. It was a bit like maneuvering an aircraft carrier to its berth.

Other than the popping cork and occasional chime of tinkling stemware, the back-seated couple behaved reasonably well. The temptation was too much for Evan and guest. Consequently the champagne flowed sixty minutes before intermission. Once their collective thirst had been slaked they settled in to enjoy the evening's splendid selection of Mozart, Verdi, Puccini, Bizet, Strauss, Brahms, Von Weber, Rossini, Tchaikovsky, Sibelius, and Gershwin. Hard feelings aside, the philharmonic played an unbiased repertory embodying, among others, the great German, Italian and Austrian composers. Their compositions had been created long before the Axis madness had ever crystallized. And sweet music saturated the house, delighting the appreciative throng.

Something spontaneously wonderful happened in the confines of Brisbane's elegant music hall this thirty-first night of December, 1942. At the evening's conclusion, the orchestra boldly struck the initial notes of Beethoven's Fifth Symphony, unmistakable in its emphasis. The reverberation rocked the comfortable audience to attention. People sat more erect, craning necks in anticipation of the powerful strains to follow. Seated in the sixth row, a silver-haired gentleman in shiny tuxedo stood with right arm extended high for all to view, his first two fingers thrust upwards and splayed in defiant pride. A richly-dressed woman at his side joined him in gesture, and within seconds, pockets of Australians scattered about the hall rose in support, twin fingers stretching aloft.

Like a great contagious wave everyone surged to his feet, some with tears unashamedly wetting cheeks and chin. The musicians played with particular fervor having been caught up in the emotion. Horns and strings echoed in acoustical grandeur. Spines and napes tingled in electrifying sensation. Time stood still as unity and brotherhood bonded the congregation in unspoken patriotism.

"V," the twenty-second letter of the English alphabet, had become a symbol for millions resisting the yoke of Nazi oppression—V scrawled on walls in European public toilets and kiosks. A fist with index and middle fingers spread and extended was offered and returned—freely by citizens in unoccupied lands, clandestinely where Hitler's shadow loomed.

Everywhere, people tapped the Morse Code V, dit-dit-dit-dah. They clinked it with cocktail glasses, rang it on doorbells, and buzzed it on buzzers. Trucks and autos insolently beeped its cryptic promise on back roads and boulevards. Brave men and women kept alive the spark of resistance and the dream of freedom by humming or whistling the opening bars of Beethoven's Fifth Symphony, bom, bom, bom, baaaah (code for dit-dit-dit...dah). For the Czechoslovaks it stood for Viterstvi; for Frenchmen and Belgian Walloons, Victoire; Hollanders and Belgian Flemings shouted Vryjheid; and in the Slavic Balkans, cries of Vitestvo... victory and freedom. Danes, Norwegians, Poles, Canadians , Greeks, New Zealanders, Indians, South Africans and even those under Soviet domination flaunted the ubiquitous V.

And buttressing the vortex of every V stood the valiant British who rallied the free and gave hope to the chained until the Americans joined their righteous fold. In the United States people wrote their servicemen on V Mail, and tilled Victory Gardens as gestures of solidarity with the world, as well as sustenance. If ever there was a sign of the time, the V was it. Indeed it was an era of crusade, and V represented its sacred cross.

And in Brisbane, as the orchestra dramatically swung into a second vigorous encore, strangers cheered and hugged openly to proclaim the gallant

Aussies and their global brethren would not be bullied by jackboot or tabi. Through determination, guts, and the will of God, they would persevere!

"Really, won't you join us at my place? I'm having a few friends for midnight cocktails and a bite. You must, you must, I insist!" Lady Rita was used to getting her way, and tonight would be no exception. She had a knack of imposing her agenda, regardless how trivial. Holding Marla's hand close to her chest she playfully teased, "I won't let you go until you say yes!"

The younger woman knew she was trapped, especially with Evan egging her on. She looked to Andy for assistance, hoping he would whisk her from this predicament. But he smiled amenably, "Whatever you wish, honey."

Oh you're no help, Andrew Sabre Delane, she fumed inside.

"We'd enjoy that very much," Colonel Maxwell blurted, delighted to have found a place to go with Gwen. Through much of the performance he had twittered, trying to figure out where he would take his date, what he would say one-on-one. Rita Benton had provided sanctuary. Gwen, thrilled, smiled her approval.

Helpless, Marla Whitfield, nodded her willingness to join the party. "Fine," she said. *Just ducky!*

"Then it's settled," Evan said. Rita's Rolls should be waiting for us at curbside. It's almost ten o'clock now, so we have plenty of time for diversions."

For diversions! What in bloody hell is that madman talking about? Marla's unflappable appearance belied her suspicious thoughts.

Fifteen minutes later. they crammed into the silver-gray Rolls-Royce with Evan seated up front alongside the chauffeur. A bucketed magnum of Dom Perignon, cooled in chipped ice, greeted the passengers. Gordon Maxwell did the honors, popping and pouring as the big auto wove its way through North Brisbane, no one paying particular note to their route.

The revelers toasted the Royal Australian Navy, King George, Franklin D. Roosevelt, the bloody Marines (twice), ex-Prime Minister Robert Menzies, Frank Knox, and Clark Gable. Preempting a feminist backlash, Andrew rapidly added Amelia Earhart, Greta Garbo, and Madame Chiang Kai-Shek to the flock. A second cork popped and the boisterous group, growing tipsier with each salute, hailed an expanded pantheon of celebrities. Winston Churchill, the Lord Mayor of Brisbane, Dorthy Lamour, and Errol Flynn all achieved emphatic recognition. Rita, a fellow Tasmanian, was particularly fond of Errol. Generals Slim, MacArthur, and Vandegrift were next on the hit list as the sleek sedan approached Victoria Bridge. Evan motioned the driver to pull off to the roadside.

The car rolled onto the shoulder and parked, with the insouciant lieutenant commander announcing his intention to leave for a few moments. Not to worry, he would return before they could open a third bottle. Not allowing anyone to protest or query his mysterious exit, he quickly departed. "Oh my Lord, he's really going to do it, really going to do it!" Rita said hilariously, her voice rising an octave, her chest in pronounced accompaniment.

"Do what?" Marla asked. A silly grin formed, the combination of alcohol and empty stomach taking its toll. "Jump off Victoria Brizhhgg?" She slurred the final word.

Rita gulped another sip. "Oh no," she cackled. "Nothing that severe." The ridiculous conversation fueled by happy champagne caused Lady Benton to jerk her arms apart, shattering the glass against the window. Shards fell to the thick carpeting. "Oh dear." Seeing no one was cut, she matter-of-factly dropped the stem and continued. "I'm sure Evan will explain it all when he returns. But suffice it to say, it's madness like this that makes me so fond of that boy." Inasmuch as Lady Benton and Evan Whitfield were roughly the same age, she no doubt used the term *boy* affectionately, in the figurative sense.

"To that great Australian hydrographer and defender of the British Empire… Evan Whitfield!" The sauce was also getting to the suddenly extroverted Maxwell. He handed Rita a fresh glass and poured a round. "Here, here," they chorused. Clinking to Evan's good health, they worked their way into the third magnum.

Several more minutes passed before a jaunty pink form strode off the bridge's entranceway and briskly approached the Rolls. Straightening an askew bow tie, he paused, allowing the dutiful chauffeur to open the door. Once inside he grinned like a prankish child. "Any bubbly remaining?" Rita handed him her half-full glass from which he greedily emptied its contents in a single, quick belt.

"You devilishly nasty boy. Did you actually do it?"

"Of course. Some things are a matter of personal ethics."

She cackled aloud, gripping Maxwell's thigh to restrain her convulsive laughter. "Tell them, Evan. Do tell them."

"Tell us," they all demanded, like denied school children.

"Well if you must know, I pissed off the center of Victoria Bridge, straight down into the river."

"Bravo, Evan, bravo," Rita complimented in beaming admiration.

"You what?" Delane asked, not believing what he had just heard.

"Well, when I was in the Philippines, temporarily deserted by my own Navy and yours, I felt somewhat abandoned, and justifiably so! For months I was jockeyed around from jungle hut to pineapple shack, hiding from the Japanese, never knowing who was truly my ally. Those Moros are a mercenary lot. Any one of them could have sold my head to the Japs for a sack of rice. Can you imagine this exquisite face mounted on a stick?" He puckered an exaggerated smile causing an imbecilic, bucktoothed grin. "So several weeks before I met you, Andrew, I made myself a solemn promise. Call it a bond with my conscience if you prefer, but nevertheless an irrevocable pledge. If I escaped that tortuous locale and returned safely to Brisbane, I would piss dead center off Victoria Bridge on my first New Years Eve home. *Voila mon amis*! Tonight I honored that noble declaration."

"Bravo, Evan, bravo. And those damned British think we're so sodding provincial!" Rita was ready to sponsor him for knighthood had she the authority.

"Easy, my sweet, you'll explode right out of that magnificent gown," he tempered. She climbed over the assemblage of shoes and legs to plant a long, juicy kiss on her champion's mouth. He accepted it casually. After Rita clumsily reseated herself Evan continued. "When a man is desperate like I was, he needs a goal, or perhaps more accurately, an oath to see him through. Makes no difference if it's serious or ludicrous. Polonius' appropriate words ringeth yet tonight, 'To thine own self be true!'" Whitfield played out the drama, raising a veed fist to the ceiling. He hesitated, amusing himself aloud with a poor pun, "So V, my companions, is also for Victoria Bridge!" His raptured audience applauded and howled.

"Damned fine gesture, Evan. Damned fi—worthy of the Royal Shakespearean Navy I'm certain." Maxwell, loose as the proverbial goose, was enjoying himself for the first time in months. Gwen kissed his cheek in the fun of the moment.

"Go on," Andrew encouraged his fellow denizen and escapee of the Zamboangan peninsula. "Provide some information. After all, I'm supposed to be an intelligence officer these days."

"There's not a whole lot more except for the precise math," Evan winked. "The bridge is one thousand, forty-one feet long. So figuring one long step to a yard, I paced off one hundred seventy-three-and-a-half steps to the middle, climbed the restraining wall and unbuttoned. My balance was sure, hand steady, kidneys poised. Without doubt the longest pee I've ever attempted. And successful at that!"

"That's a lot of Dom Perignon," Maxwell quipped. Evan laughed uncontrollably, slapping the dash board. They all laughed as the Rolls roared off in the direction of Queen's Park, north to Benton Hall.

What Marla had expected to be an intimate circle proved to be a gala group of New Years merrymakers. Cole Porter's "Begin The Beguine" rolled out of the impressive baby grand piano and flooded the great room. The hostess' sweeping entrance was met with "oohs" as the two dozen or so guests made sure to actively recognize Lady Benton's arrival. No one wished to incur her displeasure, no matter how petty. Wartime champagne, especially the highfalutin variety, was difficult to come by. She bathed in the attention, flitting from one clique to the next. Compliments were devoured like so many plankton in a sea of beluga. Puffing smoke through a dramatic six-inch cigarette holder, she affected theatrical poses, highlighted by one word responses like "divine" and "superlative."

Colonel Maxwell selected two effervescent glasses from a passing servant and reached one out to Gwen, holding it to her lips while she set down an empty canape plate. Cesar Romero couldn't have pulled it off more suavely. He stared into her receptive pupils, a smoldering look of desire. The cage had opened. She moved closer, the wine working its magic. "Dance?" he asked, cocksure of himself.

"I'd love to," she answered in a throaty whisper.

Sucking in a self-conscious waistline, he whisked her into his arms and foxtrotted through the night, crooning as they glided, unaware of anything but each other.

"Telephone, madam," a skinny, cadaverous butler apprised in sotto voce. "Long distance. I believe it's Sir Harry in Sydney."

"I'll take it in the den, Morgan. Thank you." Rita moved quickly, acknowledging the nods of guests while en route.

She sat on the tufted arm of a rich, leather chair and lifted the phone. Expecting him to be impatient and perhaps a bit testy, she affected her warmest salutation. Hopefully it would disarm his temper. "Harry, darling," she gushed. "I've missed you so."

"Don't give me that sodding syrup. Where the devil have you been? I've been calling for hours!"

"You don't mean Morgan didn't tell you?" She waited a moment before continuing, hoping Sir Harry would calm his ire. "Why, I've been to the philharmonic as the guest of the Whitfields. Sat in their private balcony box, I did. Very charming people, quite proper. The cream of Australian society."

"Don't give me that cream crap. Eighteen months ago you were just another sodding, big-titted secretary unable to spell 'Whitfield.' Meanwhile I've got some bloody witch doctor down here who's talking about packing my balls in shaved ice. And you're celebrating with caviar and champagne? Well, you can kiss my royal sodding ass, Rita."

"You shouldn't speak to me so, Harry. I'm just trying to entertain a handful of your friends. Thought it would be good for your business investments and all."

"I'll speak to you as I see fit. As for my sodding 'friends,' I haven't any… they're *your* chums. Keep them out of my bedroom! Is that understood?"

"Harry, dear, why don't you smoke your pipe, that Turkish mixture you love so much. You know how it relaxes you."

"The sodding hospital won't let me smoke. Next time the beggars want a fucking donation I'll remind them of their bloody insensitivity." Rita Benton was used to the humiliation. It bounced off her like so many rubber bullets. Harry treated partners, employees, bankers, salesmen, and anyone offering service like dirt, his spouse included. But she endured it with a tough resilience. Small price, she reckoned, to offset a lifestyle teeming with abundant luxury. Occasional sexual favors, hardly enough to break a sweat, rendered him docile. The ornery bastard's weak spot breathed between his flabby thighs. She had learned that her first week at Benton Pacific Ltd. in 1940.

Mostly, he wanted her to look stunning when together in public, a trophy for peers and aspirants alike to envy. For fifty-seven year old Sir Harry Benton, image was half the battle in his commercial manipulations. So, in effect, Rita represented a business asset toward a lifelong pursuit of money and power. Her frequent indiscretions, made possible by Harry's solo trips down south to Sydney, Melbourne, Adelaide, and Hobart, revolved around fun-loving playboys like Evan Whitfield. And bless those rare trips to Perth, over two thousand trans-continental miles away, opening wide the rear door to extended liaisons. Gossip, regardless how bizarre, was never her problem… as long as no busybody confronted Harry with lurid tales of boudoir intrigue. The spicy whispers, though, were to be expected. They went with the territory.

In fact, she enjoyed the carnal reputation, equating it with great women of history and myth. As for her paramours, they were nothing more than essential toys retained for their ability to amuse and satisfy. Like most playthings, owners weary of them over time, and Lady Rita Benton's stable of expendables had recently whittled down to but a single Romeo. Rita's behavior stemmed from a promiscuous appetite and half desire to thumb a vindictive nose at her petulant husband. In her mind, she dwelled on the enjoyable thought of an overbearing mate cuckolded in spades! She didn't loathe the old boy, simply found him a thorny pain in the arse. *Well, Evan, my randy sailor boy, looks like it's your lucky night. Let's call it a generous citizen's gratitude for our men in uniform.*

By now everyone at Benton Hall had learned of Evan Whitfield's titanic urination. One wag titled it "Victoria Falls." Amazingly, the men pressed him for exacting details, ladies satisfied to listen, inching ever so close. Each retelling fostered a more ardent explanation of the Zamboangan pledge. "Standing up there in the high wind, clad in pink jacket, I felt somewhat like the Colossus of Rhodes in blush. Once I started, the gravity flow was extraordinary. You can't imagine the pressure. Felt like all the blooming fluid in my body was plummeting hundreds of feet down to the river. Thought my bloody head would cave in, I did," he bellowed.

The crowd roared, shaking their heads, astonished and amused. "I wouldn't recommend it to the timid or weak of bladder." Rolling his eyes upward, he played the crowd like a nightclub comic. "Being a hydrographer, I can alleviate your concern. The estuary will not suffer tidal disruption," he deadpanned, communicating an end to the humorous monologue. Applause and a few congratulatory backslaps rewarded his narration, an amused sister among the listeners. Victoria Falls would become a small legend over the next few weeks, remembered both as a zany episode and a honorable debt paid in full to one's psyche.

"What was that all about?" Marla rolled awake having half-listened to Bauer's call.

"Just Roy, curious how Colonel Maxwell made out."

"I'd say he and Gwen made a fine right couple. Hopefully, they'll get on as well after the champagne wears off."

"That's pretty much what I told Roy. He also mentioned that I've been designated a Captain-select."

"What's that mean?"

"That I've been approved for a captaincy, but it actually won't happen until the Marine Corps is good and ready. According to the paperwork that passed through the Mission, it's scheduled to happen in February, but I'm not quite that optimistic. April is probably a better guess."

Marla snuggled close to his chest. "I'd say we should celebrate but I think we did enough of that last night." She giggled and kissed his chin before sliding out of bed and into a silky, saffron robe. Loosely knotting the belt, she disappeared through the doorway. Moments later, one could hear the dull clang of coffee pot and fry pan in preparation of New Years breakfast.

Following a brisk shower, Andrew donned a T-shirt and tan walking shorts. He slipped up behind her, placing his arms about her narrow waist. Marla arched her slender neck, encouraging a playful nuzzle. "How would you like your eggs, love?" she asked, enjoying the tiny kisses dancing around her ears and throat.

"Lookin' at you," he responded.

"What's that supposed to mean?"

"Lookin' at you just like a pair of bulbous yellow eyes. Like Barney Google. You know, sunny side up."

"Oh, of course, with the goo-goo-googly eyes." She leaned back to kiss his mouth. Marla loved his "Americanisms," as she termed them. "I suppose after we're married I'll have to get a Yank dictionary, so I can decipher your very foreign language."

"After we're married? You mean you actually want me to make you an honest woman?" he teased.

Bacon hissed and sizzled, like a theater audience anticipating a juicy point of contention. "Well, I would like to set a date. You know that. And nineteen forty-three seems like an appropriate year to me." She pouted her upper lip.

"Honey, there's nothing definite about the timetable of this war. It could last three more years, or seven! There are no guarantees. We've discussed it before. I'm not about to marry you only to leave behind the most beautiful widow in Queensland."

She enjoyed the compliment even though it emphasized Andy's point. "But that's precisely why we should wed soon. I don't want to wait up to seven years to call myself Mrs. Andrew Delane, or for however long it takes the bloody Japanese and Nazis to surrender. It seems we're allowing Mr. sodding Hirohito to dictate our life!" As usual, she made a persuasive plea. "Besides, you're an intelligence officer in Brisbane! That's hardly the jungle of New Guinea." She forked a noisy bacon strip, flipping it over.

"Temporarily in Brisbane, temporarily," he emphasized. "I'm not even a real intelligence officer. Who knows, once my promotion comes though I might be assigned to an infantry outfit."

"You'd like that, wouldn't you?" Marla slammed the long fork on the countertop, its whack startling Andy.

"You've already lost half a finger!" She was on the threshold of tears, her eyes wet and fiery. "Next time it could be half a leg… or worse!" The tears came in rivulets and she turned, burying her beautiful face in his strong shoulder.

"The truth is," he softly murmured. "I don't like flying a desk. The troops in the field, the ones really fighting this war, scorn rear echelon warriors. I know, I used to be one of them. There is a special contempt for officers who swill champagne and eat fancy sandwiches while they're living in holes subsisting on rancid crap. Yes Marla, I do want to be with them, although it will probably scare the hell out of me. But know this. I also love you more than anything in this mad universe, and I want to be with you through eternity. For me it's a matter of conscience as much as duty. I am what I am. Can you understand that?" She sobbed, pressing her tears tightly against Andy's wet shirt. They rocked slowly in a tender embrace, his hand gently stroking her supple shoulders. The bacon burned to a blackened crisp.

CHAPTER XIV
REFLECTION HILL

DATE: SATURDAY 30 JANUARY 1943

TIME: 0700 HOURS

LOCATION: GUADALCANAL

The Japanese have an expression. When a man is expected to die, they say his shadow grows pale. For the mortally wounded and those slated for execution, the pale shadow is a self-evident prediction. However, there are others who exude a fatalistic aura, wearing the phantom presence of death like an invisible fog. It clings to skin and cloth, traveling with the damned. The preoccupied and frivolous hardly ever sense it. But true observers, prophets of doom, those mystically anointed with the gift, or curse, can intuit death's specter in select occupations and venues.

Captain Hiro Shigura of the 38th Infantry Division saw it all about him, even in his kit mirror. Soldiers of his company, fever-ridden and wracked by painful diarrhea, had been existing on roots and grass for almost a week. Rainwater bloated empty stomachs, riflemen hoping it would pacify hunger. Jungle rot melted skin into ugly cankers. Disease and festered wounds silently debilitated every enlisted man and officer. Weakened troops were becoming a discipline problem. They balked at burying their own dead, content to let the maggots and flies gorge on the fresh decay. Lassitude had sapped the last vestiges of vigor.

Infantrymen who once meticulously cleaned and polished every screw head on rifles and automatic weapons now sat back in abject exhaustion, indifferent to pitted rust. Puttees unwound from emaciated shins were donated to medics for use as bandages, or carelessly cast along the trail. Helmets had been discarded, excess weight; besides they behaved like ovens baking brains in the merciless Guadalcanal sun. The painfully wounded often ended it with a rifle bullet in the mouth, triggered by the final flex of an obedient toe.

Perhaps this is why we have been given the 'honor' of delaying the Americans while our army hacks its way northwest towards Cape Esperance and evacuation. The weak have become the expendable, condemned to a one-way mission. My depleted company can barely keep up with the others. Logic dictates we be sacrificed. General Hyukatake himself has given the order. So be it!

Hiro Shigura would prepare a fiery speech for the men, invoking sacred duty to the living God, Emperor Hirohito, watchful lord of Nippon. "We have been granted an opportunity to punish the Yankee bullies who would rape our gentle women, defile our temples. The anguished deaths of fallen comrades will be soothed by our vengeance. They too will be observing the performance of us, their brothers. After weeks of being hunted and slaughtered like running dogs, we will trap the cruel oppressors and strike with the stabbing wrath of the Japanese nation.

"Escaping soldiers, survivors of the Guadalcanal hell, will sing praises of our brave and unselfish deed. *The Shigura Force died so that we might live.* School children from Kyushu to Hokkaido, stretching to the Ryukus and Kuriles, will light candles and recite poems to our heroism. Yes, *Shigura* would rally depressed souls, energize ragged bodies to a valiant effort, one that would usher them into the spirit world of ancestral warriors. Every Japanese soldier would be challenged to slay at least three Americans. No, four.

"Whatever meager rations still existing will all be consumed and relished… in a ritual meal, a Spartan feast. Preparation will be unerring, rifles spotless, bayonets honed. Destiny has placed us all on this tortured island, at this time, in this precise spot for but one preordained purpose. Our shadows are undeniably pale. Yes we will die, but not like fleeing dogs—like Samurai!"

DATE: TUESDAY, 2 FEBRUARY 1943

TIME: 0950 HOURS

LOCATION: GUADALCANAL
           WEST OF TASSAFARONGA

Virtually all of the 164th Infantry Regiment had pulled back after engaging the enemy with little pause for the past month. The Americal Division's other two regiments, the 132nd and 147th, would pinch the Japs in a crushing pincer movement somewhere near Cape Esperance. Corps planned to link up the Americal with the advancing 25th Infantry Division around 9 February and, along with 2nd MarDiv, pummel the reeling enemy into Savo Sound. Thus would end the Guadalcanal saga.

Unfortunately, no one at XIV Corps or Halsey's command realized the Japanese were loading troops onto fleet destroyers, skillfully evacuating them in a brilliant maneuver reminiscent of a small scale Dunkirk. Imperial Staff had reluctantly approved the withdrawal, abandoning the jinxed island after six months of brutal combat. Between nine and eleven thousand men would be extracted from under the Americans' napping thumb. Yet the Bushido Code viewed it as nothing more than cowardly retreat. In Tokyo, generals and admirals avoided each other's disgraced eyes. Loss of face demanded the satisfaction of hara-kiri, honorable suicide, rather than suffer the pain of humiliation. A few did just that. Others rationalized the army was merely recoiling like a deadly viper preparing to unleash a renewed strike. Plentiful reservoirs of venom awaited the cocky Americans. The Guadalcanal force had been a pittance of the imperial arsenal.

The American press referred to December and January as a "mopping up" operation. For the soldiers and Marines of the three pressing divisions, the prickly understatement rankled their collective gut like a dentist's drill. That which news writers, secure in Espiritu Santo and New Caledonia, chronically dismissed as a "mop-up" involved hideous hand-to-hand homicide in oppressive heat and slime. Indeed, the three divisions would endure over 800 KIAs and in excess of 2,200 wounded. Disease would seriously affect the health of thousands more. Rear echelon service troops picked up on the news articles and, as a result, unwittingly perpetuated the metaphorical "mop." Soon it became ingrained, part of Guadalcanal's historical lexicon.

Though the regiment had been ordered off the front, Woody Luzak's company remained, temporarily plugging a gap. Once the line could be shortened up, they would fall back for rest and refit. The Canal had beat him up. Twelve pounds lighter with a yellowed pallor from months of Atabrine, he looked much like he remembered his brother. Atabrine, a synthetic quinine substitute, staved off malaria, but it left one's complexion a sickly amber. Sitting on an ammo box, he scrubbed his teeth and gums with a calloused fingertip while holding a letter from Nancy in his free hand.

Dated October 4, it bore wonderful news. A father…he was to be a father, probably sometime in mid-spring.

Things were moving fast for "the best damned platoon leader in the third battalion." That's how Colonel Hall had complimented him last week when pinning on his 1st lieutenant's bars. The promotion had been both premature and unexpected, not that he didn't deserve it. With the promo came an elevation to executive officer of Item Company, number two officer overseeing 170 men and fellow officers. His duties were more administrative than actual command, but it represented a necessary progression on the career path to Company Commander. The colonel intimated that he was being groomed for that very post.

"Woody, you'd better get up ahead with second platoon. They're reporting that brush has been cleared to their front. Fresh cut. We might be walking into a kill zone."

Maybe the sneaky bastards have chopped out a field of fire for their machine guns, Woody thought as he pictured the scene in his mind.

"I told 'em to stay put until you get there." Luzak's musings had been cut short by Item's CO. The lanky captain hawked up a wad of sour phlegm and spit. "Take a radio man. We'll use the identical call signs as always."

"Yes, sir." Woody hopped off the olive-drab box and snatched up his Garand, cleaned and oiled a half hour earlier. Yesterday he almost lost it fording the Bonegi River.

Pfc. Carl Gruber, a radio strapped to his shoulders, stepped forward from behind the captain, and Woody addressed him. "Are you familiar with the signs?"

"Yes, sir, lieutenant, same as the last two weeks."

"Let's hear them, just to be sure." Exec. Officer Luzak would leave nothing to chance.

Gruber smiled. "Cough Drop in honor of the Old Man." The captain had developed a persistent hacking cough in December and been unable to shake it. His conversations rasped and choked, sometimes barely comprehensible. In dubious recognition of the condition, one of the platoon leaders suggested "Cough Drop" as the company's call sign. The wheezing captain, in good humor, approved it. Why not? "The CO is *Cough Drop Boss*," the private continued.

"You're *Cough Drop X*. First, second, and third platoons are *Cough Drop One, Two* and *Three*. Weapons platoon, *Cough Drop Boom*!" Carl Gruber, a grain elevator operator from St. Paul, Minnesota didn't stand too tall, but his powerful build made up for any altitude limitation. The radio looked puny strapped to his wide shoulders. Under the amusing moniker of "The Bavarian Hog Wrestler," the muscular Gruber had taken on all comers in a Noumean beer joint. Company members had quadrupled their money parlay betting on Gruber's prowess arm wrestling, or plain old "wrasslin," pinning two beefy Air Corps mechanics in the sawdust one raucous night.

Unfortunately, the audience's post-match exuberance caused several fixtures to be torn from walls and ceilings before the MP's hustled them outside and confiscated IDs. Carl was busted down from corporal to Pfc., having taken an unfair share of the rap for the drunk and unruly. The stripe would return in March, assuming he kept his nose clean. Since that evening, though, every swingin' dick in the battalion had grown to know him as "Hog Man," "Hoggy," or just "Hog." Most of the men found him fun to be around. He wore his reputation cheerfully, enjoying the notoriety.

Woody and Hog moved out at a fast clip, having already alerted Cough Drop Two that they were on the way. They dog-trotted past Weapons Platoon's 60mm mortar section dug in behind a small slope. Company First Sergeant Perry and the platoon sergeant were laying prone atop the high point, trying to get a fix on the shallow hill roughly less than a half mile ahead. From their perspective, even with binoculars, all they could make out was a sweeping green mound, lush with giant ferns and a broad-leaf umbrella. Misty shrouds hung in patches like gauze, the rising sun boiling earlier precipitation to smothering vapor. "See anything?" the lieutenant asked.

"Not a damn thing, sir. I reckon we're about eight hundred yards from the crown of that bump out there," the first sergeant said, pointing. "Lieutenant Mobley went up front five minutes ago. He's gonna be our forward observer. Took a radio operator with him. We've got the other here."

"How many shots will you boys need to register some Willie Peter on top of that pimple?"

The grimy platoon sergeant removed his helmet and massaged a scalp dank with perspiration. "The base plates are set in pretty well. I doubt they'll shift. Ground's rock hard for a change. I figure two shots… one to get a fix and another to adjust on target. Maybe three. Of course it depends how accurate the FO's guesstimate is." The man knew his stuff.

131

Woody had seen his mortar section perform with uncanny accuracy. Luzak reckoned two might do it, but three was more probable. A little white phosphorous might cause a few Japs to scatter if they were hiding up there. *Good way to get them to tip their hand.* "Okay, stick close to that radio," he reminded, before he and Hog proceeded toward the position in question, the unyielding sun on their damp backs. They jumped a tiny stream and moved hunchbacked through trampled vegetation for five minutes until reaching second platoon's rear security. Obvious visual identification rendered the password/countersign somewhat redundant. Even so, the lead sentinel challenged them as a matter of discipline and because Lieutenant Luzak might chew him out for being lax.

"Jelly Belly!" the sentry called out, and the officer responded, "Hillbilly." Double *L* had become an extra safeguard against infiltrating enemy inasmuch as no *L* sound exists in the Japanese language. Tongue-tied, any *L* was corrupted into an *R*, ergo, Jerry Berry and Hirbirry.

Shigura was pleased. The men had reacted well to his exhortation. Some openly wept and embraced each other, knowing the last few hours of their lives would have purpose. Joyful resignation overcame despondency. Frazzled bodies were propelled to renewed vitality by the boundless human spirit. Dutiful death became necessary springboard to an eternity of honor.

Three lateral bunkers were gouged and scratched from the soft earth one hundred fifty yards below the hill crest. Palm logs had been cut from the reverse slope and fitted on sunken posts to form sturdy roofs. Reinforced with haversacks and canvas packed full with muddied dirt, the pill boxes should resist small-arms fire and light mortars. The center-most and largest bunker housed two Nambus, each of which would interlock its fire with the single-crew-served machine guns in the two smaller positions. Fifty to seventy-five yards separated each, so their fire would be mutually supporting. He had angled the left bunker slightly to help protect against being rolled up.

Captain Shigura had but eighty-six able men and one officer. Second Lieutenant Kimura would control the center bunker and (via a shallow belly trench) utilize messengers to communicate with Sergeants Hataki and Murayama commanding the two flanking fortifications. Camouflage concealed the guns but the Americans were no fools—it was doubtful they would walk in blind once they discovered the macheted field of fire. At staggered points between the bunkers, the company commander had posted riflemen spaced in zigzagged fox holes. And farther down the hill they had dug a half dozen spider holes in which the most sickly soldiers poised stoically with hand grenades, the first line of sacrifice. Back at the summit, Shigura could observe all from a long transverse trench containing about twenty riflemen, including two medics brandishing Arisakas. Defense in depth, though abbreviated, would make the Yankee barbarians pay dearly for every millimeter of soil. A single small mortar sat ready on the rear slope with a meager supply of nine rounds. Aiming stakes had been hammered into preparedness to guide the deadly missiles. Shigura would save the mortar until an opportune moment when the Americans least expected it.

Protecting his right flank, a prohibitive swamp, virtually impassable, would help channel the enemy into his guns. But to be sure, he sent two snipers wading into the tangled marsh to cover the possibility of infiltrators. The last morsels of food had been consumed, medicine depleted. Nothing remained but men, bullets, and the impregnable resolve of Captain Hiro Shigura.

Kneeling, he faced northwest toward his beautiful homeland, and silently chanted a Shinto supplication. The pensive captain thought of his family near Osaka and contemplated his life, trying to focus on memories of boyhood. Life was uncomplicated then. Mother clipped his silky black hair in bangs, tending to dress him in fresh, spotless shorts and shirt, often with a maritime pattern. Maybe she knew something about a sailor's more civilized lot—starched clean whites, fastidious existence without privation. Army life in contrast offered this morning's filthy, mildewed uniform, soiled by dysentery, hanging on an underweight, sore-laden body. War had already claimed an older brother last winter in frozen Manchukuo. How would his parents handle his own death? Who would care for their saddened old age?

Months earlier, Hiro had mailed them a lock of hair and nail clippings, hardly a legacy. Young relics of an imperial warrior. A tear rolled down a tanned cheek. He caught it on his fingertip and examined its pristine nature for a moment before touching it to his sword pommel. Slowly rotating his hand, he worked the salty liquid until its wetness disappeared. *The essence of man is salt and water. He sprang from the sea, laboring millions of years to do so. And yet, even today, and another million years hence, the products of his labor, sweat and tears, are the identical solution that created him.* Shigura nodded a meditative understanding. Now that his fate was determined, he allowed himself to ponder the root of life. Perhaps this recognition, this snatch of philosophy, was really a form of prayer. Nonetheless, he was at peace with his soul.

Shifting his musings to more martial concerns, Shigura unsheathed the gleaming sword of the samurai and held it high in quiet tribute to his emperor. *Morituri Te Salutumus!* He had never had circumstance to wield its terrible destruction, to slice an enemy to ribboned defeat. Maybe this would be the day, his last day.

"Up there at the top, a flash! Did you spot it?"

Luzak had seen it, so had the FO and platoon leaders squatting beside him. Third platoon had come on line with the second to form the attack force should an assault be necessary. Already digging in, first platoon, at their rear, would be held in reserve. Weapons platoon sent up four .30 caliber light machine guns to establish covering fire.

"Cough Drop Boss, this is Cough Drop X. Do you read? Over."

"Cough Drop X, this is Cough Drop Boss. I read. What the hell's going on? Over."

"Boss, we've spotted a reflection atop the hill. Trees and growth have been cleared away. Has all the signs of a showdown. Suggest we drop a few rounds of Willie Pete on the summit and face. Maybe they'll panic and reveal themselves. Over."

"Good idea. No sense in running up that hill until we know what we're up against. Let's hold off though until I get up there. Understood?" The captain had his assessment. Now he would take personal command of the operation.

"Roger Wilco and out."

By the time it took the C.O. to come on line, a four-man patrol returned after having probed Reflection Hill's open flank. They reported a broad sight line had been cut from midpoint on the hill down to its base.

"Well, that probably tells us where they've got their gun set up," Woody observed. "Just follow that corridor."

"Let's get it started," the captain called to the F.O. At 1030 hours a hollow *whunk* echoed. Seconds later, a muffled explosion and telltale smoke rose somewhere beyond the crest.

"We're long," Lieutenant Ted Mobley, the forward observer, shouted into the radio. "Drop one hundred."

A second *whunk* sounded and swished overhead. This time, squiggly arms of hot phosphorous erupted high on the incline, suspended like an abstract white lily. He yelled into the open line. "You're registered! Lay in six more rounds of high explosive."

Rapid explosions perforated the ridge in rapid succession. Huge clumps of shattered green vegetation shot skyward, immediately pattering back to earth in a slow shower.

Shoulders and head of a small khaki figure materialized from a hidden pocket and, screaming unintelligibly, hurled a long-handled object. The throw was weak, traveling no more than forty feet. It seemed every gun in third platoon erupted at once. Like a scarecrow caught in a hurricane, the soldier flew apart even before his grenade exploded harmlessly. The action caused the swamp-side bunker to open up and within seconds the hill was ablaze with Nambus and Arisakas spitting lead.

Prostrate GIs hugged the soupy soil behind the protection of a shielding earthen fold. Flattened out in the saddled depression, Woody shouted to the CO, "Man alive, must be more than a platoon up there!" Coughing twice, the captain nodded. He wisely decided to pull the two forward platoons back to the reserve line under suppressing mortar fire. A few scouts and the FO would remain.

Having moved rearward, they checked casualties. Two wounded, two dead, including Lieutenant Joe Hermann, second platoon leader. "Shit, Woody, you'll have to take over his platoon. Let's make sure our flanks are secure and then we'll have an officers' powwow to sort this fuckin' mess out." The Old Man was younger than Luzak but somehow he seemed older.

Up at the crest, the irate Shigura cursed the premature fire of his troops. He had emphasized fire discipline during his briefing, all for naught. The Americans must have his bunkers identified by now. Any semblance of surprise had disintegrated. His troops, sick and exhausted, had worked non-stop preparing their hasty bulwark. Over-fatigue dulled their patience, sapped self-control. The rattled soldier who let fly the first grenade had been delirious the previous night, his fever dangerously high. Oguchi the medic had feared convulsions. Hunkered in that spider hole, his nerves must have shattered. Nevertheless, the Americans had halted…*buying precious hours for our brothers struggling toward Cape Esperance*, Shigura reassured himself.

The CO recognized frontal assault would chop his force to pieces, playing into the Jap commander's trap. No, there would be no battle of attrition. Not if he could help it. *Maybe I can keep them busy trading shots while we work a force around them…*"Luzak, let's huddle. I've got a plan!"

They had been trudging in a wide arc for two hours. Periodically, a scout would nervously shinny a tree to ascertain their bearings, to get a fix on Reflection Hill. Second platoon had dropped packs and K-rations back at the jump-off point. Weapons, water, and ammo constituted their "travel light, travel silent" directive. Dull echoes from Browning .30 caliber machine guns and an occasional mortar *whump* maintained the comfort of an audio lifeline. The rest of the company were harrying the Nips while Luzak's encircling force slipped behind. Fatigue uniforms, wet and clammy, clung to bodies like an extra layer of skin. The temperature was especially muggy.

Another thirty minutes passed before Tech Sergeant Manny Alcazar returned from the point. Holding up a clenched fist, he signaled the column. Like a string of dominoes the strand of thirty-six men froze in place, spaced out at five-yard intervals. To Lieutenant Luzak, Alcazar reported his two scouts were near the base of The Hill's reverse slope. "We smelled shitty cigarette smoke. Good thing. Two Japs in a mortar pit smokin' and jabberin' like they was sittin' in the bleachers watchin' a fuckin' ball game." He grinned a bit wild-eyed and pointed to a sheathed trench knife. "Gottem both, we did!" Enemy blood, dark and red, soaked his right sleeve.

"They only had nine rounds. I left Cookie and Maskell up there in case the cocksuckers sent a runner down from the top."

"Good work," Luzak said. "How far from the mortar pit to the top?"

"Tough to tell for sure. But it must be about a hundred and fifty yards or so."

Woody thought for a moment and quickly calculated his next steps. "Sergeant, get the squad leaders up here pronto. Gruber, see if you can raise Cough Drop Boss."

Adrenaline pumped through their veins at a previously unexperienced level. Spread out over a skirmish line covering nearly the length of a football field, second platoon knelt in restrained eagerness. It had become personal, seeking to avenge Lieutenant Hermann. A twelve-minute mortar barrage would commence at 1348 hours. At 1350, the platoon would scale the incline and pause roughly seventy yards from the reverse summit until weapons platoon's mortar gunners had completed their lethal business. When the final high explosive round dropped at 1400, Luzak's charges would assail the crest, lobbing grenades over the top. Hopefully, no friendly "long rounds" would overshoot the hill into their midst.

Woody checked his Bulova just as the first 60mm missile slammed into the Jap position, then another and another. Blunt explosions sounded in waves. Machine guns joined in. *Good, the Japs will be expecting a frontal assault after softening 'em up.* From his position Luzak could see smoke and dusty debris above the hill's mounded horizon. Mortar fire continued to roll in. The skirmishers rose to their feet and began a methodical advance.

Bursting through the verdant jungle growth, a young Japanese runner, ostensibly delivering a message to his own mortar pit, ran directly into an unflinching BAR man. Surprise lasted but a few seconds as the young GI ripped a short burst into the man's torso. So commonplace had death become that the veteran platoon paid no mind to the crumpled corpse. They pushed through the wet tropical brush, breaking the straight line only to skirt trees and impenetrable stands of bamboo-like plants. 1357. Second platoon halted, waiting the next stage. Removing his magazine, the BAR soldier who had dispatched the Jap messenger replaced the spent bullets to a full twenty. He clicked it in place under the housing and calmly awaited the signal to move out.

Luzak, now at the skirmish line's center, raised his hand and turned left and right for the men to see. His purpose was twofold. Naturally he wanted to alert his soldiers so they'd all advance together on cue. But he also wanted them to know he was *leading,* not pushing them. All three squad leaders emulated the lieutenant, arms uplifted. Emphatically jabbing a pointed finger up the hill, Woody took the first step, squad leaders doing likewise.

The platoon moved out. Hog Man, a pace behind the officer, maintained an open line to Cough Drop Boss in case the mortars failed to let up. The precaution turned out to be unnecessary. Coordination was perfect, the last blast shook the air with about thirty yards yet to cover. Luzak pumped his arm like an engineer yanking a whistle cord, the signal to pick up the pace. Thumb over clamp, he pulled the pin ring, holding the grenade high for his pressing troops to view. Riflemen did the same, waiting the lieutenant's heave so they could unleash their own pineapples.

The ground was not uniform fifteen yards below the top. For some it was steep, others relatively level. Luzak let it fly, the clamp snapping free from its lethal package as the grenade left his hand. It arched high and long above the silhouetted brow. In seconds the sky was cluttered with dark bomblets streaking like a flock of angry bats. They swooped over the hillcrest, booming sporadically, a staggered string of hellish shrapnel seeking soft flesh. A great roar went up from the charging Americans as they surged over the summit, firing Garands and automatic rifles from hip and shoulder. They poured a killing sheet of lead into the high trench destroying dazed and wounded survivors of the grenade attack. Two dozen ripped bodies littered the slit, among them Captain Hiro Shigura, clutching a tasseled sword. Unyielding fragments had torn the blade and its samurai master into a twisted jumble of man and steel. Firing into the trench, Luzak leaped across and continued downhill to the open rear of the bunker.

Craters, smoking footprints of the mortar barrage, dotted the bruised landscape. Very little vegetation remained. Most had been liquefied to a viscous slime, like pea soup, making footing treacherous. More importantly, second platoon was over the hump. The butchery became point blank. Stunned Japanese, confused and punchy, had been expecting an attack to their front. Now they were being shot in the back without seeing their executioners. Whooping dog faces swarmed over the two flanking bunkers blazing away at the helpless defenders. Nipponese lurking in blind spider holes popped up to fire and hurl their terrible potato mashers. They in turn were subdued by a hail of semi-automatic rifle shots blasting their slumping bodies into ready-dug graves.

The center bunker, most substantial and fortified of the three, had been the least vulnerable to the attack. Japanese soldiers tossing grenades uphill and sniping with Arisakas held the Americans at bay, while a Nambu crew reset its fearsome weapon. Its noisy rat-a-tat zipped out a protracted burst, dropping four riflemen. Shot through the abdomen, a sprawling GI attempted to jam a fresh clip into his Garand. The machine gun blew him away, one shot puncturing helmet and head. Under withering fire of the big gun, approximately twenty Americans scrambled back to the crest trench. They threw out enemy corpses, using them as a protective shield, Shigura's lifeless remains among the cadavered wall. Perhaps ten Japanese defended the large principal bunker. Several more fired from nearby holes clustered around the besieged pit.

Having suffered a gunshot wound to the thigh, Woody Luzak flattened out in a belly trench extending in a twisted path from the defiant bunker. No more than twelve inches of cover protected the lieutenant and Hog, prostrate behind him. The radioman tried to press a field dressing inside Luzak's torn pant leg without exposing himself. They lay about seventy feet from the bunker, listening to the enemy scream high-pitched taunts and curses at the Americans upslope. By this time, the second Nambu had traversed 180 degrees and it too barked sharply. No one had to remind the forsaken defenders of their pale shadows. Clairvoyants needn't apply. Surely they would perish in each other's company, true to their vow. But first they looked to slay as many Yankee dogs as destiny's clock would permit.

On Item's line, first and third platoons couldn't fire for fear they would hit their own, the killing field was that intermingled. If they advanced, the company risked being peppered by second platoon shooting downhill from the high trench. Squirming toward the bunkered Nambus, Woody reached into a canvas utility bag slung diagonally from shoulder to hip. Four fragmentation grenades remained. Damn, his thigh hurt! The bullet must have hit the bone or lodged against a raw nerve. His foot wouldn't respond as he attempted to push off. Hog realized the problem and thrust both Woody's boot heels, propelling him along the shallow ditch.

Atop the crest, those who could maneuver a peek had enough of an angle to witness what the Japanese could not. Like oversized worms, the two men inched closer until they approached a slight elbow. Woody determined the bunker opening must be just beyond it, perhaps twenty feet, no more. He slid a pineapple to Gruber, motioning him not to toss until Luzak threw his. Setting a single grenade in front of him, he gripped the other two. Looping free fingers in each ring, Woody pulled with a steady force until each drew clear. Breath came in short, quick bunches as he released the clamps, allowing the fuses to start their rapid burn. *One one-hundred, two one -hundred.* Springing off his functioning leg, he catapulted beyond the bend and pitched a right-handed grenade into the small side entrance and over an improvised poncho sand bag. On target. The other one flew in an awkward lefty push, more like a shot put. It landed against the sand bag, failing to gain complete entry.

Quickly he crabbed backwards as the imperiled bunker crew's panicked shouts cut the air. Simultaneous explosions rocked the big emplacement forcing a concussive wave to ripple through the belly trench. "Now!" Luzak and Gruber charged the mangled access, tossing their last frags inside and diving for cover.

The smoking entry hole was broader than before, the bagged sill having been blown inside. Four ticks passed before twin detonations staggered the collapsing structure. Again a rush of shocked wind jolted them. Snatching his Ml, Woody hobbled into the choking cloud of translucent dust when a terrifying blast erupted from within the pit's ruptured bowels. It lifted him off his feet skyward, blowing his body backwards as though a giant fist has slammed him from spleen to throat.

Woody had absorbed the compacted force of a Jap grenade cache ignited by his own explosives. The battered officer flew in reverse, bowling over his radioman. Blood leaked from ears and nose. A thick palm log had caught him square in the upper body, his helmet rocketed twenty feet high, tumbling in a lopsided roll down the rise. Shards of burnt debris and splintered wood penetrated limbs and cheeks. Trenched American riflemen rushed down and poured unrelenting fire into the smoldering pile of dilapidated timbers and ripped carcasses. Fanning out they finished off every spider hole and fighting position. The concentrated carnage on so small a hill was horrific.

"Medic! Medic! Medic! Medic!" Gruber screamed wild-eyed as he helplessly cushioned the broken body.

"Medic's dead," someone called out. "Caught one in the chest from that fuckin' Nambu." The angry soldier fired his remaining clip into the devastated bunker. He knew it was futile but didn't care. Not one bit.

To those about him, Woody appeared lifeless, limbs immobile, eyes fixed in an unblinking squint. But in a distant, hollow kind of way he heard those inquiring voices. "Is he dead?" a haggard GI asked.

"Don't know. Maybe," another answered. "He was one tough sonuvabitch. Took out the whole fuckin' bunker. Him and Hog."

Woody's dulled brain tried to function. *Maybe I died,* he thought. *Maybe this is what it's like to be dead. Just a painless kind of non-feeling, a numbed head stuffed full of swirling, wadded cotton.*

"He's alive, goddammit. He's going to live. Get out of my way!" Gruber lifted Woody in his blacksmith's arms and began running downhill toward the other two platoons coming up. To his rear, bunkered ammo continued to cook off in occasional pops. "Where's the aid station?" he shouted.

"Back at the jump-off, Hoggy." The squad leader jerked a thumb, indicating the general direction. Gruber frantically picked up his trot. Looking up, he spotted a medic waving him on. Double-timing through the ranks of advancing riflemen, the Bavarian Hog Wrestler stampeded downslope like a wild boar. Reaching the aid point, he lowered the limp body. "Fix him," he sobbed. "Fix him."

So much for "mopping up" on Reflection Hill.

In Havre de Grace, Nancy Swift Luzak felt a sudden chill. She slipped into a bulky yellow cardigan and stood at the bay window. Cradling her swollen belly, she stared over the ripping Chesapeake current into the bleak winter sky.

Author's Note: In the years after World War II, the Americal Division *was given the numerical designation US 23rd Infantry Division. The name* Americal *came from a combination of America and New Caledonia, the latter being where the division was formed.*

Author's Note: The butcher's bill for Guadalcanal reached 1,592 KIA and 4,283 WIA for U.S. ground forces. The Japanese suffered 28,146 army dead, and lost approximately 1,000 prisoners. Somewhere between 9,000 and 11,000 troops were successfully evacuated. Japanese and U.S. naval losses were probably in excess of 1,600 men for each side.

CHAPTER XV
THE BASH

DATE: THURSDAY 30 JUNE 1943

TIME: 1120 HOURS

LOCATION: WEST OF KAIOURAN, TUNISIA

The Five-O-Five's regimental staging area covered roughly thirty acres of parched, sandy soil. Not much vegetation grew here, and that which did was puny, an arid, scrubby brush trampled or smothered with canvas. Pup tents and roomier general purpose(GP) tents were laid out in neat, geometric company streets by battalion. Two thousand years earlier, Roman legionaries probably used similar *castra* patterns during their occupation of Carthaginian North Africa. Now it was camp to the 82nd Airborne Division's 504th and 505th Parachute Infantry Regiments, and the 325th Glider Infantry Regiment, as well as four airborne field artillery battalions, engineers, and various combat support elements. Commanded by Major General Matthew B. Ridgway, the division had been leapfrogging east since its arrival in Casablanca, French Morocco, on May 10 after departing Fort Bragg. Eight days by rail in stifling boxcars had seen them relocated to Oujda and Marnia (also in Morocco) where an insect-infected "pup-tent-ville" became their temporary base.

Practice jumps and rugged training took up almost a month before the hardened troopers, on June 16, yanked out pegs, rolled shelter halves, filled in latrines, and mounted transport. Destination Kaiouran, a moslem holy city situated in Tunisia, one thousand miles east. The trek passed the division through Algeria, utilizing vehicles both military and civilian. Some, the lucky, flew, escaping the murderous heat. Most though, traveled via cattle cars or jarring deuce-and-a-halfs. Hordes of black-faced flies compounded the discomfort. Disappointed, the All-Americans were too late to fight, the

German Afrika Korps and Italian desert forces having already capitulated. British Tommies and their commonwealth allies had borne the great brunt of battle, with the US Army's best divisions having participated since November 8 and 9, commencing with Operation Torch. The US 1st, 3rd, 9th, and 34th Infantry Divisions, along with the US 1st and 2nd Armored Divisions, had seen much action, and after a rocky baptism had distinguished themselves well. Communiques and news articles now referenced them as *veteran outfits*. The 82nd trained and retrained, but so far hadn't gotten into the melee. Impatient and testy, the sky soldiers were eager for a real test.

For Colonel "Slim Jim" Gavin's 505th Parachute Infantry Regiment, the anxiousness had been primed by "the word," the absolute latest poop. Everyone, officers and EMs, believed their first combat jump would come in July. The sixty-four-dollar question though, was where? As was to be expected, a myriad of nickel answers ran rampant. Depending on to whom you spoke, the Eighty Deuce had been tapped to invade: Sardinia, Sicily, the Italian mainland, Corsica, Yugoslavia, Crete, or Greece. Additionally, a host of more exotic locales kept popping up. One wilder rumor, half serious, had them parachuting into Berlin. Betting pools flourished, ignited by the most recent poop. Location represented part of the lottery equation. Exact date and hour of departure further complicated the prediction. No one professed it to be a precise science! Each morning new rumors surfaced, ranging from rational to preposterous. Sardinia and Sicily, however, seemed to be the most prevalent. One had but to examine the relevant geography of the crowded Mediterranean to conclude those two massive islands as logical choices.

First Lieutenant Philip Primo didn't know where the Five-0-Five was going but he had already been assigned his mission. Wherever, whenever, he would lead a reinforced platoon in capturing a small bridge, designated only as *G-Bridge*. The battalion's new commander, Major Mark Alexander, had specifically selected Primo for the task, assigning him two bazooka teams and a pair of .30 caliber light machine guns to accomplish it. The extra bodies swelled his platoon to forty-nine troopers. Instructing him that the ideal bridge-seizing strategy was to snatch both ends at the same time, Alexander directed the lieutenant to leave at sun-up for Hamia, more of a map point than a small village eight miles southwest.

Hamia existed as a crumbling crossroads. Sand and grit blew almost constantly, blasting the pitted stucco of the junction's three tired buildings: a bus transfer station; a ramshackled cooperative storage building which housed produce during better days; and a two-story combination residence and cafe operated by a short-legged Frenchman, Henri Caron, and his half-Berber, half-French wife. Hamia's value to the troopers was a long stone bridge spanning its dried-up river bed. Here the platoon would rehearse the assault and capture of G-Bridge—until they got it right. During the lieutenant's briefing he had been informed that there was no certainty the bridge would be defended, and if so, to what extent. As a consequence, Primo would prepare for several contingencies. The axiom "practice makes perfect" would be as appropriate as any for the next three days' exercise.

"Andrews, John Joseph, Pfc.," the lanky redhead barked.

"I guess I'm your bazooka man, sarge. Battalion reassigned me to your outfit. What's going on?"

'You'll find out when we do," Sergeant First Class Lennart Aarborg sourpussed. "Turk" Aarborg had picked up his nickname in grammar school twenty years past as result of a driven propensity for a sweet, white confection, Bonamo's Turkish Taffy. For a Swedish-American to be monickered "Turk" took a heck of a stretch…no pun intended. Home in Sioux Falls, South Dakota, most folks didn't even know he possessed a first name. To them he was simply "Turk." Aarborg had long since given up the chewy candy but the handle stuck. "Where's your tube?"

"Outside in the jeep that brung me here," the young paratrooper answered.

"They send anyone with you to load that thing?"

"Nope, just me." Jack Andrews smiled.

"Shit, I guess we'll have to locate someone to team up with you. For now you'll report directly to me. Get your gear and stick it in my tent for the time being. That's it next to that Tunisian excuse for a tree." He nonchalantly backhanded a wave toward the platoon's bivouac. Roughly two dozen tents neatly sat on a flat piece of terrain protected from wind blast by a small hillock.

"Andrews, John J., Pfc. reporting as ordered, sir." The lieutenant returned Andrew's crisp salute.

"Have you reported to Sergeant Aarborg yet, Andrews?"

"No sir. Just got here. Hitched a ride in that chow truck." He pointed to a three-quarter ton four-by-four. Troopers had dropped the tailgate and were unloading canisters of hot food—probably franks, beans, and scalloped potatoes—sent to them by the battalion mess.

"What's your specialty, Andrews?" Primo chewed on a two-inch cigar stub, frayed from extended service.

"Rifleman, sir. I just joined the Five-O-Five two days ago, kind of a late replacement from the states. The sergeant major asked if I had any experience loading a 2.36 three-inch rocket launcher. I had done it a few times in training so he told me to get on down here." Andrews, broad-chested and thick-necked, removed his helmet, running fingers through short dark hair, cut white to the scalp on each side.

"Okay, welcome to the platoon. We're supposed to be receiving a couple of M-9 bazookas. Looks like you're going to be half of one of those teams."

"M-9, sir? I believe I loaded an Ml-Al. Is there a difference?"

"Same equipment, only the M-9's tube breaks down into two pieces. Easier to jump with." Primo removed his own steel pot swathed in camouflage netting and rubbed the dull itch. "Better report in to Sergeant Aarborg. He's the big horse over there testing the walky-talky."

A few minutes later, the Turk cursed in disbelief, sure someone was pulling his leg. He grabbed both men purporting to be Pfc. John Joseph Andrews and checked their IDs and dog tags. Sure enough, astounding as it might seem, defying the astronomical odds of probability, the Army had unwittingly accomplished the near impossible. They had assigned two men with the identical name in the same remote Tunisian boon-dock, even maneuvering them into the selfsame two-man bazooka team! "This is one for the fucking books! Let's all go talk to the lieutenant before they commit me for a Section Eight."

The four men chatted in a tight circle, Phil Primo nodding slowly, though his eyes kept darting from one Andrews to the other. He stroked his shadowed chin, asking, "Does either of you have a nickname?"

"Jack!" Both men answered in harmonic unison.

Phil Primo allowed a short grin to creep across his mouth. "How did I know that," he chuckled, "Well look, I don't have time to screw around so here's how it's going to shake out." He touched a finger to the redhead's field jacket. "Henceforth you will answer to and identify yourself as 'Redjack' and you," he said, pointing to the husky brunette, "are Blackjack. Is that understood?"

"Yes, sir," they answered in a staggered echo.

"Sergeant Aarborg, let's keep 'em in the same team. At least this way we'll always know where they are. On surface it would seem to alleviate confusion, but I guess there'll be times when it'll be compounded bullshit as well. Does that make sense?" He started to explain his complicated comment but thought better of it. "Screw it. Let's get some chow."

DATE: MONDAY 4 JULY 1943

TIME: 0800 HOURS

LOCATION: HAMIA, TUNISIA

For three days they had captured and recaptured Hamia's ancient stone bridge using different avenues of approach. They also rehearsed defending the span once it had been seized. Timing was all important in the event the actual G-Bridge's surrounding landscape didn't permit the platoon, split into groups on both river sides, visual contact with each other. To keep it simple, Primo developed two tactical plans which were designated the *Sight Plan* and *Blind Plan*. Off the two plans, similar sub-schemes were practiced to account for various possibilities like armor or pillboxes. This morning, Independence Day, they ran through the Blind Plan before sunrise. He would allow them a C-ration breakfast prior to acting out other tactical components and alternative scenarios.

"Hartz, get me Second Battalion HQ. I want to talk to the Major." Major Mark Alexander's star had risen meteorically. Three years earlier he had enlisted as a buck private, scaling the ranks in uncustomary speed. One week ago Gavin promoted him from XO to CO of 2/505. Primo had been instructed to check in at 0800.

"Sir, Major Alexander is on the line." Hartz handed him the talk-piece extending from the jeep-mounted radio. He took it.

"Alexander here."

"Sir, it's Lieutenant Primo calling per your instructions."

"Yes, Primo. How's your progress coming along?" The authoritative but friendly voice was faint.

"We had an outstanding run-through in the dark hours this morning, sir. Went real smooth, even better than the one you observed yesterday. I'm confident we're prepared for all contingencies. I've scheduled a new round of bridge defensive tactics for the remainder of the day."

"Fine!" Alexander was positive he had selected the right officer for the job. "If you're that certain, bring your boys back here later today after you've wrapped things up."

Dry-mouthed, Primo bit his tongue working up some saliva before making his pitch. "Well sir, as you know, the men have worked hard, really busted their tails. With your permission I'd like to keep them in Hamia tonight and throw them a little party. There's a cafe here and no place to get in trouble. Not even a camel to steal. They could use a break."

Alexander didn't have to think twice. He knew in less than a week the All-Americans would be leaping into Sicily with Primo's unit among the vanguard. "It's a deal, lieutenant. No firearms at the party. You've got an aggressive bunch there. Keep it under control. I want you standing tall at reveille here tomorrow, zero six hundred."

"Yes, sir, zero six hundred. Thank you." Phil gave a thumbs-up sign to Pfc. Hartz who slapped his hands and yipped. "And, sir?"

"What is it, Primo?"

"Any word on where we're going?"

"Not yet. Enjoy the party." Click. Click.

Uncle Ray had always taught his nephew to estimate the value of a job and negotiate a fixed price for the whole package. Never hire them by the hour or else they'll string it out and suck your blood. Ray's first rule…go for the contract! This piece of business philosophy did not fall on deaf ears. For the stipulated sum of three hundred twenty-five dollars and four cartons of American cigarettes, Henri Caron agreed to supply all the wine (raw Algerian *vin ordinaire*) the platoon could consume between 2000 and one hour past midnight. He would also feed them grilled goat basted in a spicy piquant sauce, rice, beans, bread, and a bottle of cognac each for Phil and the Turk.

Primo also convinced Henri to throw in a metric fifth of sweet vermouth to boot. Some might call it the privilege of rank. He preferred to think of it as a spiff for orchestrating the deal. To the critical observer, the issue was somewhat academic for he planned to share it with his wild herd. And for entertainment, the Carons would provide two scintillating belly dancers and American phonographic music. At under $6.70 a head, the lieutenant reasoned he had haggled a package worthy of Ray Romanek. Helmet liners were passed and filled with great willingness: six bucks from each GI, nine from the sergeants, and twenty-five from 1st Lieutenant Primo. So much for the privilege of rank. Packs of butts were collected with the eventual aggregate generously exceeding the promised four cartons. They decided to give them all to Henri and Louise Caron as a *bon chance* gratuity. The resultant smörgåsbord of brands included Lucky Strike, Chesterfield, Phillip Morris, Old Gold and Camel, among several others. American cigarettes fetched an exaggeratedly inflated price on the open black market in Tunis. Henri would barter the tobacco trove into a handsome profit.

One might have thought it was prom night revisited. Men washed and preened at the Hamia well. Singing and good-natured ribbing sounded along its two gritty cross streets. July 4 had been a long hard day but no one remembered the sweat. All that mattered was tonight's bash. They hadn't celebrated in a long, long period. For some it would be the last time they would get a little crazy…ever.

Impatient troopers, noisy and pushy, surged into Cafe Caron as the clock struck eight. The room was situated three stairs below ground level. Wonderful aroma of roasted meat curled its way to the landing, greeting the nostrils of tough, young paratroopers. Rosemary, mint and pepper dominated a variety of delicious smells. Yelps of satisfaction sang out as men elbowed their way into the cellar bistro. Six rectangular dining tables filled most of the room. Platters heaped with rice and goat sat at the center of each. Crusty loaves of circular bread piled high in wicker baskets. Bowls containing beans cooked in a savory sauce and ceramic pitchers of dark red wine surrounded the main course. In the kitchen, number-ten sized tins of peaches were being opened in preparation of dessert. Turk Aarborg had bargained a "special" transaction with the battalion mess sergeant earlier that day. Hours later, a dusty jeep materialized, dropping off a case of scarce cling peaches in syrup.

At the far end of the room stood a permanent bar from which huge wine jugs cradled in woven straw were being drained of their rich maroon liquid. Several skinny native boys, probably thirteen years of age, served as waiters. Turk had filled their pockets with Hershey bars and "cigarettes for papa" during the pre-meal preparation. Wide-eyed, the cheerful adolescents watched in awe as the warriors seated themselves to feast. The buzz of conversation and shuffling jump boots was rendered silent by a stentorian "Ten-hut!" Rising to attention, the platoon stood straight and rigid. Even the boy waiters snapped to.

Entering the room, glass in hand, a beaming 1st Lieutenant Philip Primo shouted, "As you were!" Immediately a great cheer went up from the troopers. They thought highly of their leader. He was one of them. Perhaps he drove them hard but that was to be expected, they were airborne… all the way. When push came to shove he stood up for the platoon. Tonight's bash was proof positive of his commitment. A few clenched fists pistoned the air as the cheers grew more raucous. Phil blushed a smile. He was the hero fullback in a victorious locker room all over again.

"Settle down boys, settle down," he calmed the boisterous group. "I've got a few words to speak before we get into tonight's activities. First let me dispense with the bad news. Four deuce-and-a-halfs and a jeep will be departing here at zero five fifteen hours. Be on one of them! I promised Major Alexander we'd be standing tall for reveille at Kaiouran. Drunk or sober!" A chorus of laughing "boos" serenaded the information. "I'm delighted to see you still hold me in great affection," he feigned a wince. They cheered anew, applauding and stamping boots in a show of genuine fondness. Primo held up his glass.

Unlike the others who imbibed deep red wine, his tumbler contained a dark amber fluid, a concoction of three parts cognac, one part sweet vermouth. No doubt there are a few purists who choke the thought of mixing Courvoisier with vermouth. But for Phil, the union was the inspiration of six weeks without a decent cocktail. So, welcome the "Cognac Manhattan." Slurping a half-inch from the rim he exclaimed, "Damn, that's fine wine!" The aware soldiers roared their approval, a few rebel yells punctuating the ovation.

"Troopers, we've trained hard. Hell, the entire Five-O-Five has trained hard. But our team has gone the extra mile." He paused for effect. "And we've done it together. Right now for my dollar, you're the finest platoon in the Eighty Deuce. Soon we'll have to prove it. In one week's time, maybe less, all of us will be going out the door in quest of fulfilling the important mission for which we were especially selected." He held up his glass high and sought out every prideful eye before him. They all raised their drinks in similar fashion. "To G-Bridge… wherever the fuck it is!"

"To G-Bridge," they toasted, "wherever the fuck it is!"

As the noisy meal wore down and the men prepared for some heavy-duty drinking, Sergeant First Class Aarborg banged a spoon on an empty plate. It took twenty seconds of banging and hushing before the room quieted.

150

"Boys," he called out, "we've got a surprise dessert coming, peaches and, of course, wine. Now I want you to save a little room because them fuckin' peaches cost me a bottle of genuine French cognac." The redundancy was lost on the platoon, most of whom couldn't spell *cognac.* "So instead of behaving like a bunch of predatory dogs, I want you to savor dessert and the enormous personal sacrifice that went into it."

"But we are predators!" a trooper yelled out. "Primo's Predators!"

"Primo's Predators!" A chant chorused throughout Cafe Caron, accompanied by clinking glasses. They had rechristened themselves, "The Predators." Morale had always been sky high. Now it stretched to another galaxy. *Esprit de corps,* the soul of every human fighting machine, had achieved a new stratum. Primo's Predators. Bring on the G-Bridge… wherever the fuck it is!

A scratchy phonograph with warped turntable wobbled out the musical strains of Bing Crosby crooning "White Christmas." So it was the Fourth of July! Who cared! Besides, no one had promised them a jukebox. Bing represented a nostalgic voice from back home, a link to family and girlfriends in Buffalo, Tupelo, and Salt Lake City. The tables had been cleared and groups of noisy men playing cards chatted or engaged in good-natured horseplay. Excited conversations touting the obvious superiority of the Dodgers, Cardinals, Tigers, and Yankees echoed about. For many who had cut their drinking teeth on beer and whiskey, the unfamiliarity with wine showed. They guzzled it in prodigious quantities. Soon, language slurred and unsure footsteps wove serpentined paths to the outdoor slit latrine. A blue-gray layer of cigarette haze clung to the low ceiling. It never had a chance to dissipate, continually fed by exhaled streams of cloudy nicotine. Jokes were told and retold. Men laughed and howled. Amusement came easy.

Phil Primo had disappeared for a short while. Now he returned with a flat wooden box tucked under his thick arm. Slipping and bulling through the crowded bar, he placed the parcel atop the counter, sliding it through a maze of green bottles and ashtrays. "Cuban Panatellas!" he shouted above the din. "One for everyone!" The lieutenant had already pocketed four or five of his precious stogies, leaving the rest for his Predators. Snatched up quickly, the cafe was soon filled with a fresh smoky layer pushing up against the first. Taller men stood with heads projecting into the cigar fog. Youthful troopers commented in mock sophistication how the fine quality of imported Cuban tobacco had no peer. Rich leaf, slow burn, mellow aroma. The manipulative power of advertising had drummed the touted catch-phrases into the depths of their unsuspecting brains. Now they subconsciously parroted them in conditioned response.

The spate of vulgar conversation and swinging lilt of Helen O'Connell's "Green Eyes" were suddenly interrupted by the ringing chings of tambourine and finger cymbals. The olive-drab wave of troopers rippled apart as two barefoot women with heavily mascaraed eyes swept through the cheering throng. Cat calls and strident whistles greeted the entrance. Earthy propositions questioned their virtue. Monsieur Caron climbed a chair and, ducking below the low smoke, asked for quiet. Motioning the GIs to form a wide circle, the diminutive impresario made a brief announcement in heavily accented English. "American soldiers. Tonight I present to you the dancing sisters of Hamia." He radiated a happy glow. Henri had been tipping a few vins himself.

"Yasmin—with the feet of passion!" She stepped forward in a graceful whirl, her tambourine shaking a noisy fanfare. A colorless shawl dropped to the floor exposing Yasmin's short, plump torso, somewhat on the greasy side. A musky perfume was in strong evidence, masking bath-less weeks in the hot Tunisian hinterland. A stiff red satin halter girded her flabby bosom. Shiny black beads hung from the dancer's neck almost to her pot belly. The latter sported a cheap costume jewel clinging to her navel. There wasn't much to admire, but in this crowd of horny drunks, Yasmin-with-the-feet-of-passion could have passed for Hedy Lamar.

Attempting her most sultry look, Yasmin took a brass bowl from her bony sister and tossed in a coin with a loud clunk. Placing it on the floor she gestured to the applauding Predators, encouraging them to follow her example with their own pocket change. "And the beautiful sister lady," Caron continued like a circus barker. "A beautiful dancing bird of gold, the wonderful woman—Shalia!" The heady Frenchman was getting caught up in the toastmaster role, overdoing the intros.

Shalia curtsied deftly and twirled off her shawl like a matador's cape, revealing a grimy, mustard bra-like top piece, hardly a bird of gold. Searching for metallic metaphors, "Pig iron might be more accurate," a sarcastic Turk Aarborg observed. Upon closer inspection it was in fact a brassiere. Evidently, genuine belly dancer halters were difficult to come by in war-wracked Tunisia.

Shalia's wide mouth glistened with dime-a-dozen red lipstick. Her swarthy body was considerably slimmer than Yasmin's. It appeared the scrawny waist, hips, and belly were a single curve-less body part. The only way one could distinguish this belly dancer's belly was the phony emerald set in her navel. An S-shaped scar, wide and reflective, marred an inside bicep, completing the unattractive package. "Maybe it stands for *Shalia*," an intoxicated trooper pointed out.

"More likely *Scarecrow*," another offered.

Shalia chinged her finger cymbals while big sis developed a drumming rhythm on the tambourine head. The soldiers got into it, clapping a beat as the two dancers rotated around the circle, undulating hips and abdomens in a grinding, seductive motion. Anklet bells added to the Casbah mood. A few coins found their way into the brass bowl and the women nodded their approval to the donors. More coins followed and the dancers picked up the action, bellies vibrating in a controlled spasm. Sweat rolled from their long black hair and under the beaded bands which decorated their heads. Perspiration mingled with the musky fragrance to form a pungent odor contributing to that of cigars and slopped wine. The rowdy ring of men grew tighter. "Take it off, take it off," they hooted in mock desire.

Moslem women, particularly those who are Arabic and Berber, have the peculiar ability to effect a piercing, high-pitched call from their vocal chords. To westerners, its shrill sound is electrifying, almost eerie. Mouths open, tongues wagging like tuning forks to accentuate the tremolo, the two women startled the gaping Americans. A few jumped back to their own laughing embarrassment.

An inebriated Corporal Dillon kneeling in front reached out, attempting to pluck a navel souvenir, but fell on his face in failure. "Schweinhund!" Yasmin castigated him. Obviously the ladies had performed earlier that year for the boys in the Afrika Korps. In their defense, some would offer the creative arts, dance among them, should reside on a loftier plateau beyond world politics. Hey, these were just a couple of tough broads trying to hustle a few bucks in an impoverished land inundated by warring strangers. Stepping a chubby leg over the immobile corporal, Yasmin bounced next to her glistening sister, twisting and gyrating their baggy harem pants until the bowl overflowed with crumpled dollars, cigarettes, and a rolled condom... compliments of the War Department. Abruptly they scooped up shawls, bowl, and short-fallen coins and rushed from the dance floor waving as they fled. Showtime had concluded. Some cheered, others booed. One well-oiled trooper clapped slowly. That's show biz!

Caron would have preferred they extend their performance, for less wine was consumed during the entertainment. A rush for the bar ensued as GIs slapped palms and fists on the surface, giddily demanding more "red stuff." Drunk as they were, the platoon recognized their commander had shared his prized panatellas. Though most weren't cognizant of top quality Cuban cigars, they appreciated the sentiment and what it represented, a special bond. Too many Cognac Manhattans had rendered Phil glassy-eyed and a tad wobbly. He leaned back against the rough bar, listening to the gratitude and nonsensical babbling of his shit-faced troopers.

A private, Corcoran, who claimed to be from Death Valley, preached to his equally soused buddies. "Did you know," he hiccuped, "there are twenty ways to kill a man with a rope?"

"No shit," an impressed Pfc. Drago answered. "I only know one." His line of vision went directly over Dillon's head straight to the motionless ceiling fan. Not knowing better, a passerby would have taken him to be speaking to the stationary blades.

"Only one?" Corcoran queried. "What's that?"

"Shove it down his fuckin' throat and make him eat it until the son, the son, the son-of-a-bitch dies of fuckin' rope poisoning." He burped indifferently.

"Christsakes, I never thought of that! Twenty-one, now there's twenty one." He belched a fume of gassy goat meat, causing even the most intoxicated to shrink in retreat.

About this time a challenge worked its way through the wine-soaked paratroopers. Which of the three squads among Primo's Predators were the platoon's finest knife-throwers? Five men from each squad, hopefully the soberest, would compete for the right to raise Old Glory on G-Bridge. Lieutenant Primo himself would impartially judge the "tournament of honor," as a piss-eyed Drago called it.

Stepping over the yet prostrate Corporal Dillon, he who would snatch the navel's treasure, two troopers positioned a round wooden cocktail table so its flat surface faced the knifesmen twenty feet away. Paratroopers possess a well-documented obsession with knives. They carry them in boots or strapped to legs, in pants and breast pockets, even on their waist belts. The requirement is quick access to cut themselves free of chute harnesses and tangled risers in the event they become snared in trees. Seldom, however, are the blades used for such utilitarian purpose. More often than not, they are instruments wielded in tournaments of honor.

A white doily, one of Louise Caron's hand-crocheted patterns, was pinned dead center, serving as bullseye. The inebriated marksmen withdrew their throwing daggers and waited in turn. First Squad: Two bounced off the table; two stuck in the wood off-center; one clean miss—it continued to the wall where it crashed into a photo portrait of Charles DeGaulle. Primo made a mental note.

Second Squad: All five bounced off the table, the fifth trooper vomiting an instant prior to the knife leaving his hand. Boos and hisses pursued them back to the bar. Third Squad: Three bounced off the table, one of which rebounded, almost striking its catatonic thrower; one stuck in the edge of the doily; the last sailed amiss narrowly impaling the beleaguered yet unflinching General DeGaulle.

Heavy hangs the burden of leadership. Primo declared third squad the victor inasmuch as they had plunked the doily. To them would go the distinction of hoisting the flag. Naturally first squad protested, claiming two sticks in the wood was at least worth one in the doily. Decisiveness being a key component of leadership, Lieutenant Primo didn't budge.

Outside by the latrine, a half dozen careening winos christened themselves "Predator" using Algerian red for baptismal fluid. The platoon's sole Jew, a staggering Pfc. Bachman, was moved to inquire, "Does this mean I'm a Christian? My grandmother's gonna shit!" before passing out. So ended the uncouth evening that in future recollections was always referenced as "The Bash."

CHAPTER XVI
G-BRIDGE

DATE: FRIDAY, 9 JULY 1943

TIME: 1950 HOURS

LOCATION: KAIOURAN, TUNISIA

Grim-faced troopers of the Eighty Deuce had been rolling into the airstrip since 1600 hours. By now all of the 3,045 jumpers had eaten and assembled. Due to a lack of C-47 gooney birds, only the 52nd Troop Carrier Wing was available to drop a svelte representation of the division this first night. Two days earlier, General Ridgway had met with his commanders to inform that First, Sicily would be the target of a massive airborne/seaborne invasion, Operation Husky, the scale of which the world had never seen. It would involve combined British and American Forces, each responsible for its own area of engagement. Second, because the 51st Troop Carrier Wing had been loaned out to the Brits, only Gavin's 505th Parachute Infantry Regimental Combat Team and the Third Battalion of the 504th would actually jump at about midnight July 9/10. Additionally, cannoneers of the 456th Parachute Field Artillery Battalion and Baker Company 307th Airborne Engineer Battalion would leap with them, along with signalmen, medics, and a handful of US Navy support personnel. The irate remainder of Tucker's 504th would not drop for another twenty four hours. Embittered All-American glidermen of the 325th Regiment would have to bide their time.

For the Predators, their G-Bridge target had been finally identified, Ponte Girasole! "Jeer-A-So-Lay," they had been told was the correct pronunciation. Italian for "Sunflower."

"Can you beat that?" a trooper yapped. "Ponte Girasole, Sunflower Bridge. Who would have thunk it?"

"What'd you expect the *G* stood for, 'Golden Gate?'" his striped-faced buddy wisecracked.

"No, George Washington Bridge, asshole," he said. All the Predators, in a gaudy show of fierce bravado, had shaved their heads leaving but a crested Mohawk strip running from forehead to nape. Warpaint being in short order, the men ran a thick black streak of burnt cork from lobe to lobe, along cheek bones, under each eye and across the nose bridge. Their coiffure and cosmetic make-up were not that unique. Many of the All-Americans had donned a similar warrior display confirming that conformity is a willing slave to fashion.

The Five-O-Five was slated to jump when the hands reached straight up, inland from the Sicilian coastal town of Gela. Like a passel of ruptured ducks, the Predators waddled in three groups to as many C-47s separated from the other transports. Each man lugged in excess of a hundred pounds: main chute, safety chute, Garands, Tommy guns, carbines, grenades, ammo, bazookas and rockets, entrenching tools, canteens, bayonets, knives, field jackets, map cases, tethered bags holding light machine guns with their linked cartridge belts, rations, and spare equipment of every variety.

Helmets swathed in camouflage netting hugged white-scalped skulls where razors earlier had whisked the remnants of stubbled hair. Chin straps secured the steel pots as they clumsily duck-walked to the revving goonies. Several quacked for emphasis. July heat reflected off the runway, wilting uniforms with an uninterrupted sweat. A medic had been attached to their little band, totaling the reinforced platoon to an even fifty soldiers, two sticks of seventeen and one of sixteen. Primo, Aarborg and Sergeant Burdette, a squad leader, were the senior men in each craft, serving as jumpmasters, number one out the door. Sergeant Stanway in Primo's stick volunteered for the numero uno slot, stating he was born on the first of January: first day, first month, nineteen hundred and twenty one. "A reasonable request," Phil countered, "But in the language of my noble ancestors, Primo means first!" End of debate.

Obviously the initial man to enter the aircraft will be the last to exit. Trooper seventeen, the same puking Corporal Dillon who had distinguished himself at The Bash, was awaiting the man behind to provide him a boost into the plane. "Look!" he yelled, pointing to the curvaceous, blonde belly dancer painted on the fuselage with the words *Sugar Baby* stylishly highlighted in yellow. A transparent veil covered her red luscious lips. This was a gorgeous, buxom Hollywood belly dancer, unlike the horsey pair who had entertained at Hamia. "Must be fate," Dillon beamed. He stretched and gently patted the exaggerated star sapphire decorating the fantasy lady's navel. "Good luck, *Sugar Baby*," he said over a bulky shoulder. Each succeeding trooper repeated a similar touch, echoing "good luck, *Sugar Baby*," upon entering the hollow, metal tube which would carry them to an uncertain rendezvous at Ponte Girasole.

The other two C-47s in their mini-squadron, *Texas Lil* and *Kitty Kat*, both sporting provocative females, soon swallowed their eager sticks and taxied in line. Dusk arrived as similar patterns of sky soldiers "saddled up" and embarked straining transports. Operation Husky had begun. Sicily, rugged steppingstone to the European continent, would be breached before the sun rose again.

The Predators' three-and-a-half hour flight plan was identical to everyone jumping this night. As they lifted off into the fading light, a golden glow hung close to the disappearing western horizon. Flying southeast to a gathering point near Chergui Island, the great mobilizing armada of 266 C-47s worked their way into formation before departing due East to the Malta checkpoint where searchlights of immense candlepower guided the slow-moving transports, providing navigators with an accurate beacon to plot their dogleg north. Perhaps they also shone in premature welcome of Dwight Eisenhower, overall commander, who would shift his nerve center in North Africa to a Maltese headquarters once Husky kicked off. As they swung into the final seventy-mile stretch from Malta to Sicily, the pilot dropped down to a harrowing altitude of 200 feet, hopefully under the Axis radar screen. Indeed sea spray spattered windshields and wings. The beautiful *Sugar Baby* would see her seductive brilliance pocked and bleached by a salty, white residue.

Moments before arriving at the Maltese landmark, paratroopers in the *Sugar Baby* stick, tense and silent, were startled by an eerie whistling sound in their midst. It cut through the engine hum and buffeting wind like chalk on a classroom blackboard. Emanating from the plane's tail-end, the concerned Predators were relieved to determine that the high-pitched whine originated from the nostrils of Lieutenant Primo's fullback nose. While other men were absorbed in personal thought and prayer, while some smoked quietly and chatted in hushed tones, the boss man dozed in relaxed composure. Nerves of steel? Or had the exhaustion of the last forty-eight hours caught up with him? Nevertheless, the amused stick marveled and joked about Primo's strident nap. Sensing the sixteen pair of observing eyes, Phil shook himself alert and stared at the aisle of ashen faces. "A little nose music for the Predators," he said loudly. They all laughed, but it was a reflexive, nervous response. Stomach pits were overly taut. Realizing their tightness, he stood and faced up the walk, thinking of something settling to say. Most had removed their steel pots. Some contained pictures of girlfriends in the helmet liner suspension.

The cockpit door swung open. The co-pilot's youthful face, pasty in the dim cabin shine, showed itself. A crushed billed cap, cocked at a backwards angle, sat atop curly brown hair. "Coastline's dead ahead boys," he shouted. "As soon as we reach it, we're going to bank left to the west and fly along the surf. We'll continue until we sight the Acate River. Then we swing north at six hundred feet and into your drop zone." He smiled, closing the cabin door. Moments later it reopened, only the leather sleeve of an A2 flying jacket in evidence. "And good luck!"

"Helmets on!" Primo hollered. "Cigarettes out." He gave them a half minute to make the adjustments. It was time, he figured, to loosen them up a bit. "Everybody enjoying the ride?"

"Yes, sir," they screamed, eager to be stimulated, wanting to be riled from their collective funk.

"Who are we?" he asked.

"Predators!" came the reply.

"Okay, Predators," he grinned. "I know it's customary to yell 'Geronimo' upon exiting the aircraft. However, this beautiful night it will be *Sugar Baby*! Is that understood?"

A raucous chorus of cheers filled the cramped cabin as men chanted "*Sugar Baby, Sugar Baby, Sugar Baby!*"

"Is that positive with you, Corporal Dillon?"

"YEEEEOOOHH," came the howling response from deep inside. The troopers laughed like hell. The jittery ice of nervous tension had thawed to a thermal puddle.

The twin-engined big bird creaked and shuddered as the pilot banked sharply. Flying parallel to the shadowed beach, the formation gained a hundred feet of altitude in anticipation of reaching the split where the Fiume Acate empties into the Mediterranean. Virtually every All-American would be jumping north by northeast of Gela. The Predators however, would penetrate a few miles deeper and slightly to the west. *Deeper and slightly off-center, that's us,* Primo smiled inside. He checked his wristwatch just as the sweep second indicator crossed the twelve, causing the minute hand to jump one increment. *Midnight!*

Today, July 10, 1943, over 160,000 men would initiate the first phase of Operation Husky. 2,600 ships and LSTs would support and carry the amphibious assault divisions through the surf of Licata, Gela, and nearby Scoglitti in the US 7th Army's sector commanded by George Patton. Meanwhile, Red Devils of the British 1st Airborne Division would swoop in from the sky, while Montgomery's Eighth Army, seasoned victors of the desert campaign, planned on crashing the eastern beaches at Pachino, Nota, Ayala, and Cassible. A melange of 14,000 military vehicles plus 600 tanks and 1,800 various-calibered guns of the allied artillery would be floated ashore. The greatest air-sea invasion ever conceived was underway and Ridgway's All-Americans would spearhead the brutal intrusion. In the cabin's dull, hazy light, Phil Primo unfolded a creased mimeographed sheet and silently re-read Slim Jim Gavin's exhortation to the Five-O-Five. At this very instant the gallant Colonel sat in the lead plane, preparing to jump with his feisty RCT.

Soldiers of the 505th Combat Team: Tonight you embark upon a combat mission for which our people and the free people of the world have been waiting for two years.

You will spearhead the landing of an American force upon the island of SICILY. You have been given the means to do the job and you are backed by the largest assemblage of air power in the world's history.

The eyes of the world are upon you. The hopes and prayers of every American go with you… The term American Parachutist has been synonymous with courage of a high order. Let us carry the fight to the enemy and make American Parachutists feared and respected through all his ranks.

Attack violently. Destroy him wherever found. I know you will do your job.

Good landing, good fight, and good luck,

Colonel Gavin

Lurching starboard, the plane followed a northward track. They had reached their final checkpoint, the Acate River. The pilot climbed to 600 feet above the rolling Sicilian landscape and leveled off. On his feet, peering directly above the cabin door, Phil Primo anticipated the gleam of red light. The moment it flashed he yanked open the hatch, allowing a blast of cool air to rush inside. "Stand up and hook up!" he screamed over the engine roar. Stiff from nearly four hours on their duffs, the excited troopers readjusted cumbersome loads and shook out the kinks as they fastened static lines to the anchor cable. "Check equipment," he barked. This was not a superfluous routine. Every man counted on the trooper to his rear to scrupulously examine harness and gear. Those carrying tethered bundles held their loads in front. Like seventeen cramped sardines the GIs wiggled into position and shuffled toward the exit as best they could manage. "Sound off for equipment check!" They did, loud and clear.

Aboard *Texas Lil*, Sergeant First Class Turk Aarborg reminded his troopers that, "This ain't no sand lot game, boys. It's the real thing, the World-Fuckin-Series!"

And on *Kitty Kat*, Sergeant Buck Burdette encouraged his stick by reading Colonel Gavin's message aloud and then punctuating it with a forceful "Let's do it!" Both were received by spirited shouts.

Phil Primo braced in the open door and sucked the invigorating wind in huge gulps. With one eye searching the Sicilian blackness for a clue of what awaited and the other observing the impending green light, his thoughts paralleled those of the Turk. *This will be unlike any football game I've ever played. Lord Jesus, please watch over me.*

GREEN!! Gurgling "Sugar Baby" as an unbridled gust slapped his face, the fullback stepped into the inky, summer night. In a matter of seconds, sixteen overladen Predators tumbled after him. Probably every paratrooper who jumped this hour screamed "Geronimo," except those in Primo's cocky stick. To a man, like pouncing birds of prey they all shrieked "Sugar Baby!"

DATE: SATURDAY 10 JULY 1943

TIME: 0450 HOURS

LOCATION: NORTHWEST OF BISCARI STATION SICILY

Unbeknown to Lieutenant Primo, for the most part the 505th Regimental Combat Team had been strewn far beyond their appointed drop zones. Weather and navigational confusion had dispersed men in small packages, preventing large scale units from linking up. For the platoon, though, the jump had been as accurate as could be hoped. It had taken about an hour to gather the troopers and begin the push north, using the Acate as their guideline. Two scouts, about a quarter mile to the unit's front, probed the way. At 0430 the column's point man spotted a crouched silhouette approaching him. Dropping to the ground he called, "Halt. Who goes there?"

"Friend," came the return.

"Password?"

"Has anyone seen my brother George?"

"Which one, the Sheriff or the Marshal?" Both men laughed. They'd known each other since jump school. The password-countersign combo for Husky One, the airborne phase, had been designated "George" and "Marshall," honoring the Army's great Chief of Staff. His genius and leadership would formulate the American master plan and implementing war machine for both theaters. However, for a couple of dog-face privates roaming Sicily, the war was a tiny span of mortar and stone called *Ponte Girasole* and a superlative leader named First Lieutenant Philip Primo.

The returning scout reported to the boss man that they had advanced along the east bank until a dirt road appeared, sweeping in from the right and bending upriver. At the elbow, a blue-enameled sign proclaimed, "P. GIRASOLE 4 km" in white block letters. Beneath it reaffirmed a fresh wooden equivalent in German Gothic, *Sonnenblume Brucke*.

"Only two-and-a-half miles to target," Primo whispered to Turk and the three clustered squad leaders. "I want us to be in position before sun-up. The river's fairly shallow here. Good a place as any to ford." He read the luminous glow on his thick wrist. "I've got 0455. Make sure you're synchronized. Let's get your team across, Turk. We'll cover you from here. Make sure we stay in radio communication. If that fails for some reason, we hit the bridge at 0600. Call signs are 'Predator One'–me, and 'Two'–you. Got it?"

They all responded in the affirmative. In minutes, Platoon Sergeant Aarborg and third squad, reinforced with a light machine crew and the Redjack-Blackjack bazooka team, slipped into the Acate and forged its seasonally dry breadth. Once the eighteen men reached the west bank, Turk gave his scout a three-minute head start before signaling his force to move out.

At 0542, the Predators on both sides sprawled into position, the machine guns occupying high ground about four hundred yards from their respective bridge entrances. They could just about make out the bridge as the sun was yet stuck behind a large hill to the east. Girasole, a small farm hamlet, sat on Primo's right. He had retained the bulk of his platoon in the event the town had to be stormed. Stealthily, his forward squad crept toward the bridge, moving over dry crumbling terrain with little cover. As the morning sun hoisted itself over the hillcrest, Lieutenant Primo and his troopers stared in confused disbelief.

"Predator One, do you see what I see?" Turk's voice crackled.

Primo removed his helmet and massaged the Mohawk strip. "Yeah, I see it. 0600. Let's move in and take it anyway. And stay alert for a trap."

Girasole Bridge, focus of meticulous planning and countless hours of expended energy, had been reduced to an amorphous drift of quarry stone. Spilled into the riverbed like discarded slag, the ancient arch's shattered spine no longer spanned the muddy flow. Deep-rutted tracks gouged the surrounding banks, crushed to compacted silt. A large yellow dog stretched awake at the east entrance, a sleepy sentinel indifferent to neither the rubbled heap nor the troopers entering the quiet village. A crowing rooster broke the spell, as if to announce to the Paesani that the Americans had arrived.

No more than two dozen buildings comprised Girasole, old and tired. Fingers of sunlight formed, distorted shadows playing against dingy stuccoed walls. The villagers, mostly old men and older women garbed in funereal black, stared out from leathery faces weathered by long years scratching bare subsistence from the weary Sicilian earth. Curious children, sullen but unafraid, examined the baggy-panted intruders from behind studded doors and dusty windows. Adolescent girls and young women no doubt had been hidden away in wine cellars and attic lofts. A generation of young men had disappeared, sucked up conscripts in Mussolini's disintegrating war machine. A middle-aged man, perhaps fifty, wearing a threadbare blue suit and tasseled sash, strode forth from a shadowed portal. Ostensibly, the maroon ribbon represented his badge of office. Recognizing Lieutenant Primo as the head man, he smiled beneath a curling salt-and-pepper mustache. "Inglese?" he asked.

Primo studied the official before responding. He determined a stern facade would command respect, something on which the ritualistic Sicilians placed great stock. Mustering up as much Italian language as he could recall, Primo answered. "No. Siamo Americani." He removed his helmet exposing the Mohawk. Surely it would terrify the man into volunteering information.

Unmiffed by the bizarre coiffure, the Sicilian beamed a broad smile. "*Ho un cugino a* Brooklyn!" He had found common ground, a cousin in Brooklyn. Perhaps the young officer knew of him? "*Americani!*" he joyfully shouted to the villagers. "*Sono Americani!*" The people feigned unbridled joy as though their American brothers had returned home from a brief sojourn. This was how they disarmed forceful interlopers. Survival, a Sicilian art perfected over centuries of foreign incursion, had preserved their lives and everyday culture. Mainland Italians blamed all that was negative on the unforgiving island's residents: the economy, the falling lira, crime, even the weather. Alienated and ostracized, they survived by any means available. As a prelude, though, one must size up his adversary. In this instance, however, the *Americani* held all the cards. "*Il ponte,*" Phil asked. "*Che passato?*" *The bridge, what happened?*

"*I tedeschi stupidi hanno fatti,*" the man raised a frustrated palm skyward. *The stupid Germans did it!* He went on to explain that a panzer column had passed through four days earlier and managed to place two massive tanks on the bridge simultaneously. The great weight was too much. It collapsed, sending one of the huge Tiger tanks into the muddied Acate. The second dangerously teetered over the ruptured span. German recovery vehicles winched out the hanging Tiger, destroying much of what remained. After a half day's inspection and debate, the battered tank was righted with much effort and it too hauled out of the muck. Signore Spano, the *sindaco* or mayor, blessed himself, stating that two *Tedeschi* died and another was severely injured in the mishap. The following day, a group of engineers from the Italian Army's 4th or Livorno Division stationed nearby assessed the bridge damage, judging it beyond repair. They too cursed the Germans' folly. Adding a piece of potential intelligence to his excited narration, Spano informed that the Germans mentioned they would have to use the Ponte Dirillo about five kilometers north.

After Primo explained the situation to his non-coms, Turk cocked his head and asked the question all had been thinking. "Does this mean we have to take D-Bridge?"

"No. Our orders state that if we're unable to secure Girasole, we are to head southeast toward the railroad tracks and follow them to Biscari Station. Try to join up with the regiment or straight legs. Besides, we have to inform our own tankers that the bridge is down or else they'll be making a beeline to a dead end! We'll rest up on that hill until noon. A couple of the guys banged up their ankles and can use a break."

At this very hour, inspired amphibious troops of Patton's Seventh Army were striking, the initial shock forced by three powerful infantry divisions landing abreast, enhanced by several Ranger Battalions. The 3rd, 1st, and 45th Divisions, running west to east, would hammer the interior and link-up in part with the scattered paratroopers. Once the beachhead had been seized, the US 2nd Armored Division would blast out north and west. When required, the 9th Infantry Division, yet in North Africa, would join the assault. The impatient 504th Parachute RCT's two remaining battalions, in tandem with regimental artillery and engineers, planned to jump later that night at captured Farello Airfield. Or so it was devised.

Meanwhile the British Eighth Army, like an unstoppable tidal wave, was surging ashore, the 5th, 50th, and 51st Infantry Divisions and their commonwealth brothers of the 1st Canadian Division in the fore. Commandos and the 1st Infantry Brigade splashed in with them. Red Devil glidermen, surviving a catastrophic landing, had already been at work slugging it out with Axis infantry. Their parachutist comrades would jump later. In reserve, the British 78th Infantry Division and restless armored units readied themselves in North Africa, poised to join when Monty summoned. The scope of invasion, unlike any other ever contemplated, now raged with brutal consequence.

DATE: SUNDAY, 11 JULY 1943

TIME: 0845 HOURS

LOCATION: BISCARI STATION

Swollen ankles, possibly broken, and a progressively aggravated knee were worse than originally thought, severely hampering the group. Cutting cross country, avoiding open fields, and hugging the rolling wood line had also taken longer than expected. To the south, the muffled pops of gunfire and explosions gave testimony to the fierce action they had yet to enter. Overhead, Luftwaffe ME-109s and an occasional Italian Air Force Macchi Folgore 202 zoomed en route from strafing runs along the beach and Allied supply ships riding at anchor. Each time, the platoon would flatten out, seeking concealment.

Open olive groves and tile-roofed farm houses dotted the warm Sicilian campagna compelling caution. Once darkness fell, the going got even slower. Around midnight they took a long break while Lieutenant Primo checked compass and map in an attempt to reorient and land-navigate toward Biscari Station. Just before sunrise, a panting scout returned. Railroad tracks 300 yards ahead! All they had to do was follow the choo-choo line east.

At the station house, a sentry in paratrooper jumpsuit lowered his Tommy gun and waved them in. He signaled they were to double-time, "on the hop!" Meeting Primo halfway, the man called out "Hurry, sir. The old man needs you pronto!"

"Which old man," the lieutenant gasped, still heaving from the final sprint.

"The old man. Colonel Gavin!"

Standing outside the station keeper's battered cottage, a boyish Slim Jim Gavin reached out his slender hand to shake Phil's as the younger officer attempted to salute…a bit of Alphonse and Gaston on the threshold of battle. "Lieutenant, am I glad to see you!"

"Yes sir. I'm Lieutenant Primo, Second Battalion. Our mission was to capture Girasole Bridge but when we got there it had already been destroyed. Villagers told us Kraut panzers were supposedly using the Dirillo Bridge farther north. Someone had better notify our own armored people before they walk into it."

"Got that?" Gavin asked a lanky captain listening in the doorway.

"Yes, sir," the man responded. "I'll try to get the word to them at once."

"Primo, Kraut armor is about a half mile northeast of us at a place called Biazza or Biazza Ridge. I've got a handful of troopers up there trying to hold back a Nazi column. If they bust through, they're going to chop up the flank of the 45th Infantry Division fighting its way up from the beach. Let's move 'm out!"

"Yes sir!"

Unbeknown to American field commanders, Field Marshal Kesseiring had slipped two German panzer divisions across the Strait of Messina to bolster Sicily's defenses. The veteran Hermann Goering Panzer *Fallschirmjaeger* Division, a mix of armor and paratroopers, had assumed a counter-attack position a few miles inland from where the All-Americans had jumped.

167

This unit was about as well-equipped, well-trained, and elite as the Germans had. It was they who were attempting to smash through Biazza Ridge. In fact, combined German-Italian units were counterattacking the American perimeter from Gela to Scoglitti. Through a remarkable stroke of misfortune for the Nazi panzer column, Gavin and a number of troopers had been dropped mistakenly twenty-five miles to the southeast of their planned DZs, right smack in the path of a Tiger-E heavy tank company.

Tigers, fifty-five tons each of crushing steel, spit 88mm projectiles with vicious accuracy. Also referred to as the Tiger I, its massive V-12 gasoline-burning engine cranked out 700 horsepower at a top speed of twenty-three miles per hour. Two 7.92mm machine guns helped protect its five-man crew from individuals foolish enough to challenge. Lightly armed American paratroopers were at this instant confronting the formidable Tigers as Gavin hustled the Predators to the Biazza high ground. Rather than defend the approach, Gavin decided to attack the counter-attackers. All-Americans separated from their units rallied behind the inspirational Gavin to galvanize makeshift platoons. Combat engineers and artillery troopers converted themselves to infantry. Field grade officers commanded hastily thrown-together squads and uttered the two most stirring words ever to energize a battlefield. "Follow me!"

The stubborn handful of Five-O-Fivers desperately hanging on below Biazza Ridge were being shelled by 60mm mortar fire. Dead and bleeding troopers lay about the pocked landscape. The living maintained a tenacious base of fire, holding back enemy grenadiers descending the ridge. Scattered GIs, lost during the night, heard the sound of battle and showed up to join the firefight. Gavin was determined to take the high ground and, rifle in hand, directed the excited Five-O-Fivers to form a skirmish line. Before jumping off, he sent a message to 250 troopers of his Second Battalion to move quickly to Biazza. Lead elements of the 45th "Thunderbird" Division's 181st Infantry Regiment, perhaps two platoons, showed up spoiling for a fight. Troopers wounded a day earlier limped out of aid stations, scrounged weapons, and struggled north.

Storming up the forward slope, the aggressive Predators poured a withering fire on the surprised Germans. The platoon's two machine guns had been commandeered to cover the entire assault force. Rage most often takes on an accompanying vocal release and today was no exception. Screaming curses and exhorting those about them. the gutsy dog faces punched their way through a hailstorm of bullets and grenades. Impacting fire and shrapnel mercilessly slammed men backwards. Some managed to ignore the shock and righted themselves, angrily returning rifle fire with a retaliating vengeance. Primo tried to look away from Sergeant Stanway who caught a round flush in the upper lip, an ugly crimson mustache erupted before he pitched over dead, landing face-first in the crumbly mustard-colored earth.

"Let's get these bastards, get 'em good!" the fullback screamed. "Don't let up." The uneven skirmish line serpentined like a great undulating wave. Some forward ripples had progressed to points ahead of others. A young soldier of the Wehrmacht rose to hurriedly hurl a potato masher. Phil and the man on his left emptied their Garands into his chest. Rolling his eyes, the lieutenant saw Corporal Dillon offering a wild smile.

"Sugar baby!" the corporal howled. "Sugar-fuckin-baby! YEEEOOHH!"

Eight Predators including Primo and Dillon had almost reached the ridge crest's lowest finger. Like a weaving spine, the high ground bent toward them. *If* we *can overrun this piece of horizon, my boys will roll up the flanks like a spool of wire.* "Grenades," he urged his aggressive little band. "Grenades!" In a moment, a half dozen pineapples arched a lethal rain on the horrified defenders. Detonations blew dirt and pulverized debris sky high, the harmless fallout drifting down on the anxious All-Americans.

"NOW!" Primo bellowed, and over the top they went, firing Tommy guns and Garands on the fly. Slumped corpses, some balled up in a small trench, evidenced the effectiveness of their grenade assault. Having achieved the heights, the men spliced left and right to slam the enemy's flanks. More troopers followed, like a swell of instinctive gravity pulling them to the locus of least resistance. Primo led a small group flaring along the high ground. Working their way from foxhole to foxhole, they quickly dispatched unsuspecting *Panzergrenadiers* before they could react. Caught between the frontal and flanking assaults, German soldiers began withdrawing piecemeal from the high ridge. Approaching a small knob, he heard rapid automatic weapon fire emanating from a concealed position. Noticing a bobbing angular helmet in profile, Phil crawled forward.

Normally machine guns have a staccato rat-a-tat-a-tat sound as each exploding cartridge fires. But the rate of fire ahead was so fast it came out as one long distinctive raaaaaaaat, putting out a stream of unending lead like a fire hose. *Must be a MG-34 or MG-42,* Primo deduced. Veteran officers of the independent 509th Parachute Infantry Battalion had told him of the dreaded weapon in North Africa. Its unmistakable chatter became easy to identify, even in the din of a monstrous battlefield. Creeping forward, he reached for a grenade. The cupboard was bare, no pineapple surprise today. He'd have to do it the old fashioned way. Opening the bolt on his Ml, he extracted the half-empty clip, replacing it with a full load. He jiggled the bayonet to insure it remained securely attached to the stud. All fine. The fullback tensely waited for an opportune instant to overwhelm the crew. Perhaps a break in fire would indicate a fresh linked belt was being readied. Feeding time represented the ideal moment to charge.

The gun fell silent and Phil sprang to a low crouch, rushing the position in gridiron strides. The square-jawed gunner spotted him too late. Two killing .30 caliber rounds slammed into the startled man's cheek causing the light machine gun to fall sideways on its bipod. The terror-stricken assistant started to throw up his arms and yell "Kameraden" at the same split second Phil fired, clipping the man's shoulder. "Kameraden," he sobbed, "Kameraden." Barely restraining his instinct to shoot, he motioned the young German to lie down.

"On the ground, Fritz." He had captured his first prisoner.

In another five minutes the attackers swept over the ridge, cleaning out nests of remaining enemy. The exalted GIs occupied vacant German foxholes, simply facing the other way. Heat and battle exhaustion afflicted one and all. The silent sun perched straight up. No time for congratulations nor pause, the Tigers were coming!

Pursuing troopers ran into the fiendish monsters just as enemy mortar and artillery fire began dropping on the ridge positions. Two bazooka teams slithered downslope and into the approach lanes. A huge gray Tiger, ominous black crosses decorating its steel skin, roared into view and fired at an All-American pack howitzer positioning itself on the heights. Short! The high velocity round spumed a geyser of splintered gravel twenty feet forward of the stationary .75mm gun. While the Tiger gunner reloaded, a two-man bazooka team stood to let fly a point-blank rocket. It bounced from the beast's armor plate like spit balls off a brick wall. The angered giant spewed machine gun fire at the helpless infantrymen and clanked over their twitching bodies with a crushing finality.

The howitzer roared a direct fire shot. It exploded several feet in front of the tank causing it to rock slightly. Thinking better, the crew maneuvered the Tiger behind a dilapidated farmhouse wall, there to wait a safe opportunity. Pockets of troopers infiltrated a timeworn olive grove extending from the lower slope. They continued to snipe at retreating German grenadiers, when the unmistaken rumble and clanging of steel treads echoed through the orchard. Panzers! Tigers hastening to reclaim lost ground? Elite Hermann Goerring Panzer *Falischirmjaeger* were not about to allow a rabble of lightly-armed American sky soldiers to hold the upper hand.

Roaring between rows of olive trees, ripping low-hanging branches from their wizened trunks, three Nazi tanks came into view. The good news, they were not Tigers. Three Mark IV tanks, swift thirty-ton brutes, dashed in triangular attack formation, the center panzer in the lead. Machine gun fire flashed from their gun ports, intent to mow down and overrun the scattering GIs. Kneeling behind an uprooted stump, Redjack sighted his 2.36 inch bazooka at the passing Mark IV, leftmost in the group. The projectile flashed out of the tube in a smoking whoosh heading directly at the gasoline-fueled engine. Heat pushing out from the back blast radiated past the alert Blackjack ready to seat a fresh round. A yellow-orange explosion belched from the panzer as the rocket slammed home. Gas and ammunition started cooking off as the choking crew attempted to escape a fiery death. Instead they were cut down by riflemen secreted among the trees, more merciful than a fiery tomb perhaps, but equally savage.

Snatching another rocket by the stabilizer fin, Jack Andrews, the brunette, seated it in the tube, his deft fingers hooking up the ignition wire. In one motion he pulled his hand free of the circular opening and slapped his partner's helmet, signaling a live load. The two Predators in a predatory frame of mind raced around the motionless crew and smoldering panzer, dark oily smoke yet curling from the open turret hatch. Pursuing the remaining pair of Mark Vs through a grassy swale they skidded to a halt, the red one firing again from an erect kneel. The shot missed the bullseye. Instead it struck the left track, causing the clanging tread to slither from the wheels like a gigantic caterpillar. Stuck in the saddled dip the driver engaged the right track. It immediately pivoted the crippled machine in a herky-jerky one-hundred-eighty-degree arc, its cannon pointed at the pair of helpless troopers.

In a flash it was over. "Missing In Action" is a polite term often used for men not missing but simply blown to smithereens. Such was the case with the two Jack T. Andrews. Their scorched particles were fused into a grisly residue, one with the Mediterranean soil. Neither Red nor Black would distinguish them any longer. Trapped in the small gully, the driver ground screeching gears in a futile attempt to free the hamstrung vehicle.

"Grenade," screamed the enraged fullback. A private named Castine handed him one. Dropping his Garand, he took off in a flat-out sprint, covering ground in quick strides, end zone to end zone. Reaching the gully lip, he hurtled himself onto the lurching steel box. The hot engine grate tore flesh from the fisted knuckles clutching the lethal pill. Ripping out the ring pin, he regained his balance and clawed at the hatch. It flew open, almost throwing him off. Thrusting his fist into the turret cavity Primo release the grenade and jumped free. Inside, the alarmed crew shouted to no avail. Agonizing seconds ticked by. Unable to capture it and purge its deadly force they scrambled out of the certain coffin, one clinging to a slung Schmeisser machine pistol. Hugging the scorched earth they waited the detonation. It didn't come. A dud?

A half circle of five riflemen rushed the dazed crew, unsure of whether to shoot or claim prisoners. The panzer soldiers made the decision easy. "Kameraden." For them the war was over… kaput. Twelve seconds later the lazy fuse burned through the grenade stem and blew, detonating cannon shells inside the disemboweled Mark IV. It ruptured in a great earsplitting growl. A young German blessed himself and thanked God.

The main body of enemy tanks came on with a vengeance, intent on climbing the slope and dispossessing its new tenants like fleas from a stable. GIs scrambled back to their lofty perch as German 60-mm mortars fell on the hill, escorting the tanks in with a rolling barrage. The critical moment had arrived. Suddenly the grove and fields erupted with thunderous explosions. *My God, those are 155's! Ours! Tearing up that Kraut armor.* The deadly rain cascaded in continuous salvos ripping steel like cardboard boxes. Thunderbird artillery had zeroed in with an entire battalion of the big howitzers. Shock waves reached up to the ridge, vibrating the elated troopers with a welcome tingle. Down below, burning hulks dotted the Sicilian countryside. Those that could, retreated… docile and momentarily defanged.

Around 1900 that evening a half dozen American Sherman tanks pulled into the approach below the ridge, followed by an equal number of half-tracks tugging anti-tank cannons. Soon they deployed along the line, firing in support of troopers pressing forward. The pugnacious defenders had won, licked the best soldiers the Hermann Goering Division had to offer. But it didn't come without a steep price tag. Many troopers died this day, among them fourteen Predators buried on Biazza Ridge. Eleven others had suffered wounds. Fifty-percent casualties. On to the next ridge.

DATE: TUESDAY, 13 JULY 1943

TIME: 1350 HOURS

LOCATION: SICILY

Reunited with the Second Battalion, the skimpy platoon of Predators struck north. Things that happened three and four days earlier seemed the distant past. They had learned that twenty three C-47s carrying brother troopers from the 504th had been shot out of the sky by friendly fire. Allied naval and beach defenses, despite being alerted to their impending presence, had riddled a serial of paratroopers flying in to Farello Airfield from Kaiouran, along with airborne engineers and artillerymen. The slow flying, low-altitude transports were fat sitting ducks for nervous gunners. A total of 318 troopers died in the debacle, in addition to Air Corps flight crews. Many others were wounded. Of the 144 aircraft slated to drop their troopers at Farello, one of every six was blown from the night.

Earlier, the bulk of the Hermann Goering's armored infantry attack had been focused on the US 1st Infantry Division near Gela beach. A furious battle left sixteen destroyed panzers smoking on the long plain. Shermans and a Ranger battalion had joined the melee to stem the aggressive Nazi thrust.

Thunderbird riflemen from the 45th Division's 180th Infantry Regiment swarmed over Ponte Dirillo and captured it intact, thereby securing an uninterrupted path for the big guns being hauled up to punish the reeling Axis forces.

Meanwhile the US 3rd Infantry Division, "Rock of the Marne," tore into the Wehrmacht's 15th *Panzergrenadier* Division. Tanks of the US 2ndArmored Division's Combat Command A landed ashore and together the two outfits forged a front some fifty miles wide. The Italian 4th Infantry Division (Livorno) attempted to help their German allies stuff the advance but were soon swept aside. The westernmost flank was secured. Much farther east, First Lieutenant Phil Primo had been rooting out pockets of Italian soldiers, remnants from the July 10 counterattack by the fascist regime's Mobile Gruppo E. Within the group's antiquated arsenal were several pieces of German equipment, specifically *Sonderkraftfahrzeug* scout vehicles and light-armored cars. The latter employed a 28mm anti-tank gun, sometimes a 20mm cannon, plus machine gun. A Predator had just caught one of the scout vehicles near a collection of communal farm buildings, the ancient stones of which had probably stood for centuries. The two-man crew had halted for a piss stop, only to be spotted by the platoon's point man, Pfc. Corey, who shot them both, killing one. Bleeding heavily from a shattered wrist, the agonized Italian raised his good arm, shouting, "*Non sparare, non sparare!*" The bullet had splintered the bone, the ineffective hand dangling like a limp bird.

Hearing the shooting, Primo and his troopers rushed toward the old buildings. They had been probing ahead of combat engineers loaded down in a M-3 Half Track. The engineers were seeking out a facility to store heavy equipment coming up to their rear. From afar the collective farm buildings seemed an ideal depot to stockpile spools of barbed wire, bridging material, mines, various explosives and other tools of their hazardous trade. Enemy vehicles were prized trophies not solely because of the status they afforded their captors, but because foot soldiers could pile personal freight aboard.

Field packs, rations, and extra ammo would find their way inside the *Sonderkraftfahrzeug* which, like an obedient pack mule, would soon follow in formation. A small American flag was already being fixed to the rear mounted antenna, the same flag the knife-throwing champion third squad had won the right to raise over G-Bridge. They would mooch gas from the engineers to guarantee extended range.

The jubilant troopers were standing around congratulating Corey on his war prize, watching the medic aid the bleeding prisoner whom the men called Gino. Lieutenant Primo unfolded the map and penciled an "X" to indicate their location. Leaning against the armored car with his jump boot resting on the hub, he stuffed the map into his shirt and was attempting to return the stubby pencil to a breast pocket when a *braaaat* split the air. Another followed as ricocheting bullets slammed off the armor into his thigh and foot. *Braaat!* The flag-fastening trooper spilled off the turret onto the packed dirt. Phil dragged himself tight to the vehicle. Again a burst raked their position.

The Predators hugged the vehicle, keeping it sandwiched between them and the shooters general direction. Primo clutched his muscled leg as if to contain the biting pain. The ricocheting slugs had flattened out, tearing abnormally jagged punctures. Seeing blood, the medic rolled to him and ripped away the saturated pant leg. Deftly he applied field dressings to the two thigh wounds, another man maintaining pressure. *Stop the bleeding, protect the wound, prevent or treat for shock,* Phil thought to himself. Next the medic slit his laces and removed the perforated boot. A round had creased the instep without much damage.

"Breda!" Gino howled. He had been hit again, this time by his own people. His khaki trousers oozed a blood-red trickle near the hip. A Breda Model 30 machine gun was the culprit, firing from a hidden position somewhere in the aggregate of pocked buildings. The Breda had them pinned down.

"Anybody got it spotted?" Turk called out.

"Hell, no," came the response.

The platoon sergeant tried to peek out from behind a fender, attempting to get a fix on the shooter. A whizzing stream of 6.5mm bullets kicked up chipped gravel, spraying the peeker. He jerked back hurriedly. "I think there's only one gun."

Laying behind the wood line, the engineers' Half-Track had the sniper spotted. "Let's hit it!" a young corporal shouted. Tracks bit into the hard earth as the driver kicked the M-3 into gear. All 147 horsepower surged as the speedy vehicle roared to support the troopers. Its churning cleats flung out lumpy divots of sod and gravel. Clutching the fearsome .50 caliber weapon, dreaded by Italians and Germans alike, the corporal unleashed a fearsome red burst at the loft opening high on the largest stone barn.

Inside, an Italian private realized too late that he had bitten off a slab too large to chew. Granite chips and a splintering wooden sill flew about him. Reloading the Breda, he foolishly reset the hinged, side-mounted magazine and squeezed off a short spurt. Down below the incensed 50, mobile and hostile, barked over a hundred rounds at the loft. The big slugs tore out the frame and slammed into the Breda's steel bipod. A flock of angry rounds flew into the opening as though drawn by a magnet. Each five-round sequence embraced two balls, and one each incendiary, armor-piercing, and red tracer bullets. Ugly chunks of the Italian's upper body were splattered among the rafters and ancient beams, another of Mussolini's legionaries dead in an imperialist war doomed from inception. The pit bull of fascism would be transformed into a whimpering Nazi lap dog. Sicily lost would take the Italian government out of the conflict, though the people would suffer greatly.

Back at the field hospital, Major Mark Alexander chatted quietly with a short, bald army surgeon, bespectacled and wearing a white smock. The doctor shook his head in a negative manner. Alexander nodded slowly in reluctant agreement. He turned, and spotting Primo propped on a cot, strode to him with a confident bounce.

"Hi, Primo." He flashed a concerned smile, looking down at the leg and foot swathed in rolls of clean, white surgical gauze.

"Good morning, Major." Phil had just been shaved and sponge-bathed, a clean T-shirt covered his strong chest.

"Doc says you're going to be okay, thanks to those tree trunk gams of yours. But it'll take a while before you'll be jumping out of planes again."

"Yes, sir. Looks like I'm leaving the Five-O-Five. Shipping me back to the States for some re-constructive surgery. Guess I'll have to learn how to walk all over again."

The major held out a pair of silver bars connected at the flanks. "Well, if it's any consolation, your captaincy came through. Congratulations, Captain."

"Thank you, sir, it's very important to me," he said softly. He took the bars. Turning the conversation, Primo asked, "And my boys. How are my troopers?"

"As you know, they've been shot up pretty badly so we've pulled them off the line and integrated them into a reserve platoon for the time being."

"Good, sir. They need the break. I haven't had time to put them in for commendations yet. Some of them were phenomenal. Give me something to do while I'm lying on my ass."

"Fine. I welcome your recommendations," the tall major approved. "By the way, some of Colonel Gavin's staff witnessed your gallantry on Biazza Ridge and have put you in for a Silver Star. Seems like you were the lead dog in that show. You're one hell of an officer. I hate to lose you."

"Thank you." Moisture had collected in the fullback's eyes. He yanked a corner of bed sheet and blotted the dew of emotion. "I hate to leave," he whispered.

"Oh, one last thing," the major recalled, reaching into a breast pocket. "I almost forgot." He withdrew a cellophane-wrapped cigar, slightly bent. "One of your troopers, a Corporal Dillon, asked me to give you this. He said to tell you it was a Sugar Baby from Primo's Predators. In fact he seems to call everything a Sugar Baby."

A flood of tears rolled down Phil's clean-shaven cheeks. He made no effort to stem the flow. Alexander touched his stubbled Mohawk and softly slipped away.

Sicily evolved, like many battlefields, as a struggle for ridges and bridges, for junctions and passes—Biazza Ridge, Piano Lupo, Ponte Primosole, Tumminello Pass—brief bitter actions repeated over again. On August 17, General George Patton, gloating and victorious, entered Messina, the final triumph in the Sicilian campaign. Montgomery, pushing up from the south soon joined him. Inexplicably, the Allies had failed to prevent the Germans from evacuating troops and vast quantities of tanks, artillery and munitions across the strait to the Italian Peninsula. Like the Japanese at Cape Esperance and the British at Dunkirk, the attackers had lost a glowing opportunity to heap a more pronounced defeat on the enemy. Yet Sicily represented a smashing success. It took the reluctant Italians out of the war and forced the jackboots of Hitler disheartened, but far from defeated, Wehmacht back into Fortress Europa.

CHAPTER XVII
PICNIC

DATE: THURSDAY, 19 AUGUST 1943

TIME: 1030 HOURS

LOCATION: WALTER REED ARMY HOSPITAL,
                 WASHINGTON, D.C.

A plump Army nurse wearing traditional white from cap to shoes offered a caring, maternal smile. "I'm sorry, lieutenant, but Doctor Karoyan will be tied up for fifteen or twenty minutes. Won't you take a seat? There's a whole stack of new magazines arrived yesterday… *Life, Look, Colliers, The Saturday Evening Post*…"

"That's okay, Nurse Ryan," he murmured. "I'll just plop myself in the corner. I picked up a Washington Post on the way." He held the folded newspaper for her to see.

"You're looking very fit and tan. I suspect medical leave agrees with you."

"Thank you. I'm back to my old weight, and been getting plenty of exercise catering to the whims of our baby daughter." Woody, like all new fathers, welcomed every opportunity to inject baby references into conversation no matter how remote the subject. Irene Marie Luzak, was almost four months old, the joyful recipient of her glowing father's unabashed attention. Nancy and he doted on the tot, placing her in bed cuddled between them, listening to her coos and chatting gushy baby talk. It was a wonderful feeling like no other.

Woody Luzak had been on the mend for over a half year. It took that long for his body to shake off the residual shock of Reflection Hill. No shrapnel entered him, the explosive hardware having been smothered and absorbed by the sump and surrounding Japanese defenders. However, the overpowering concussive force and cartwheeling palm log had smashed most of his ribs and traumatized internal organs. Smell and hearing had temporarily disappeared. Ultimately his spleen had to be removed. Jagged splinters and volcanic stone had penetrated arms and legs, inciting an ugly spray of tiny festering pits. Woody's collarbone and right ulna were fractured along with several fingers. An angry gunshot wound to the thigh had severed a nerve, and a terrible concussion compounded the grim wreckage. Indeed his anatomy had been stunned into a dormancy lasting several weeks. His mangled body already underweight and debilitated by jungle fever, clung to life, fragile and desperate. Comatose and within the narrow shadow of death, his struggling heart continued to tick, pumping oxygen along the arterial viaduct of the living. Submerged in a strangling black void, his stupored essence fought back staving death's embrace.

Guadalcanal's medical facility, yet primitive, necessitated he be airlifted immediately to a more sophisticated hospital if he were to survive. A Navy PBY, reeking of sulfa and alcohol, evacuating critically wounded Marines to the US Navy Fleet Hospital in New Caledonia, offered to haul out his gauzed and plaster-casted body to Noumea. There, after much consternation, he regained consciousness and recovered in agonizing segments enough to be declared out of danger. By early March a sedated Woody, still aching, was steaming northeast to Hawaii on a crammed hospital ship. From there he would be transported to the States and ultimately Walter Reed. A long, tedious healing followed. Bones knitted, bonding themselves to pre-injury strength, although a few ribs still formed a pained kink when twisted into an uncomfortable position. July saw him released, minus his spleen, for a thirty-day recuperative period, officially termed "medical leave."

That same day, Swifty, with baby Irene napping in her arms, proudly stood by as a piece of unfinished protocol played itself out. Undersecretary of War, Robert P. Patterson, pinch-hitting for Secretary Stimson, arrived with a major from General Marshall's staff to confer upon Lieutenant Woodrow Luzak the Army's second highest decoration, the Distinguished Service Cross.

"Medals are symbolic badges, pieces of fabric and thread, metal and enamel," the Undersecretary philosophically summarized. "Let us all remember it is the soldier who wears them whom we honor. Do not dwell too long on the medal but look to the man behind it!" Having awaited completion of Patterson's presentation, the major awarded Woody the Purple Heart with oak leaf cluster signifying a second award, one for the soldier's bullet wound, the other for the explosive injuries suffered later at the bunker.

The brief ceremony ended with congratulatory handshakes and a tearful kiss from Nancy. They walked out into the muggy Washington summer and drove to Havre de Grace for thirty days of familial bliss.

"Doctor will see you now." Dark, curly haired George Karoyan wore the gold oak leaves of an Army major, but hardly ever encouraged subordinates to address him by rank. His was a wartime commission made necessary by the swelling number of casualties streaming back to the U.S. from the European and Pacific battlefields. Doctor first and foremost, Karoyan dispensed with the military pomposity so often postured by his medical colleagues working in home front comfort. "Hot damn, Luzak, if you don't look terrific. How's it going?"

"That's why I'm here, Doc. This is supposed to be my final check-up." Woody smiled and held out his hand. Karoyan grabbed it and shook heartily. His purpose was more than friendship, attempting to discern a wince, a weakness, or any sign of discomfort. "What are you trying to do, shake something loose inside?"

"Who, me?" the doctor feigned innocence. "Strip to your socks, big boy." As Woody undid shoes and necktie Karoyan took him through a series of diagnostic questions, all of which received negative replies. He removed his khaki shirt, careful not to wrinkle the starched creases. Draping it neatly over a metal chair painted a glossy olive-drab, he made sure not to finger the lustrous collar brass.

"Nice ribbons," the doctor observed gesturing to the two rows of colorful honors stacked above the closest pocket flap. High on the left shoulder, a royal blue cloth patch bearing four white stars of the Southern Cross announced him to be a warrior of the Americal Division. More revealing than any of his decorations were the DSC and clasped Purple Heart. To those in uniform who saw him, regardless of service branch or rank, came a special respect. Soldiers, sailors, and Marines are able to read cryptic ribbons like an astronomer reads the heavens, each star cluster representative of a specific constellation. So it is with striped fabric rectangles neatly aligned; they told of campaigns fought and heroism by degree. Even crusty Doc Karoyan, indifferent to military protocol, held a particular reverence for men who had entered the eye of the tiger. God knows he had pieced together and rebuilt enough of them.

Woody nodded quietly, not caring to comment about the ribbons. His pants and trunks were off, T-shirt in the act of being stripped over his head. Thirty days of pull-ups, push-ups, stretching exercises and sit-ups had restored much of the muscle tone. Karoyan signaled to the polished steel examination table and Luzak responded by hopping upon it, ignoring the chill. He stretched out, allowing the doctor's experienced fingers to probe and tap various parts. Inspecting the scar left by the spleen removal, the physician emitted an approving grunt.

"You're a remarkable man, Woody. This beat-up body has responded one hundred percent. And you can still count to twelve by threes so I guess your brain's okay too!" He winked a smile. Luzak sat up and the major shone a scrutinizing light beam into his eyes and ears. "You're a friggen miracle, that's what you are, my friend. I hope you say your prayers at night cause someone, maybe a guardian angel, must be watching over you. If I didn't know better, when they wheeled you in here five weeks after sustaining your injuries, I'd have said Woody Luzak had fallen out of a ten-story window! Luzak must mean 'lucky' in Slavic. Get the hell out of here," he laughed. "You're as fit as Joe Palooka!"

"Thanks, Doc," Woody said, sliding into his underwear. "There's a whole chain of people like yourself from the Solomons to Walter Reed who made the miracle happen. Most I've never seen. I owe a lot of people a very big debt. Even the Navy!"

"Woody, I can declare you fit for duty on Monday, or grant you an extra fifteen days recuperative leave. It's your call, son."

Woody's head cocked. He rolled his tongue inside the smooth cheek walls, pausing for an instant's thought and allowed himself an impish grin. "That fifteen days will do real fine, Doc. Real fine."

The rugged-looking patient wore **a** dark blue robe with white caduceus embroidered on the breast pocket. He edged off the bed, easing into a pair of white terry slippers. Scuffing with a slightly pronounced limp across the ward's shiny linoleum floor, Captain Phil Primo fished a slender cigar from his pocket and peeled the cellophane wrapper. As everyone in the ward had learned this past week, the officer had two strong inclinations—a liking for Cuban cigars and a peculiar tendency to whistle loudly while sleeping. A fellow captain, a good-natured foot-amputee from Kansas, concocted the invention of a whistling cigar which purported to satisfy both habits.

"If you could find a way to include whiskey and vermouth in that thingamajig, I'd buy a thousand," Primo told him. He passed through the ward's swinging double-door to the main corridor, planning to hit the open air terrace for an unrestricted smoke. As he strolled the mini-limp worked its way out and moved to a fluid stride. Hell, he had taken tougher hits in the Boston College game, or so he told the surgeon who removed the Breda's twisted slugs from his muscled leg, trivializing the painful damage.

"Excuse me, is that the officer's ward you just exited?" A suntanned first lieutenant, erect and square-shouldered in tailored khakis, stood directly to the fullback's front. "Yep, it sure is," Phil responded, noticing but not staring at the beribboned soldier, "Who are you looking for?"

"A Captain Primo. Do you know him?"

"Intimately. You're talking to him."

The uniformed man thrust out his hand, two fingers a bit gnarled, and smiled. "Captain, I'm not exactly sure how to explain who I am without confusing the hell out of both of us."

"You're not from the whistling cigar company, are you?" Phil deadpanned, then gritted his teeth in a playful smirk as he clasped the hand and shook it.

The humor was lost on the unaware visitor. "Did I miss something?" he asked.

"No, no, forget it," the fullback laughed. "Just a bit of self-directed sarcasm. We get a bit stir-crazy in the ward."

"Okay, if you say so, Captain." He cleared his throat and began anew. "My name is Woody Luzak and my sister Stella is married to your Uncle Ray's brother, Vic Romanek. Doesn't exactly make us blood kin, but there's a connection there somewhere. Anyway, Stella and Ray are coming to visit my wife and me tomorrow. We live in Maryland not far from here. Stella's never seen our baby so she's coming from New Jersey for the weekend. She phoned last night to say your mom, Aunt Rose Marie, and Ray, were also driving in from Connecticut to haul you back on furlough. So I'd like you to be our guest, along with your folks, at my place for a cookout Saturday. Whew, got that out all in one breath!"

"Woody, do you smoke cigars?"

"On occasion, when there's a reason."

"Well, this is one of them." Phil reached out and gave his new friend a long-armed hug. "Let's move to the terrace. We've got a lot to talk about."

One hour later, the two men wound down their conversation with an exuberant parting. They had talked of the Army and buddies lost, but not dwelling on the anguish. There was no bitterness, only memories of special friendships evaporated by cruel war. Chatter touched on Tony Luzak and Woody's reunion on The Canal.

They compared amusing notes on the Romanek brothers, discovering Ray and Vic had remarkable similarities—headstrong but without a demanding demeanor, mentally tough with a kind heart, homemade everything from sausage to wine presses. Loyalties, character, and family were more important to the brothers Romanek than the fast buck or cosmetic facade. The Romaneks cut through the superficial like acetylene through tin plate. Opting for a few frills lifestyle, premiums were placed on good food, basic booze, and a loving woman with whom all was shared. A life, a philosophy almost primitive, with no pretensions… except when playing cards. That was a game of playacting and bullshit, of cackling victory and scornful defeat. Yeah, games like pitch, casino, hearts, and pinochle were designed for hyperbole and intense argument. Woody and Primo had the Romaneks figured out, alright.

After a while, a silent bell stirred Phil's realization that this Luzak must be the same officer who had impressed Nick Callahan at OCS, the very man who unselfishly big-brothered Nick through the demanding course. They spoke of their mutual fondness for the slender Callahan. Primo commented that in jump school he, like Woody, had become the Kid's partner, helping to guide him over the rigorous shoals of paratrooper training. Double Manhattans introduced to the young lieutenant at the Fort Benning Club and their powerful effect became a source of sidesplitting laughter. Phil embellished the tale, injecting witty commentary regarding the hurricane-force hangover which followed. The laughter caused a stitch to stir in Luzak's ribs and he begged Phil to belay the humor.

It felt good, though, to laugh, to interact, to be alive and secure. Neither realized that as they bantered, Callahan's 503rd Parachute Infantry Regiment was en route from Australia to the contested hell of New Guinea. Tomorrow, August 20, the Five-O-Three would disembark at Port Moresby and begin initiating a gutsy series of airborne strikes against the stubborn Japanese. And the Kid would be dropped into the thick of it. Like a couple of gabby washerwomen, the two veterans covered a wide swath of conversation, moving away from Callahan. The subject matter, as one would expect, revolved around matters military…rumor and counter-rumor. Instinctively, without braggadocio, each recognized the other to be a fine soldier. A lasting friendship would form this hour; their camaraderie buttressed by common experience and its inherent hazards.

DATE: SATURDAY, 21 AUGUST 1943

TIME: 1130 HOURS

LOCATION: HAVRE DE GRACE, MARYLAND

A pair of sawhorses supported three two-by-twelve inch planks to create a crude but effective picnic table overlooking the balmy Chesapeake. Checkered yellow oilcloth covered the form, an odd mix of ten unmatched bridge chairs and kitchen chairs completing the ensemble. Off to the side, a large sparkling block of ice rested in a galvanized wash tub, surrounded by chilled beer bottles. An ice pick lay atop the block, available to chip off small chunks for mixed drinks. The azure Maryland sky embraced nary a cloud, a perfect day warm with soft breezes off the big bay.

Vic and Woody had built a temporary barbecue pit where the sloping lawn began to drop off to the water's edge. The ground was soft and with minimum effort they had shoveled out six inches of soil roughly three feet wide and two feet from front to rear. Horseshoed bricks surrounded most of the pit with a blackened grill set on top, held in position by its own weight. Irregular chunks of charcoal, probably ash wood, sat heaped in a corrugated cardboard carton, the words *Nabisco Saltines* on each of the long sides. The shiny charcoal reflected the overhead sunlight off its facets like fractured obsidian. Woody stared at the glitter, his mind tumbling back to Reflection Hill and the horrid events of that fateful day. Flashes of gored men and the closeness of death caused a quick shiver to course up his spine and shudder neck and shoulders.

Big Vic noticed the spasm and the sour look on Woody's face. "Something wrong?"

"No, nothing." He spoke without emotion, unconvincing. "I guess there's some baggage that will travel with me forever."

Inside the cottage, Stella and Nancy butterflied the sausage, prepping it for the grill, Polish-style kielbasa made by the Lemko Club boys back in

Jersey. Sauerkraut flavored with onion and pepper browned on the stove. A pot of shallow water sat ready to boil awaiting the gas flame. Sweet corn from Connecticut would be steamed as soon as Ray, Rose Marie, and Violet arrived with Philip. Baby Irene had been napping for two hours as if to prepare herself for the day's activity.

The long-hooded 1940 LaSalle coupe rolled down the gravel fork to the little cottage by the bay. Eight honey-smooth cylinders in a straight block propelled the graceful silver-gray machine effortlessly, its three-speed unwinding transmission allowing virtual ease of shifting anytime. Ray had borrowed it from Joe Petri, a wrecking contractor in New Haven who owed him a few favors. Besides, Ray convinced the gent it was his "patriotic duty" to volunteer the LaSalle. After all, it would be fetching home a wounded hero, ergo, an ambulance of mercy in the national interest. To clinch the deal, Ray promised, in absolute good faith, that his nephew would write an appropriate letter of recommendation to the Holy Cross admissions director on behalf of Petri's son, currently a freshman at Notre Dame High School in West Haven. Ray would hold Phil to the deal even if the teenager was a moron.

Elbow hanging out the window, the older Romanek wheeled the gleaming classic between Woody's 1937 Chevy and his brother's Hudson of the same model year. Seated beside his uncle, Phil Primo worked the door handle. It clicked open with a solid snap. The LaSalle was built to last, a marvelously designed piece of machinery, superbly engineered and crafted. Multiple coats of lacquered paint and polished chrome encased its comfy passengers. Fat white-walls, freshly scrubbed clean, showed off her deep-treaded Firestones. The officer swung out his thick legs, the highly buffed jump boots and bloused khaki trousers, proud symbols of the airborne, the first to exit. He pushed the coupe's seat forward and took his mom's waiting arm, assisting her out.

True to her name, she wore a summer-weight, purple pastel blouse with an ankle-length white pleated skirt, the latter in contrast to the fashion of the times. Hemlines were almost knee-length these days inasmuch as the production of textiles mainly devoted itself to wartime needs—uniforms, tenting, parachutes, medical paraphernalia, etcetera. As a result, manufacturers of civilian attire made do with a limited amount of fabric. Much to the pleasure of ogling males, women's legs were revealed with greater exposure each passing year. A necklace of walnut—sized, pearlescent beads graced her neck while a floppy-brimmed hat in eggshell white topped off the pleasing package. Violet's eyes still misted. The emotional reunion with her boy a few hours earlier at Walter Reed had left her trembling and sobbing.

For the week prior, she had been unable to sleep in anticipation of today. In fact, the entire year had been a nervous, gut-wrenching existence, not knowing where Phil was until he phoned from the military hospital in D.C. He wrapped an affectionate arm around her quivering shoulders and slowly walked her toward the cottage, while Ray helped Aunt Rose Marie, glassy-eyed herself and feeling almost the same tender sentiments as her twin. The tears no doubt represented a mix of joy and relief, of love and thanks. Young men, somebody's children, droves of them, were dying in previously unheard of locales, Savo Sound and Coral Sea, the skies above Vella Lavella, Rabaul and Schweinfurt, the beaches at Gela. Blue Star mothers thrashed in the restless nightmare of a Gold Star prospect.

Ray Romanek keyed open the spacious trunk and began removing its bounty. Big Vic and Woody came across the short lawn to help. The brothers bear-hugged each other with loud back slaps and hearty bellows complimenting how great they looked. Woody, clad in casual pants and polo shirt, introduced himself to Ray. They had never met before. All three unloaded containers packed in dry ice: Italian sweet sausage, roasted peppers and onions, a small mason jar of preserved wild mushrooms, another larger one of green olives, and a gunny sack holding thirty ears of sweet corn. Two apple pies cradled in balled newspaper rounded out the glut. Coupled with Stella's liberal contribution, it would be a delicious picnic of great duration. Break out the Brioschi and Bromo Seltzer.

Phil tiptoed into the kitchen and whispered hello to Nancy and Stella, careful not to rouse the baby. Too late, she was awake and hungry, and let them know it. "Great lungs," the fullback laughed. "Sounds like the Turk!"

"Who's the Turk?" Nancy smiled.

"A platoon sergeant I was lucky enough to serve with. A heck of a man with a very loud voice."

"Well, Turk Luzak doesn't sound very feminine, so I think we'll stick with Irene," she laughed.

Woody stood off to the side, spotting the Silver Star and Purple Heart side-by-side among the rainbow of ribbons. Phil clutched a small valise his mother had brought from Ansonia. Inside, comfortable civilian clothes, "civies," fresh washed and folded shirt and slacks, along with a soft pair of cordovan shoes, awaited. "Use the bedroom over here to change," Woody offered. "You can leave your uniform on the bed or hang it in the closet, whichever you choose."

"Thanks, Woody. And I'm sure you've heard it before—you've got yourself one beautiful wife and baby."

August in Maryland usually means excessive heat and humidity, especially during the sun's vertical mid-day hours. But the fortunes of weather were kind this day to the little group picnicking on the Luzaks' grassy yard. The meal was as much a dinner of thanksgiving as a summer outing. Stella said it all for everyone when she offered thanks to God for the safe return of the two soldiers. Raising her wine filled glass, she spoke patriotically of deliverance from "our nation's enemies," and asked the Lord to protect and bless her brother Tony and all of America's sons and daughters in uniform. Seemingly concluding her invocation, the big-boned defense worker stepped a slack-covered leg onto a chair and pointed her glass toward Irene. "As the child's godmother…" she welcomed the baby into the family. Stella was enthralled with the "next generation." Her newly bestowed godmother status perhaps filled the void of her own fruitless union. She had married too late to bear offspring. The early adult years had been dedicated, willingly, to raising her two brothers. In some ways she regarded Woodrow as her very own baby… and now he had one.

Meanwhile the child played on a yellow quilted blanket, indifferent to the fuss. Vic, however, wore an impatient smile on the threshold of exasperation. He caught Stella's eye, politely suggesting that her benediction had run its course. Sipping homemade Dago Red on an empty stomach in Nancy's kitchen had loosened her tongue and lubricated emotions beyond her normal extroverted level. A gallon jug, the product of Ray and Rose Marie's cellar press, saw its measure drop by almost one fourth. Months at the Eastern Aircraft plant with little respite earned "the old gal" the right to unwind once in a while, Vic reasoned. Besides, today was a special event. "Her baby" had recovered from the punishing depths of incapacitating injury, and likewise, Phil, whom she hardly knew. And now the unexpected honor of *godmother*. She relished the limelight and basked in its glow—but everyone was hungry!

Realizing she had been rambling more than a tad, Stella abruptly blurted the three-word phrase which has always provided political orators a swift and graceful egress. "God bless America!"

"God bless America," and "Amen!" they responded. Clinking utensils and plates serenaded the summer air for about two hours along with happy conversation of days past and future hopes. More than twice, Violet Primo tenderly squeezed her handsome son's forearm without a word. Their eyes would meet and communicate more love in a fleeting blink than language could ever affirm. Thirty days in Ansonia—yes, she would have him home for a full month.

After Rose Marie's high-crust apple pies had been devoured, and coffee (with Ray's optional anisette) had been served, the captain ambled down by the small bluff. Hardly a hobble accompanied him as he enjoyed the soft Chesapeake breeze. Cup in hand, he sat in the dry grass gazing out at distant sailboats. A kaleidoscope of images flashed through his brain, a mix of the pleasant and ugly including the Hamia bash, grisly specters of men consumed by flame and steel, the Five-O-Four splattered over the Sicilian sky by his own side's guns, the ridiculously sashed official at Girasole. Only five or so weeks had passed. And yet it felt as though that compartment of his insignificant life had been sealed decades ago and deposited in the timeless vault of eternity, an infinitesimal episode shelved in the great cosmos of endless space.

He sipped the dark coffee laced with liqueur, greedily inhaling the licorice sweetness, rolling it across tongue and gums to absorb and savor. In a sense he was tasting life, deliberately experiencing its petty indulgence. The interred of Biazza Ridge would never again know the simple treat of coffee or pie, or sense the warm touch of a mother's affection. The contrast between the Maryland shore and the hellish cauldron of Sicily was not lost on his pensive soul.

"Got room for one more or is this a private party?"

Phil glanced up to see a cheerful Woody Luzak dropping to a squat beside him, a mug cradled between his hands. "I welcome the company," he answered softly. An awkward moment followed. Both men wanted to talk but neither wished to broach the other's privacy, to trespass on the private domain of things personal. Finally Primo broke the stillness. "What's your next step, Woody? Or should I ask, what's Uncle Sam got in store for you?"

"I think I've lucked out, at least temporarily." Luzak broke the squat and sat back, propping himself with a free hand. Squinting out at the Chesapeake water, he swigged hard at the coffee. "A colonel named Wallace has kind of become my patron the last few years. He runs what amounts to a public relations group at Aberdeen. Wallace pushed to get me into OCS." Woody drained the mug's remaining liquid. "While I was 'relaxing' at Reed, Colonel Wallace turned out to be my most frequent visitor. Other than Swifty."

"Swifty?"

"My wife," he chuckled. "Nancy's last name was Swift."

"Swifty," Phil repeated. "I like that!" His face lit up.

"So, as I was saying, Colonel Wallace offered to have me assigned to Fort Myer right in D.C., at least for the short term."

"Doing what?"

"Don't know… maybe a doorstop?" Woody allowed his mouth to form a tight grin. "From what I've seen at Reed, the Army's got enough doorstops… important ones too. And a lot of them are wearing stars." They both chuckled.

"How big is Fort Myer? I mean D.C. isn't that huge to start with."

"A little over six hundred acres. They refer to it as a military reservation, but I'm not sure exactly what the hell they do there."

"Probably got a lot of typewriters," Primo shrugged.

"Sure, someone's got to fight the paper war," Woody scoffed more in humor than contempt. "A lot of carbon paper moves through there. You know, memoranda in triplicate, copies of copies, the bullshit war." Luzak yanked a long grass shaft from the sun-baked lawn and played it between his teeth. "How about yourself?"

The fullback flopped onto his stomach, supported by akimbo elbows. His face took on a serious tone. "I'm going back if they let me. Too many reasons not to."

"You want to talk about it?" Woody asked, giving his new friend the opportunity to bare a decision no doubt troubled by conscience. He too had gone through a procrastinating period of soul-searching.

"Not really. How about you?"

Now it was first Lieutenant Luzak's turn in the barrel, if he so opted. He deliberated for a quiet minute. "Well, as long as we're playing true confessions… " Woody braked his response, catching a deep breath. "I think after my Fort Myer stint is played out, I'm going to request a combat command."

"Are you nuts?!" The voice cracked like a rifle shot. Nancy Swift Luzak, angry tears flushing her eyes, confronted the two men. But her challenge was directed at her startled husband. Obviously, it was all news to her.

Author's Note: Even though the Americal shoulder patch was not officially authorized until December 20, 1943 many wore it months prior to that date.

CHAPTER XVIII
WEDDING

DATE: SATURDAY, 27 NOVEMBER 1943

TIME: 1130 HOURS

LOCATION: BRISBANE, AUSTRALIA

Jacarandas, bougainvillea and flame trees graced the imposing mansion's long driveway. Evergreen shrubs, mainly sculpted oleander, leathery and lush, dominated the landscaped gardens artfully framing the crowded parking area. Autos, virtually all British, mostly Bentleys and Rolls-Royces, a single sporty MG, gleamed splendidly in the late morning sun like so many regal carriages-in-waiting at the ducal palace. Inside, the groom stood straight as the anecdotal string, his calm eyes belying the nervous knot tangling guts and stomach acid into nauseous panic.

Events had bulldozed a comfortable, loving relationship into the permanence of binding matrimony. He glanced at the white-uniformed Naval officer to his left and forced a weak nod, hardly reassuring. Evan Whitfield, best man and imminent brother-in-law, responded with an "I told you so" smile as broad as Anzac Square. Resplendently outfitted in dress blues, Roy Bauer, standing next to the Australian, tilted his head forward to catch a glimpse of his fellow Marine similarly liveried. Roy also teased a puckish grin. A silver-haired organist gushed out the repetitive strains of Beethoven's "Ode To Joy," her bony fingers smoothly easing one note into the next. Passive Reverend Jonathan Tilson, slight, with receding, oily hair plastered tight to a hawkish skull, clutched a black, leather-bound prayer book. His relaxed show of patience counterbalanced the impending spouse's flush of paranoia.

The powerful smell of fresh flowers flooded the great room, its sweet pungency reminding him of wakes he had attended back home in North

Carolina. Andrew repeated a masking smile toward the minister, wondering if the scrawny man ever shampooed or soaped his unctuous locks. Seventy plus well-dressed Brisbaners barely filled the makeshift chapel, most women exhibiting pleased smiles, the men somber…or so it seemed to Delane. Other than Roy, Colonel Maxwell and Gwen Cash, the attendees were either relatives or longstanding friends of the bride and her parents seated in the front row. Occasionally a flash bulb popped, triggered by a gangly, pasty-faced photographer in shiny charcoal suit and black tie. *More moribund than joyous,* observed the groom.

Numbed by the fragrance of cloying pollen and the mesmerizing organ, Captain Andrew Delane's mind journeyed back to late October and a pivotal discussion with Colonel Gordon Maxwell, for it had unleashed the chain of circumstances leading to today's decisive finale.

"I'm sorry, Andy, but you're much too valuable to this office, to this mission. I can't release you to the infantry or anyone else for that matter! You've become a key player in our intelligence scheme. What I'm saying is fact, not flattery. We've been over this before." The Colonel jerkily pushed a Lucky between his lips and struck a light from the waning book of C-ration matches. He dragged in deeply and exhaled, conscious not to blow the smoke in his subordinate's direction. "Don't press me on this one. Our friendship shouldn't become a consideration. Know what I mean?"

"Sir, I'd never overstep that line!" Andy bit the thin line of his lower lip.

"I know. Maybe I'm letting my own thwarted expectations, my inability to get into action, cloud my comments—if I can't go then neither can those around me. Do you think that's what is motivating me?"

Maxwell's dilemma was obvious. His group had grown, commensurate with the increased USMC involvement in theater operations. The staff had quadrupled since Delane's arrival almost a year and a half ago. Roy and Andy split the day-to-day workload, each supervising a half-dozen junior officers and sergeants, plus a bevy of typists and support personnel serving both sections. Continuity of command and ongoing projects were crucial to the unit's effectiveness.

"Colonel, I'm aware of your situation. It's just that I'm so damned frustrated, having flown a desk here in Brisbane through the entire Guadalcanal fireworks. I know you understand, sir, because you're going through the same agony."

Maxwell clenched the butt in his lips, running both hands through the short, fading hair at his temples, kneading the scalp and tanned ears. "At least you got into it on Bataan and Corregidor. My combat experience on a scale of one to ten is a big fuckin' zero! Hell, the only Jap I've ever seen is the Green Hornet's faithful Japanese companion, Kato. Come to think of it, someone told me that these days Kato's miraculously become a faithful Filipino companion!" He laughed heartily and removed the cigarette. "With the instant flash of an editor's imagination, our friend Kato has undergone an ethnic metamorphosis of astounding magnitude! Next thing you know, the Katzenjammers will be Cubans!" They both giggled a bit. The politics of war and shifting allegiances had reoriented the perceptions of comic strip enthusiasts, radio serial fans and statesmen alike. If only world conflict could be as easily solved by the creativity of a scriptwriter's pen.

The humor must have tickled Maxwell's generosity bone. In a moment of spontaneous empathy he proffered what he felt to be a fair compromise. "Against my better judgment, Captain, I'm going to offer you a labor-management proposition worthy of Samuel Gompers. And once having proposed it, I want you to promise to stop badgering me about a transfer. Understood?"

"Well, sir," he emitted a sly smile. "Before I commit to what amounts to surrender, I'd like to see what you're putting on the table."

"You're on," Maxwell countered, enjoying the repartee. "On or about November 1, the Third Marine Division will be assaulting Bougainville up the Solomon chain. You've worked on much of the coast-watcher information and mapping vital to the operation, so I'm not telling you anything you don't already know. What you probably don't know is that about three weeks later, the Second Marine Division will strike Betio Island, spelled B-E-T-I-O but pronounced 'Bay-show.'"

"I'm aware of it," Delane declared. "In the Gilbert Islands Tarawa Atoll. As a matter of fact our hydrographer friend, one Lieutenant Commander Evan Whitfield, and the RAN have advised Kelly Turner's staff that the coral reef approaching Betio requires shallow-draft landing craft, shallower than we've got. Apparently Admiral Turner's people are confident our new amphibious tractors, though in limited numbers, will overcome any obstacles." The captain raised a questioning if not skeptical eyebrow.

"Obviously you're cognizant of everything going on in the Pacific. Why is it I still act surprised?" He puffed out a skinny curl of smoke. "Yeah, that's the one, Betio. Either case, Bougainville or Betio, I guess I could send in an intelligence observer to check out the landing and serve in some kind of liaison role. Interested?"

Andy's face lit up. "Yes, sir!"

"Well, it's your deal, your choice. Which will it be, Bougainville or Betio?"

Captain Delane jumped up from his armchair and moved across the room to the huge map hugging the office wall. Using his pinky stub he traced the two options. "Christ, sir, that whole Tarawa Atoll is nothing but a speck of fly-shit in the deep blue sea. By the time the Navy's big guns and flyboys do their job, there won't be enough Japs left to do spit." He turned to face his boss. "I'll take Bougainville!"

Evening light had all but extinguished as Marla and Andy nibbled on macaroons, the remaining two of a batch purchased earlier from the little bakery on Edward Street. Pink Garden Villa was particularly picturesque when early dusk danced its warm glow through the tall west windows. Pink turned a neon magenta and white reflected like pearlescent sea shells. A soft radiance played across Marla's lips and hazel-green eyes, her golden hair accentuated by the sun's final rays. Andy sipped a few drops of treasured Drambuie, an earlier gift from Jock, allowing its sweet strength to slide along his tongue. *How positively decadent,* he chided. *The Whitfields are spoiling me rotten.*

Ambivalence continued to haunt Andy's conscience. Brother Marines and GIs were prepping to slam the Japanese on New Guinea, Bougainville, and Tarawa while he, like a pseudo Brahmin, luxuriated with Muranese crystal, sucking down expensive cordials in his pink castle. A magnificently beautiful woman was keeping him, sharing bed and ample larder. Each night and weekend he lived the fantasy of every serviceman—hell, of every man. This was the stuff of cinema: sailor and showgirl, cab driver and socialite, peasant and princess.

"Honey, I've got a few things on my mind," he started. "The night is especially beautiful and the mood so amorous I feel I should speak in whispers so as not to disturb anything."

Contentment shone from her raptured eyes, conveying the love pulsing deep inside. For her too, the last seventeen months had been fairytale-like. "Marla's Yank," the family called him. In her romantic mind she attached to him a litany of character traits: polite, handsome, considerate, fun, educated, passionate, well-spoken, athletic, honest, heroic, and Single! The latter descriptive had left her annoyed, not so much at him but at the prevailing circumstances which discouraged marriage. Andy's military status could change overnight, thrusting him in harm's way. If so, his conscience, unselfishly noble, didn't desire a young, grieving widow bound to his remembrance. No bereaved survivor would be sacrificed on the pyre of his memory.

"Yes, darling, it is a time for hushing," she answered softly. Marla also sipped a slender, crystal goblet of Drambuie. The superb concentrate of honeyed scotch coated and glistened her sensuous lips, inviting her cross-table partner to stretch to her. He kissed her candied mouth, tasting the moist spirit lingering there.

"Marla, I have to go away for a short while. But hold on, don't be over-alarmed. Let me finish before you start asking questions."

Marla Whitfield sat back, steely eyes riveted on Andy groping for precise words. "In forty-eight hours, I'll be leaving to do some, uh, liaison work. Unfortunately it's classified so there's no way I can disclose where. However, in all probability, I shouldn't be in any danger. There's no exact timetable, but I expect to be gone approximately seven to ten days, that's all."

"Why, Andy, I—"

"There's more," he cut her off. "The possibility of me being transferred to a fighting outfit in the future is most remote. Colonel Maxwell virtually informed me that I'll be riding out the war working for him. That means the Land Down Under will most likely remain my home base." He cleared a lump before lubing his pipes with another nip of Drambuie. Reaching into his pant pocket, Andy withdrew a small square box covered in fuzzy, purple velvet. "So I guess that means it's safe to get married after I return."

Opening the lid, he removed a diamond ring, the stone brilliantly cut but modest in size. "Marla Whitfield," he gently asked, "will you do me the honor of becoming Mrs. Andrew Delane?" He reached out to grasp her left hand quivering in delighted anticipation.

Marla, the voracious reader of reams of English literature, solver of bushels of crossword puzzles, could only squeal a strident, "YES!"

He moved to her side of the table and with the palm of his hand tenderly rubbed small circles on her back. He kissed the wet tears about her eyes and cooed, "I love you." That night, after countless pledges of endearment and predictions of eternal happiness, the lovers slept snugly wrapped in each other's arms.

DATE: MONDAY, 1 NOVEMBER 1943

TIME: 0730 HOURS

LOCATION: BOUGAINVILLE

Cape Torakina, forming the southern point of Empress Augusta Bay, had been selected as the landing site for the 3rd Marine Division's invasion of Bougainville. To confuse the Japanese, the Marine Corps conducted decoy attacks in strength on the enemy-held island of Choiseul and in so doing paved the assault to the largest of the Solomons, Bougainville. Captain Andrew Delane had overstepped his authority, convincing an intelligence officer of the 9th Marine Regiment that he should accompany its 3rd Battalion assailing a beach sector coded RED ONE. The division's two lead regiments, the 3rd and 9th, would storm the high dunes. With them, Marine Raiders in force would help breach the initial line of enemy resistance. On their heels, in subsequent waves, would come engineers plus the divisional artillery regiment, the 12th Marines. Several days would pass before infantrymen of the 21st Marines, departing Guadalcanal on November 4, would complete the 3rd Marine Division's rotation. And soon army units, specifically the American and 37th Infantry Divisions, would join the action.

The LCVP in which Delane rode through the swirling surf of Empress Augusta Bay contained close to forty Marines. Peering over the bulkhead, the captain immediately determined the beach to be inadequate. Landing craft were being spun by invisible rushes of undertow, only to be uncontrollably propelled sideways by whipsawing waves. Many had simply been beached rather than risk jeopardizing their passengers. Red, Yellow, Blue, and Green beaches collected the steel litter of small ships aidless against the tide. In a few cases, they crashed into one another, bending landing ramps like tin cans, jamming some inoperable.

Marines laden with the tools of death struggled over the sides, taking their chances in the shallows. As craft were pitched onto the sand, the succeeding assault waves had nowhere to disembark, so the coxswains let them ride in, plowing into already strewn vessels. Delane's craft wheeled in the closing surf. Helplessly it had saddled a rolling wave, its port side leading the way. Had Jap gunners been evident, a broadside target would have presented an unmissable target. With a crunching lurch, the LCVP slid through wet sand

and careened to a wobbly halt. No one had to blow a whistle or shout "last stop" as a disorderly gaggle of men exited anyway they could.

Armed with only a holstered .45 caliber pistol, Andy raced to the high dune obstructing the view beyond. *Shit,* he cursed, *if a half-decent hydrographer had scoped out this place, maybe we could have avoided all these pile-ups.* A quick check of his wristwatch showed it to be 0743 hours. Salvos fired earlier from the destroyer fleet's five-inch guns and TBF Grumman Avengers out of New Georgia had ushered the shock troops to the shore. Fortunately there existed no Japanese where the 9th Marine's had landed. Farther south along stretches of Blue Beach, the 3rd Marines were not so lucky as bunkered weapons raked their approaching craft.

Overhead, Val Dive Bombers and a flight of Kates harassed the shoestring strip of beach. Eventually they were shot down or driven off by Allied fighter planes, mostly New Zealanders, until combined American Navy, Marine and Army Air Corps fighter cover, designated AIRSOLS for Air Solomons, could establish an umbrella screen. Still, a number of enemy aircraft were able to penetrate early on and strafe the beach approaches and sitting duck transports stationary in the expansive bay. Aggregates of Marine infantry collected themselves and rushed the bluff-like dune in a dead sprint. Andy scaled the thirty feet of sand comprising the natural embankment's face and carefully surveyed what he expected to be the jungle beyond. To his amazement, all that stretched ahead was an unending swamp, virtually impenetrable. The flooded morass explained the absence of Nip defenders.

Men looked to their leaders for instructions. Perplexed officers radioed for directions. Plow ahead or skirt the barrier? Gyrenes trained for such contingencies waded into the slimy web to ascertain its depth of field and probe for lurking defensive positions. On hold, the 9th Marines temporarily dug in. After a short interval the scouts emerged only to confirm what all suspected. The swamp was impassable. Later someone recalled that it was "like running across ten yards of Sahara and suddenly dropping off into the Everglades!"

The 3rd Marines had not encountered the same hazardous surf. Instead they were channeled smack into the limited yet deadly enemy beach defense. Delane could hear the gunfire and vibration of muffled explosions, their dull thuds fracturing the morning humidity. First Battalion-Third Marines had come ashore in the heart of it, their landing boats under fire from both

Cape Torokina and close-by Puruata Island, an offshore isle simultaneously under assault by Marine Raiders.

As an "observer," Andy had the flexibility to roam the battlefield. Trotting along the protective dune base he pushed south, laboring in the soft, restricting sand, now reflecting glaring heat from the equatorial sun. Crouching low, he weaved through clustered platoons and company H.Q.s, attempting to establish situational control as more men sloshed ashore and bunched up. He rapidly crossed Yellow Three and Two, empty of Marines, and entered the Blue sections where disciplined leathernecks of the 3rd Marines pressed inland. With great courage, they attacked and destroyed a small network of bunkers, one of which in particular housed a 75mm gun which apparently had blown quite a few LCVPs out of the sea with the lethal accuracy of point blank fire. *How could our Naval gunfire booming murderous high explosives on the assault area have missed such a seemingly obvious target so close to the waterline?*

Scores of dead Japanese lay in clumped heaps where they had been mowed down fleeing grenades tossed into the bunker's mouth. Flies and various tiny insects already bristled about the corpses. Delane pushed his way inside the dark pit. A narrow gun port looked out at the Bay. The 75's line of sight was direct, able to fire like a gigantic rifle. Shell casings and the acrid stink of gunpowder permeated the enclosure. Her crew evidently enjoyed little tolerance to traverse the weapon, the portal lacking any width, providentially for incoming craft off to the left and right. Elevation though had not been a problem. Peering out of the commanding gun port, Delane's naked eye could make out the mighty armada of crisscrossing destroyers and what appeared to be a cruiser perhaps four miles out. Marine grenades propelled by arm power, puny in contrast to the Navy's floating cannons, had done what the ships had unwittingly ignored.

DATE: THURSDAY, 4 NOVEMBER 1943

TIME: 1030 HOURS

LOCATION: ABOARD THE USS GENERAL R.B. PETERSON
                 TWELVE MILES WEST OF THE
                 SHORTLAND ISLANDS

Three days following D-Day, Captain Delane, freshly showered and clean-shaven, reclined in the quiet stateroom of a transport to Guadalcanal. Once there he would catch a hop out of Henderson Field to Australia. Fortunately for him, Bougainville had been somewhat of a surgical episode, in and out like a thin scalpel. He knew the horror had hardly begun for the men expanding the beach-hugging perimeter. Counter-attacking Japanese would contest the American incursion with merciless ferocity during the ensuing bloody months.

Delane used the voyage to organize his notes into facts supporting two conclusions. First, amphibious landings required highly accurate hydrographic and topographic data, both tidal and beach, to maximize the effectiveness of landing operations and prevent a disaster of catastrophic proportions should craft get hung up on shoals, cross currents, etc. Second, supporting Naval gunfire had to do more than blindly saturate the beach. Initially it must identify and hone in on specific targets. Gunnery officers on ships eight thousand yards from the impact area required more than binoculars to guide the potential supremacy of their guns. More diligent intelligence, it would seem, should be able to surmount these challenges. In Brisbane, he would prepare a report backed up by clear-cut examples of the Bougainville experience. Perhaps it would encourage a better assessment for the Tarawa invasion later in the month. The brief would include recommendations urging the formation of an intelligence group geared exclusively to deal with future seaborne intrusions.

Strains of Lohengrin shook Andy from his reverie and directed wide-eyed attention to the spiral staircase garlanded in bowed ribbon of snowy white and gold. He caught his breath as Marla appeared at the upper landing. At once, all qualms evaporated. If he had harbored any nervous reticence it fled with the angelic sight of his exquisite bride. Dressed in a white, silk two-piece suit cut at the knee, she smiled with a great show of happiness, proclaiming open confidence in her decision to marry. Lily of the Valley and Baby's Breath embracing a clutch of ivory camellias were held close to the wide cloth buttons securing her smartly cut lapels. A small pillbox hat understated with half-veil in pristine white perched above the creamy white earrings. A mid length strand of exquisitely matched pearls embellished her long throat. Complimenting high heels accentuated the young woman's statuesque height, resembling "a goddess descending from the Olympian clouds," as one agog guest whispered louder than his spouse would have wanted. A rush of excitement jangled along Andy's spine as he soaked in the dazzling vision.

The wedding and its suddenness had thrown the family into social turmoil. Cynthia and Jock had always assumed their only daughter would wed in a cathedral with several hundred in awed attendance. Fittingly, a colossal reception would follow, with dignitaries and vassals from the sprawling corporate empire respectfully paying homage to the lords of Whitfield Pacific. Instead, a "simple" house wedding would suffice with a meager smattering of family and special friends. Undoubtedly, the unexpected dash to matrimony caused some tongues to wag, suggesting the eager bride to be pregnant. Incorrect as that rumor was, once the gossip seeded itself it became more difficult to defuse. Denial only stimulated "where there's smoke there is fire."

Marla's option was one of conscience, as she dissuaded her reluctant parents, intent on an ostentatious show. "When Australians are voluntarily making untold personal and financial sacrifices for the war effort, I won't flaunt our wealth with a grandiose church spectacle and high society reception. I am most content to forgo such pomp for a house wedding and lunch, small and simple! No Anglican cathedral, no bishop, no pageant!" And so it was agreed with hugs of love and great respect.

At the staircase bottom, Jock Whitfield, feudal master of commercial enterprise, offered his daughter an arm and proudly walked her to the little group knotted about Reverend Tilson. He kissed his "baby" on the cheek and shook Andy's hand before retiring to Cynthia standing in the first row. They held hands, finding strength in each other's grip to stifle the swell of joyful tears.

CHAPTER XIX
PAVUVU

DATE: THURSDAY, 30 MARCH 1944

TIME: 0915 HOURS

LOCATION: PAVUVU, RUSSELL ISLANDS
       60 MILES NORTH OF GUADACANAL

"What kind of horse shit are you dealing, Luzak? I understand you've got one hell of a reputation as a first class Marine, but I'm not about to swallow this 'last order' story without some kind of corroboration." The personnel officer pushed a wrinkled utility sleeve across his upper lip, dispersing tiny beads of collected sweat. Over the years, Major Ed Hollis had heard many strange requests supported by phantom substantiation; however, a supposed command given two years earlier on Corregidor represented the flimsiest yet.

Master Sergeant Anton Luzak had arrived on the God-forsaken island of Pavuvu two days earlier. *God-forsaken* is a phrase overworked by humans relegated to environments of ill favor. But for those who would breathe the unending ilk of decaying coconuts and crushed land crabs sun-boiled to a putrid stench; and when crawling scads of itching, stinging insects and pilfering rats take up housekeeping where men choose to inhabit; and again when humid slime and torrential rain foster jungle rot to aggravate crotch and pit, then truly it is a place of no consequence to the lord. Perhaps unforgiving Pavuvu's only saving grace was the view from afar, looking in to Macquitti Bay, postcard tranquil.

First Marine Division veterans, after four months warfare on New Britain, mostly in the western Cape Gloucester sector, would be steaming aboard "sweat box" troop transports to the Pavuvu paradise after sustaining 1,393 battle casualties, while all but wiping out the Japanese 17th Infantry Division. Fatigued and sickly, they were expected to land sometime after

April 27. Needless to prophesize, their disappointment with the "rest area" would be massive. Luzak's premature arrival had been prompted by Colonel Julian Frisbie, regimental commander of the Seventh Marines, who sent an advance party ahead to insure the Seventh's future location would be the most optimum available, dry and high. As it turned out, no such neighborhood existed.

"Sir, I just learned yesterday that the Raiders were disbanded on Guadalcanal in January or February and the men were used to re-form the Fourth Marines, the very same Fourth that was destroyed at Corregidor. I'm one of the few to escape, ordered out by Colonel Howard on a special mission. He foresaw that the regiment would someday be reconstituted and it would take old China Marines like myself to rekindle its spirit, kind of a link to the past." The old salt surprised himself by the eloquence with which he pleaded his case. "So you see, Major, this is an order I'm obligated to obey. And scuttlebutt has it that the Fourth has occupied Emirau Island. Even though there was no fighting, it was my duty to have been with them… and I wasn't!" Tony's jaw tightened, locking his teeth in a bitter grimace.

Hollis could discern the fire raging in the leatherneck's eyes. This was no frivolous transfer request. Emotions meaningful and honorable dwelled before him. Tony Luzak, battle-scarred warrior extraordinaire, owned a service record heavy with exploits and recognition achieved by only a select few. "Luzak, either you've got a pair of stones larger than Errol Flynn or you're telling the truth. And I'm inclined to believe it's the latter."

"Thank you, sir."

"But if only there was a document or some piece of evidence to support your claim." The Major's quandary was obvious. Not only was he heeding the military's most self-serving tenet, "cover thy ass," but he also required tangible justification beyond sentiment to warrant Luzak's transfer.

"There is, sir."

"There is?" Hollis' slump perked to attention.

"I escaped The Rock with a First Lieutenant Andrew Delane. Last time I heard, he was assigned to the USMC Mission in Brisbane, some kind of hush-hush billet. Lieutenant Delane was privy to the exchange between the Colonel and me. Sure, he heard the whole thing. I'm confident he'd remember it even though so much was going on." Tony's enthusiasm caused him to speak at a quick clip. He punched his palm with a loud slap.

Perspiration spread out in expanding blots from the armpits and collar of the Major's wilted uniform. Morning steam flooded both their bodies even though they stood virtually inactive. A paltry effort of exercise would no doubt render saturation complete. Soon, some twenty-thousand-odd Marines, exhausted and irritated, would be swarming over the island's swampy grunge. The dismal forecast predicted tropical rain in great persevering waves.

"Fortunately, dispatches are being forwarded to Brisbane all the time. If this Delane is still there, it should be a simple matter to obtain his confirmation." Major Hollis had come over to Luzak's side. Accommodating (for a personnel officer), he actually was plotting to assist Tony. Living legends have a way of enlisting assistance. "Of course it will have to be cleared through your chain of command."

"Of course, sir. Under normal circumstances I would have approached Colonel Puller with this request. As you are aware, he's in Cape Gloucester."

"Puller's XO of the Seventh now. Isn't he?"

"Yes, sir. But word is that before long he'll be commanding his own regiment, probably the First Marines. Strange as it may sound, General Rupertus doesn't share this kind of information with me." Luzak offered a tight grin to emphasize that he spoke in jest. Tony wasn't very good at humor so he wished to make sure Hollis didn't misconstrue wit as impudence. One could never tell about personnel officers.

Timeless clichés by the score had been overused in explaining the reconstitution of the Fourth Marines on Guadalcanal. Analogies were drawn from Bible and classics. Overnight it became a veteran regiment in that most of its aggressive fighting men were drawn from the broken-up Raider battalions which had fought brilliantly on The Canal, Tulagi, Bougainville, the Makin Island foray, and other actions. The regenerative power of the Fourth was likened to the great mythical phoenix bird rising from its own ashes, reborn and more powerful. And also like the indestructible salamander of mystic folklore, it had withstood the consuming flame of an arsonous enemy, converting the heat to forge a steel of greater strength—durable, resilient beyond conquest.

The restless souls of Corregidor's fallen, of the Shanghai garrison, of Sam Howard, and Salty Waters had stirred a new beast, steeped in tradition, hellbent on avenging the past. Regeneration, re-dedication, and revenge— the three *R*'s of the re-minted Fourth Marine Regiment—provided motive and purpose for the rancorous business down the line. And throughout the

Corps, loyal Marines who had served a pump in the Fourth, who pridefully referred to themselves as "China Marines," cajoled and pulled strings over long distances to rejoin their old regiment. Such is the residue of espirit de corps. The time-worn compulsion to rally to the colors was never in greater evidence.

DATE: SUNDAY, 16 APRIL 1944

TIME: 1315 HOURS

LOCATION: PAVUVU, RUSSELL·ISLANDS

The unending drizzle of rain pounded a monotonous drumbeat on Hollis' corrugated metal roof. Outside, a jeep with leaking canvas roof splashed to a halt, its ponchoed driver indifferent to the muddy spray. Letting it idle, he slipped the gearshift into neutral and pulled up hard on the hand brake. The messenger sloshed onto the pallet leading to the entrance and handed the seated clerk typist a damp, webbed courier bag. On the way out, a crunching splat sounded as his heel inadvertently crushed an unlucky land crab. Its anthracite bluish black shell and gooey innards hugged the floorboard like a rotten egg dropped from the ceiling. Pretending not to notice the damage for fear he'd have to clean it up, he hurried to the little vehicle and plowed through puddled ruts toward his next delivery.

"Anything for me?" the Major asked from across the room.

Opening the bag, the bespectacled clerk withdrew two envelopes, one of the large, yellow manila variety, the other small and white. He unwound the red wax twine securing the wider jacket flap and peeked inside. "Looks like a roster of replacement troops coming in aboard the General Howze." He quickly eyeballed the cover sheet. "Seems like there's been a delay though, sir. Won't be here until, uh, 'E.T.A. 3 June.' The Howze will be hauling out Marines being rotated back to the States, according to the order. Lucky bastards," he added.

Hollis responded with a barely perceptible grunt of acknowledgment. "What's in the other envelope?"

"Marked 'Personal' for you, sir." He got up and walked it across to the curious Major.

MEMORANDUM

FROM: USMC MISSION, BRISBANE AUSTRALIA 1600 8APR44

TO: HOLLIS EJ MAJ PERS OFF FIRST MARDIV PAVUVU RUSSELL/ SOLOMON ISLS

SUBJ: LUZAK ANTON J MASTSGT

PURSUANT YOUR REQUEST RE CORROBORATION, THIS IS TO SUBMIT VERIFICATION THAT I WAS PRESENT WHEN COL S HOWARD, COMMANDING FOURTH MARINES, INSTRUCTED THEN GUNSGT LUZAK, ANTON J TO "CONSIDER IT MY LAST ORDER (TO YOU)" THAT IF AND WHEN FOUR MARREGT IS RECONSTITUTED LUZAK TO JOIN SAID REGT. MY UNDERSTANDING THEN, AND NOW, LUZAK REPRESENTS A MANDATORY LINK BETWEEN OLD AND NEW.

ABOVE TOOK PLACE CORREGIDOR ISLAND PHILIPPINES ON OR ABOUT 13 MAR 1942

DECLARE ABOVE STATEMENT ACCURATE TO BEST MY RECOLLECTION.

DELANE, ANDREW S CAPT USMC

CHAPTER XX
POWER

DATE: MONDAY, 3 APRIL 1944

TIME: 0725 HOURS

LOCATION: BRISBANE, AUSTRALIA

The officer passed through the lobby security Marine and, dismissing the open elevator, decided to travel via the staircase. He took the steps two at a clip as if to exercise the sleepy languor from his calves. Married life and the disarming serenity of Pink Garden Villa had caused him to dally an awful lot lately. Normally he'd arrive at the Mission before 0700. But the relative isolation of PGV had lulled Delane into a morning lethargy, comfortable and untouchable in his stuccoed cocoon, immune to the pressures of duty. Still, a troubled conscience, restless and driven, sniped at his soul with arrows of self-imposed guilt. Bougainville, instead of placating feelings of inadequacy, had only served to remind him that he was delinquent, a malingerer avoiding the gut essence of his chosen profession. Circumstance had maneuvered him into a job billet in which decanter supplanted canteen, paté superseded K-Ration. Today, April 3, Delane would be shaken from apathy and injected into an adventure of scintillating peril beyond anything he would have contemplated.

He briskly wove his way through the blocky military desks manned by busy Marine specialists processing and analyzing data entering the Mission's nerve system. Ringing phones and the clatter of typewriters added to the activity. The big room seethed with a bustle of officious energy. Messengers entered and departed without a word. Those delivering, thrust out yellow-hued vouchers for signature. Pick-up couriers themselves signed similar slips acknowledging receipt of sealed correspondence. Moving to the communal coffee urn, Delane drew himself a mug before slipping into his office.

To his surprise, Colonel Gordon Maxwell sat behind the Captain's desk, ostensibly in anticipation of his arrival. Trying to read the senior man's mood, Andy set the ceramic cup on a bookshelf bragging a photograph portrait of Marla. Was he perturbed, or simply anxious to initiate a new project? Technically their workday didn't start until 0730; however, the unwritten code encouraged officers be present a half hour earlier, both to set an example to the enlisted men and to get a jump on the day's business.

"Rough weekend?" the colonel greeted.

"Not especially, sir." *Is the old man being sarcastic or am I over-suspicious?*

Maxwell rolled a dummy grenade paperweight between his palms, a nicotine-stained index finger showing a stubborn saffron pallor. He returned it to a short stack of typed reports next to the phone and stood. Gesturing the captain to take his spot, he moved to the right as the two men rotated positions in an unspoken choreography of sorts. They both sat, continuing to stare at each other with looks of uncertainty. Situated in the middle of the desk blotter sat what appeared to be a memorandum, lying flat but exhibiting soft creases where it had been folded. "This arrived in this morning's dispatches. What the hell's it all about?" He slid the sheet closer to Delane.

SECRET FROM: CINCPAC 1030 2APR44

TO: MAXWELL, GORDON COL USMC

USMC MISSION/BRISBANE AUSTRL

SUBJECT: PERSONNEL TRANSFER

BELOW LISTED PERSONNEL TO REPORT IMMEDIATELY TO AIB HQ BRISBANE. RE TDY ASSIGNMENT UTMOST IMPORTANCE. FULL COOPERATION NECESSARY.

DELANE, ANDREW S CAPT USMC

1.) UNTIL FURTHER NOTICE DELANE NO LONGER ATTACHED USMC MISSION BUT WILL CONTINUE DRAW PAY AND ADMIN THROUGH MISSION.

2.) MAXWELL TO ACCOMPANY DELANE AIB BRIEFING ASAP. TO COORD STINGMAN, RJ MAJ USA NLT 3APR44

BY DIRECTION: MCBRIDE, F.X. REARADM USN

CC: RITTER, A.K. BRIGEN USMC

After digesting the order a second time, a perplexed Delane could only shrug. "I have no idea, sir. Not even an inkling."

"You're not pulling a fast one on me are you, Andy? **I** thought we made a deal—you observe the Bougainville operation and forget about transferring to a combat outfit."

"Colonel, I swear to you that I haven't gone behind your back. Besides, the Allied Intelligence Bureau is hardly an infantry outfit. Hell, they conduct behind-the-scenes sabotage and cloak-and-dagger stuff. That's way out of this marine's league."

After MacArthur escaped Corregidor for the comparative sanctuary of Australia, he ordered the formation of the AIB under the auspices of his chief intelligence officer, Major General Charles Willoughby, who soon developed a reputation as a brilliant but stern intelligence czar. Perhaps *kaiser* would be the more appropriate descriptor inasmuch as Willoughby had been born in Germany, christened Karl Weidenback before Americanizing it. To this day, **he** spoke with ponderous accent. Seemingly, the Kato syndrome reached all levels of endeavor. Fiction wasn't its only province.

The AIB's tentacles embraced operations of the most clandestine and destructive nature beyond traditional information-gathering. Included within its arcane structure were branches devoted to Special Operations (a mild pseudonym for sabotage and assassination), Propaganda, and a division so secretive it had no name, though its mission involved intercepting and decoding Japanese transmissions.

Additionally, AIB oversaw Australian "coastwaters" dispersed throughout the Solomons and other island chains, surreptitiously reporting Japanese air and naval movement. The latter, under the banner of Operation Ferdinand (like the flower-sniffing bull of storied note), proved to be invaluable especially during the Guadalcanal effort. A lesser known facet of the Allied Information Bureau was its Philippine Section, headed by Courtney Whitney, Sr. since the middle of 1943. Whitney was brought in as a bird colonel and ultimately would rise to the rank of major general. His knowledge of the Philippines was broad and in-depth, having lived twenty years in Manila practicing law. During World War I, Whitney had served as an Army pilot, so this was no civilian pretender. It was into this byzantine Philippine Section that Andrew Delane would be absorbed and disappear from the Brisbane scene without so much as a postcard to his bride of four months.

"Well," Colonel Maxwell mused aloud, "I guess I'd better get hold of this Major Stingman pronto. AIB is serious stuff."

At 1400, US Army Major Rudy Stingman, deeply tanned and gaunt, slid the knot of his maroon necktie snug against the top button and smoothed its breadth tight to the chest. Stingman looked more like an insurance salesman than someone with his thumb on the pulse of guerrilla activity on Leyte. Loose-fitting and crumpled, his gray and white seersucker suit gave him a somewhat frumpy appearance, which belied the bulldog inside. Maxwell figured him to be thirty-two at the youngest, assuming the receding chestnut hairline to be premature. Like many in military intelligence he preferred the inconspicuous garb of the civilian world. It permitted him to move freely and meet with agents and various contacts without arousing curious inquiries. Better to travel inconspicuously in the public landscape.

Stingman's meeting room was equally indistinguishable. Only an overblown black and white photostat of Leyte served as wall decor, if one chose to call it that. A small wooden table, rectangular and plain, surrounded by folding metal chairs, furnished the austere room. The word "functional" quickly leaps from one's vocabulary. Two black telephones sat on the block tile floor in diagonal corners. Several folders marked with orange grease pencil were piled to the Major's right, weighted by an oval ashtray containing remnant debris from earlier conferences. Chair legs squealed against the bare tiles as the three men piloted them to a tighter perimeter.

Rudy Stingman spoke with a serious voice, though non-threatening. Introductions finished, he got to the point straight away. "Captain Delane, you've been selected by the AIB for one reason only, more specifically for one man only… Antonio Rizal!" He searched Andy's eyes for reaction but none came. Andy had his antennae out, seeking to sense vibrations of information, to determine what the Secret Orders stipulation of TDY, or "temporary duty," was all about. "You do know him, don't you?" the major probed.

"Yes, of course, sir." Like a witness in a court of law his laconic response provided only the most niggardly affirmation.

"He wants you!"

Maxwell withdrew a pack of smokes and offered it around. No takers. He expertly flipped the package to his conditioned lips and extracted one. Snapping a veteran Zippo, the colonel inhaled a puff, holding it for several seconds while he studied Stingman's inexpressive almost colorless eyes. "Sorry to disappoint you, major. But also my wife, I'm a married man."

Andy's mouth formed a hint of a smile. Both Stingman and Maxwell emitted perfunctory laughs before the major again took hold of the conversation.

"Gentlemen, let me provide a bit of background as to what's going on. AIB's Philippine Section essentially is laying the groundwork for the reconquest of the commonwealth. We control a guerrilla army of over 175,000, scattered throughout the archipelago under the umbrella of USFIP—United States Forces in the Philippines. Unfortunately, we don't have the unity of command inferred by the acronym. Huks in Luzon, some of whom are communists, splintered tribes acting unilaterally when it suits them, Moros in Mindanao, and so on. But where we have American officers in place, USFIP has been able to establish an impressive network of radio stations and weather reporting stations. My responsibility is the island of Leyte, almost 2,800 square miles with a spine of volcanic mountains running almost the full length of its north-south axis of 120 miles."

Stingman stretched out to the mounted map and casually indicated the axis line with pointed finger. "Much of the area is cultivated, sugar, tobacco, coconut, rice, the usual things. Rock asphalt, sulfur and manganese are the principal mining products. Technically the Province of Leyte also includes several lesser islands." He held up a file brochure. "It's all in here. Hand these over before you depart." He pushed the flat of his palm alongside the thinning hair. "There are roughly one million people inhabiting Leyte and virtually every one of them hates the Japanese with a savage passion. The Kempei Tai's ruthlessness has guaranteed that!"

Akin to the Nazi Gestapo, the Japanese secret police, Kempei Tai, committed daily atrocities against the Filipino guerrillas and general population with bestial indifference. "MacArthur's committed. He will return to the Philippines and wrest them from the enemy. For sure. The question is, in which sequence will our troops invade the individual islands and where will the actual landings take place?"

"And how does Rizal fit into all this?" Maxwell asked.

Major Stingman gazed across the table. "I'll take one of those cigarettes now, colonel, if they're still available." The head of the USMC Mission slid the pack of Camels to him and was about to offer his Zippo, but Stingman already had torn a match free from its book. Shaking out a butt, he quickly lit it. Three words—boldly simple yet more meaningful to a nation's expectation of freedom than any national symbol, graphic or otherwise—leapt from the match cover. The searing, indelible brand, "I Shall Return," saw itself proliferated on matchbooks throughout the great archipelago. Filipinos, regardless of their proficiency in English, rallied to its promise of hope. Similar to the "V," MacArthur's dramatic pledge of "I Shall Return," sacred and honor-bound, provided vital impetus to growing resistance. Fanned by the AIB, the sentence was printed on myriad items smuggled into the islands. Cigarettes, matches, pencils, chewing gum, candy bars, sewing kits, and packages of every variety carried the phrase, usually reinforced by a representation of the U.S. and Philippine flags. Often the wrappers of such packages were purposely discarded where the Japanese occupation forces would find them. Psychologically it caused the enemy to seethe and worry about MacArthur's coming. Foolishly they had allowed him to escape the strangulation of Bataan and Corregidor. That fatal flaw, magnified by Mac's prophetic vow, ate at the Niponese penchant for pre-destiny. Evading capture had set stars in motion that ordained his messianic advent which no human force could prohibit. And for the defiant citizens of Panay, Mindoro, Cebu, Palawan, Bohol, and the entire scattering of islands huge and diminutive, "I Shall Return" allowed them to silently thumb a collective nose in haughty contempt. *Yes, our day will come!*

"Yes, I'm interested, myself," Delane said. "What is Rizal's role?"

"Leyte is one of those islands," Stingman began, "that we'll have to invade. That's no military secret. The Japs know it as do we. However, so will Mindanao, Luzon, Negros, and a host of others. Antonio Rizal heads up the guerrillas, indeed the resistance movement for all of Leyte."

"Really!" Andrew said. "I thought his home base was on Mindanao, specifically Zamboanga and Misamis Occidental provinces."

"It was," the major continued, "but he was promoted for his diligence and given control of Leyte and its attendant island of Biliran, just north, and has done a fine job there too, I might add. The problem is that Rizal has political aspirations. He views himself as an intellectual leader, above the squabbling political hacks who would guide the nation following liberation. He is fearful that many are nothing more than Yankee puppets who will footdrag the achievement of independent nationhood."

"Antonio is also half Moro which would seem to provide him some kind of advantage if played correctly." Delane was into it. He sensed Stingman's narration would no doubt spin a devious web of intrigue and maneuver… *but where do I fit in?* "So, where's the problem?"

"The problem, Captain Delane, is that in exchange for his devoted cooperation, Rizal wants Uncle Sam to commit political support to him personally…or at least a guarantee."

"Why no give him that guarantee? He's more than competent by your own admission. And my experience with him, albeit limited, convinced me that he's both ethical and brilliant." Andy leaned forward, his face no more than fifteen inches from Stingman's, swarthy and dry from outdoor exposure.

"If only it were that simple. Unfortunately, Rizal has formed an alliance of sorts with Luis Tarluc, leader of the Huk resistance, or Hukbalahaps, on Luzon."

Andrew Delane screeched his chair back a foot in order to cross his legs, resting ankle on knee. "I guess I'm in the dark. Who's Tarluc?"

"A communist! And a bona fide, fire-breathing rabble-rouser, I understand." Colonel Maxwell's interjection struck to the core of the issue.

"Precisely," the major confirmed. "Now that's not to say Antonio Rizal is a commie, but it's the old birds of a feather association. Perhaps this bond with Tarluc is one of those pragmatic relationships necessitated by war. You know, political expedience often makes for strange bedfellows! My superiors in the AIB, all the way to the Secretary of Defense and the State Department, I'm certain, aren't about to endorse a suspected communist. Plain and simple!"

"So, what is it you require of Captain Delane?" Maxwell was starting to twitch.

He had dealt with AIB in the past, and didn't trust them wholly even though he respected their effectiveness.

"As a result of our refusal to back him, a long-range pissing contest has erupted between Rizal and AIB's Philippine Section. He's become most suspicious of us, maybe fearing a double-cross of some sort. I don't know for sure. The fact is that he has declared our last two agents unacceptable! There is little dialogue between us other than coordinating supplies shipped to him via submarine. Like petulant lovers, Rizal and AIB are estranged, hopefully in the short term. We need a liaison with Rizal to help orchestrate his movements and assistance for the impending invasion. Our last agent exacerbated things by calling him an 'opportunistic demagogue' in a transmission which Rizal overheard, supposedly inadvertent. In short, the whole fuckin' thing has gone sour!" The frustration in Stingman's face caused it to flush a beet-red through the deep tan. He plunged the smoldering butt in the ashtray causing the coal to flatten out, dispelling sparked particles onto the table surface. "And that, Captain Delane, is where *you* enter! Rizal claims that the only, I repeat, *only* American he would trust in his midst other than Q-10 is you, Captain!"

213

The outwardly unruffled Delane tried not to expose the apprehension churning inside. "I guess I should be flattered."

"Captain, it is our intent to place you on Leyte for the purpose of reestablishing solid cooperation with Rizal's organization."

"And to spy on the man who saved my life?" Andrew's voice was matter-of-fact.

"In a word, yes!" Stingman's cold eyes froze an icicled beam between himself and the Marine.

"Christ," muttered Maxwell, "I was afraid of this. AIB is stealing one of my best men to perform some political hand-holding." He hammered a fist to the table causing the ashtray to rattle.

"Sorry, but our needs supersede those of the USMC Mission." The major spoke with a sympathetic friendliness, nothing cocky. "Neither General Willoughby nor I mean to leave you stranded on the beach, colonel. It's just the way things worked out."

"Beach!" Delane rose quickly and moved to the map. "You've got stations reporting on weather, troop movement, supply depots, air support, topographical boogie-woogie, etcetera." His hand revolved in a large circle about Leyte's periphery. "But the Army's amphibious troops have to come ashore somewhere. And that somewhere must be conducive to a landing in terms of coastal defenses and the beach, surf, tides, currents, depths, and so on. Major Stingman, we Marines, in concert with our naval cousins, are supposed to be experts in amphibious operations, but our experts stupidly paid zero attention to the hydrography of Tarawa, resulting in a God-awful fiasco.

"Earlier we stumbled into a somewhat similar problem at Bougainville, but fortunately there were few Japs available to slaughter the assault waves. If you or the Navy are not already developing this information, then you should, and I know how to get it done! Additionally, it will give me a tangible purpose beyond hand-holding Rizal."

"Interesting," Stingman observed. "I just assumed the Navy would have that info. What would you suggest?"

Delane smiled. *The plot thickens,* he mused. "There is a Royal Australian Navy hydrographer who escaped from Zamboanga with me in '42."

"Yes, I read it in your file. Whitman, wasn't it?"

"Whitfield. Lieutenant Commander Evan Whitfield," Andy corrected. "Not only is he a first-class hydrographer but he's familiar with the country, its people, and customs. Also he's a friend in good standing with Rizal, which makes him all the more ideal for this operation."

"Excellent!" the seersuckered man exclaimed. It was the first time his voice had shown any emotion throughout the meeting.

"Of course you can't just order him to go. You'd have to put in an urgent request."

"Don't worry," Stingman said, "I know how to handle that!" Then as an afterthought he inquired, "Does this Whitfield have any weaknesses I should know about?"

"Just two," Maxwell chipped in.

"What's that?"

"Big-titted women and Dom Perignon," he laughed.

They all laughed before Stingman said, "I suspect they're both in short supply on Leyte." Then, pushing the files to Delane, he asked, "Are there any questions that come immediately to mind?"

"Yes, sir," Andy said. "When do I leave, and who or what is Q-10?"

"Forty eight hours! You fly to Milne Bay on New Guinea this Wednesday. The following morning, a sub will carry you the rest of the way. All transmissions will be made directly to me, code name 'Stingray.' You will be identified as 'Electric Eel.' If Whitfield makes the trip, his moniker will be 'Electric Eel Two.'"

"How fitting. But I'd have thought Hydro-Electric Eel to be more appropriate."

"I get the humor," Stingman patronized before proceeding. "As for Q-10, he's one of our most valuable agents in Leyte. A Navy commander by rank, he moves like the fog from Tacloban to Hilongos. No reflection on you, Captain, but Q-10 is too valuable to remain exclusively with Rizal. He needs the freedom to roam at will. Q-10 will contact you once you've established yourself with the guerrillas. He'll be your superior on Leyte. It's important you understand that. I'll cover all this tomorrow during a more in-depth briefing. Incidentally, he's been such a thorn in the Japs' side that they've placed a reward of fifty thousand dollars in gold on his head."

Chick Parsons, alias Q-10, was the stuff of living legends. Operating on Leyte and Luzon, his harrowing exploits would become so extraordinary that the Kempei Tai elevated him to a position so exalted as to warrant the incredible bounty mentioned by Stingman.

"Colonel, captain, I know you both play by the rules but I'm duty-bound to remind that all we've discussed is highly confidential."

"Understood," Maxwell said. "And Major, there's something else you should know."

"Whats that, colonel?"

"Commander Evan Whitfield is the brother-in-law of Captain Delane." Maxwell waited for a note of surprise. It never came.

"Yes, I knew it all the time. I was just fishing with that Whitman bait. But thanks for your candor, colonel."

Outside the street air was cool. "Why do I have the feeling Stingman played us like a Stradivarius?" Delane said.

"Because he did. And besides, his name isn't Stingman."

"Really?" Andy was genuinely surprised. Sometimes he didn't give his boss enough credit for experienced intuition and perceptiveness, like sons and fathers. "Then who is he?"

"Chick Parsons, alias Q-10. Take your pick and call him what you wish."

The revelation hit Delane like a bucket of Rita Benton's chilled shrimp. It stopped him, immobile in his tracks. "You mean…"

"It's a tough business, bud. You're playing on a whole new playing field, very different from information-gathering at the Mission. Welcome to the varsity. Rule number one, trust very few, and watch your flanks and ass. Everything you do from here on must be weighed every which-a-way, militarily, politically, and most of all personally from a life-threatening perspective. I hope you understand what I'm attempting to communicate because, Andy, you are in the hot seat. Don't expect people to bail you out—your survival hinges on your own suspicious instincts.

"There are those who would sell out their own sister or Q-10 in the blink of an eye simply to advance their own cause. That's why agents like Q-10 have to insert buffers such as you, kind of like human shock absorbers. He cheats the prospect of capture and death only through subterfuge and misdirection. Christ, fifty thousand in gold makes him ripe for every Judas on Leyte. In the States, folks dream of a million dollars. Filipinos fantasize of a thousand! And now you will be exposed to circles of potential Iscariots where every player carries an ace up his sleeve. Find your own protective ace, Andy! Blackmail, perjury, coercion, and bribery are all instruments of the secret agent's profession. Manipulation through fraud and deceit is as commonplace as dirt.

"Rizal, Tarluc and the AIB will conspire as one only when it is of common benefit. Beyond that, each has his own agenda. Murder is termed 'execution,' larceny twisted to 'requisition.' War accelerates the cheapness of life…what's another corpse on the pile! The routine of slain civilians and enemy soldiers has it become easy for leaders of the movement to liquidate adversaries, or even petty nuisances, for that matter. Because on the surface, they view themselves as freedom fighters and vindictive crusaders, above any rules. You must understand their motivation and willingness to perpetrate anything!" Maxwell hesitated with the cognizance that his warning to Delane had spiraled into a philosophical diatribe.

"Please, colonel, go on. This isn't empty skepticism you're offering. It could save my life!"

"Okay, put this in your backpack for future consideration. The FBI, OSS, AIB and all the intelligence and counter-intelligence masterminds from Moscow, Berlin, London, and Tokyo always seek the one piece of leverage that will lead to dominance on the battlefield or the corridors of government. They will stop at *nothing* to achieve it. And the identical mindset trickles down to all their attendant organizations and subgroups. Those pawns caught in the nutcracker of power struggles are expendable like so many chess pieces. If there's a message here it's don't be a pawn, be a player. They stand a better chance to survive and play another game."

Andy stood agog, feeling naive and empty. At the same time, he sensed a new respect for his commanding officer. While he and Roy Bauer, officious and mildly self-important, cranked out reams of "intelligence dope" like a pair of eager beavers, Maxwell had been dueling atop the hill, protecting turf. Until now he had sheltered his underlings from the vicious in-fighting for control. Now for the first time, Andrew Delane comprehended that internal forces beyond his cozy dominion struggled for the mastery to dictate policy, to determine the fate of the unsuspecting, and in many instances to reap personal advantage. His father-in-law, outwardly benign and brimming with altruism, understood the true issue of power as did captains of industry and influence brokers in every venue. Visions of megalomania prompted by Maxwell's lecture crystallized in Delane's mind. He would become even more analytical of its scope and ramifications over the next few weeks, replaying history over again in his mind. With a suddenness he had become infatuated.

Power is never bestowed, he recollected from a collegiate poly-sci text, *but seized!* Rizal knew this, as did the kingpins controlling the politico-intelligence community. Survival and power drove such men. Maxwell's mysterious trips to Hawaii this past year no doubt went beyond strategic meetings. Negotiations and markers to be called in during future "chess games" were part of the horse trading. It was apparent now. Ambitious officers operated on a different plain, swapping information among their own, bartering secrets, even extorting favor. Some did it in the patriotic national interest, some for personal aggrandizement and glory, others driven by ideology or the preservation of a military culture…still it came down to *Power!* In its quest, the ruthless engender scant respect for honor and friendship, for the end justifies the means.

"Suddenly, colonel, I know exactly what you mean. And I appreciate your signals."

"I hope you do, Andy. I sincerely hope you do! As you've probably figured out by now, even though I expect you to share everything with me, there is much about Gordon Maxwell and what I do that can't be disclosed. Do you understand?" Before the younger man could respond, the colonel offered a deal, the deft reciprocity of which was blatantly clear. "I could be one of Electric Eel's ace cards—although a long distance one. But I can't help unless you maintain a link with the Mission." The contract was obvious. *Keep me informed and you've got yourself a reserve lifeline.*

"Yes, sir. The last few hours have enlightened me beyond the sun!"

"Good," Maxwell said, "because I do care about you and Marla, and Roy too. You're all fine people. In some ways I envy you." He paused to place a firm hand on Andy's shoulder. "So let me say it in even simpler terms. There could be one hell of a crossfire between Rizal and AIB. Don't get caught naked in no man's land or they'll shoot you full of holes!"

He speedily lit a fresh cigarette and exhaled, using the moment to mull how much more he should divulge. Until now he had generalized, putting out nebulous storm flags. "According to my contacts, Andy, I'm on the list for a star. As a general officer, my intelligence role will expand greatly. It has to, I know too much. Who knows, I could even be permanently integrated into AIB and be its highest ranking Marine."

Andy nodded, slow and deliberate. His friend was letting it all out. "Roger, sir," he whispered. "I know your call sign."

"If the shit gets too deep on Leyte, get word to me and I'll try to yank you out."

"Much appreciated, sir. And on a more cheerful note, congratulations on the star." They strolled a bit farther in the pleasant Brisbane air, crisp and dry.

"Oh, Andy, one thing troubled me in there. Why in hell did you volunteer Evan for a highly dangerous assignment?"

Captain Delane adjusted his fore and aft cap, or "cover" as the Corps identifies all hats. "Well, colonel, between us subterranean intelligence Marines, I guess I can share another piece of dope."

Maxwell grinned a receptive acceptance.

"This weekend, Evan confided that several crises were strangling his freedom and threatened to humiliate him. First of all, Rita Benton has been progressively imposing physical demands of the most sordid nature. She's wearing him down to a frazzled nub. This I found more amusing than cause for alarm. Second, she often speculates how wonderful it would be if Sir Harry met with a deadly accident. Evan views this as a gambit by lovely Rita to enlist his service in dispatching the old boy. The prospect has frightened him so much he's willing to abdicate his cushy job in Brisbane.

"Consequently, Lieutenant Commander Whitfield approached his superior officer, a commodore I believe, requesting an immediate transfer far from Australia. For him, even New Guinea would represent hospitable refuge. According to Evan, his C. O. emphatically refused, castigating him with, 'Whitfield, you're nothing more than a bloody snot whose offensive behavior and promiscuous reputation is an embarrassment to the RAN!'"

"Maybe he was right," Maxwell chuckled.

"Perhaps, but Evan responded by slamming the steel-cased door with great verve to show his displeasure. Unfortunately, the commodore's fingers were crushed in the slam. Whit swears it was unintentional. His boss believes the contrary and is bringing our friend up on charges. Saturday, Evan asked if there was any way his 'American brother' could influence his transfer to a U.S. base." Delane issued a toothy smile. "And today the AIB presented an option made to order. Of course I didn't realize then the political menace to which you've just alluded. Anyway, it's Whit's to accept, or decline."

CHAPTER XXI
CIPHER

DATE: MONDAY, 24 APRIL 1944

TIME: 0340 HOURS

LOCATION: LEYTE ISLAND, PHILIPPINES

Laboring up the narrow mud road, twin carabaos strained at the wooden yoke. Pale moon glow bounced from their massive shoulders tugging at leather harnesses, supple and dank with lathered sweat. In excess of five-and-a-half feet tall, the thick-muscled beasts snorted in concert with the overladen wagon's ancient beams creaking from stress. Though reinforced for special freight, the old cane wagon, bowed and deformed, rolled unevenly. Small fierce men in tattered khaki, some wearing frayed straw hats, trudged ahead and to the flanks.

In addition to magazine fed M-1 carbines, a few flaunted cavalry sabers strapped high on the waist. Inexplicably, an earlier shipment of Tommy guns destined for Filipino fighters had been mis-sent elsewhere, and in their manifest cargo the U.S. Quartermaster bureaucracy inadvertently substituted the sabers, relics from a backwater supply depot. Converted into jungle-clearing machetes and instruments of decapitation upon ambushed Japanese, they soon became very popular among the guerrillas. Of course they would have preferred the Thompsons. However, this was a resistance of innovative partisan warfare where nothing of value is wasted, and vital necessity motivates the mothers of invention. Consequently, the sabers became symbols of menacing opposition as well as functional cutlery.

An elderly peasant guided the water buffaloes, steering them with touches from a slender, polished stick, tapping either their haunches or widespread horns. Pine wood crates of varying proportions, several the size of a refrigerator, were symmetrically stacked on the wagon, their weight distributed so as to discourage an imbalance. Following behind, at least twenty bearers struggled with smaller boxes and waterproof canvas bags. The nocturnal caravan had been on the trail for close to four hours but covered no more than five miles. An American submarine had delivered the supplies along with two tall Caucasians to a beach rendezvous southeast of Abuyog.

Leyte's geography is laid out on a vertical line, the island pinched to its most constricted point in the center, roughly where Abuyog sits. From there it flares out at the upper and lower reaches like a distorted figure eight. A mountainous spine of tangled jungle forest runs the length. Ahead of the wagon but well behind the lead element, the visitors trudged in silence, loaded down with cumbersome packs.

They had departed Brisbane nineteen days earlier on a R-4D transport plane, the US Navy's designation of the Army Air Corps C-47. Known by many names, the workhorse "Dakota," as the Aussies and Brits called it, flew a course directly north to the Louisiade Archipelago before swinging due west toward Milne Bay at the easternmost tip of New Guinea. With a range of roughly twenty-one hundred miles, the trip fell comfortably within the transport's range. The tedious air voyage approximated fourteen hundred bouncing miles at an altitude of about eight thousand feet. Alternatively christened the Douglas Skytrain, goony bird, and also the DC-3 by its commercial clientele, the dependable twin-engined aircraft cruised at significantly over two hundred mph. Seven hours aloft was about all it took until touchdown at Milne. Yesterday the pair had been provided an in-depth AIB review of the sticky political situation, as deep as possible in twenty-four hours. The following evening, Delane and Whitfield hooked up with an American sub headed for the Surigao Strait and the southeast coast of Leyte.

When their rubber rafts came ashore in the moonlit stillness, they were hailed by a guerrilla identifying himself as Captain Rafael Criquel, "a trusted follower of Rizal." By way of recognition, he showed Major Delane a filigreed silver compass, the very same gift the American had bestowed on Antonio when they fled Zamboanga in early May, 1942. No other credentials could have been more valid. Criquel would lead them, along with the material of resistance, to Rizal's hidden redoubt.

Delane had been half-promoted to the temporary rank of major in order to equalize his rank with Lieutenant Commander Whitfield, RAN. In some circles he would be referred to as a brevet major. This way there could be no conflict of command. Even though Evan enjoyed greater tenure, or time in grade, the Marine was in charge, clearly. If and when they returned to Australia, Delane would revert back to captain. But for the duration of the Leyte assignment he would sport the gold oak leaves of a field grade officer. Sparse recompense for the chancy months ahead.

They had almost reached a small cane field where the jungle rose in a continuing sweep to the central cordillera. Suddenly a commotion sounded to their rear, followed by an agonizing wail trumpeting through the darkness. A timeworn harness strap had snapped, causing one of the straining carabao to lose its equilibrium. A hoof slipped into a rutted crevice, the full weight of the collapsing animal fracturing its foreleg like old wicker. Pained, the crippled beast lay on its side, the huge body heaving in ponderous agonizing breaths. Splintered bone, stiletto sharp, protruded through hide surrounding the ankle. No choice was open to the peasant other than to slit the throat deep and clean with a razor-edged machete. Within minutes, gallons of rich, sanguine fluid flooded the trailway, mixing with already moist earth to form a muddied, red gruel. Fresh meat was in short supply and soon the guerrillas' sabers had dismembered the carabao, reducing it to hefty slabs.

Rafael Criquel ordered the band to unload the wagon and manhandle its cargo into the hidden jungle mass. Guards would be left behind to protect its unwieldy bounty until others could return to haul it inland. Meanwhile, the old man guided the surviving buffalo in a semi-circle, towing the empty wagon away from the bloodied soil. Tears clouded his sad brown eyes. The butchered carabao had been more than a source of livelihood. He had raised and trained it, like a pet, from a calf. Now nothing remained other than gory mud and the remnants of a hacked carcass already drawing insects of the night. Within days maggots and scavenger birds, rodents and dehydrating sun would reduce the carrion to a pile of ivoried bones. Only a bleached skull, hollow sockets and smooth horns, would survive the ravage of nature's recycle.

Turning to a guerrilla sub-lieutenant, the elder inquired for compensation. The younger man angrily rebuked him. His "contribution" represented but a "pittance to overthrow the Japanese enslavers. For the cause! For victory!" He arrogantly shoved the old man and whirled imperiously to direct the transfer of supplies into the heavy growth.

Criquel sprang to the offending sub-lieutenant like an enraged jungle cat, seizing his shirt front, and raised a hand as if to cuff him with a backhanded blow. His threatening fist froze, suspended, but the intent was clear. "The people are our strength, you fool! You are fortunate Rizal is not present to witness this act. He would have you punished beyond my angry words. You treat our people no better than the Japanese. Remember the words of Rizal—the people are our strength!" He released the sheepish man who apologized for his haughty behavior. Rafael Criquel nodded. Even in the shadows of early morning darkness his eyes could be seen boring an ired beam into the guerrilla's cowering pupils.

Reaching into his grimy shirt, Criquel removed a small drawstring sack dangling about his neck. He removed several wrinkled banknotes and striding to the old fellow, took the peasant's bony hand and pressed the bills into the palm. The ancient one mouthed a thankful smile absent of many teeth. The captain hugged him gently and whispered, "Grandfather, this money is not much, not nearly enough to replace your fine carabao. But it is all I have."

Then he pulled a matchbook from deep within a flapped pocket and held it in such a way as to capture the dim moonshine. "And I give you this, the promise of MacArthur." The book did not have to be read to ascertain what was meant. *I Shall Return*, the message so ingrained in the phraseology of every Filipino, was as sacred as religion itself. Taking the matches, the old gentleman kissed the cover and touched Criquel. He spoke not a word. Instead, he turned away and spryly performed a little hop-step en route to the wagon, the jig his way of acknowledging faith in the guarantee of liberation. Stroking the remaining carabao, he uttered something sentimental and soothing, then the two of them ambled off into the blackness, the squeaking wagon in tow.

DATE: THURSDAY, 27 APRIL 1944

TIME: 1530 HOURS

LOCATION: LEYTE, PHILIPPINES (RED SEVEN)

Red Seven camp was small, containing less than fifty men concealed in its near invisible embrace under the verdant canopy. Huts, slightly elevated, constructed of sturdy bamboo, served as shelter from the damp rain forest carpet. Thatched roofs afforded protection from sporadic showers typical of the climate. They had eaten well these past few days, feasting on sinewy carabao steaks and a sort of native stew gleaned from less desirable cuts. Rizal maintained a series of self-sufficient encampments throughout his command. He had learned that larger concentrations of men attracted detection through the collective odor of cooking fires and human waste, and from the sounds of activity, regardless how subdued their efforts. Many whispers become a roar. Observation planes logically possess a greater ability to spot the presence of many, versus the scant. So the leader elected to spread his guerrillas in small pockets scattered throughout the long chain of mountainous knobs and valleys, connected via runners and, in some cases, radios.

This particular base functioned as a principal supply point as well as nucleus for southern Leyte. It also contained a transmitter capable of reaching far beyond the Philippines. Radio lifelines served a dual purpose, cranking out the information of intelligence and soliciting supplies and AIB direction. During the day most of the soldiers relaxed or slept, movement usually relegated to things mundane. Weapons were scoured and oiled continuously, the rapid oxidation of jungle rust surfaced overnight in the oppressive humidity.

Many Filipinos, slight and diminutive, preferred the compact, lightweight M1 carbine over the now traditional M1 Garand. Even though it was inferior in stopping power, accuracy and range, the carbine was ideal for their close-in purposes. Also the fifteen-round magazine afforded its handler a seemingly constant stream of semi-automatic fire. One hundred and ten such weapons were included in the submarine's largess. Several men diligently cleaned the gunk of protective cosmoline from the little rifles in anticipation of distributing them to their brothers farther north. Such was how the streamlined killer force expended their daylight hours. Night, however, was the time of stalking and sabotage.

As was his custom, Antonio Rizal moved from camp to camp in the company of a handful of companions and ranging scouts. He had yet to convene with his new AIB contacts. Priority and caution guided his schedule. His was an unpatterned deliberateness. No one was ever quite sure when he would show up. "Always expect me, then you won't be surprised," he had admonished a miffed subordinate. Rizal had a way of keeping folks on their toes.

Curious, Delane thought, *that this camp is designated Red Seven. Is there a symbolic connection between Red and Communism? Or am I suspicious beyond reason? After all, the Navy and USMC always color-code their amphibious assault beaches, red included. And One-One, First Battalion First Marines, takes consummate pride in referring to itself as Red Death. Why am I so paranoid? Damn, AIB's got me leery about things as innocent as color! Cincinnati Reds, Boston Red Sox, Detroit Red Wings, Johnny Walker Red Label—the beat goes on. Stop!!*

"What's going on, old boy? You look as though a bloody jackaroo's wrestling inside your head." Evan entered the hut they shared, carrying an armful of second-hand clothing, the type worn by field hands and fishermen. Most were of a coarse, off-white cotton. Perched atop the pile sat a wide-brimmed straw hat, saw-toothed and misshapen. Hemp-like twine circled the crown base in lieu of a decorative band. It fed down through openings aside the brim for about ten inches, meeting at a tightening slide of blue-white seashell. The improvised lanyard allowed the wearer to remove the sombrero without losing it, hanging off one's back. And that's precisely how Whitfield would wear it for the months ahead, charting tides and shoals of beaches suitable for veteran US Army shock troops to land.

"My brain is like a goddamn pinball machine, Whit, ideas careening off the sidewalls fast and furious. By the time it'll take me to explain a single thought, my fertile cranium will be banging away at a bonus bumper and into another dimension. Know what I mean?"

"Not really. I think you've already succumbed to jungle madness. Perhaps you should double your Atabrine intake." Evan set the pile on a wood table crudely fashioned from a crate panel. He lifted the straw chapeau and placed it atop his head, pushing up one side brim, Aussie style, for his amused roommate to admire. "How do I bloody look?" A self-mocking smile accompanied his inquiry.

"Like Pancho Villa, bandit patriot of Queensland."

"Who in sodding hell is Pancho Villa?"

"A Mexican shoot-'em-up character who terrorized the Rio Grande about thirty or so years ago."

"Righto, I like that! From this day hence I shall be known as Pancho Villa." He squinted an eye and grimaced to punctuate his new alias before they both broke out laughing.

"No matter what you call yourself, Lady Rita will track you down and strip you naked. She's probably cruising Surigao in one of Sir Harry's racing boats at this very moment," Delane teased.

The naval officer winced. "Don't bloody remind me of that she-bitch. She's half the reason I'm hiding out in the sodding bowels of Leyte, risking my beautiful head rather than subject an unwilling body to her insane perversions." He pushed the hat rearward so it fell dangling between his shoulder blades.

"Well, Pancho Villa, I thought insane perversion was something you've sought since the first tremor of puberty!"

"True, brother-in-law, true. But Rita's appetite for, shall we say pleasures grotesque, has reached the stratum of half-Amazon/part Harpy. The more debauchery she devours the greater her craving. I never imagined in my wildest dreams that I'd ever reach the point of supersaturation—like a submerged sponge incapable of absorbing any more." Evan's tirade, emphasized by animated expressions, proved doubly entertaining. Flailing arms accompanied his outright exasperation.

The monologue had elevated Delane to sidesplitting laughter. He had grown to care deeply for the Australian. They had shared much together since their friendship was sealed on Mindanao two years past. Certainly Whit represented the catalyst in his introduction to Marla. Resultantly, the marital bond had extended their camaraderie to the more cementing relationship of family.

He was about to respond to Evan's outpouring when a movement rippled through the quiet camp. No noise or commotion agitated, just a mild stirring, signaling an event. Indeed, the great guerrilla chieftain and inspirational leader, Antonio Rizal, had arrived. Scourge of the Japanese occupiers and legend in his island universe, with a temptation of seventy thousand dollars in Hirohito's gold hanging above his sleek black hair, unquestionably he had made his mark. Rallying his people, marshaling support from abroad, and brutally destroying the soldiers and material of Nippon, the name of Rizal was reverently whispered wherever countrymen congregated in Leyte's captive cities: Tacloban, Barugo, Hilongos, Isidro, Abuyog, and Ormoc. He walked with an air of great confidence, the very strides inspiring those about him to swell chests, to tuck in grimy shirts, to straighten belts swaying blades and canteens. Pride shone from the undernourished faces of the staunch army of Red Seven. Truly he was a demanding taskmaster. But for him they would sacrifice blood and limb without question. He was Rizal!

Planned reunions usually take place in bars, restaurants, homes or lobbies, seldom in the equatorial vapor of a mosquitoed jungle. The tall Filipino gracefully stepped into the open-walled hut. He had aged since last they had seen him. Streaks of silver lined temples and narrow sideburns. Playing prey and stalker interchangeably had taken a physical toll, both in the superficial sense as well as tired joints and debilitating ailments common to the torrid zone. But the keen mind ingrained by an indefatigable will and the methodical precision of an experienced engineer had never betrayed him. These assets and a unique perception into the psychology of ally and foe alike were his most powerful resources.

"Aha!" he said. "This is truly a treat beyond optimism. I was expecting you, Andrew, and an unidentified Westerner, but I had no idea it would be Evan Whitfield of his majesty's Royal Australian Navy. It pleases me." He moved quickly to them, wrapping his wiry arms about their shoulders. Like a trio of ringed dancers they hugged and rocked in an embrace of companionship knitted by months of mutual anxiety in Mindanao. Actually for Delane, the adventurous voyage aboard El Corazon Blanco had been the genesis of their fellowship. "Only Gunny Luzak is missing. Or did you stow him away in a crate?" Rizal slapped their sweaty backs and guffawed heartily. His eyes radiated the gleam of delight.

Amicable as always, Evan seized Antonio's shoulders, momentarily holding him in place. "I'm terribly pleased also, my friend. And I've brought us something special to commemorate our days in Zamboanga and to celebrate this auspicious reunion."

Grabbing a small maritime-gray trunk containing the tools of his hydrography trade, he flicked the twin hasps and playfully opened the lid. Evan performed like an excited child on Christmas morning. Amid the gauges and drafting instruments slept a towel-wrapped object shaped much like a bowling pin. "Dom Perignon," be boasted, wide-eyed and emphatic. "If there remains any of that God-awful *filet de carabao*, I suggest we wash it down with this sodding magnum!"

"Excellent, my friend. I see you haven't lost any of your appreciation for, how shall we say… " He searched for the proper expression, then smiled. "For the civilized refinements in life."

Andy moved closer to Rizal, their searching eyes showing signs of experience gainfully mature since their earlier association. War has a way of accelerating maturity. "Antonio," his voice came out hoarse. "You have been in my thoughts much these past few years. I had hoped for nothing more than your deliverance from the clutches of the Japanese. But I learned my hopes for you have fallen short of your ascendancy into a select ring of Filipino leaders. I am proud to call you comrade and renew our friendship." The choice of the word *comrade* was not coincidental. He was chumming the depths of ideology, and would continue so over the ensuing weeks, searching for reactions and return signals.

"It is kind of you to honor me, my friend. You are as diplomatic as you are thoughtful, major." Smiling, he touched Delane's collar brass and finger-tapped an oak leaf. "You are ascending swiftly yourself—a major already. I knew from the beginning you were a good man, and obviously your marine hierarchy is in agreement."

Delane was about to play down the major rank and disclose its temporary nature. But rather than modestly pooh-poohing it, he preferred to say little. *Better he shouldn't know. Let him think it's a routine promotion. Bide my time. Don't even let him know of my intelligence background until the appropriate point in time. Maybe it'll be my ace in the hole.* "I guess I've just been lucky, Antonio."

"So it seems. Now tell me, how have you found your accommodations here at Red Seven?"

"Splendid," Whitfield piped up. "Plenty of fresh air, good for the constitution. And Captain Criquel has been most helpful in settling us in."

"Ah yes, Criquel. He is a good man."

"And most compassionate," said Andy. "There was an incident during our trek from the beach. An old drover lost a carabao to a busted leg. One of your men apparently treated the gent harshly, but Criquel interceded and handled him with respect and kindness. Although I couldn't understand the language, I was able to comprehend the feeling. To his credit, he acted skillfully and with humanity."

"Good, I am glad to hear that. After all, the people are our strength." Rizal's voice grew softer. "A population's hostility should be directed at the oppressor, not within."

Sounds like something out of the Communist Manifesto, Delane reckoned. *But then again, perhaps it's the rhetoric of fervent patriotism?*

DATE: Tuesday, 9 May 1944

TIME: 0730 HOURS

LOCATION: LEYTE, PHILIPPINES (RED FOUR)

He had arrived at Red Four a half dozen days earlier. Farther north and situated high atop the mountains, the climate was cooler, especially at night, and overall more comfortable than Red Seven. Delane was chatting with the two US Army AIB radio operators who called the camp home, although they never transmitted directly from the small base. Each evening they would melt deeper into the volcanic highlands and set up their station, receiving and tapping out coded information: weather, enemy troop movement, and factual tidbits overheard by native sweep-up boys tidying the Jap barracks and garrison headquarters in Leyte's southern cities.

Theirs was only one of a number of strategically located radio points. Staff Sergeants Barney Brown and Donald "Duke" Gillette went to tedious effort to constantly relocate the daily transmission, never broadcasting from the identical position twice. Japanese radio wave hunters given enough time could catch their signal and, through triangulation, pinpoint them.

Half of the Mutt-and-Jeff team, the string-beaned Duke, possessed an Abe Lincoln profile, two inches over six feet but seemingly taller due to a gaunt, sallowed face and disproportionately elongated arms. He stood in comical contrast to his best friend and switchboard partner—Barney's physiognomy reminded one of some mongrelized dogs which appear to be the products of genetic conflict, like cross-breeding Great Danes and Dachshunds. His robust torso and head perched on very short, albeit sturdy, legs. When seated he emitted the impression of full size, however, once he rose there would be but a marginal stature gain. Standing or sitting, he was virtually the same height. "Stubby" was probably the most common adjective invoked by those describing his truncated frame... and no doubt he was tired of hearing it. Both men grew up in Los Angeles, but never knew each other until they were teamed in Brisbane back in '43.

Barney and Duke were small-talking to Delane, describing their modus operandi during their seven month tenure, when a small patrol of silent but obviously jubilant guerrillas entered the camp. With them they carried an assortment of captured weapons and several burlap sacks stuffed with the loot of a successful foray. Lieutenant Orlando Garzon, commander of Red Four, descended the hut step and approached the patrol leader, round faced and carrying an old crescent scar beneath one eye.

Rizal had departed the previous evening to travel north for meetings with a representative of Major Jesus Villamoor, also known as Ramon Hernandez and nicknamed Monching. To further confuse the issue, AIB listed him as W-10. Villamoor's guerrilla army oversaw all resistance activity on the huge island of Panay to the west. His trusted agent Castaneda (Delane had learned) was on Leyte seeking assistance on behalf of the legendary major. The gallant Hernandez Villamoor, evasive and mysterious, carried a large price on his scalp, hence his many aliases to keep those who would pursue off balance.

Garzon was older than most lieutenants, exuding an air of experience and high confidence. He spoke to the patrol leader who related his band's success. They had bushwacked a staff car and accompanying small truck around midnight. Evidently the vehicles had become lost and wandered off the main road. Incredibly, the Japanese thought they had stumbled on a group of night fisherman and hailed them, seeking directions to Hilongos. "We shoot-shoot all five. Two officers," informed the cocky patrol leader, and explained how they pushed the vehicles off the cart track into a shallow ravine covered with thick foliage. They slashed tires and smashed the engines, insuring an inability to serve the enemy again. Handfuls of gritty earth were dropped into the fuel tanks for good measure. A fire was out of the question for it would attract attention. Better to force the enemy to waste his resources seeking out the missing convoy.

Stripping the corpses of weapons and valuables, the guerrillas methodically severed heads from the slain soldiers. It was during this ritual decapitation that they realized the most prominent remains belonged to the infamous Captain Akiro, reputedly the Kempei Tai's most sadistic enforcer. Benitez, the grinning patrol leader of the sickled scar, shook out a trophy from his burlap sack. After rolling to a stop, the grotesque head of the aforementioned Captain Akiro stared open eyed up through the leafy screen. A small hole between cheekbone and eye demonstrably showcased the caliber accuracy of a guerrilla carbine. *Quid pro quo*, the Romans phrased it—this for that. The Japanese had been publicly beheading Filipinos since their conquest, as punishment and object lesson. Two could play the game though. Neither party owned a monopoly on atrocity.

A man carrying a thick bamboo stick sharpened at each end thrust it into the damp ground, working the shaft in a tiny circle until it stood erect and unwavering. Predictably, he ceremoniously lifted Akiro's head aloft before spiking it. The impaled memento would decorate the camp for over a week until there was opportunity to bowl the knobby ball in the vicinity of Kempei Tai headquarters at Tacloban. The battle of terror and psychological dominance continued. Quid pro quo.

From the very same sack, Benitez retrieved a small book printed in Japanese characters and Arabic numbers. Scraps of gore, the debris of Akiro's butchered cranium, clung to the cover. Spotting its potential value at once, Delane asked to examine it. He squatted as he inspected the unintelligible columns of digits and symbols. Over his shoulder the macabre skull appeared to stare at the booklet as well, its unseeing eyes fixed and passionless. Uncomfortable as he might be, the Marine showed no spookiness. "Duke, Barney, if I'm not mistaken this is a cipher book…what do you think?"

Barney removed a short-bladed knife from his belted sheath and shaved off the gore before leafing through. "That's sure what it looks like to me, major." He passed it on to Duke who bobbed his long neck in agreement.

"He say take book out box bag, carry by Kempei Tai Jap," Garzon explained in broken English.

"You mean a brief case?" Andy asked.

"Yes, I think. My English no very good. Beef case."

"No, brief case," Delane politely corrected.

"Brief case," he repeated. "Important stuff?"

"Yes, lieutenant, I think so. Very important." The Marine took the book and turned to the radio team. "I'm no expert, but this might be a key element of the Imperial Japanese Army secret code. The Kempei Tai man must have been transporting it to headquarters at Hilongos. If so, we must get it into the hands of AIB's cryptoanalytical section. This could be dynamite! It's imperative we radio AIB at once. Grab your gear ricky-tick and let's move out to a point of your choosing."

"Yes, sir," they responded immediately and sprang to action.

Ninety minutes later, the three-man band set up shop on a small perch high above an agricultural valley. Tiny white specks of workers and draft animals were scarcely visible tilling geometric rows. Delane assumed they were cultivating pineapples, a principal crop of the island. Morning mist began to disappear, burned dry by the solar blast furnace rolling across the cloudless Leyte sky. Temporary Major Delane had scribbled out a concise message which Staff Sergeant Gillette encoded with efficient precision. The process was painstakingly slow. Meanwhile, Barney Brown set up the radio key, antenna, and bicycle-style pedal generator.

"All set," he said.

"Me too," said his partner. "You riding or blabbing today?" he grinned through a stubbled beard.

"I'll climb in the saddle. You rode last time, Duke."

"Sure you can reach them pedals, Barn?" Gillette teased.

"Kiss my ass at Hollywood and Vine." Brown stretched onto the seat and began pumping. His powerful, compact thighs and calves soon had the generator whirring like a Singer sewing machine. A slight glimmer lit up the panel, its glow indicating a readiness to transmit and receive. Gillette sat cross-legged, his head hovering above the key, and rapped out the coded message from Electric Eel to Sting Ray.

URGENT.

USFIP AMBUSH NETTED JAP K.T. CIPHER BOOK. MY POSSESSION. AWAIT DIRECTIONS HERE 30 MINS.

Listening through the headset, Duke jotted the return signal code onto a small pad and translated its succinct response.

MESSAGE RECEIVED. DIRECTIONS FORTHCOMING 30 MINS.

Delane thumbed through the enemy code book in an impossible effort to make something of its cryptic tables and matrices. In reality he was only killing time. The super sleuths at AIB with pools of linguists and mathematicians, and instruments ranging from already-primitive cipher wheels to state-of-the-art detection equipment, would be able to crack the code using the Kempei Tai book. The ability to read intercepted Japanese dispatches at will would be an incredible feat of espionage if, in fact, Captain Akiro's little secret publication was the key. Stencil codes, angle codes, whatever, they were all mumbo jumbo to Andy.

Damn, I'm an infantry officer trained and retrained at Quantico for this very specialty. Months of small unit tactics, fire and maneuver, etcetera, etcetera, all for naught. To date my resume includes anti-aircraft fire control, chair-borne intelligence, and now amateurish spying in the boondocks. At least Evan is performing at his chosen profession.

Whitfield, surprisingly well-disguised in fisherman attire, left a few days before to begin charting the eastern beaches near Dulag. Insouciant as was his temperament, the lieutenant commander, now code-named Pancho Villa, expressed his desire to dine on a sea-provided diet rather than the stringy cuisine of jungle fowl and carabao. He would be working under the nose of Japanese Army sentinels and Navy patrol craft combing the beach areas. Danger was dismissed as a petty nuisance by the Aussie as he attacked the science of navigable water.

Delane had propped his back against a smooth-barked tree trunk and begun to fantasize, his thoughts drifting to Marla and the crisp-sheeted comfort of Pink Garden Villa. Three weeks ago his world had been snug, the only anguish stemming from the self-imposed guilt of not being where the action was. *Well here you are, Mister Delane, you of the ambivalent conscience, up to your ass in spiders and Japs for God knows how long—if you survive!* His reverie was shaken by Duke. "Here it comes!"

CRITICAL

RETURN BOOK TO AMBUSH SITE ASAP. JAP MUST NOT KNOW YOUR POSSESSION. ACCOMPLISH AND CONFIRM.

Incredulously, Delane stared at the transmission trying somehow to read between the lines. "What is Stingray up to?!"

"Beats the shit out of us," Duke shrugged. "Guess it wasn't so important after all, huh, major?"

Delane remained silent, the gears churning inside his deductive brain. "On the contrary," he thought aloud. His voice rose with excited revelation. "We've already got it. Sure, that's it, AIB's already got it!"

"Got what, sir?" the stubby one asked.

"The code, man, the code! AIB already owns the Jap code but the Japs don't know it!"

"You mean the boys in Brisbane are already reading the Japs' mail?"

"You bet, Barney. But if the Nips figure out we've captured it here on Leyte, they'll be forced to change it as a security precaution. That's why we have to return this little beauty to Akiro's headless person and make the enemy think the guerrillas unknowingly overlooked it."

True, three-and-a-half months earlier, an Australian Army recon patrol in pursuit of the retreating Japanese 20th Division near Sio, New Guinea, stumbled upon an abandoned military trunk half-submerged in the muck of a stream bed. To their astonishment (and good luck) it contained the complete cipher library of the Imperial Japanese Army. Rushed to Brisbane, the AIB soon began reading enemy transmissions. Its bounty had provided MacArthur with information of the most extraordinary nature and contributed enormously to the developing strategy which time again successfully leap-frogged US Army troops up the New Guinea coast, cutting off and slaughtering trapped concentrations of baffled Japanese.

DATE: WEDNESDAY, 10 MAY 1944

TIME: 0345 HOURS

LOCATION: LEYTE ISLAND, PHILIPPINES (AMBUSH SITE)

The stench smothered the surrounding jungle, all but suffocating the two men lying in wait. At first light they would sift through the gory jumble of five corpses and four heads attempting to locate Akiro's briefcase. Unseen animals, probably rodents, could be heard scurrying inside the windowless staff car snacking on human carrion. Buzzing insects, thousands, swarmed about, gorging on the ready-made feast. The guerrillas had efficiently crammed the carnage into the one vehicle. Like an oversized roaster, it had sucked in yesterday's fiery sun, and in little time accelerated the chemistry of decomposition, converting bloated flesh and organs into putrefying gas, its pervasive stink serving as an olfactory beacon to colonies of flies and slithering insects. For the first ten minutes or so, all Delane's body could do was gag in reflexive horror. He tried inhaling through his mouth hoping to avoid the overpowering foulness, but it only made matters worse. The taste reeked in his mouth, causing innards to wretch. Finally the physical revulsion subsided though his nostrils worked overtime in a vain attempt to filter out the malodorous rot. Benitez stretched out beside him, quietly sucking on a stick of sugar cane, indifferent to the polluted air and grisly remains. *Just another ho-hum incident in the life of a guerrilla fighter,* thought the Marine. *Marla, I'm coming home, baby. No more hero stuff.*

CHAPTER XXII
TRANSITION

The spring and summer of 1944 witnesses enormous victories in campaigns either initiated exclusively by the Americans, or in which the U.S. fights as an allied co-participant. Overlord, the greatest invasion enterprise ever conceived, preceded by three airborne divisions, forges a tenacious toehold in Normandy. Turk Aarborg is slain in the vicinity of Ste Mere Eglise. A buck sergeant named Dillon is shot through the chest while destroying a German weapons carrier near Chef Du Pont. He is awarded the Silver Star.

The intrepid amphibious landings, subsequent major battle for the Normandy interior, and dramatic breakout at St. Lo represent the war's most ambitious logistical undertaking and force of arms by the western allies. Troops and heavy armor, multi-battalions of powerful artillery, pour into the breech from their springboard in Britain. Every village, every hedgerow, every farmhouse becomes a desperate conflict. Irreplaceable losses in manpower and equipment are heaped on the Germans in staggering numbers, the most costly at the colossal pincer that historians will identify as the Falaise Pocket. It is a killing event of prodigious dimension.

Almost ignored by the world audience is mid-August's Operation Dragoon, the spectacular airborne/seaborne incursion into southern France along the picturesque Riviera. Here the energetic US Seventh Army surges ashore and soon engages in a piston-like thrust, ramming up the Valley of the Rhone into the underbelly of ancient Gaul. Axis-occupied France is being compressed like a perforated bladder hissing and leaking its shrinking contour.

Relentless round-the-clock aerial bombing shatters Nazi military installations and industrial capacity in the heart of the Vaterland. From the east, the Russians, in a grinding drive of attrition, relentlessly pound Hitler's reeling war machine. The Soviets sustain horrific losses, yet they doggedly storm along a titanic front stretching from the Baltic to the Black Sea. Red Army hordes with apparent unlimited human resources, Georgians, Siberians, and Uzbeki, keep charging in endless waves too turbulent to stem. Wehrmacht and SS legions are slammed back through the Ukraine and Belorussia into Bulgaria, Rumania, Hungary, Slovakia and Poland. The Allies, sensing a collapse is imminent, throw in fresh reserves, well-trained and amply outfitted, anxious to execute the *coup de grace*.

Though the western alliance brims with warranted confidence, the spiteful hierarchy of nazidom prepares last-gasp counter-offensives which will cause Russian, American, and British commanders huge consternation and extend the hideous slaughter beyond rational expectation. But then, war is irrational behavior, the tenured scale of which often determines its historical identity: the Hundred Years War, the Great War, the World War. Duration and scope are the denominators of epoch calamity, not people, for it is bigger than nations and belligerents.

World War II and its attendant exterminative policies are no exception. The statistics of carnage and devastation will exceed all others.

Overshadowed by Normandy headlines, focus in the Pacific is concentrated on the blood-chilling battles for the Mariana Islands, viciously contested since mid-June. Three Marine and two Army divisions, plus a USMC brigade, capture the three bitterly-resisted volcanic islands of Saipan, Tinian, and Guam. Master Sergeant Tony Luzak's 4th Marine Regiment along with the 22nd Marines will fight on Guam as components of the First Marine Provisional Brigade. The 3rd Marine Division and the US Army 77th Infantry Division constitute the Guam attack force along with the brigade. Lessons of past amphibious debacles are heeded as the Guam operation goes off textbook-perfect, though casualties run appallingly high, as they do for the entire Marianas campaign.

Brother gyrenes and dog faces of the 2nd and 4th Marine Divisions and 27th Infantry Division have already wrested the excessively difficult Saipan from Japanese control after three-and-a-half weeks of savagery. The USMC overruns neighboring Tinian in short order, with inordinate loss of enemy life. Luzak picks up mortar fragments in the shadow of Guam's Mount Santa Rosa. The wounds are termed *minor*. His reconstituted regiment has been blooded in a searing hell of fire and shrapnel, and acquitted itself with distinction. In the following months they will be integrated into the new-to-be-formed 6th Marine Division and projected into the entrenched bowels of the Pacific Theater's last and greatest battle.

Back in June, the way had been paved for vanquishment of the Marianas by the US Navy's formidable air fleet under the able Vice Admiral Marc

Mitscher. Part and parcel to the ground slugfest, American carrier pilots obliterate the enemy's ability to support those dug-in Japanese holding the islands. To the west, 330 aircraft of the Rising Sun are blasted from the tropical sky on June 19 alone, at a cost of only twenty-nine American planes and fewer throttle jockeys. Posterity will record it as the Battle of the Philippine Sea, but swabbies of Nimitz's command will exhilaratingly dub it the Great Marianas Turkey Shoot.

To compound the enemy's dilemma, torpedoes fired by U.S. killer subs sink two large Japanese aircraft carriers the very same day. In the following hours, Grumman Hellcats, punishingly swift new fighters, will spit their deadly saliva into scores of Zeroes, Vals, and Kates, plummeting them into the flotsamed Pacific spittoon. More attack planes locate yet another carrier and send it to the ocean floor while damaging two others plus a battleship and cruiser. By August, the final land offensive is concluded and Guam declared secure. The Marianas campaign ends as a one-sided thrashing of pivotal importance. Tojo's predicament is of backbreaking eminence because Army Air Corps long-distance bombers ranging from the islands can now strike the Japanese nation itself.

In what many will castigate as an unnecessary sacrifice of unacceptable proportion, the Palau Islands are assaulted in September. Doggies of the 81st Infantry Division and 1st MarDiv leathernecks capture the two staunchly defended islands of Pelilieu and Angaur. Heroic American casualties are wastefully high as they are recklessly, almost negligently, ordered into withering Japanese defenses cleverly conceived in depth. Marine divisional leadership is excoriated and ultimately relieved.

Pressure on Hirohito's fading dominion is also being exerted in the China-Burma-India theater by British commonwealth forces, many of which include Indian, Gurkha, and Burmese units. Australian General William Slim skillfully maneuvers his army to take strategic advantage of the enemy's overstretched supply lines. Chinese nationalist forces, controlled in part by American General "Vinegar Joe" Stilwell, along with a relative handful of US Army Marauders, capture key enemy airfields, further diminishing logistical lifelines to the empire's home islands. Much of the action is supported by fighting assets of the Air Corps' 14th Air Force, commanded by Claire Chennault.

More than one million Japanese soldiers are tied up in China, clinging onto the far-reaching perimeters of occupied territory and suppressing interior rebellion. The partisan armies of communist leader Mao Tse-Tung and his political and ideological adversary, Chiang Kai-Shek, unleash an un-orchestrated hodgepodge of resistance. Though they lack any semblance of unified coordination, their effect is to absorb enormous resources of the Japanese military machine which could be expended against MacArthur and Nimitz.

Summer of 1944 also sees the Japanese brutally extricated from the largest island in the southern hemisphere. New Guinea, in excess of 345,000 square miles, about equal to that of Texas, Oklahoma, and Massachusetts combined, falls into Douglas MacArthur's hands with seizure of the final bastion, the Vogelkop Peninsula. The protracted struggle for New Guinea is a series of ferocious brawls,constantly moving westward, primarily along the island's northern coast. Because it lasts for over two years, debilitation from tropical disease is monstrous. If you were there long enough, you caught it. Monsoon rain and stifling ninety-plus-degree heat incubate a glut of infested filth, parasitic fungi, and blood-sucking insects. The US Army, with its Royal Australian allies, overcome the cruel environment and stage a sequence of outflanking amphibious and parachute assaults , which cut off and annihilate stubborn isolations of imperial Japanese troops.

Brilliant strategic actions confound the enemy into a reeling state of reactive defense. Their initiative is sapped, a force stripped of momentum. Airfields with planes still on their strips are blown to extinction by Air Corps bomber crews and accompanying P-38 Lockheed Lightnings. Some might think of New Guinea as a single, gigantic battle of frontal assault, methodically pushing enemy resistance into the horizon. In truth, it is a campaign with many disconnected battles. Key individual islands, dwarfed by massive New Guinea, like pilot fish about a ponderous leviathon, have to be bombarded and stormed by gritty GIs of General Walter Krueger's Sixth Army and their stalwart Anzac allies.

The litany of killing fields from Milne Bay to the Vogelkop is too excessive to enumerate in total: Buna, Kokoda, Lae, Madang, Wewak, Aitape, Hollandia, Sarmi, Wakde, Biak, Sansapor, and nearby LosNegros in the Admiralty Islands. Mercifully, around July 30 the swamp fighting and dune warfare ends. New Guinea's ostensibly unquenchable blood-thirst has finally been slaked. Resultantly, MacArthur's next major hurdle to Tokyo lay open before him, the insular grail of his discontented crusade—the Philippines and vindication—*I Shall Return*!

CHAPTER XXIII
LEYTE

DATE: SATURDAY, 23 SEPTEMBER 1944

TIME: 1420 HOURS

LOCATION: LEYTE, PHILIPPINES (RED FOUR)

"Are you a communist?" Delane surprised himself with the question, harsh and sharp like the tropical lightning that cracks the strait between Leyte and Samar.

The unflappable guerrilla chief stood and readjusted the tarnished belt buckle supporting his wrinkled khaki pants stained with damp mold. He peered beyond the thick, segmented bamboo posts supporting the command hut's dripping leaf roof. Soaking rain and air laden with stifling humidity blanketed the camp's denizens, resigned to discomfort. The ever-present cycle of jungle rot saw its recurrent stages, devouring slimy clothing and trappings necessary to sustain and preserve the partisan community. "Is that what you've been fishing for all these months?" Rizal's sharp, dark eyes pierced his inquisitor. "I will say this, my fisherman friend, your question is more of a harpoon than a baited hook!"

The frustration grew apparent on Delane's unshaven face. Unkempt hair, dank and clinging, gave him a motley appearance, the cheeks drawn and fatigued. Climate unkind and constant coupled with the gnawing threat of Japanese discovery had taken a debilitating toll on body and nerves. "You've never declared a governing philosophy of any conviction, Antonio. It seems you espouse particles of ideology from a convenient spectrum of politics."

The major had breached the most difficult terrain. Now he imposed a more aggressive assault. "First you come from one direction, then another. I'm never quite sure if you're cleverly avoiding a declaration… or a man without conviction?" The last phrase was purposely stinging, striving to motivate Rizal into identifying his true colors. The two had been sparring on and off since Delane's arrival, and the marine felt it was time to force the issue.

"My friend, I am committed to whatever economic and political system will best serve the Filipino people!" Rizal stroked a lengthy hairshock greasy with weeks of neglect. 'To alleviate your anxiety, let me state unequivocally that my political leanings are more toward a socialistic democracy. Communism represents repressive economics . No matter how hard one works or how much one avoids work, his reward is the same. Hardly equitable!"

He flicked a yellow green insect from his forearm and into the drizzle. "If you need a label, I suppose I'm a social democrat."

"Well, Antonio, I'm very pleased to learn of your democratic principles. For a while there, I must confess, your behavior carried all the earmarks of a commie!" He smiled but Rizal didn't return it.

Rizal took on a pedantic demeanor, pacing the confines of the abbreviated floor space. "You Americans invariably manage to squeeze the two under the same umbrella. Learn to make the distinction between totalitarian communism and democratic communism. For you it is all the same! Just as there is democratic capitalism, the world also has experienced the error of fascism which is nothing more than industrial capitalism driven by a reptilian dictator. Hitler, Stalin, Mussolini, is there a difference? Tyranny is tyranny, whether it emanates from the left or right. Which would you prefer, tranquil life under a benevolent autocrat, or the terror driven mob of revolutionary France crazed by the liberal guillotine of democracy?

"My friend, your own Thomas Jefferson preached that a democratic constitution supported by the people is the ideal arrangement, but he also knew the people must be enlightened and led by elected leaders of moral character."

"Like yourself?' It was not a challenge, more of an encouraging invitation to continue.

"I think so. What do you think?" Rizal had spun the table, forcing Delane to evaluate the Filipino's political potential.

The Marine also rose to his feet as if to neutralize Antonio's advantage. "You know I have great admiration for you and what you've accomplished as an organizational genius and military leader." He breathed deeply, pulling in the heavy air. "Antonio Rizal has forged a resistance network of impressive note, but how will you assume political supremacy at the conclusion of hostilities, when the Jap is driven from your nation? Will you simply seize power? Will it grow from the barrels of your army's carbines, or will free elections be the instrument of your political fortune? It's my understanding that there exist ambitious forces which will assert control by squashing the competition. Some believe the seizure of power is the most important political prerequisite regardless of methodology—the means are justified by the end."

"Do you feel I am one of those…squashers?"

"Not you, but perhaps Luis Tarluc and his Huks seek to dishonestly fill a political vacuum on Luzon… and it could spread elsewhere aided by allies already in place through the resistance movement."

Rizal allowed an admiring smile. "Andrew, you are more astute than I had imagined. I thought AIB had sent me someone who would expedite and coordinate. Instead my camp is host to an intelligence agent perhaps?"

"Touché." Delane was pleased with the non-hostile nature of their discussion. He sensed Rizal enjoyed the repartee. "After having authoritatively led the Leyte resistance throughout most of the war, will the great Rizal be content to stand aside simply because he might lose something as petty as an election? I suspect there will be an enormous temptation to subvert the system."

Antonio leaned forward, his knuckles on the small crude table between them. The emphasis in his tone shifted more to oratory than conversation, the words emphatic, facial expressions underscoring his pronouncements. "Andrew, there are some in the Philippines, indeed the world, who would put personal ambition ahead of country and family, who would tread the path of deceit before friendship… greed before loyalty. Those who do, ultimately die in the arms of that monster of conscience we call the devil!"

His half-Moro eyes glowed with the fire of sincerity. "Do not confuse my patriotism with personal aggrandizement or a blind addiction for power."

"I'm not confused. I simply wanted to hear it from the horse's mouth."

"Unfortunately, sometimes people are unable to distinguish my horse's mouth from my horse's ass!" Rizal permitted himself a slight snicker. "Well, no one's perfect!" They laughed together.

The guerrilla raised a booted foot, resting it atop a bench fashioned from a stenciled supply crate. It too showed signs of jungle fatigue, the leather pitted and stressed. He wore no weapon nor rank, not any sign of authority.

For him such symbols were unnecessary. Perhaps his lack of ceremonial tinsel, his humble uniform, spoke to the stature of the man. Presence alone drove those who surrounded him to an unflinching following, willing to commit their lives to Rizal's control.

Blind obedience? Not really, because they knew the man fervent and judicious. Theirs was an open-eyed allegiance. He lived and breathed with them, enduring the same hardships, subsisting on handfuls of rice and stringy meat if they were lucky enough to snare unsuspecting fowl or pigs. One beat ahead of the equally violent Japanese, he traveled by their side along circuitous mountain trails avoiding patrolling aircraft, laboring under torturous loads and chafing straps. Their existence and his were one in the same.

Machete in hand, he would hack overgrown vines and low hanging branches blocking the narrow jungle footpaths. Callous and bruise discolored palms and knees. This was no rear echelon elitist; this was Rizal!

"There is no doubt in my mind that the chains of Japanese oppression will be snapped. But our liberation will be costly. The enemy will sacrifice Filipinos like biblical lambs to buy time, to extend the inevitable. And to satisfy the perversion of their samurai blood lust. If I possess any political ambitions I will not corrupt their pursuit, prolonging the suffering, so I can negotiate a loftier post war position for myself. Rizal would do nothing selfish to endanger the swift liberation of his people, to jeopardize the day of emancipation. If you have fears, they are ill-founded, my friend. My cooperation with AIB and the promised return of MacArthur is absolute!"

A tingle of guilt flushed Delane, looking a bit sheepish after Rizal's declaration. "Antonio, I… "

"That is what you wanted to hear wasn't it? That was the purpose of your fishing expedition? Let me add, Andrew, that I think there is a political future in my life, but two things are very certain. First, I will not slow down or accelerate my organization's military commitment contingent on promised Yankee support for my personal growth. Prostitution, political or carnal, is repulsive to my character. Also be assured, after the war all my energy will be directed toward establishing the Philippines as an independent republic. I will not be a puppet of Washington or anyone else." Rizal's attitude was firm and persuasive, flecked with strains of passion. "Have I answered all your questions, spoken and implied?"

"I believe so, Antonio. I hope you understand it is my duty to determine your level of compliance with AIB. Now I know."

"On the contrary, Andrew, you have my deepest respect and friendship. In fact, my professional esteem has grown immeasurably." Rizal held out his hand for Delane to grasp. He took it and pumped slowly, their eyes locked.

"And what are your immediate priorities," the temporary major asked, smiling.

"Just one. Set the table for MacArthur's promise and kick the Japs off of Leyte."

"I'm in solid agreement with that," Andy grinned. "On second thought, there is something about which I'm curious."

"Spit it out, as the head engineer at Clark Field was fond of saying."

" What about Tarluc?"

"You are persistent."

"That's why you respect me so much."

"Andrew, I'm sure there are those from Whitney to Willoughby who suspect that because I cooperate with Tarluc I must be a communist. Certainly Luis is an admitted Marxist. He reasons we are an agriculture nation and supplier of raw materials to the industrialized powers. Therefore, Filipinos will remain under the boot of economic imperialists while we are milked and live in squalor. I am sympathetic to much of his evaluation but disagree with his solution. For me, communism creates more problems than it solves. Regardless of Tarluc's ideological leanings, he is dedicated to purging Luzon from the Japanese slave masters. I deal with him because it is militarily expedient for me to do so. In truth I watch Tarluc closely… and Tarluc watches Rizal… closely."

DATE: THURSDAY, 28 SEPTEMBER 1944

TIME: 0830 HOURS

LOCATION: LEYTE, PHILIPPINES

Blue hues ranging from pale aquamarine to vibrant turquoise danced and dazzled in the low morning sun. Pools of shimmering light exploded like tiny sapphires in the shallows stirred by bare feet. Cutting a slender trail where its narrow keel had been dragged through the white sand beach, the little boat crunched to a stop as three fishermen relaxed their grip. Bandana in hand, the tall Filipino mopped his swarthy neck shadowed under a sawtoothed hat. As he blotted, the others pulled circular throwing nets from inside the hull. They had been netting off the boat since sunrise slowly working their way shoreward. Only a few small scavenger fish comprised the morning's catch.

Succumbing to the tide, the vessel had bobbed its way to the coast from a point roughly twelve hundred yards out. So they decided to fish the shallows, wading into the soft surf flanking the Surigao Strait. Perhaps their luck would improve. The tall one hunched as he walked the high tide mark, often tamping the packed sand as if to stomp a cramp from his arch. In reality he was testing the sand's ability to support weight. This was the third time Evan Whitfield had investigated this particular coastal strip and its strand of crescent beach. Reaching inside his threadbare shirt, he removed a small notebook and began making shorthand notations using a stubby pencil dangling from a sweaty cord about his neck.

Easing into the water with barely a splash, his two companions began casting for the small schools of marine life which hug the warm shoreline. Maintaining the appearance of busy netters in search of the sea's bounty, the men maneuvered about, gesturing and jabbering in typical native fashion to convince prying eyes of their legitimacy. For months the Australian had been meticulously charting those beaches and approaches which he felt could foster a major amphibious operation. On more than one occasion he had eluded Japanese discovery by the narrowest of margins. Evan had learned to walk in a compact manner so from afar his appearance would be shorter, more in keeping with the guerrilla fisherman who supported and protected him.

Risk came with the assignment, but Whitfield's indifference to potential enemy detection alarmed even his most daring Philippine friends, who by now all called him Pancho Villa. Pancho swam about suspicious reefs measuring depths at various tide levels. A six-inch error could rip the bottom from a landing craft swollen with assault troops. Still he questioned, at least in his own mind, whether a Leyte invasion was truly imminent. Were his painstakingly diligent surveillances only insurance in the event some whimsical strategist desired more options, more plausible islands for his planning board? Logic concluded that Mindanao would be the first island to be stormed. And its enormous dimensions would require a prolonged campaign, pushing a Leyte incursion into the distant future.

Skin tanned to a leathery teak from too many hours in the blistering sun, covered his entire body excepting crotch and buttocks. Short cropped hair stained dark by a concoction of local flora, barks, and betel nut juice passed him off as a Philippine of mixed ancestry when observed from a distance. Squinting to narrow his eye slits he could even fool close-by onlookers into thinking him an indigenous inhabitant. A skimpy diet had slimmed his physique to that of a marathon man, an angular frame covered by wiry hide virtually devoid of fat. Absentmindedly he played his fingers along a slender rib cage when one of the men, Javier, called to him.

Coming down the beach roughly a quarter mile, maybe more, from the north trudged what appeared to be a small patrol of three Japanese soldiers wearing soft field caps and slung rifles. Casually, Evan meandered to the boat, moving indifferently so as not to rouse curiosity. Reaching into the craft he withdrew a net and small gutting knife which he tucked into his belt. Crouch-walking to shrink his silhouette, Whitfield stepped into the warm, lapping surf beyond his companions. Deeper water would facilitate the illusion, making him out to be shorter, and provide the Japanese with less distinctive features to observe. Posterior to the beach, he lowered the hat brim and cast the net expertly, emulating many Filipino fisherman he had watched.

Evidently the patrol thought the jungle line just beyond the boat would allow generous shade for a short smoke break. They plopped under a thick palm, removing canteens and light packs to enjoy the respite, stacking rifles about the trunk. Nonchalantly admiring the deft net throws, one gave appreciative applause when the deepest Filipino flung his long and high. Unfortunately for Evan, a type of dolphin fish, about a two-footer, ensnared itself, thrashing and splashing to escape. Silvery reflections of wriggling fish and sun-catching droplets entertained the Japanese audience, a pair of whom trotted to the water's edge to take in the action. Evan had no choice but to haul in his prize. Javier, recognizing his friend's plight, waded to him hoping to exchange his net for Evan's while the Filipino dragged the fish beachward and deposited it in the hull.

Well-intentioned, a young Japanese, caught up in the excitement of the catch, ran into the water to assist. His enthusiasm caused the three men to get caught up in a flailing mass, Evan's straw sombrero falling to the churning surface. The laughing Japanese flashed out a hand attempting to save the hat when his eyes locked on to Whitfield's. For an instant time stood still as the soldier's brain computed the hazel green irises before him.

The hair was different too. Off balance and open-mouthed, he started to react a moment before Javier jerked him below the waterline and slit his throat in a quick, deep slash.

The Japanese standing flatfooted at the high water mark barely understood what had happened when Javier dashed ten yards from the flat surf and plunged his filleting blade into the man's abdomen and tumbled him to the wet sand. Instinctively, Evan charged the confused soldier idling beneath the shade palm. Fast on his heels Mongron, the other guerrilla, also sprinted for the palm, his net still clutched in both hands. The soldier realized too late the danger approaching. Futilely he made a fumbling attempt to snatch an Arisaka and wheel it toward the rushers.

Evan impacted the man in a tackling, sprawling bear hug, the rifle trapped between them. Pain ripped through the Aussie's ribs as his full weight collapsed along the rigid bolt and rear sight. ignoring the anguish he allowed his heaviness to immobilize the enemy, smaller by some sixty-odd pounds and considerably shorter. Mongron leaped onto the jumble, and with Evan pinning the Jap's flailing upper limbs, managed to slip and tug the fishnet over the trapped man's head and torso. He twisted the twine tightly constricting the shoulders and bound elbows. Like a methodical python he circled the web lower and lower encasing forearms and hands in a doomed chrysalis. The Filipino shouted to Pancho Villa to finish him off.

Whitfield's responding thumbs and fingers wove a deadly path through the netting surrounding the terrified soldier's neck. Locating the knob that forms the Adam's apple he plunged both thumbs and squeezed with all his power. Looking into the helpless face all he could think of was a biology text book of his youth depicting a white rabbit in the choke of a huge boa. Only the long ears and pathetic, misshapen face protruded, the snake's muscular coils crushing its body into a suffocating bag of pulp. But it was the bunny's eyes he recalled vividly, bulging in a defenseless plea to a photographer intent on capturing its dramatic expiration. Strangling beneath him, the Japanese's eyes goggled in a silent beseechment. The distended lids remained open. It seemed the harder he squeezed the more the orbs dilated. His own pupils were less than twelve inches from the gurgling open mouth and eyes… the pained, begging eyes. Evan could look no more.

He twisted his face away and, summoning all his strength, throttled an extra measure of power into a grip already vice-tight. Gasping, his knuckles trembled in an uncontrollable spasm about the limp throat. "Pancho, stop.

Pancho!" He heard the voices and felt Javier tugging his shoulders, snapping him from the frenzied convulsion. Whitfield had never killed a man before… and he would never forget the picture now indelibly imprinted in his mind's eye, like the biology book photo. Off to the side, his prey's cigarette still smoldered. A matchbook lay a few feet away… "I Shall Return."

The ribs pained him immeasurably, perhaps two or more were broken. Unable to bear any weight, he watched the guerrillas float the boat and load aboard the dead Japs and their paraphernalia. Mongron would sail out a few miles and dump the remains into the swallowing waters of the Surigao. But first he would weight their pants with large stones to prevent a telltale carcass from washing up on the long stretch of beach.

As the little vessel worked its way toward the eastern horizon, Javier smoothed the sand, erasing traces of the boat's keel track and covering the struggle site. Another routine patrol of the empire had disappeared. Three young Japanese soldiers, possibly one-time peasants, good will in their hearts, had been cruelly snuffed like the fish they sought to help harvest.

DATE: SATURDAY, 30 SEPTEMBER 1944

TIME: 1900 HOURS

LOCATION: Leyte, Philippines (Red Four)

Tuba juice, a homemade concoction, primitive and pungent, favored by Leyteans of the more remote hamlets, flowed from a recycled gallon jug latticed with rattan. Javier poured the bittersweet fluid, refilling the Australian's outstretched canteen cup. The alcoholic components were a mystery to Evan. No one explained to his satisfaction the base ingredients. All he cared about though was its prodigious consumption helped smother the fire living within his rib cage. His preference would have been for the rich dark rum distilled from the island's bountiful sugar cane crop, but none was available this day. Rum was far more potent, hence more anesthetic than the jungle juice he now gulped in greedy swallows.

Normally Rizal forbade alcohol in his camps—that is, for recreational purposes, fearing it would encourage insubordination and an overall breakdown of caution. However, it was permitted as an antiseptic and painkiller which suited Whitfield just fine. The silly smile stitched across his lips belied the nightmare wrestling inside. Images of the pop-eyed Japanese, tongue being squeezed from an unwilling mouth like paste forced from a tube, remained vivid in his brain's cinema. Replaying the memory, his mind distorted the morbid truth, twisting remembrance into a grotesquely exaggerated picture, eyes bulgier, tongue purpled and over-distended. Perhaps the tuba juice would anesthetize his grappling brain. *Oh God, I hope it does. I don't want that bloody image residing in a life of dreams.*

Over the months, Javier had become ever-present, almost permanently, at his side. Bearer, guide, and personal bodyguard, the Filipino had protected him well. Indeed by observing Whitfield, Javier had developed a basic understanding of hydrography and thus often was able to anticipate the lieutenant commander's needs. Though uneducated, he harbored a desire to learn the science of tidal flow and currents, things he already comprehended from a lifetime living off the shallow sea. And Evan, who tended toward impatience, went out of his way to explain much to Javier the student. "More tuba for Pancho Villa," the Australian slurred, tapping the kidney shaped cup atop the table crate.

"Okay, okay, Pancho Villa." The guerrilla grinned a broken-toothed smile. 'We make big pain go away." He hoisted the large bottle and glugged a generous pour. "You get better. We kill more fuckeen Japs. Me cut. You make big choke!" He wrung the jug neck with both hands to demonstrate the act, the technique overstressed.

Evan winced. Javier assumed it originated from the rib injury, which can make even breathing a hurtful exercise. But this agony stirred from the conscience. Some things, black things, dwell forever, constant in a lifetime of forgotten incidents, ever-fresh down to the tiny buttons on a victim's shirt. Whitfield knew this would be one of them, no matter how much tuba juice, crude rum, or Gordon's gin he guzzled. The specter would consume him always.

DATE: MONDAY, 9 OCTOBER 1944

TIME: 1400 HOURS

LOCATION: LEYTE, PHILIPPINES

URGENT

Q10 ARRIVING VIA PBY 10 OCT. ETA 0700. POINT LD22. SECURE AREA. CONFIRM.

Rizal passed the wrinkled message to the Marine major who read it silently and routed it to the Australian seated across the table.

"Something important, very important, is in the wind, my friends. Q-10 would never risk a daylight flight into such a dangerous environment unless the most crucial business is at hand." Rizal retrieved the note from Evan's offering hand and reread the brief communication. Usually the agent slipped in during the murky hours by submarine, unannounced but to a select few after much secrecy and precaution. But to arrive by noisy flying boat in the coastal waters of Japanese-held territory represented mind-blowing peril beyond derring-do.

The trip would be Chick Parsons', A.K.A. Q-10, eleventh hair-raising visit to the Philippines. Unbeknown at this time to guerrilla bands which had been instructed to step up sabotage, MacArthur and Halsey had made the decision to bypass Mindanao in the short term, and stipulate undeveloped Leyte the focus of their combined might. Leyte, the archipelago's initial target of invasion, had risen to paramount importance in the commanders' flexible strategy, owing to the pounding US Naval air had been raining on Japanese sky power in the central Philippines. Dwindling enemy air assets encouraged the Americans to storm Leyte and thus be that much closer to Luzon and its supreme prize, Manila. The accelerated Leyte timetable called for D-Day on October 20.

Parsons' mission is to pave the intrusion, affirming appropriate assault beaches and coordinating volatile guerrilla actions: dynamiting Japanese telephone poles, blowing up supply dumps, crippling bridges, expanding convoy ambushes, badgering the enemy at every opportunity, forcing him to retract his tentacles away from the eastern beaches. Parsons, Q-10, the Stingray of AIB, would oversee a crush of pesky mayhem, ushering in hardened Army units of the dismounted 1st Cavalry Division, the 24th and 7th Infantry Divisions, plus the 11th Airborne Division—all veteran jungle fighters of New Guinea and islands dispersed throughout the Pacific breadth.

New to combat will be the highly trained and motivated 96th Infantry Division. Dog-faces of the battle tested 32nd and 77th Infantry Divisions will initially be held in reserve. As a prelude to the invasion, 6th Ranger Battalion is charged with seizing three peripheral islands screening the entrance to Leyte Gulf: Sulvan, Dinagat, and Homonhon. The northeastern beaches just below Tacloban are the intended landing sites, and more than coincidentally, the focal point of Evan Whitfield's most pronounced attention. Some outfits will hit the surf farther south. Two months into the fury the 77th, with "old soldiers" averaging thirty-two years of age, compared to twenty-four for most units, will assail the northwest beaches near Ormoc.

The Imperial Japanese 35th Army will inundate Leyte with reserve forces during the fray and suffer devastating losses to the grinding GIs, while exacting a bitter toll in return.

"Holy mother! If Leyte is to be invaded soon, I'd say that is cause for a tuba toast… to supplicate my rib pain of course." Whitfield touched a self-mocking palm below his chest.

'There is none," the Marine said.

"No tuba juice! Are you certain?"

"Absolutely, there's none left on the whole friggen island. You drank it all."

Rizal emitted a concurring cackle. Pancho Villa had become somewhat legendary among the local guerrillas, fed in part by Javier who bragged excessively about his friend's enormous capacity for the intoxicating liquid.

DATE:	TUESDAY, 10 OCTOBER 1944
TIME:	0653 HOURS
LOCATION:	LEYTE, PHILIPPINES POINT LD22

Hugging the waves, the dark speck zipped in over the horizon like a skimming tern. Twin engines buzzed in smooth unison as the pilot skillfully set down the bulky PBY Black Cat on the tranquil surface, a white rooster tail spraying skyward from the hull. He taxied as close to the western shore as he dared before a side hatch popped open. Nearby guerrillas pushed off four small wooden craft and paddled energetically to the braking "Cat." Within moments two figures made their way from the plane's belly, stepping into a little boat. Several large supply cartons were also off-loaded, and in moments the mini-squadron shoved off for the beach. Having transferred its passengers and cargo the PBY roared out to sea, retracing its wake, and disappeared away from the sun. The entire operation lasted no more than five to seven minutes.

As he stood admiring the splashy take off, Andy wished he would have been able to stow away, fetus-like, in the big bird's hollow womb. His hand-holding duty had left him feeling used and manipulated. He longed for Marla's arms and the insulated comfort of Pink Garden Villa.

Assembling in the clumpy jungle bordering the sandy stretch, Chick Parsons, shadowy super-agent of the AIB, made brief introductions. "Good to see you again, Antonio, Delane. Say hello to Colonel Frank Rouelle, US Army. Let's get the hell out of here!"

The mysterious Q-10, laconic and intense, offered no more information regarding Rouelle. Chick functioned on a need-to-know basis exclusively. The men engaged in a round robin of handshakes and polite nods before trekking into the hills. Following that evening, Delane would never see the undefined Rouelle again.

After interviewing Rizal, Whitfield, and Delane independently at Red Four the next day until after sunset, Q-10 laboriously transcribed his notes onto two small 3x5 cards and encoded them using ciphers unknown to the two radio operators. Indefatigably he summoned Duke and Barney and trudged to a transmitting perch distant from the little base.

At dawn he was up and about before anyone, anxious to survey other camps with Antonio, Rouelle, and a handful of scouts. Undercover agents secreted in the Tacloban work force were also on their clandestine itinerary. They were gone before Delane and Whitfield could see them off or bid good fortune.

Lying on his rattan sleeping mat, the Marine mentally reviewed the preceding night's conversation with Parsons. Among other observations, the AIB man wanted to learn of Rizal's connection to Tarluc and any political leanings Delane had been able to ferret out. The temporary major related facts of long past discussions between Antonio and himself, as well as his own judgments, instincts based on the man and his character.

Parsons listened quietly, drinking in his agent's comments, occasionally scribbling a one word notation, a buzzword, on a small, lined file card. Periodically he would ask a terse question designed to determine qualitative evaluations of guerrilla strength and reliability. Steely-eyed and impassive, he sucked in information like a demanding sieve, culling the important from a wash of data, scratching down a note here and there. Near the conclusion, Andy in turn queried Stingray about the Kempei Tai cipher book. "AIB already owned the code before we found the K.T. man's book, am I correct?" he asked.

The most Q-10 would commit to a confirmation was, "Something like that." Avoiding further quizzes, he purposely steered the discussion to probes directly related to Leyte and its invisible partisans waiting to spring like so many vipers. As they wound down, Commander Chick Parsons enlightened the Marine with news he had suspected since the October 9 message announcing Stingray's impending arrival.

"Delane, unless I discover something here to offset our plans, the US Sixth Army is preparing to invade Leyte on or about October 20. This will be preceded by days of massive air and naval shelling." Parsons paused, not so much for effect but to measure the impact in Delane's eyes. Poker-faced, Electric Eel simply gave a comprehensive head bob and casually finger-stroked six days' growth of scraggly stubble decorating his upper lip, the humble beginnings of an ugly mustache.

"Now having provided you with this knowledge, I must confine you to the environs of this camp until D-Day. And of course, don't tell anyone!"

"Will you inform Lieutenant Commander Whitfield?"

"I don't think so. I understand he's really been doing a number on the tuba juice." Parsons smiled for the first time. "He's a good man, that Whitfield, though, risked his ass every day to analyze the coast. His work will be invaluable to the invasion."

"I'm glad to hear it. If it all had been a futile gesture, no doubt Evan would feel cheated."

"And you're a good man too, Andy." It was the first time Stingray had ever addressed him by his first name. "Whether you realize it or not, you've been able to maintain an important link between AIB and Rizal. As a result, I've been free to pursue other duties. It was more than comforting to know your steady hand was on the tiller here with Rizal. This probably sounds corny, but I gambled by placing my trust in an untrained agent and you came through with flying colors. You have my personal gratitude."

'Thank you, sir. It's nice to be appreciated. And I say that in earnest." He bit his lower lip. "However, I must confess to tremors of paranoia these past few months, feeling a bit unloved, perhaps abandoned. I'm sure you've been under enormous pressure yourself, far beyond anything I've experienced." Delane shuffled his boot soles on the rippled bamboo that served as a flooring. "And for what it's worth, I have tremendous respect for your ability to quarterback this incredible espionage enterprise. I know you work Luzon, too. You're a brave, brave man and **I** salute you!"

Parsons sat still, yet absorbing the compliment. He knew he had used Delane unfairly. But hell, that came with the territory, as the expression goes. He whispered a soft, "Thank you." The secret war had taken a toll on his emotional self. Recapturing his composure he conversationally added, "Oh, it almost slipped my mind. General Maxwell contacted me a few days ago. Asked me to pass on his best wishes and to inform you that your Mrs. is expecting a Marine in January. Congratulations."

"You mean… "

"Yes, you're going to be a daddy. That Maxwell seems to know everything that's going on, both at home and on Leyte!"

Delane had been feeding Maxwell information for months, keeping open an alternative lifeline to Brisbane. Was Stingray alluding to this? Did he know? Delane was too stunned to care. He was to be a father. "Wow—a heap of fantastic news today."

"Well, I'm also burdened with some disheartening news too. Whitfield will be on the first transport out of Leyte, but I'm afraid you're going to have to remain, helping to coordinate between advancing army units and the resistance fighters. Your assignment will be to contact Colonel Spencer Marzen on the G2 staff at Twenty-four Corps north of Dulag the twenty-second of October. It'll be sticky business trying to link up. Got it?"

"Marzen, G-2 staff, Twenty-four Corps, north of Dulag, twenty-second October," he parroted, still numbed by thoughts of fatherhood and Marla carrying their child. "Sticky business," he footnoted.

"Leyte will be a bitch, Andy. No doubt the Nips will attempt to reinforce the island once we've landed. It's going to be a bitter bloodbath probably lasting months. Once Marzen releases you though, you're free to return to AIB in Brisbane. They'll process you back to the USMC Mission and a lengthy furlough, I'm sure."

"Hot damn—I'm going to be a father!"

DATE: SUNDAY, 22 OCTOBER 1944

TIME: 1015 HOURS

LOCATION: LEYTE GULF, PHILIPPINES,
                           NEAR DULAG

The Navy's big guns had commenced banging the beaches and inland installations on the nineteenth. Overhead screaming Avengers flying off carriers of the same fleet swooped upon Japanese defenders of the 16th Division. Ironically, the 16th was the unit responsible for much of the brutality punished on American and Filipino prisoners at Bataan, two-and-a-half years earlier. Now they would be the first to suffer MacArthur's wrath upon his return to the commonwealth. Cover fighters, powerfully nasty new Navy Hellcats and Marine Corsairs, occasionally streaked in low to unleash streams of .50 caliber revenge, tearing up troop movement beyond the beach. Four divisions comprising the X and XXIV Corps landed abreast and stormed into the swampy jungled morass. By October 22, they had carved out a secure perimeter and were battling inland, fighting through cratered earth and a pall of black smoke.

There was no way for Delane to plod through the fury erupting along the front lines. With Javier at his elbow, the two men had worked their way south, weaving around steamy marshes and suspected enemy concentrations. They pushed east toward the huge gulf. Once they reached blue water, they planned on completing the final leg of their U-turn, traveling north along the beach until they met up with GIs holding down the operation's left flank. Hopefully the soldiers wouldn't be in a trigger-happy frame of mind.

They trudged lightly, carrying only carbines, ammunition, and twin canteens. Major Delane had trimmed his hair and shaved the struggling mustache, trying to appear as American as possible. He had also chucked his soft cap for that very same purpose, wishing not to be mistaken for a Jap. Knotted about Javier's neck hung a filthy white towel. Optimistically, when waved it would encourage sentinels to think twice about sending a burst of lead in their direction.

Several times during their hike they had disturbed invisible nests of infuriated insects. The tiny bastards swarmed about heads and throats, anywhere skin and hair was exposed. Andy wished he hadn't discarded his cover prematurely, as his scalp crawled with a hundred itches. Javier, stoic and undistracted, ignored the discomfort without so much as a twitch. Spotting a dinky rivulet, the clever Filipino nodded a knowing glance and motioned Delane to follow him. He realized the streamlet would flow to the ocean, or at least empty into a larger creek heading to the beach.

Laboriously they twisted through steamy walls of sharp vegetation, exposed roots, and barring vines. No trail existed where they wished to go and the stream banks existed as flats of slick, sucking mud and jutting tree shoots, sharp and unyielding. Finally the duo observed the bed widening before them. It flared through the wood line to the beach where, enjoined by other running water, it formed a broad estuary. To the north, dull rumblings confirmed the combatants were indeed involved in the hideousness of killing. Delane placed an arm about his spunky companion's shoulder and squeezed a *well done* hug.

Having scouted a vantage point where they could spy along the strand without being observed, they rested for about twenty minutes, sipping halazoned water. Gray silhouettes—hundreds of them, maybe a thousand, some riding at anchor, others steaming in graceful, lazy sweeps—decorated the gulf like a Newport regatta. The powerful sight exhilarated both men.

They were about to shove off when the alert Filipino spotted figures carefully snaking along the tree line in their direction. A patrol... but whose? Javier unknotted the towel and let it hang free, barely breathing as he studied the patrol growing larger. Andy squinted while cupping a hand to his sweat-beaded forehead ,warding off the glare. "Gaiters," Delane whispered, "I think they're wearing gaiters, not puttees. And the helmet outline looks like ours."

The Filipino had no idea what his major was talking about. And neither would the reconnaissance GIs of the 7th Infantry Division who were cautiously advancing toward them. For what the Marine Corps called *gaiters* the army termed *leggings* and civilians referred to as *spats*. Semantics aside, the soldiers were Americans!

Within minutes they had flagged the doggies and were safely in their midst, although a few tense moments had preceded the reception. Not yet having completed his mission, the patrol leader released a single scout to escort the officer and guerrilla back to his company command post. Two hours later, they were passed on to XXIV Corps' beach area farther north.

"Delane, sir, Major USMC, and Sergeant Javier Palacios, USFIP, reporting in." He didn't know if the Filipino possessed a rank but "sergeant" sounded good. Besides, he was in a generous mood, and Javier seemed to be enjoying the status. Standing at a casual excuse for attention, they saluted Colonel Spencer Marzen.

Examining the bedraggled pair, Marzen returned an even more casual salute, the response more of a wave. "Electric Eel, isn't it? You boys look like you came from hell." Marzen, slender and graying, winked through wire rimmed glasses.

"Not quite, sir, but we were close." Delane was ebullient, he couldn't stop smiling. The beaches hummed with American slang. Soldiers muscling supplies through the sand and onto wheeled and tracked vehicles were everywhere, noisily swearing instructions. Cavernous LSTs emptied hulking loads of munitions and rations. Artillery pieces were hitched to tractors and wheeled off ramps and through ruts of wet sand. Javier marveled, as did Delane, at the swell of activity stretching as far and long as could be viewed. The roar of straining engines filled their joyful ears with a symphony of liberation. Leyte was being torn from the heinous grip of Tojo's legions, the first glorious step in the reconquest of the great commonwealth, soon to be republic. Beyond doubt, MacArthur and his historic oath had returned in overwhelming force.

"Sir, in spite of our exuberance, neither of us has slept in forty-eight hours, and speaking for myself, I haven't showered since a sub dropped me here last April. Do you think we could escape to that LST for some running hot water and a nap?"

"I don't see why not. And if the navy is unable to scrape up some clean duds for you folks, I'm sure there's a quartermaster somewhere around here who can help out." Colonel Marzen checked his wristwatch. "It's almost sixteen hundred now. I'll give you until zero-seven-thirty hours tomorrow to clean up and catch a few winks. Twenty-four Corps' Intelligence is set up about a quarter mile up that bulldozed road to my rear, I'll see you there."

Delane had to restrain himself. His near-giddiness was more that of a fraternity boy than a Marine Major… but he was truly overwhelmed by the spectacle encircling him. He began moving in the direction of the angular LST when an afterthought crossed his mind, bearing a twinge of guilt for not having brought it up sooner. "Colonel Marzen, my partner Lieutenant Commander Whitfield of the Royal Australian Navy is up in those hills laid up with busted ribs. Probably at a guerrilla camp designated Red Four. Has anyone heard from him? Perhaps you could check with your counterpart at X Corps."

"Oh yes, Pancho Villa!" Marzen said, an admiring look flashing in his blue eyes. "They brought that wild man in yesterday morning, along with a couple of AIB radio operators. Whitfield collected some serious shrapnel in his legs, evidently from friendly naval gunfire.

"Before the medics put him under with morphine, he claimed it would take more than 'blind-assed-Yank naval gunnery from preventing me my appointed piss off Victoria Bridge come New Years.'" Marzen effected a horrible impersonation of an Australian accent but the words were genuinely Evan's.

The Marine laughed with eyes clouded by wisps of emotion. Even Javier understood his old comrade in the "sodding science of bloody hydrography" was safely in the hands of his American brothers. "Where is he, might I ask?"

"Out there somewhere." The G-2 man's olive-drab sleeve swept in a seaward arc. "On a hospital ship. Once they've patched him up, I imagine he'll be transported out on the first available boat. Maybe he's already shipped out."

"Well, it's good to know he's out of harm's way. I can only hope Rizal, Q, and the rest of them are equally fortunate."

"Rizal is dead!"

The words rocked Delane and Javier alike. Death declares a finality beyond something as clinical as a heartbeat or brainwave. It affirms the demise of wit and character, of dreams and emotions. Major Delane steadied himself on the shoulder of the shocked Filipino at his side. "How... " His voice sounded weak and trembling. The joy of this glorious day came crashing down inside his shocked soul.

"By his own hand."

"Suicide, Rizal? You must have your facts wrong, man."

"Colonel Rouelle radioed the news yesterday. It happened near Dagami. Evidently he shot himself to prevent capture."

"I—I'm flabbergasted." The distraught Marine's earlier excitement had been deflated to limp anguish.

"As I understood Rouelle's transmission, Rizal and his group stumbled into a concentration of Japanese traversing the highlands. I suspect they were being redeployed from the west coast to our combat zone. Rizal walked right into it. A fire fight broke out and he was hit, shot badly through the chest and knee. No doubt the chest wound would have been mortal in time."

The colonel removed his steel pot and shook the silver-haired head, perspired and matted, his eyes sad, not relishing the prospect of continuing the morbid conclusion. "Rizal ordered his party to withdraw and leave him to die. They refused to abandon him, so he handed a map case and a few personal effects to his second in command. The rest is nobly unselfish. He pressed the muzzle of a Colt to his temple… and made the retreat an easy decision, one without second thoughts or guilt."

Despair gasped from Delane, a hissing, moaning, "No…no." He searched for something to kick, a carton, a stump, anything. On a beach cluttered with inanimate targets none was immediate. So he booted the uncaring sand in a vain show of torment, the spray harmlessly falling a few yards away.

"You have my sympathies. I understand he was quite a man."

"That he was, colonel." The words came out hoarse and throaty, like someone who is suffering the hungover aftermath of a nightlong binge. Delane took a deep breath and held it, trying to muster the energy for a deserving response.

"Antonio Marcos Rizal was a patriot in every sense of the word. His people viewed him as a savior, and rightfully so, a father figure who sacrificed personally on behalf of villagers and field hands. More than a swashbuckling resistance warlord roaming the hills, he represented the best of leadership. Rizal literally ate the same rations as his guerrillas for close to three years when he could have enjoyed more sumptuous fare by virtue of his position. But he elected to dine out of the same lean pot, to drink from the camp's communal cistern.

"Did you know he was an electrical engineer, colonel? And he conceived solutions to everyday problems with an engineer's precise, dispassionate logic… while possessing a heartfelt empathy for those in poverty, for those whom the next meal was uncertain. Serving as mediator and judge, he settled a myriad of petty squabbles. And the litigants always respected his decision because he was *Rizal*, a man of intellect and fairness. He was *Rizal*, who promised to reform the system once he had driven the Japanese from their nation.

"Half-catholic, half-Moro, he owned a hybrid's sensitivity for the issues that touch the whole of society and its segments. We would talk long into the dark nights about his peasant constituency, not so much the psychology of how they acted, which he understood in a very analytical way, but more of social needs and the soul of a collective people. After our discussions, I often would think back with the realization I'd been lectured. But in retrospect, Antonio had a manner of stimulating new thoughts." Delane exhaled a sigh of fond remembrance. "I guess you could say he also wore the philosopher's mantle. Yes, colonel, he was quite a man, the most exceptional I've ever known."

Colonel Marzen, touched by Delane's impromptu eulogy, reached out to both men, paternally patting their shoulders in a silent reaction of condolence and sharing. Sagging under the painful news, a weeping Javier allowed the Marine to prop a supporting hand under his utility belt and steer him toward the LST. Unfortunately the ship's showerheads would be unable to cleanse the sting of loss. Only time would ease their grief.

DATE: MONDAY, 23 OCTOBER 1944

TIME: 0830 HOURS

LOCATION: LEYTE, PHILIPPINES

Dulag Area "Catamon Hill," the communications officer confirmed to the signalman manning the field telephone. Delane and Javier had just entered the 96th Infantry Division's command post with Marzen. The colonel had come forward a half hour earlier from his Corps position near the beach and had sent word for the two to join him. Delane had experienced the two most rejuvenating showers of his life, none would be better. After the second, he scraped and scrubbed the slimy green mold from his boon-dockers and sprinkled their innards with clouds of disinfectant powder.

Wearing clean army fatigues and helmets, they moved toward Marzen, huddled over a topographical map in the canvas-topped revetment serving as headquarters. Several other officers also gathered about. "The Japs have emplaced a significant number of artillery pieces on Catamon Hill." He pointed to a cluster of concentric circles ringed asymmetrically around a smudged number designating the hill's elevation. 'They're pounding heavy stuff right on top of our infantry trying to advance through the swamp approaching the hill base... here." His finger indicated an area forward of the outermost ring.

"Our flyboys are tied up supporting heavy action in the 7th Division's sector. We've been blindly responding with counter battery fire from both Divarty and Corps Artillery but we can't seem to pinpoint the bastards." His eyes searched the two new arrivals. "Are you familiar with the area?"

Javier, his undersized head swimming under the new steel pot, made eye contact with Delane. He jerked his head up and down, anxious to share knowledge, yet silent, unsure of his poor command of English. The Marine excused himself from the group and took the guerrilla aside. "What is it, Javier?"

"After swamp water, ground cut like no fat snake. Go up top Catamon." He made a fish-tailing motion with his hand, serpentining it upwards. "Jap no see. Much bush," he added. "Good for sneak."

The Marine turned back to the group. "Javier here has lived in this general locale all his life. He says that once beyond the swamp, there's a narrow 'no fat' ravine, overgrown with concealing foliage. Evidently it twists all the way to the summit."

A full bird colonel, commander of the Division's 383rd Infantry Regiment, punched fist into palm and excitedly approached Delane. "Major, would you and your scout be willing to move up to the front and guide our men to the ravine? That is, unless Colonel Marzen can't spare you." Marzen nodded his approval.

"We'll do anything we can to help, sir." Delane said.

The regimental C.O. called out to a tight-jawed, younger officer listening near the field radio. "Captain Luzak, get these men up there pronto. I'll ring up Second Battalion to let them know what's happening."

Three men moved quickly at a crouch, following a string of commo wire to their destination, when a shell whizzed in from Catamon Hill and detonated about a hundred yards to their front. Instinctively they jumped into a deep crater and awaited more shelling. None came. "Must've been either random fire or a long round," the army captain observed. "Let's wait a few minutes to be sure."

"Sounds good to me," Delane agreed. "By the way, did the colonel call you Luzak back there?"

'That's right, Major."

"L-U-Z-A-K?"

"Yes, sir. First name of Woodrow. Have we crossed paths before?"

"Well, it's not the most common name. I thought perhaps you might be familiar with another Luzak—Tony Luzak, a marine NCO I served with. And one tough S.O.B. I might add."

The captain shrugged one of those *Well, I'll be damned* smiles. "Cripes, sometimes I think there's only eleven people in the whole friggin world. Yeah, that tough S.O.B. is my brother. Where'd you hook up with him?"

"Corregidor originally. Then he and I escaped on a little boat ride to Mindanao. We even served in Brisbane together for a short while."

Woody issued an approving look of wonderment and extended a muddied hand. "Woody Luzak, major. Glad to make the acquaintance."

"Andy Delane. Likewise."

Catamon Hill is overrun the following day. Its conquerors enter the environs of Leyte's torturous embrace and slug out an ever-broadening perimeter, annihilating the enemy 16th Division in the process. At first the Japanese are content to let the Americans take the island with limited resistance, husbanding their resources for the imminent Luzon campaign. But somewhere along the decision tree they shift strategy, determining to engage a furious land battle and a concomitant naval war of immense dimension.

Two imperial divisions, the 30th and 102nd, are landed at Ormoc on the island's west coast while the clash at Catamon Hill still raged. For six more weeks, the vicious land war disputes every anonymous lump large enough to be called a hill. Reinforcements surge onto the island from both combatants while mighty sea vessels exchange thunderbolts of destruction, sending scores of fighting ships and scorched crewmen to a watery cemetery.

Kamikaze attacks, incomprehensible to the Americans but nevertheless effective, heap murderous devastation on the U.S. fleet. By early December, the Japanese have committed over 60,000 soldiers to Leyte, pledged to either stuff the Sixth Army or die for the emperor. Having run up against near impregnable defenses in the north near Carigara, the Americans loop the 77th Infantry Division in a daring amphibious assault to the enemy rear near Ormoc. The "old men" envelop the Japanese in a slaughtering pincer with the 11th Airborne and 7th Infantry Divisions. Also around Ormoc, US 24th Division infantrymen savagely expel the dug-in enemy

1st Division, dislodging them with TNT and flame throwers. By Christmas, all MacArthur's strategic objectives have been torn from enemy control and the weary Sixth Army pulled off the island to refit for Mindoro and Luzon.

Fresh American divisions from the Eighth Army move in and are given the task of "mopping up" the yet formidable Japanese holed up throughout the island. This bloody affair lasts until May of 1945. US Army casualties total over 3,000 killed and about 12,000 wounded. For the Japanese, 60,000 would be buried in Leyte's damp volcanic earth. Only 400 surrender and most of those are wounded or shocked, unable to fight to a glorious death for Bushido and emperor. Inferior Japanese tanks have been blown to scrap metal and an enemy ill-planned parachute attack snuffed out during the bloody contest.

Naval losses are staggering on both sides, with the enemy suffering the great majority. Japanese air power has been attrited to a strike-less capability. Other than "divine wind" kamikaze capacity, they are reduced to a defensive force almost exclusively. For the most part, the seas and skies have become American, and the grinding land forces of Uncle Sam hold a powerfully supreme upper fist, though long months ahead will contend the issue.

DATE: SATURDAY, 23 DECEMBER 1944

TIME: 1430 HOURS

LOCATION: BRISBANE, AUSTRALIA (USMC MISSION)

ELECTRIC EEL BATTERY LOW ON JUICE. REQUIRE IMMEDIATE RECHARGE. PLEASE RETRIEVE ASAP

Brigadier General Gordon Maxwell balled the transmission slip and grunted an approval to the second lieutenant standing by. His promise to lend a helping hand was being reeled in. "Evidently, army G-2 people on Leyte are unnecessarily hanging on to Delane like a long-lost security blanket. It's about time we snatched him," he barked. "Call AIB and confirm Major Delane's immediate release back to this mission. And then cut top priority travel orders ricky-tick. I want him out of Leyte on the first available PBY heading south!"

CHAPTER XXIV
THE COOP

DATE: TUESDAY, 30 JANUARY 1945

TIME: 1845 HOURS

LOCATION: MINDORO ISLAND, PHILIPPINES

Streaks of translucent pink and gray striped the western skyline, the reluctant sun preparing to submerge below the lazy South China Sea. The corrugated Officers Club near the airstrip soaked in horizontal rays, its configuration looking more like a roadside hotdog stand than a drinking establishment befitting officers and gentleman by act of congress. *The Coop* represented an informal fraternity of sorts rather than a bona fide saloon—no chairs, no tables, standing room only. Still, it served a practical function until time and material permitted more luxurious digs. In its midst a relaxed bedlam prevailed as young officers, most of them company-grade variety, tippled horse piss beer and a smattering of spirits.

Mindoro had been assaulted via sea by the independent 503rd Parachute Infantry Regiment in tandem with the 24th Infantry Division's 19th RCT on December 15, fighting sporadically through January 4, with light resistance. Due to Mindoro's geographical enormity, another eleven days were required to root out Japanese remnants stubbornly holding out.

Within hours of official repatriation, two-by-fours, sheet plywood, and rippled metal roofing hastily appeared and an elongated three-sided shack, christened *The Coop* by its mocking patrons, opened its largess to an appreciative overflow. Serving a limited selection of the above- mentioned booze and warm brew from 1700 to 2100 hours each evening, rain or dry, its rowdy customers were almost all exclusively airborne or air corps with a few Yank and Aussie engineers. Soon rear echelon service troops would flood the island, prepping fields and depots in support of the massive invasion of

Luzon already underway. More substantial structures would sprout in time to slake and sate their recreational appetite. By then though, the sky soldiers would be long gone.

Shouldering his way among the boisterous crowd, the husky captain clenched a skinny cigar dead center between incisor teeth. Puffing perfunctory "excuse me's" through the lengthy stogie, he pushed to the counter where a pointy-faced tech sergeant volunteered as bartender. "Double Manhattan on the rocks," the officer shouted, holding out a crumpled five spot.

"No ice, sir," pointy face responded. "No vermouth either, except for some private stock locked in the cupboard. Belongs to another officer. Christ, he thrives on long cigars and double Manhattans, too. You guys must have attended the same Sunday school"!

"His name just wouldn't happen to be Callahan, would it?"

"Right on the money, Captain. You know him?"

Phil Primo's face lit up, buoyed by the inference that Kid Callahan evidently had survived the Five-O-Three's New Guinea parachute assaults at Nadzab and Noemfoor Island in addition to the recent amphibious undertaking on lightly defended Mindoro. "Well, sergeant," he jabbered through the stationary cigar hardly moving his lips, similar to a vaudeville ventriloquist, "I'm Callahan's godfather, and I'll personally absolve you of any restrictions he might have placed on said vermouth. Now why don't you pour me an inch, and about three more fingers of your smoothest whiskey." Phil emitted a determined smile, though he knew it was a tough sell.

"Sorry, sir, but even a godfather requires permission from higher authority when it comes to Lieutenant Callahan's stash." The sergeant was dodging effectively. Looking beyond the persuasive captain, he seemed relieved to glimpse a familiar face. Returning his gaze to Phil, he suggested, "Captain Godfather, perhaps you could check directly with Lieutenant Callahan yourself—he's standing about twenty feet off to your left wing if you wheel around—the one trailing a cloud of cigar smoke."

'Thanks!" Primo eagerly whirled, anxious to reunite with his old buddy from Fort Benning jump school days.

Engaged in rapid conversation, First Lieutenant Nick Callahan bantered excitedly with a small circle of young officers while weaving to the bar area. Starched fatigues and close-cut hair framed a sun-tanned face and neck. The years had matured Callahan since he and Phil had hoisted an overload of doubles the summer of '42. Boyish Nick had filled out frame and face, the latter handsomer and more square-jawed than Phil remembered. Like a prideful big brother, Primo glowed at what his influence had wrought, at least in part.

Veteran of two combat jumps and an amphibious landing, Callahan had scrapped through the fiendish hell of New Guinea and lesser struggle for Mindoro, leading men and displaying savvy initiative in the process. Rock hard yet lean, he carried himself with a confidence that only comes with experience. He stretched out the cigar stub, attempting to signal the barman's attention when his eye caught the fullback's grinning puss. "Holy shit, is that who I think it is?!"

"It sure is, young trooper. And where'd you pick up those nasty smoking and drinking habits?" Phil hooted above the chattering din.

"From you, you crazy son of a bitch! Man it's good to see you." The two stumbled into each other's embrace and bear-hugged heartily with much heavy backslapping. Reeling in an off-balanced promenade, they bounced into surrounding drinkers before pushing apart to assess each's appearance.

"Still whistling in your sleep?"

"Like a traffic cop! Say, Nick—I hear you've got the only vermouth on Mindoro. Tell you what, you put up the vino and I'll spring for the hard stuff!"

"Let 'er rip. My mama raised no fool!"

'Then who in Chicago raised you?" the fullback chuckled.

"Be civil, Phil," he playfully cautioned. "I've got two quarts squirreled away for future emergencies."

"And I flew in this morning with three boxes of Dutch Masters Panatellas!"

"Sounds like a deal is in the wind. Wanna get married?" Callahan yipped like a coyote as the two shook hands, cementing barter of the most symbiotic benefit.

They reminisced for hours, rambling long and deep into the Mindoro night. Tropical skies spanned warm breezes as a thousand glimmering stars eavesdropped overhead. Exuberance graduated to sober reflection as they touched upon experiences of the last two-and-a-half years. The Kid had picked up two Bronze Stars on New Guinea. He gratefully attributed "luck of the Irish" and a threadbare scapular (still dangling around his neck) in seeing him through the thick of monstrous combat without so much as a scrape. A cousin, Pat Shanahan, had not been so fortunate, having lost a foot to a Wehrmacht antipersonnel mine at Anzio.

The Coop had been shut down for an hour, but they had managed to garner a couple of oversized Manhattans, nursing them through whispered conversation. Clusters of men sat similarly on the ground, chatting quietly and dispatching the final dregs of canned beer and spirits.

Primo had volunteered for the first available airborne replacement contingent shipping overseas. Because he oversaw troops in training at Fort Bragg in North Carolina, he assumed that his new outfit would be in the ETO. Deemed one hundred percent, Phil's leg had been given the green light by Army surgeons at the Bragg post hospital. Other than a few shiny purple scars, lumpy and free-form, he stood prepared to again meet the test of combat. When orders of a Pacific assignment reached him he had been surprised, but then the appeal, or more appropriately the uniqueness, of being one of a relative handful of troopers to jump in both theaters, brought a gleam of titillation to his adventurous soul. Something to thrill his grandchildren.

Though a fairly modest man, Primo always savored pursuing a pedestal apart from the pack, whether on the gridiron or field of combat. It wasn't so much the limelight as it was accomplishment beyond the ordinary. In his own mind, personal achievement represented an acceptable goal as long as its pursuit remained within the team concept, something he believed in with unabashed zeal. Had Phil known he was destined to participate first-hand in arguably the most recklessly daring parachute assault of the war, he might not have been so porky.

DATE: MONDAY, 5 FEBRUARY 1945

TIME: 0900 HOURS

LOCATION: MINDORO, PHILIPPINES

Twice within nine days, the Five-O-Three had been placed on battle-ready alert to jump on Luzon in support of Krueger's Sixth Army surging in from Lingayen Gulf. Elements of Eichelberger's Eighth Army, mostly glider infantry of the 11th Airborne Division, were also in the thick of it. The Eleventh's 511th Parachute RCT had successfully pulled off a vertical assault on Tagaytay Ridge the third of February. The same day, the 503rd had been instructed to depart Mindoro and leapfrog jump beyond the 511th. According to plan, the two regimental combat teams would pinch the enemy in their swift jaws at a point between Highway 17 and Luzon's Nichols Field.

Colonel George M. Jones, energetic and youthful, looked much younger than his thirty-three years. As regimental commander of the Five-O-Three, he had just received disappointing orders canceling the unit's Luzon jump. Frustration was apparent. His troopers were ready to go. Pre-jump SOP had been in place for forty-eight hours: weapons and radio maintenance, parachute bundle procedures, supply package preparation, jump-stick assignments, plane designations, along with schedules for takeoff and a myriad of jumping procedures. For whatever reasons, the plug had been yanked.

The "stood-down" 503rd was all gussied up with no place to dance! ...or so it would seem. But Colonel Jones knew better. An old airborne comrade in arms, temporarily appointed to planning at Sixth Army, had forewarned him that a most formidable task was coming his way, one so audacious it would electrify the imagination of ally and foe alike.

Through the "old boy" buddy-buddy channel, Jones had ascertained his unit had been selected to air drop onto heavily defended Corregidor Island, that treacherous pimple of rock and sand guarding the entrance to Manila Bay. As the troopers subdued beach defenses, a battalion of the 24th Infantry Division's 34th RCT would depart Mariveles at the tip of the Bataan peninsula and storm The Rock by amphibious assault. Together they would eradicate Japanese resistance. Incredibly, the jump would take place in the frightful exposure of broad daylight.

February 7, 1945, Colonel Jones, commanding officer, 503rd Parachute Regiment , received Field Order 48 confirming the operation. Later amended on February 11, the revision stipulated the entire RCT to be dropped, including its field artillery battalion and a company of engineers. The official order was merely a formality. Jones and his staff had been scoping out the target for days.

DATE: MONDAY, 12 FEBRUARY 1945

TIME: 0900 HOURS

LOCATION: MINDORO, PHILIPPINES

Like a punt returner, Primo twitched, feeling all alone as he awaited Colonel Jones' orderly to summon him. Phil had requested the meeting, hoping to clarify his position within the unit. So far he had been a fifth wheel, doing odd jobs without a command of his own. The upcoming Corregidor jump had juiced him up, as it had every trooper on Mindoro. However, his undefined role left him feeling somewhat diminished. An exact mission, one with a leadership part, would be more to his liking. *I should be commanding a company! Instead, I'm counting chutes and rations. Dicking around with the regimental S-4, inspecting riggers, checking for leaky radio batteries—* and all the necessary prerequisites which "someone else" had always handled.

He was rattled from musings of "poor-me" paranoia by a young corporal entering the anteroom off Jones' makeshift office. "Captain Primo, the colonel will see you now." Sucking up a lungful of humidity, an apprehensive Phil Primo approached the open planning room door and knocked.

Hunkering over a topographical relief sand table and recent aerial photos of the island in question, a pensive Colonel Jones looked up and interrupted Primo before he could respectfully report, as per the military courtesy chapter of every officer's handbook. "Captain, it's going to be hairy, but I think the Japs are convinced an airborne show is so insane that they'll never expect it. Surprise and only surprise is the key!" Jones was thinking aloud as much as sharing an obvious conclusion.

No doubt MacArthur's thinking for ordering such a risky endeavor was every bit emotional as strategically practical. *Ours is not to reason why.* Besides, Mac's G-2 estimated only 850 Japanese troops defended The Rock. A regiment by air and a battalion by sea should be able to overwhelm the enemy after a frightening period of pre-invasion bombardment. Unknown to Jones and everyone else on the American half of the ledger, more than 6,000 Japanese soldiers and imperial marines infested each defensible position from Topside to Hooker Point, and the murky environs of Malinta Tunnel.

"Yes, sir," the junior man agreed. "Everyone's primed and confident."

The commander of Rock Force, as the Corregidor assault units were now designated, had recently overflown the island to confirm drop zones and general familiarization.

"Captain," he abruptly stated, "I've got a staff meeting here at zero nine fifteen, so let's make it swift."

Phil cleared his throat, bracing himself for his own appeal as well as the anticipated rebuke. "Colonel Jones, I realize you're a busy man... "

"Get to the point," the West Pointer restively encouraged.

"I want a company, I want a command!"

Rock Force commander eased out a disarming smile, comforting to Phil's expectation of reproach. "Captain Primo, you're right, I am a busy man. Unfortunately, too preoccupied to personally meet you and all the officers new to the Five-O-Three. In the past, I've always made it a point to do just that. So let me take this opportunity to apologize for my delinquency."

"No apology necessary, sir." Primo nervously shifted weight to his other foot.

'Thank you. However, I've managed to spin through your service record and let me compliment you on its impressiveness, especially your stint in Sicily with the Five-O-Five. Fine outfit. You're probably not aware, but Jim Gavin is an old friend from way back. Have you ever met up with him?"

"Well, sir, as the expression in the ranks goes, a finer officer never shit between a pair of jump boots than old Slim Jim Gavin. And as a matter of record, I hooked up with him first-hand at Biscari Station and a piece of contested real estate called Biazza Ridge."

Jones laughed aloud at the profane overpraise common to men in uniform. "I guess you're aware he's a general these days, top dog in the Eighty Deuce."

"Yes, sir. Jumped them into Normandy and Holland."

"Nijmegen, wasn't it?" Jones butchered the Dutch pronunciation.

"Yes, sir, colonel. Although I've never heard it pronounced the same way twice. I believe, however, NYE-MEE-GAN is the way it goes. The Hundred-And-First hit Eindhoven and the Brits landed at Arnhem at the same time the All Americans jumped. From guys who were there, I heard those poor Limeys and Polish troopers really took a pasting."

Jones nodded. "Well, Captain, I'd enjoy chewing the fat all day but the clock is ticking and I've got things to do. So let me be as succinct as possible." The bird colonel hesitated as if to gather his thoughts and choose words selectively. But the two he picked were as basic as they come, uttered repeatedly from commanding lips at Fort Ord, Fort Jackson, Camp Mackall, and wherever petitions surfaced, "Request denied!"

Before the captain could offer even a breath of protest, Jones continued. "Primo, I've got more captains than my table of organization requires. My company commanders are all experienced and established. It would be foolhardy to switch people around at this late hour merely to satisfy seniority. But I recognize your competence and outstanding record. You'll be jumping as a supernumerary, as part of my regimental staff. That's the best I can do. If casualties warrant a command replacement at the company level, I'll consider you at that time. Needless to say, you're at the head of the list. Any questions?"

"No, sir." *I know a stone wall when I see one.*

'Then you're dismissed." Jones offered an assuring smile to show he was not unhappy with the eager captain. He liked them aggressive.

Phil Primo snapped to attention and saluted smartly. "Airborne, sir," he called out.

"All the way," Rock Force commander responded, returning the gesture.

The fullback executed a perfect about-face and departed, empty in his request but satisfied in the recognition his superior had afforded.

"Warden" Jones, as the troopers had monickered him, liked to think he could outmarch any man in his outfit, any time, any distance, any terrain. Hard training humps had influenced several jokesters to laughingly refer to the Memphis native as their "Tennessee Walking Horse." Nicknames aside, their confidence in his ability to plan and lead stood unquestioned.

As he stared for perhaps the thousandth time at the miniature sand table representation, he couldn't help but wonder about the future. Swooping in at daylight with unpredictable crosswinds threatening to sweep parachutists beyond the skimpy drop zones could slam men into craggy cliff-sides, or helplessly overshoot them into the choppy sea. All this, while they floated , sunlit, at the mercy of Jap gunners plinking away like Sunday skeet-shooters. The prospect for calamity loomed ever-present.

Normally, a stick of troopers contains roughly eighteen jumpers who exit the C-47 aircraft one after another in a matter of seconds. *Impossible,* he thought, *on the narrow confine of Corregidor.* Only six parachutists will most likely be able to jump at a time. Then each clumsy Gooney Bird would have to loop a wide circle, come in exposed for another gutsy pass and drop the second six. The process would be repeated yet again to unload the third half-dozen paratroopers. So three sticks of six would comprise each crammed plane load, armed to the teeth and determined to oust the Japs from almost three years of cushy occupation. Squatters rights would soon be trampled by the double-buckled jump boots of the Five-O-Three, and veteran amphibious dog-faces of 3rd Battalion, 34th Infantry Regiment.

Friday, the sixteenth of February, around 0830, would see the first sky soldiers step into the bright morning slipstream and hit the silk. Rock Force, fierce and motivated, had a confirmed appointment to retake that blackened lump of ash and smoke, cratered and gouged like Dante's sulfurous netherworld. Hell has many names, and Corregidor for most would become a fitting synonym.

Colonel George Jones would lead his command with tight-lipped resolve, recognizing fully the potential for disaster. Reality dictated that a certain margin of casualties was inevitable. But the historical chill of Little Big Horn and the Light Brigade of Crimean note, examples of unnecessary, callous disregard for one's troops, penetrated his conscience. The Rock Force mission treaded on a similar possibility. Detailed planning, kind weather, and an unsuspecting enemy would be infinitely more important than Lady Luck's favored glance. But just in case, he knew most of the men had hedged their bets with rabbit feet, four leaf clovers, and a plethora of assorted coins, crucifixes and female accessories carried in sweet memory of wives and girlfriends halfway round the globe. Religious conviction, superstition, and a meticulous scheme, the ABCs of survival, would ride with every trooper when the green light flashed.

DATE: TUESDAY, 13 FEBRUARY 1945

TIME: 1930 HOURS

LOCATION: MINDORO, PHILIPPINES THE COOP

Training had been especially strenuous the past few days and Colonel Jones realized his troopers needed a pressure valve to bleed off the tension all were experiencing. Under the limiting circumstances, no better physical release existed than a raucous evening at The Coop. Big band sounds of Benny Goodman, Glen Miller, Artie Shaw and a select few others rocked the Victrola, blaring trombones and clarinets in the evening heat. Beyond the other end of the airstrip, enlisted men caroused in a festive night of their own. Sentries were posted around the perimeter not only for security purposes, but to prevent drunks from wandering into spinning propeller blades. Air Corps night flight interceptors stealthily landed and took off regularly, guarding against possible enemy surprise attacks.

Callahan and Primo mixed freely with other officers of the Kid's 3rd Battalion, including its commander Lieutenant Colonel "Big John" Erickson, legendary survivor of hideous wounds suffered on New Guinea, destined to be first man on Corregidor. For two days every platoon had entered a special briefing tent to inspect their particular zone of action indicated on the sand table mock-up. Erickson insisted individual squads be double-briefed right down to each rifleman. Large, strong, and Hollywood handsome, Erickson, by virtue of earlier wounds, could have been shipped stateside had he so elected, but his loyalty to Jones and the Five-O-Three insisted he heal up and stick around till the finale. The plan was the 3/503 would spearhead the leap into the gullet of Corregidor.

Similar to the historic bash at Hamia, Phil ponied up a box of panatellas for the boys even though he barely knew but a fistful of them. The ritual donation wandered his mind back to his Predators and the special bond that connected them. Within less than thirty seconds, the flat carton had been emptied of its aromatic missiles and The Coop capped with a gray layer of tobaccoed haze. Guzzling Manhattans in no small number, their circle soon became the focus of bleary-eyed activity, exceedingly vocal.

Among the inebriated lot basked a pair of uniformed Red Cross ladies, approaching forty and a bit overweight... old broads! Well-groomed and issuing the remindful fragrance of perfumed talcum, they were the recipients of countless free drinks and insincere offers of matrimony. Like bloodhounds frenzied by criminal scent, young second lieutenants, inexperienced in love but hell-bent on asserting their masculine prowess, zeroed in on the two like a Norden bombsight... if one is permitted to mix similes. Inside the noisy ring, men took turns jitterbugging, twirling the gals in a dizzying twist of spins and kicks. "Chattanooga Choo-Choo" played and replayed a dozen times, Tex Benecke's high pitched whine carrying the solo lyrics, the volume knob cranked to the max until the overworked needle snapped and only a screeching static reverberated through the club.

Molly, the more seasoned of the Red Cross women, and certainly the drunkest, picked up the pace by singing "I'll Be With You In Apple Blossom Time" to the roar of sentimental troopers enjoying the old favorite. And Molly's voice wasn't half-bad. Certainly her stylistic rendition overcame any octave deficiencies. Though tipsy, she controlled and deflected the soldiers' admiring pats, several of which invariably touched her wiggling derrière. Gloria, her partner, joined in and they picked up the beat in a swinging Andrews Sisters version. It was obvious they thrilled to the center stage. And they in turn brought a smidgen of cheer to vibrant young men, many of whom would exude the merry energy of life for but a few more days. Certainly these tootsies were no neophytes, having been down the road of hard knocks, scrambling to co-exist in a man's environment, coaxing and imposing when necessary to obtain the requisites of a gypsy lifestyle. Prior to the war they had toiled as bar maids and hostesses before their physical assets faded and a younger generation supplanted their talents. Both had been married for a brief tenure to "skunks," as they giddily termed their exes.

Periodically, when the mood stimulated or an advantage could be leveraged, a roll in the hay was not out of question. Self-respect still rode high in the morning mirror. A girl does what a girl has to do. Gloria and Molly wound down the final strains to cheering applause and boot-stomping on the hard packed gravel. Catcalls and whistles stridently resounded through The Coop and into the sweaty evening. Live entertainment was difficult to come by on Mindoro, regardless how amateurish.

Invariably when large groups are enjoying a night's conviviality a minuscule minority fucks it up for all. "Who gives a rat's ass about apple blossoms!" The voice belonged to a newly joined second lieutenant, *pissed to the gills*, as the colloquialism goes. Wobbling his way to the women, he waved a ten dollar bill. "Let's see your cherry," he challenged. The din subsided to a soundless hush. Flushed with the obnoxious brazenness of too many boilermakers, he grinned a cockeyed air of superiority. Most of the officers were embarrassed but intrigued enough to see what followed.

A few, close to the confrontation, Callahan included, moved to usher the ladies out of the spotlight but Molly held them off. Hands on hips she faced her baby-faced antagonist, and with a sneer bordering more on disgust than contempt, addressed him in a manner disdaining his sophomoric inexperience. "Sonny, what makes you think **a** babe like you would know what the hell you were looking at? Besides my cherry's been banged so far back toward my asshole I use it as a stop light for kiddies like you!" She couldn't have stunned him more with an arrow through the balls.

A hooting uproar rocked the corrugated roof. Men guffawed and finger-pointed, over-supporting her prickly attack, purposely deriding the humiliated lieutenant. Their intent was to punish him to a crushing mortification. He had played and lost. Red-faced and stuttering, hopefully he was drunk enough to develop a protective amnesia. A foolish rookie, barely a year out of college, had chosen to joust a very tough broad, and predictably came out second best. Stripped and whipped. One of life's more valuable lessons—never duel with a swordsman—had been administered free of charge. Then again, the Red Cross also dispensed hot coffee, Hershey Bars, and Gillette Blue Blades without asking so much as a nickel in return.

CHAPTER XXV
ROCK FORCE

DATE: FRIDAY, 16 FEBRUARY 1945

TIME: 0820 HOURS

LOCATION: ABOVE THE SOUTH CHINA SEA

A parade field and sloping, nine-hole golf course crowning Topside had been designated as drop zones for the Five-O-Three's parachutists. If successful, the descending troopers would immediately occupy the advantageous high ground.

Commanders rejected Kindley Field as an alternative DZ, though it would have made for an easier drop site. Its position at the low-lying tail end of the pollywogged island would require scaling Malinta Hill and Topside from below and into the teeth of cliffside bunkers. Operational planners deemed it more feasible to seize Topside from the sky by vertical assault and then battle across and down the heights. Obviously, landing risks presented by the summit's treacherous terrain were weighed carefully but considered worth taking vis-a-vis the Kindley Field option. Attacking downhill offered gainful incentive, an inherent momentum aided by the effect of gravity—the most Newtonian of military principles.

Unwitting American strategists had been advised, erroneously, that a force of only 850 Japanese defended the island, a number of whom no doubt were rendered ineffective during preceding weeks of bombing runs and naval gunship salvos. In actuality, more than seven times that figure readied themselves for what the island commandant, Navy Captain Akira Itagaki, expected would be an amphibious attack on the sea-level beaches. (The captain was half right.) His logician's brain work was sound enough. Corregidor's asymmetrical perimeter represented but one square mile, hardly conducive to an airborne enterprise. Historically, the Americans almost exclusively came though the surf aboard specialized landing craft. This had been the *modus operandi* from Tarawa to Luzon, and the murderous island hops in between. Itagaki would not piddle away his resources countering a phantom prospect, and a paratrooper invasion was (to his thinking) highly irrational for the systematic plotters of Krueger's Sixth Army. The fortress island's twisting narrowness and unpredictable wind currents discouraged drop zone potentiality. Undersized and cratered from weeks of impacting explosives, the golf course's and parade field's DZ usefulness had been disqualified. When compounded by airborne doctrine, which prefers dark-hour intrusion, only lunacy would compel a daylight raid. No, the foreseeable American dogs would force the beaches, and there his disciplined defense would slaughter them.

Coastal artillery and anti-aircraft emplacements had been taking a horrific pounding since January 23 when workhorse B-24 bombers of the Thirteenth Air Force began dropping loads of heavy demolition bombs, five hundred pounders, from altitudes around 17,000 feet. The split-tailed Liberators manufactured by Consolidated each hauled a payload of twenty-six bombs, whistling them down onto Corregidor's bunkered defenders. Burrowed deep in Malinta Hill and a network of emplacements hollowed out through the island, direct hits and shock waves slew and maddened Japanese troops. Herds of four-engined brutes flew at will over the tiny target, disgorging an endless stream of destruction. Buildings of substantial construction, corrugated metal warehouses and supply sheds, were blown sky-high only to rain twisted debris, jagged and scorched, all over the blackened surface, including the diminutive golf links and parade ground. Soon thereafter, flights from the Seventh and Fifth Air Forces joined to pummel virtually every inch a bomb's trajectory could reach from head to tip. Anti-aircraft positions were eventually subdued to smoldering rubble.

Between January 28 and February 7, American airmen would average bomb-loads totaling one hundred tons per day, with no respite in sight for the beleaguered foe. Unrelenting Army Air Corps fighters, with absolute impunity, zipped in at low altitude, selectively seeking out gun pits, cave mouths and tunnel entrances, releasing thousand pounders at angles allowing maximum penetration.

Explosives deployed, they would fly 360 degree circles and roar in just off the deck in screaming strafing runs, coughing out hot ribbons of .50 caliber machine gun fire. Squadron after squadron of P-38 Lightnings, P-47 Thunderbolts, and P-51 Mustangs timed their sorties so the enemy had little time to catch his breath. Powerhouse Merlin engines propelled the silvery

Mustangs at maneuverable high speeds and ranges unknown to the Japanese air services. Superiority rode in the cockpit of every American pilot, confident in equipment and training. Indeed, air supremacy had become a fact of the battlefield. Philippine skies buzzed with the sleek steel and aluminum raptors of Yankee engineering. Twenty-four hour work shifts at Martin, Boeing, Consolidated, Grumman, North American, Chance-Vought, Bell, Lockheed and a myriad of tireless sub-contractors cranked out an ever-evolving river of superb, dependable aircraft, spelling inevitable doom to the shrinking empire. Production lines from Long Island to Los Angeles guaranteed that American industry would match its fighting men's tireless dedication. The mills of Pittsburgh and Birmingham devoted three shifts daily to driving a spokeless rising sun into a retracting, shrunken void, collapsing on itself like black holes of lost galaxies.

Standing in the open door, the rush of Pacific wind felt cool and drying. Perspiration rolled freely, coursing along his torso until it welled about the constrictions caused by the taut harness straps. Third Battalion/503 had saddled up several hours past, enplaning at 0700. Chutes and gear prompted sweat to pump liberally, soaking his two-piece combat suit like a dish rag. Surging air rippled the wet uniform, circulating relief to clammy armpits and groin, dehydrating soggy trunks absorbed with the tense swelter of impending combat. Nick Callahan enjoyed the buffeting, the cooling luxury afforded first man out the door.

The serial was composed of two parallel columns of Gooney Birds flying along a northerly flow from Mindoro's San Jose and Hill airstrips. Craning his helmeted head rearward into the slipstream, he could easily make out the long snake of fuselages comprising the 317th Troop Carrier Group conveying his regimental comrades. Twenty-four troopers rode in his aircraft, *Bunny Gal*, three sticks of eight. Every tenet of airborne S.O.P. was being violated this bright, sunny morning. Ideally DZs were lengthy, broad, flat, and clear of obstructions. *Saturate the drop zone as swiftly as possible with as many men as practical*, he had heard more than one expert preach time and again. Obedient to that axiom, they usually flew in patterns nine planes wide. Today they'd break that procedure and jump from a skimpy two-wide formation.

Topography dictated a dangerous break from proven precedent... the tail wagged the hound. Wind would be a bitch too, projected at twenty-one miles per hour. Practice jumps on sprawling, cushiony DZs had been canceled for a lot less. This morning's wind drift formula estimated an altitude of 600 feet, wind velocity around twenty-one miles-per-hour, and a Gooney Bird air speed factor of 110 mph. The calculated result presented an ominous projection. It determined that jumpers would drift almost 1,100 feet from plane to turf, a chilling challenge when one considers Topside's largest DZ is only 1,500 feet in length. Further befuddling the math, a six to eight man stick requires about four to six seconds to exit the aircraft, so the margins for numbers one, six, and eight are quite different. And when all these components are compromised by the pendulum effect hazarded by fickle crosswinds, an already disadvantageous prospect becomes mind-blowing.

Callahan pushed the arithmetic out of thought. *Let the slide rule boys figure it out. My job is to hit the ground, round up my people, locate the objective, and kill Japs. Let's keep it simple, Nicky.*

First Lieutenant Nicholas Callahan and the long trail of the 503rd had sprouted from modest inception at Fort Benning, Georgia, in March of '42. Actually he didn't join the outfit until later in the summer. That very same October, the entire unit picked up and made tracks to Camp Stoneman, an overseas staging area located in California, and Nick's first peek at the vast Pacific whose stretch extended to places exotic and distant, soon to become his venue of action.

With hardly a free moment to enjoy the balmy West Coast climate, the anxious regiment departed Stoneman, shipping out to Australia. Sailing south to the west side of Panama, they first picked up a paratrooper battalion stationed there, integrating it into the regiment to fill out its table of organization and equipment. A nine-month stint of rigorous training followed Down Under, honing lethal skills, perfecting jump techniques. Hearsay had it the Five-O-Three was going to Guadalcanal and up the Solomon chain, but like most rumors it was of the latrine variety... ill founded. New Guinea, instead, was to be their baptism of fire.

August, 1943, saw them deplaning at Port Moresby. From that strike-off point, they entered the great leapfrogging battles of New Guinea and an environment of cruel consequence. Two combat jumps at Nadzab and Noemfoor island off the New Guinea coast had steeled the regiment's confidence. On Noemfoor, July and August, 1944, fighting in tandem with the amphibious 158th Infantry RCT, the pugnacious paratroopers subdued the 15x12 mile island, inflicting roughly 1,900 casualties on the battered and starving enemy.

Author's Note: Actually the 503's jump onto Noemfoor off the New Guinea coast utilized a two-wide plane pattern for the initial phase while follow up aircraft flew in single file.

Near the finale of the Noemfoor operation, the Five-O-Three was augmented by the 462nd Parachute Artillery Battalion and the 161st Parachute Engineer Battalion, elevating the 503's status from regiment to a bristling regimental combat team. The artillerists' twelve 75 mm pack howitzers would serve well in future efforts. When the monstrous struggle for New Guinea finally climaxed, the unit enjoyed a revitalizing pause in preparation for its seaborne assault on the Mindoro stepstone. Now the prolonged journey, its genesis in the red clay of Fort Benning, pointed to a scorched, igneous haystack called Corregidor, jutting defiantly from the mouth of Manila Bay. Grim-faced and hostile, Third Battalion/Five-O-Three awaited the final minutes, suspended overhead in twin-engine transports.

Pensively, Callahan fingered the scapular cord clinging about the tight tendons hugging his neck. He thought through the words of *Hail Mary* while inching his face out into the drafty vibrations of the airworthy C-47's prop wash. *Holy Mary, mother of God, pray for us sinners now and at the hour of our death. Amen.*

A dozen or so planes behind Callahan, supernumerary Phil Primo, number 5 jumper/first stick, sat spread-legged, nervously shaking stiffness from knees and booted ankles. If all went according to Hoyle, in ten minutes he'd be drifting down over DZ-B, the midget golf course, disgorged from a straining Dakota of the right column. Following the jump, the entire file would then wheel clockwise in a precise loop and return to drop the next stick. Similarly, the left column would spill its parachutists over the parade ground, DZ-A, and bank counter-clockwise. Hopefully the pilots had adjusted their altimeters to compensate the difference between zero sea-level and Topside's summit elevation of 550 feet. During evening bullshit sessions, Nick related an incident at Noemfoor where several of the lead planes had neglected to make the switch, emptying their troopers from an incredibly low 175 feet, chutes opening moments before impact. Men suffering broken legs and severe back injuries cluttered the hard coral DZ, a crappy place to land in the first place. That operation had specified a jump altitude of 400 feet above the DZ, in itself dangerously short… but to step out the door at less than half that height caused hackles to stir on every trooper recalling the event.

Fidgeting next to Primo, Pfc. Joe Von Ness, a native of San Marcos, Texas, rechecked the bulging side pockets of his trousers, the third time that Phil had noticed. He fingered the pocket flap making sure the button fed completely through the eye hole. Resting snugly against his thigh snoozed two grenades. A strip of white adhesive tape firmly secured clamps to the pineapples—probably unnecessarily—as extra insurance guarding against mishap, an ounce of prevention as the adage forewarns. The only thing Prussian about Von Ness was his name. A slight, wiry man with darting brown eyes, not weighing more than a hundred forty pounds, Joe could fight, hump, and drink with the toughest in the Five-O-Three.

Raised on a scraggly, poor ranch, he had pushed livestock and shoveled manure since old enough to dress himself. The youngest and smallest of four brothers, his mettle had been tested during daily free-for-alls, rough-housing for hours among his siblings. Naturally cat quick, the twisting, gouging, and biting had prepared him for barracks life. More than one burly GI had learned the hard way not to throw his weight around Joe Von Ness. The dogged tenacity of a never-say-uncle mindset had persevered through many a scrap. While others faded, the little trooper always answered the bell for the fifteenth round. He had joined the 503rd shortly after New Guinea but in time for the Mindoro show. Today was to be his first combat jump, number 6/first stick. "Captain Primo, how much time till we go?"

"About nine minutes." Phil felt ancient next to the twenty-year old. "We'll be on our feet in a bit."

"Yes, sir," Joe said. "Lost my wrist-watch in a dice game. Rolled a seven before I could make the point." The drawl was high-pitched and twangy.

Primo understood the younger man was struggling for conversation to idle away the bulbous knot pulsating within his gut. "I hope it wasn't one of them fancy Swiss ones."

"No, sir. A cheap PX watch. But it was the only one I ever owned." Joe grinned a self-admonishing smile and scratched his scalp. His helmet sat on the walk, between boots and a brown paper bag, presumably to catch vomit. As the droning C-47 lurched, the steel pot wobbled and he reached down to restrain it. It was then Phil noticed the slender boot knife. Joe also carried a trench knife on his webbed utility belt, and no doubt a smaller folding knife, perhaps a push-button stiletto, in a high pocket. Troopers can't seem to get enough of them.

Shivs and more shivs, the fullback chuckled. *Hell, there's not a tree left standing on Corregidor to get hung up on.* Indeed, the most recent aerial photos had shown Topside devoid of anything but splintered stumps and chunks of crinkled metal buildings blown across the landscape. The big bombs had reverted the island to its 1942 surrender status. All regenerated growth and plantings had been blasted to smoky dust in a regressive, environmental cycle. Captain Primo realized his undefined role allowed him a degree of swashbuckling latitude once he hit DZ-B. *Maybe I can help this kid out,* he thought. "Trooper, what's your mission once we hit the golf course?"

"Kill Japs," he answered, matter-of-factly.

"I know that. I mean what's your specific function? Who do you report to?"

"I'm a Third Battalion runner. Supposed to carry messages from headquarters platoon to the company C.O.s and back again."

"Well, until you're able to link up, you stick close to me and we'll make it through this circus together. Okay?"

"Yes, sir. And thank you, sir," the private said, exhaling as if he had been holding his breath since awakening to this notable day.

"You bet." For Primo it was an instinctive act of brotherhood, the kind of thing a senior man does whether in the locker room or the belly of a C-47. It's what makes the team play harder, an intangible facet of something called leadership.

Unpredictably, the spark of a bond fostered nine minutes before exit would preclude a wild episode for the pride of Holy Cross and Ansonia High School. Over the next few days, Pfc. Joe Von Ness would rise to the stratum of conspicuous hero. The captain nudged him a stick of Wrigley's Spearmint Gum. The private quickly popped the stick in his mouth just as they heard, "Stand up and hook up!" The jumpmaster's voice boomed through the crammed bay. In minutes, the pre-jump regimen of safeguards and orders was complete.

Shuffling to the door spoon-like to number four, Primo waited a short minute. "GO!" came the cry, and in the next moment he was in the blinding sunshine, screaming "Sugar Baby!" It wasn't something he had planned, it just blurted out in spontaneous reflex. Before he could think *why*, the T-4 parachute tugged and his fall braked abruptly, the canopy blossomed. Billows of floating silk surrounded him as the lead components of Rock Force flooded the sky.

Below he could see the collapsed chutes and risers of landed soldiers strewing the fairways. Their warriors had already shucked harnesses and were securing perimeters, safeguarding brother troopers descending into the fray. Rock Force, inspired and deadly, had entered the first stage prepared to tear, yes, to rip the Corregidor bastion from the clutch of Japan's bankrupt empire, and to avenge the howling spirits of the Bataan Death March. For the militarists and jingoists nervously pacing the corridors of Tokyo's power palaces, it would signal the impending fall of Manila, all of Luzon, and verily the Philippine Commonwealth.

Boot met angled turf in a dull crunch as the trooper rolled fetus-like into a blackened sand trap. His chute had oscillated throughout the quick descent, crosswinds preventing a more vertical path. Each soldier had been issued two fragmentary and two white phosphorous grenades. A pair was stowed in the baggy thigh-pocket trapped beneath his rolling legs. Momentarily, a spurt of bland pain flashed along the femur, similar to plopping down on a park bench with a baseball in one's hip pocket. Gathering in the swaddled silk, he disengaged the snap fasteners and slid out of the main and reserve chutes. Almost in the same motion, Von Ness flung off the precautionary Mae West and scrambled to his knees. Peeping over the little knoll, he belly-crawled across a pitted green. Unquestionably, no golf course had ever suffered divots more damaging. Par would be unreachable for many months, regardless the handicap.

Joe traversed the gullied apron searching for the captain who had led him out the C-47's womb. Crackling gunfire reminded him to unseat the carbine strapped to his backpack. Detaching it, he snapped in a steel blue magazine and worked the smooth action, feeding a short .30 caliber round into the spotless firing chamber. Up above, swollen parachutes cascaded onto the DZ, their dangling passengers swaying in the strong wind current. Groans and angry epithets could be discerned as men tumbled cockeyed on chunks of blasted masonry and contorted lengths of metal roofing, or in bomb holes littered with fractured rock. Forty yards away he spied the caught-up form of Phil Primo thrashing in a tangle of risers. He had come down bullseye center in a shallow crater, the canopy directly atop him.

The young trooper clambered over the edge in a low stoop, calling out to the flailing captain. "Hold on, sir. I'll cut you free." Only Primo's exasperated face and askew helmet showed. Withdrawing his boot knife, the private slit a chute panel exposing the confusion of fouled lines which he deftly sliced free. Let's hear it for the blade. The fullback, looking a bit chagrined but grateful to be rid of his predicament, cracked, "Christ, now I know how a friggen mummy must feel! Thanks for the hand… and remind me to buy you a cigar."

Surveying the drop from a command plane circling high above the action, Colonel Jones instructed those approaching C-47s with eight-man sticks to trim their length to six, and decrease elevation to 400 feet in order to compensate for wind conditions threatening to overshoot soldiers onto cliff-sides or in the drink. Inflatable Mae Wests would buoy and preserve a number of splashed troopers until PT Boats could retrieve them.

Surveying the exhilarating scene from ground level, Phil Primo punched a fist at no one or nothing in particular. "Hot damn!" They had done it. Topside was teeming with hustling men consolidating and rushing to establish the perimeter, first step in controlling the high ground from which they would be reinforced and supplied by air. Now to throw the Japanese off their gun perches and bunkered caverns, on to Middleside, Bottomside, and seething Malinta Hill, secure a beachhead for the soon onrushing amphibious troops of the 34th RCT's veteran Third Battalion blowing through the surf. And together they would wrest Malinta and Kindley Field from the despised enemy, squeeze him to the last futile resort of Hooker Point and the unforgiving sea.

An awesome surprise awaited the Yanks, though, in the tenacious resistance of 6,000 unexpected well-equipped soldiers and marines of the imperial armed forces. From around the island, tracers spat long lethal arcs into the returning transports preparing to spill out their impatient second sticks. Conditions would worsen to the point where "Warden" Jones would order his First Battalion flown to the tip of the Bataan peninsula, and from there assault Corregidor via sea with Lieutenant Colonel Ed Postlethwait's battalion of the 34th RCT. Flexible and decisive, Rock Force commander George M. Jones would make several key decisions this day, sparing the lives and limbs of many who would have suffered otherwise.

Staccatoed bursts of .45 caliber sub-machine gun fire emanated from the parade field, the unmistakable chatter of Thompsons ferreting out Japanese snipers attempting to pick off suspended GIs floating earthward. Colonel Jones had dropped a wave of Tommy gunners in the initial contingent, specifically instructing them to aggressively clean out enemy counter-attackers rushing to stem the assault.

Last night, in a move aimed at hyping every trooper's level of incitement, news film was shown highlighting the Japanese conquest of Corregidor three years earlier. It culminated with the stars and stripes trampled under the victorious feet of her haughty captors. Film clips of American and

Filipino prisoners barbarously mistreated during the infamous death march also lit up the screen, inspiring pledges of brutal revenge. Whether the psychology of cinematic stimulation added telling fervor to their diligence is questionable; however, the Tommy gunners did go about their task with particular efficiency.

Incredibly, the Japanese had been caught flat-footed. Poised for an assault from the sea, they had neglected the unexpected, guarding the front porch while leaving the back door wide open. Once the shock had subsided they no doubt would attempt to dislodge the paratroopers from the summit using mortars and small artillery pieces. But with subsequent sticks still descending on Topside, no concerted resistance had yet materialized.

Enemy leadership, slow to react, was waiting for Itagaki to take charge but he was nowhere to be located, although his staff knew he had gone to Geary Point near the base of Topside's sheer cliffs. His purpose was to observe the path of American amphibious operations, which he had correctly determined were en route from Bataan's principal port, Mariveles. The commander never realized sky soldiers were alighting onto the high ground. Riddled by bullets and grenade slivers, he now slumped in a small ravine along with seven other members of his observation team; killed in the invasion's opening minutes. Unfortunately for them, they had been ambushed by twenty-five troopers of Item Company who had overshot the DZ, swept onto low-lying Breakwater Point. The Americans were weaving a trail up to Topside when they surprised the Itagaki group, slaying them all but a single aide who was taken prisoner.

Roughly one thousand troopers of Erickson's 3/503 had bailed out onto Topside. The combination of sniping gunfire, malfunctioned parachutes, and impacted bodies bouncing off the poor DZ left only seventy-five percent ready to fight, and a number of those had experienced wretched injuries. Tough and spoiling for battle, the banged up soldiers licked their wounds, regrouped, and stuck it to the enemy. If nothing else, Itagaki's appraisal was highly accurate. Topside represented the worst possible airborne drop site ever contemplated. But the DZs were now secure in expectation of 2/503's airdrop scheduled shortly after the noon hour.

Meanwhile at Mariveles, the Rock Force Battalion Landing Team of 3/34 embarked twenty-five LCMs for its two-and-a-half hour channel passage and roundabout circuit to Corregidor's south side. They would catch the Japanese somewhat off guard as Itagaki's staff anticipated a north shore assault, the shortest distance from the Bataan point of departure. At 1030 hours, GIs would storm ashore along a 600-foot stretch of sand in the vicinity of South Dock, now designated Black Beach. With partial cover fire from the airborne troops, Lt. Colonel Postlethwait's BLT would wedge its way across the sand flats, charging up Malinta Hill and through the Bottomside cauldron, thereby bisecting the island.

Ed Postlethwait had both terrified and energized his spirited veterans with the uncomplicated directive, "There's no place to go, once you're there, but forward. We simply take a hill at all costs and stay there until we've killed all the Japs or the Japs have killed all of us. The only reason you will not reach the top of Malinta Hill is because you are dead or incapable of putting one foot in front of another." Clear-cut and simple, the mission was as basic as they come, nothing convoluted, nothing fancy. Only commitment to a flesh-and-guts assault would push them up that sooty, tunneled mound belching death at every fold, and the American commander understood it—so now did his troops.

What the commanding officer didn't anticipate was the quantity of Japanese his rifle companies would assail, as intent with holding that marred landscape as his infantrymen were of seizing it. The irresistible force and near immovable object would collide with savage outcome. Navy destroyers coughing five-inch cannon fire, and rocket ships unleashing hundreds of whooshing missiles slammed earth-trembling explosives into caves and suspected bunkers overlooking South Dock. Regardless how much devastation they wrought, the battalion still had to race through a no-man's-land hailstorm of mortars and Nambu machine gun fire, plus 20mm armor-piercing and high-explosive anti-tank shells ripping into landing craft.

All five BLT waves would make it to the beach and into the Malinta rise, the Japanese return fire becoming progressively more intense for each succeeding wave. Enemy soldiers shrugging off the shock of numbing bombardment surfaced from the catacombed bowels of Malinta, intent on honoring ancestor and emperor. Fortunately for the Five-0-Three and 3/34 attempting to link up, their opponent displayed a most disorganized defense, no doubt due in part to Captain Itagaki's premature demise.

DATE: SATURDAY, 17 FEBRUARY 1945

LOCATION: CORREGIDOR

Jones' regimental command post, set up in the old Topside barracks, shattered and gutted, prepared itself for the unfolding day's gory business. The Second and Third Battalions of the 503rd had held the high ground's tight defensive perimeter throughout the dark hours. Pack howitzer gunners from the RCT's artillery battalion had several pieces in position within the distorted circle, in some cases pouring direct fire into enemy machine gun nests. The latter were restricting movement about the DZs where paratroopers were yet attempting to harvest ammo and ration bundles. First Battalion was expected to land via LCM at Black Beach early that afternoon.

The preceding night, 3/34 tenaciously held onto its foothold, sprawled on Malinta Hill in the face of fierce stabs by imperial marines. This day's orders would demand the vicious task of prying countless Japanese fortifying virtually every hole and depression pocking the slopes of Topside, Malinta and the Bottomside saddle. By afternoon of February 17, the stink of enemy corpses, bloated by the sun and picked over by swarms of voracious blue flies, flooded the nostrils of the living. Engine roar also filled their ears as a Sherman tank and two self-propelled howitzers from 3/34 went about their deadly game.

As light progressed into evening's shadow, the toll on both sides mounted. Whole networks of caves were flamed and sealed, taking their anguished defenders to painful, burning death. In some cases, squads of GIs were gunned down and destroyed in a fleeting blink, caught in cleverly concealed crossfires. 3/34's King Company saw its company commander and his replacement killed over a short span. Japanese in small suicidal groups seemingly materialized out of nowhere, hell-bent on taking as many Yankees with them as they banzai-charged perimeter points. Most were immediately chewed to pieces. Encouraged by the gleeful abandon of saki and ritualistic exhortation promulgated by sword-wielding officers, imperial soldiers and marines hurled their bodies with little chance of success and none for survival. GIs, depleted of grenades and Garands silenced by lack of ammunition, met them head-on with bayonets and entrenching tools, swinging the latter like battle axes and maces of another era.

By February 18, Japanese infantrymen had developed a bizarre, new tactic in keeping with Kamikaze actions of their air service brethren. Allowing, even enticing, Americans to engulf their strong points, the sons of Nippon would scurry to chambers underground, collecting as many explosives and combustibles as possible. When the earthwork was crawling with Americans overhead they would detonate the cache, bursting themselves to smithereens and erupting a man-made volcano. Enormous, ripping blasts surged from the earth, rocketing men from the exterior in a flailing flight of death. The prospect of destruction from below became as possible as an Arisaka bullet or mortar shrapnel. Like subterranean submarines manned by sacrificial crews, stationary compartments of lethal bombs and inflammables combusted in violent outbursts taking those on the surface to fiery death. Others nearby often suffered the painful aftermath of concussive shock, brains addled, ears bleeding.

Ancient coastal battery points buttressed the outer ring of Topside's mass. Manned by heroic Japanese, fighting to the last soldier, they became the scenes of many unreported but passionately disputed battles. Those fearing capture or wishing to mercifully die an instantaneous death, whispered solemn incantations while clutching activated grenades to abdomens and joined the spirits of ancestors long departed. For the stoic Japanese of Corregidor's isolated enclaves, self-sacrifice became a matter of honorable choice, inflicted by one's own hand or a headlong rush into the blazing muzzles of accommodating American riflemen.

DATE: FRIDAY, 23 FEBRUARY 1945

TIME: 1045 HOURS

LOCATION: CORREGIDOR

For one excruciatingly frustrating week, Primo had been something less than a fifth wheel in and about the Topside CP. Serving with the regimental S-2, helping to sort out reports filtering in from battalion and company commanders, he impatiently waited the opportunity to lead. The rattle of gunfire and detonations echoing around the command post had frazzled his temperament to that of a caged puma. Phil's language had undergone a laconic transformation, becoming terse and virtually monosyllabic, his mood bordering on the angry. He wasn't used to sitting on the bench, riding the pine.

"Captain Primo, get over to Wheeler Point and find out what the hell's going on. Captain Hill's company is somewhere between Wheeler and Searchlight Point trying to reduce a concentration of caves. We're having difficulty contacting him or Third Battalion to determine progress. Maybe there's more Nips than we thought. Get me a first-hand assessment. Better take a runner just in case." The words came from Colonel Jones who had just returned from inspecting Topside's northern positions and surveying the skinny tadpole tail of Hooker Point from high atop his Topside vantage point.

Soon the Five-O-Three's 75mm pack howitzers would slam their loads into Jap positions at the narrow end. Jones' Topside gunners would have the unique benefit of observing the cannons' lethal handiwork and adjusting their own fire.

"Yes, sir!" The fullback was in the game, coming off the bench. It wasn't the company command he desired, but at least he was getting to the action. He snatched up his carbine and tapped Joe Von Ness, lollygagging with a pair of battalion runners nearby. "Let's go!"

Thinking better, he returned the carbine with a clatter to the makeshift rifle rack and selected a Thompson sub-machine gun and pouched magazine belt from a stockpiled heap. The TSMG, as many would verify, had no equal in the reflex closeness of cave warfare—.45 caliber slugs pound flesh like a diesel piston. Without discrimination, it knocks people down.

Colonel Jones called aloud as they sprinted out the rubbled entrance. "As long as you're making the trip, haul up some ammo. Those boys must be shooting up a storm from the noise comin' from that direction." The Warden was one to gain maximum efficiency from even the most simple mission.

Outside, troopers manning a shallow ammo point revetment, protected by slabs of shattered concrete and piled stone, were passing out bandoleers of M1 clips and magazines destined for carbines and Tommy guns. Primo and Von Ness slung six bandoleers each about their necks, and filled sweat-soaked shirts with grenades. The stifling heat and wafting stench of fly-covered decay hung heavy in the roasting air.

"Got any satchel charges?" Joe asked a combat engineer unpacking explosive primacord.

"Shoo-uh, whatta-ya need—twenty, toity, or forty-pound satchels?" The accent was as Brooklyn as the bridge and Ebbets Field.

"Oh, I reckon a couple of thirtas will be rah-et fah-en." Joe's drawl provided amusing contrast for anyone caring to listen. "Them Jap caves take a lot of fuckin' blastin'!" His bay brown eyes glinted a bit like a hound's sensing a coon hunt.

High-explosive satchel charges, kind of portable bombs, had emerged during the great Pacific War as front-line corkscrews, used extensively to nullify pill boxes and bunkers. In a fiendish attempt to annihilate enemy holdouts deep inside fortress-like Malinta Tunnel and its complex of corridors, GI engineers scoured the huge hill searching for cupola vents camouflaged above vital air shafts. Having located them, they would lower hideous homemade killing contraptions into the exposed ducts. The device was crude but effective. Gasoline filled five-gallon Jerry cans taped together with phosphorous grenades, satchel charges and dynamite sticks fabricated the diabolical monster-bombs.

The devilish gizmo was detonated by lengths of fast burning primacord. Below, hopelessly trapped Japanese suffocated or burned to death. Tormented survivors were driven out into the open only to be mercilessly mowed down by platoons of eager BARs and Garands. Tripod-mounted machine guns raked tunnel entrances as choking men stampeded to escape the horror consuming their lungs. Within Malinta's honeycombed clutches, doomed soldiers of the empire purposely touched off prodigious explosions, hoping to blow up the entire hill, perhaps the island, and every living thing inside and on it. However, they succeeded in rupturing only the great hill beast's internal organs and, of course, themselves. Outside, ringing Malinta, awed infantrymen could feel and hear rooted tremors rumbling from the depths. Sediment spewed from fissures and vents, coughing acrid smoke to the heavens like a geothermal giant unplugged after eons of constipated slumber.

Trotting toward the Wheeler Point killing ground, two soldiers worked their way down a graded slope and through twisting ravines, making sure to keep their heads below the silhouette line. The heat was inescapable and so were the flies picking on a shredded carcass blocking their traverse. High-stepping over the Jap, they moved cautiously farther down the incline, not exactly positive of their destination. Muffled gunshots and shouting, perhaps English, resonated off to their right at about two o'clock. Shattered palm stumps aligned in a jagged row pointed to a small rise fifty yards or so directly ahead, but they'd have to traverse open ground to reach it.

Von Ness went first, at a low creep, pushing a satchel charge before him while the captain's Thompson protected his advance. When Joe had safely reached the other side, he slid into a shallow depression and waved on his companion, in turn, covering him with his carbine.

Without incident, Primo crossed the same sweltering ground in similar fashion, propelling the other canvassed satchel charge with short thrusts. The action was tedious and uncomfortable but it represented the surest method of travel. More than one trooper had fallen prey to Japanese sharpshooters by trying to race through open terrain. A flattened landscape virtually devoid of checkpoints made it difficult to orient themselves without standing erect, so they decided to slither up the tiny hillock and get a fix on their relative position. Shooting and screaming became more pronounced, heavy automatic fire dominating the sound waves. Listening, Phil thought, …*probably a Nambu. Reminds me of the Breda that took me out on Sicily.*

Primo motioned the inquisitive private not to show himself over the horizon. Instead the two men proceeded to crawl about, seeking a protected vantage point from which to peek over the rim. But first they unslung the weighty bandoleers and unburdened the dozen or so grenades contained in their shirt folds, placing them in a natural sump around which they built a ring of small boulders. Both satchel charges were added to the cranny as well. Worming a path just off center from the high point, Captain Primo edged to the rough lip and peered down, barely exposing himself. The reverse slope proved to be mostly perpendicular for about fifty feet before leveling off to a rocky step, and then fairly sheer again.

In the rock-strewn basin, he could make out GIs pinned down, pouring sustained rifle fire at a point just above the stony step. His angle of perspective was too vertical to determine their target but it had to be a cave or emplacement burrowed in the volcanic cliff. His guess was confirmed by a sharp Nambu braaat spewing a long noisy clip. Like a string of angry hornets, it emanated from where the troopers had been shooting. Ricochets pinged in the basin, forcing men to duck behind whatever cover they could put between them and the Jap gun.

A potato masher flew from cliff-side, clattering beyond the short step and down among the attackers. After a few seconds, it exploded, sending chunks of fragmented steel zipping amidst the stalemated Americans. Two more followed, encouraged by the shouts of impassioned Japanese, but fell short, exploding without effect. The troopers returned a crescendo of rifle fire, the semi-automatic cadence of Garands unmistakable in their deliberate eight-round sequences. Still the troopers under fire couldn't come forward enough to use their flamethrowers, the preferred technique. A squirt of fiery Napalm usually resolved such disputes.

If I can signal them somehow we're here, maybe they can keep the Nips occupied while Joe and I drop down and take 'em out with grenades or satchel charges. But how can we identify ourselves and not get shot up by our own guys?

Joe moved to Phil's side and quickly sized up the situation. "Maybe we can blast 'em out. Shit, we've got enough equipment to handle it."

"True, but how do we let our boys know our two-man demolition team is going to make the effort."

The Japanese increased their rate of fire, pummeling the beaten zone with hundreds of bullets stinging the earth, skipping into recesses, seeking out unseen torsos and limbs, tearing olive-drab cotton, puncturing muscle and bone. Shouts of "medic!" and cries of distress indicated the GIs were absorbing the worst of it. Directly above the spitting Nambu, Primo and Von Ness perched helpless to communicate with their hunkered comrades unable to advance or withdraw.

Finally Joe spat and blurted, "Fuck it," and sprang to a crouch. He tucked a loose trouser cuff into its respective jump boot, paratrooper style, hoping to insure his silhouette would be conclusive, *airborne—all the way.* Standing in plain view of the concealed troopers he lifted off his helmet and waved it vigorously along with the carbine in his right hand. Steel pot, weapon and bloused pants, he prayed, would provide enough distinctive profile to establish his American credentials. Hopefully they would look first before firing instinctively.

"You crazy bastard, get down," Primo growled.

But Von Ness brazenly spread his legs to provide even more delineation to unknown buddies of the Five-O-Three, who by now had to have seen him. Joe directed his rifle barrel down toward where he knew the cave to be and pointed to himself, indicating he was going to take a crack at the Japs. "It's okay, captain. They'd have plunked me by now if they thought I was a Nip."

Rushing back to the little ammo sump, they sorted out the nasty little store of goodies and moved them to the crest. In order to obtain a more accurate idea of what they were up against, Phil held the smaller man's ankles while he wriggled his body straight out over the edge. Joe forced his sinewy torso to a posture right-angled to the cliff, like a Wrigley Field pennant in the stiff Chicago breeze. He couldn't hold the position too long, but he was able to determine cave location and size. Sweating profusely, the fullback dragged him in, scraping Joe's belly along the snaggy outcropping.

What he had seen was more of a horizontal slit than a cave mouth, probably twelve feet wide and maybe four-and-a half-feet from top to bottom. But even that was shrunk by a sandbagged wall, leaving a maximum opening of two feet from base to ceiling. Toward the center he spied a muzzle flash from the deadly Nambu, a Type 92 heavy machine gun, punching out big slugs in a series of short bursts, mangling stone to flights of pebble chips. In fact, its efficacy was much more serious than Primo's old Breda nemesis north of Biazza Ridge. The cave slit, Von Ness calculated, was about thirty five feet below their aerie.

They discussed several approaches. Joe (the lighter man), they agreed could rappel down the cliff face, with the captain anchoring the line, and toss in a few pineapples, Willie Peters, or satchels, whatever—but no rope was available to lower him into position. Besides, he'd be too exposed. They decided instead on a two-phase plan. First, white phosphorous grenades, four in all, would be dropped straight down to the step. The blast and lingering thick smoke should dull and temporarily blind the cavemen. Next, they'd suspend a satchel charge, fuse burning, to the slit front, utilizing line fashioned from emptied bandoleers knotted together. To insure maximum effectiveness, a second round of phosphorous and satchel would repeat the initial effort.

About fifteen minutes ticked by while they peeled ammo clips from the bandoleer pouches, tying the cloth strands into a pair of skimpy but serviceable ropes. While they went about the splice work, several troopers slow-fired selective shots into the cave mouth, so as not to provide the enemy any pause or break in sound to detect the pair plotting overhead.

"Let's do it," the captain winked, a WP in each hand. Intense perspiration lacquered the broad, handsome face, tanned and toughened from weeks in the Mindoro and Corregidor sun. Stubbled growth sprouted in dense patches, especially thick about the upper lip and chin. "We pull pins on my command. Then release clamps on my second command. And drop 'em after a count of three. You ready?"

"Ready to send them all to hell, captain!" Joe was sweating hard too, his angular cheekbones reflecting a grimy lather fostered by excited stress as well as the tropical rays. Normally his light beard was hardly visible,. but eight unshaven days, coupled with the greasy filth of Topside, gave him the look of a West Virginia coal miner closing out a workshift, eyes sunken, nostrils ringed and grungy.

"Pull 'em!" Both men yanked the pins and waited a few moments, nodding their preparedness for the next order. "Release clamps." Thumbs relaxed and the metal constrictors flew free, allowing fuses to commence their quick burn. Extending the grenades as far as possible beyond the crag, they both silently counted to a quick three.

"Drop!" The canisters slipped from their tight grip, fingers pushing outward as if to guarantee their passel of wingless hawks had departed complete and en masse. Clanking on the rocky step, they bounced their metallic music for a second or two before erupting in a radial spume of crinkly, white fire, iridescent and acrid. Impenetrable smoke blinded the area, reaching up to the two paratroopers manning the height. Upon detonation, Primo set the satchel fuse and they lowered the green bundle hand-over-hand to the full stretch of its pre-measured thirty-three foot extension. Hopefully it dangled unseen, directly in front of the entrance.

Moments passed at an agonizing crawl as the fuse burned lazily, its thirty-pound explosiveness dormant until the final millisecond! Grasping the cord's end length, Phil counted off the final instants aloud, coaxing the precise moment of detonation. "Eleven, twelve… " He sensed a tug at the other end like a shad tugging hooked bait. Had a Nip spotted it and was now jerking it away from the opening? An enormous roar shook his thoughts and the humid air, splitting the moment with deafening shock. Translucent grit filled the space about them. Face down, hugging the shuddered stone roof, they awaited a sign of their effectiveness.

With dust yet clouding the blast area, Joe readied the second charge and slithered closer to the brink. Bits of stone and pebbles slid underneath, serving as roller bearings. The combination of gravity and dry sand lubricant plotted against him. Hanging onto the satchel the Texan was unable to brake his slide's momentum, partially slipping over the ledge. Had he released the bundle, Von Ness could probably have saved himself. But he clung to it, instead attempting to dig his skidding elbows into the hard surface.

Primo realized Joe's plight too late. He reached out a futile hand as the cowboy disappeared, a sickening pang of nausea clutching the captain's intestine.

Like unseated brahma bull-riders he had thrilled to in so many hometown rodeos, Joe twisted through his plummet, instinctively trying to land cat-like on his feet. Plunging through the pall of smoky dust, he indeed did land foot first in a crunching thud. Pain streaked through his ankle with a sharp crack. Self-diagnosis suggested it was broken. The good news though was that he had tumbled forward atop the bulky satchel, muffling secondary impact. The jolt stunned him momentarily as he slowly rolled in the powdery swirl of settling debris.

Von Ness had in fact fallen on the remnants of blasted sandbags, hardly spongy, but better than cleavaged stone. Hobbling to his knees, he yanked the satchel fuse, and with two hands swung the thirty-pounder over the lip toward the rear of the cave. Searing nuggets of residual white phosphorous perforated his uniform. He would deal with them after diving for cover.

Moments later, a terrific explosion whooshed from the cave. Had the gun crew survived the first blast, this one closed the deal. Just to make certain, however, troopers charged up the step and entered the smoldering mouth with guns blazing. Deeper and more expansive than it appeared, they counted fourteen bodies. As the military is fond of concluding—the position had been *neutralized.*

As a medic tended to Joe's ankle and WP burns, a platoon leader came forward to congratulate him on his daring "jump." By this time, Primo had worked his way around and down the overhang. He informed the lieutenant, who dispatched a couple of men to retrieve the ammo clips and remaining grenades up on top. Plopping next to the battered Texan, he removed a pair of stubby cigars from an inside pocket and the two lit up in celebration of their accomplishment and mutual survival. They puffed away while swigging gulps from an offered canteen. Actually, the aromatic smoke served a greater benefit, warding off gangs of the greedy blue flies already entering the cave in quest of fresh sustenance.

"Trooper," a relaxed Primo addressed Von Ness, "I think you've earned yourself some kind of star today, probably a silver one." He blew out a thin white stream and pawed his matted locks. "Looks like I've done myself more damage than them damn Japs," he drawled.

"Hell, Captain, I thought you might want to court-martial me for destruction of government property!" He playfully formed a cocky, little smile, the kind that says, I'm damn lucky to be alive!

DATE: MONDAY, 26 FEBRUARY 1945

TIME: 1100 HOURS

LOCATION: CORREGIDOR

South Dock hummed and grunted, exuding the confused bustle of military organization. With the battle winding down to the slenderest breadth of Corregidor, the brass had decided to pull out the 3/34 and reunite it with its parent 24th Infantry Division for future operations. As the last strings of weary GIs boarded vessels destined for the tranquility of Mindoro, a fresh battalion from the 38th "Cyclone" Division's 151st RCT continued to stream onto the beach.

Primo had been ordered to the wharf for administrative purposes, primarily aiding the regimental personnel officer confirming the departure of wounded troopers. They also were being evacuated this hot Monday. Actually he welcomed the duty because it afforded an opportunity to see off "Tex," as he now called the plucky private. Multiple fractures of the ankle and foot would have to be reset and screwed by an orthopedic jigsaw artist.

For Joe "Tex" Von Ness, the war had ended. By summer he would be carousing in San Marcos, guzzling Pearl Beer, and wolfing down beef barbecue and fat wursts identifiable with that long-standing German-American cowboy community. Phil located him "lounging," as the orderly overstated, in the shade. He rested upon a stretched canvas litter waiting for a navy medical party to evacuate him and others in the hobbled group.

Tags looped through buttonholes stipulated the nature of each man's particular problem: "GSW Buttock," "GSW Hip", "Shrapnel Chest," and so on, all non-life-threatening, but serious enough. The critical cases had been shipped off earlier that morning. GSW, shorthand for "Gun Shot Wound," identified the majority of those lying about, indicating how close combat on Corregidor had been. Most smoked cigarettes, or "coffin nails" as many chose to call them. Background rumbling of distant grenades and small arms reminded them that the furor still raged, and Kindley Field had yet to be taken.

Primo and Von Ness small-talked about things petty: cold beer, hamburgers, movie starlets, stuff to look forward to. Rank has a way of disappearing when men chat privately following a shared experience. A mutual respect flowed between them, one that relegated military protocol to the back burner.

The fullback had just checked the dial strapped to his wrist, 1105, as a pair of navy pharmacist mates hoisted Tex's litter and toted him toward a beached LST yawning an open ramp. At that same precise mark of time, an east island detonation angrily shot tons of earth skyward, raining fallout over all of Corregidor. Everyone at South Dock, and throughout the American-controlled sector for that matter, could only wonder as grit and crushed rock pattered about field hospital tenting and rippled the placid tide of San Jose Bay.

At Monkey Point, the Japanese had crammed tons of explosives in the form of mines, TNT, bangalore torpedoes, naval munitions, coastal artillery shells, grenades, and a myriad of other powerful instruments into a tunnel burrowed beneath a small hill. And with perhaps two hundred of their own loyal troops inside the crowded chamber, triggered a last gasp glorious firework for Bushido and emperor.

Outside, paratroopers from 1/503 were dueling nests of enemy snipers scattered about the mound. Among them crouched First Lieutenant Nicholas Callahan, who had come over from Third Battalion with a detail redistributing surplus ammunition. Like a primeval inferno spewing pungent smoke and flame from the earth's core, the entire hill erupted in a tumultuous boom. Up from its detonated bowels a monstrous shock of stone and reinforced concrete blew the hill to rubble. It was as though the devil's furnace had fulminated, split to shards. On the hill and its perimeter, mutilated men were swept upward, blown apart by the dismembering blast. A thirty-three-ton Sherman, like a child's toy, was thrown fifty yards, careening end over end.

Many died from the fracturing effect, some buried alive, while others succumbed to death by massive concussion though their bodies were virtually unmarred. Four smaller explosions followed in a delayed string of aftershocks bombarding survivors with large boulders gouged from the deep, with splintered logs and twisted steel beams. A mind boggling hole, scooped to a depth of thirty feet with a length approaching 130 feet and width of about seventy, smoldered in the after-stink of cordite. Fifty-four paratroopers died in that thunderous burst and another 145 suffered a range of injuries from walking wounded to hideous impairment. Among the latter lie Nick Callahan, his organs hemorrhaging in numbed stupor, too crippled to move.

The medics brought him into the South Dock aid station a little after noon. There was little anyone could do other than make him comfortable, though it's difficult to say whether his shocked body was in actual pain. Morphine and plasma couldn't overcome the devastation housed within his chest cavity and abdomen. Inside his singed skull, an addled brain battled to regain a semblance of awareness—where was he, what had projected him into this fuzzed condition? His paralyzed mind comprehended zero, short circuited by an unknown force.

Primo rushed into the big tent, uncaring of doctors and nurses moving to assist the glut of shredded soldiers clutching to life. Another officer with whom they had swilled warm Manhattans back at The Coop spotted the captain, informing him of Nick's dire situation. As a medical team worked him over, Phil stood off to one side gripping the younger man's unresponsive hand. Supine on a plywood table, they had snipped off most of the ravaged uniform but there was no way the medicine men could determine the irreparable damage inside.

Brown and stained, a frazzled square of woolly cloth lay among the discarded clothing. Though its holy image had faded, invisible from the jungled chemistry of sweat and humidity, Primo recognized the scapular immediately. Holding onto the hand, he stooped to lift it. He cupped Callahan's limp fingers around it, hoping the cloth would generate a spark of miraculous energy, to cure, to heal anew. But the shattered body remained statue-like, without so much as a respiratory heave. "Nick, it's Phil. I'm here. I put your mom's scapular in your hand. Can you feel it? Draw on it, Kid. Say a prayer inside."

The Kid hung on the threshold of lapsing into pre-death sleep. Unblinking, blood-veined eyes were open but saw nothing. Fighting the completeness of onrushing coma, he willed lips and tongue to gasp a barely audible beseechment. He had heard, he had understood. "Phil." His breath labored, the whispery voice ghostly. "Give mom… scap… "

"I will, Kid," Phil cried. "I will." Primo squeezed the flaccid hand while a surgeon's stethoscope probed for a nonexistent flicker. He continued gripping even while they carried the body out and into the sunlight. For another twenty minutes Phil sat quietly stroking the hair and cheeks. Convulsions of grief uncontrollably bubbled up from his stricken soul in a shuddered hiss. Kid Callahan, his little brother-by-choice, had passed on to the stillness of eternity.

Finally, a Catholic chaplain in baggy fatigues, a purplish stole about his collar, eased the teary fullback off his knees and gently ushered him aside. He administered the sacramental last rites of extreme unction, anointing the forehead and murmuring mysterious Latin in quick fashion, for there were more who required tending. The priest moved close to Phil, to utter a comforting, "Bless you, my son," and ambled off. Routinely, a team of Graves Registration soldiers checked and noted Nick's dog tags before wrapping him in a shroud of parachute silk, perhaps the very chute which had carried him to Topside ten days earlier.

Some souvenir hunter had placed a Jap helmet outside the aid tent. The khaki cloth cover with its sewn yellow star, insignia of the imperial army, exhibited a bullet hole about temple high. Collectors often added such touches as an afterthought, sort of dramatic enhancement. Destined for a den or saloon back home in Decatur or Little Rock, it represented a convenient target for the fullback's wrath. He lashed out hard, booting it across the open-air morgue, rowed with fresh corpses from Monkey Point. Sick of the grotesque sacrifice, of butchered humankind, of friends disappearing in the evaporation of direct hits, or like Callahan, bundled in death shrouds of canopied silk and stiff ponchos, tagged and commended to ever-growing lists of the KIA.

Optimistically, with the padre's closing supplication, their shadows were welcomed into a restful, if not joyous, spirit world. Someone once ventured there must be a big C-47 circling heaven from which old troopers parachuted, short cutting the pearly gates. The joke fell sour on Primo… barracks bullshit! Nothing around him much mattered. Events of the day left him without enthusiasm, sapped of energy. He cared not that 600 Japs had been obliterated in a fanatical banzai, or that Kindley Field, last major obstacle for Rock Force to hurdle, would fall in a few days. The cycle would simply start all over again, on another island or peninsula with a strange sounding name, places of which Americans had never heard.

Yesterday the Air Corps had flown in low over Corregidor and discharged a great blizzard of DDT, dusting the entire island. It drifted slowly, settling like snow, blanketing man and land. Americans and Japanese rose from scummy holes and cheered alike in a momentary truce, exercising common hatred for the ravenous blue flies multiplying in mega-swarms, inundating the scarred tadpole. The despicable insects had swelled to an ungodly number, flocking into rations and canteens, probing nostrils, ears and lips, fanning the stench of human carrion. Combatants roared in mutual glee as the powerful insecticide destroyed almost all the aggravating bastards. Literally, they died like flies.

Damn the war! The friggen flies are the real enemy. Issue every man a swatter and let's go home!

CHAPTER XXVI
WINDING DOWN

While the conflict for tiny Corregidor ebbs to conclusion, the ongoing struggle across the bloody tapestry of Luzon plays out. Labeled as *Sekigahara*—"the decisive battle"— by the imperial high command, it pits Tomoyuki Yamashita, perhaps Japan's greatest general, certainly its most successful, against Douglas MacArthur, arguably his nation's finest commander. Following the landings at Lingayen, MacArthur's veteran campaigners power inland, driving south toward Manila, prized pearl of the Orient. In excess of a quarter million Nipponese occupy the huge island, 21,000 of whom will defend the metropolis to the final trickle of blood, defiantly contrary to senior Japanese authority which has declared it an "open city."

In an orgy of irrational brutality, the Manila occupation force savagely tortures and butchers the civilian population. Although it would be difficult to punish Manilans any more than his barbaric troops had, the city commandant, Admiral Iwabuchi, now branded a renegade, spares nothing. Intent on spiteful denial, he orders the demolition of power plants, water systems, public transportation and the entire port, ostensibly the only property of bona fide military value. Genocide represents the cruelest of man's vindictive wrath, and certainly the massacre of helpless non-combatants, terror stricken women and children, heads the horror list. But Iwabuchi compounds the suffering by devastating those requisites necessary to sustain life, condemning pitiful survivors to extreme privation.

Unfortunately, to ferret out the Admiral's vandals, the Americans are compelled to shell the "open city" that never was. Block by boulevard, by back alley, by courtyard, rooftop and cellar, it has to be taken. Bitterly close combat contests every plaza and mercado, each stockyard and barrio. Tanks, flamethrowers, and bazookas bang, whoosh, and whizz lethal echoes in the downtown quarter. Japanese gun crews place 5-inch artillery pieces and 7.7mm heavy Nambus in the city's hospitals and magnificent cathedrals, extracting every smidgen of potential sanctuary. The Yanks never anticipated a chivalrous defense but the enemy employs the most indecent of tactics.

In a sense they dehumanize themselves and, therefore, make it easier for their opponents to slay them in droves, without a tinge of conscience. By way of contemporary parallel, had the Nazi's chosen a similar fate for Paris, as Hitler in fact had decreed, the relative scale of human, civil and cultural ruination couldn't have been more monstrous.

Pangs of deep emotion bemoan the hearts of outraged Filipinos. Their scorched pearl lays raped and shattered beyond imagination, splendid Manila reduced to shambles, its populace subjected to repeated atrocity. Mercifully, on March 3 the final charred remnant is ripped from the empire's grudgeful fist. The triumphant free world celebrates the long awaited news. No doubt the disastrous sight would have choked the philosopher-guerrilla, Rizal, had he lived to observe the depredation. The city, gutted and quiet at last, only awaits the victorious entry of its sun-glassed liberator. MacArthur will not disappoint.

The Luzon bloodbath will continue for months. Its central plains witness the daily slaughter of great Japanese hordes. Tank battles rage with powerful fury, extremely one-sided as swarming GIs pulverize Yamashita's collapsing war machine. The general wisely withdraws northward, taking over 50,000 men to a mountain redoubt, there to ride out the war.

Subsequent incursions to the archipelago's other islands follow rapidly, some concurrently. Negros, Cebu, Panay, Palawan, Tawitawi, Guimaras, and Mindanao are all contested, but the outcome is always the same. The unstoppable American army prevails, overcoming torrid heat and swamped terrain, feverish disease and above all, the tenacious enemy denouncing surrender. Until shadows pale to an invisible phantom, only death will honor the stoic appetite of Bushido.

Roughly fifteen-hundred miles northeast of Manila sits a mini collection of isolated, smoldering isles aptly dubbed the Volcano Islands. Among them rests a bleak lump of brimstone and dark sand but eight miles square. For lack of a more identifiable descriptor, planners describe its configuration as a "pork chop" axised on a southwest-northeast line. An extinct volcano dominates the island's narrow, southern point. Gloomy and foreboding, dormant Mount Suribachi projects upward to a mounded crest of 546 feet, yet seething pungent, sulfurous fumes deep from within its slumbering bowels. Indeed its uniformed denizens capture Suribachi's geo-thermal gasses to heat food and warm chilled bodies, especially this raw February.

Steam heat represents the island's only humane consolation. Devoid of fresh water and lacking much vegetation, exuding noxious, rotten-egg vapors, and without a harbor, why would anyone care to possess such a godforsaken heap? This infernal patch of ugliness dubbed Sulfur Island is better known by its Nipponese appellation, Iwo Jima. And to answer the question, its barren stretches embrace two airfields and a smaller strip only 760 miles from downtown Tokyo!

With the conquest of the Marianas the summer of '44, Army Air Corps B-29 Super fortresses are able to depart the hard-won aerodromes on Guam, Tinian and Saipan, and fly 3,000 round-trip miles to the Japanese home islands, raining tons of high explosive and incendiary bombs on her industrial cities, maiming munitions plants, crippling dockyards and oil depots. However, the colossal bombers are afforded slight margin for error. Should one or more of its four powerful 2200 horsepower engines peter out, or guzzle excessive gasoline as a result of navigational oversight, evasive action or weather problems, the big birds would be forced to ditch at sea, often their crews beyond rescue. Iwo Jima allows an ideal emergency stop for refuel, repair, and in some cases to drop off wounded airmen torn by ack-ack, or 20mm cannon fragments from marauding Zeroes. Additionally it would allow long range P-51 fighters to take the sky above the Volcanic Islands and screen the Super forts all the way to target, covering them during bomb runs and protecting the return trip. So it is in the best interest of the grand Pacific strategy that Iwo be wrested from the Japanese clutch. Engineers and SeaBees with ingenuity and muscle would rework the airstrips' capabilities, extending runways, strengthening surface to withstand the huge B-29s and their 20,000 pound bomb loads, constructing revetments for the accompanying Mustangs. But before all that could happen, prior to the first set of wheels touching down, three divisions of United States Marines would be challenged to undertake perhaps the Corps most adverse mission of the war.

On February 19, 1945, leathernecks of the 4th and 5th Marine Divisions, comprising two-thirds of the Fifth Amphibious Corps' fighting force, are charged with hitting Iwo Jima's murky southeast beaches, intent on bisecting the island at its slender base, thereby amputating the commanding loftiness of Suribachi. The plan is to scale and seize the mountain in the initial effort, then push north in an ever-widening coast-to-coast front, sweeping the Japs before them. When required, 3rd MarDiv, initially held in floating reserve, will join the fray, minus one regiment. During the primary assault, Iwo

Jima's restrictive confines will prohibit no more than a two-division front, relegating the 3rd to anxiously await its call aboard rolling transports.

The operation's overall Marine commander, Holland M. "Howlin Mad" Smith, instructs the lead regiment to assail the mountain while his principal strike force wheels right and surges from the low ground just ahead of Suribachi, capturing the airfields, steamrolling to Kitano Point, the northern extreme. A seven-day action is foreseen to complete the bloody grind. On paper the scheme appears well-conceived. Unperceived, a surprisingly large garrison, almost 23,000, will stretch Smith's optimistic timetable fivefold. His casualty prediction will also fall woefully short of the actual toll. Paper battles represent hypotheticals based on supposition and probability. And sometimes what is "spose to happen" doesn't, and what is "probable,'" ain't. Errors among the master planners will be further distorted by tactical inflexibility. All, however, will be overcome by the heroism of hard-nosed grunts and their frontline leaders.

In the predawn darkness, gyrenes aboard transports and landing ships breakfast on traditional steak and fixin's before rehashing tactics and call signs, double checking weapons. Finally its time! Troops cluttering transport decks descend clumsy cargo net ladders into the hulls of pitching Higgins Boats. Others on LSTs clamber down steel-runged ladders into vehicle compartments stowed with amtracs. Tense drivers prepare to churn the infantrymen through the high surf and up the steep, dingy dunes. The amtracs or DUKWs will be first to pierce the Iwo pork chop. Fast in their wake, waves of Higgins Boats will rush headlong to the uninviting beach. Three days of inadequate naval gunfire precede the assault waves. Despite Corps protests, the Marines are denied the requested *ten* days of shelling. Smith objects vehemently but the Navy is intractable.

During the "softening up" bombardment, attacking ships take a pasting from enemy guns secreted in Suribachi's ashy folds, many sailors dying in what amounts to point-blank action, especially aboard the daring squadron of vulnerable rocket ships. With the Navy's artillery booming overhead, pummeling the gray panorama, the Marines spin their way to the choppy surf. Corsairs and Hellcats continually dive upon the sandy approaches, prepping the battlefield. Huge, amber fireballs splatter the landing beaches, coded Green, Red, Yellow, Blue. Oddly the first waves come ashore virtually untouched. A smattering of token gunfire is all that greets them.

Had the seaborne barrage and aerial bombing subdued resistance? It is only after follow-up waves stumble onto the traction defying volcanic ash that the Japs cut loose. Howitzers and mortars had been registered onto virtually every square yard of beach, chopping the accumulated Marines to confetti. Skillfully, the enemy strategy has been to lure them in, and then deliver volleys of mortared steel and Nambu lead, raking the assault area in continuing sweeps, heaping maximum casualties on the bewildered leathernecks. As the tired expression goes, nowhere to run or hide. So they put their heads down and charge inland through the barrage. Marine casualties mount at a horrific rate. That first day 30,000 land on bloody Iwo, 2,500 die or are wounded. And it is only the beginning.

After much savage bloodletting 5th MarDiv's 28th Marine Regiment conquers Suribachi on February 23. Certainly the flag is raised that historic day, even though it still takes a while to toss the last Jap off the hill. As in earlier battles on islands long vanquished, many elect to remain in man-made caves and tunnel networks, ultimately grenaded or flamed, sealed for eternity. Suribachi, in effect, is transformed into a gigantic mausoleum entombing unknown numbers of Japan's brave.

A series of pre-conceived defensive lines and fallback positions typify action over the next three weeks. Cleverly designed at varying angles, the Japanese system of interlocking bunkers pours withering fire into flanks and front of penetrating Marines. Twenty-two enemy tanks blast into the American ranks. Over time, they are blown to bits by superior Shermans and accompanying infantry. Disciplined Japanese utilize the deliberately repetitive tactic of kill and retreat. However, Iwo is insular and, therefore, its perimeter limited. Eventually they will run out of real estate, backs to the closing sea. Soon futility will lash out in that most suicidal of military expedients, the banzai.

A hideous series of assaults and counter-attacks mark the action: Motoyama Plateau, Cushman's Pocket, Quarry Ridge, Turkey Knob, the Meat Grinder, Hill 362-A, and so on. Every pillbox and blockhouse represents desperate action, every cave, trench, and spider hole. Companies of marines ambushed in gorges are all but annihilated, existing on organizational tables only. Point men are swallowed up immediately, only to be replaced by others who are erased with equal alacrity. Ravines are choked by Japanese dead. Booby-trapped corpses block shallow gullies and jutting crags. Every step could be the last.

March 24 sees a pittance of diehard Nipponese clinging to a tiny enclave near the northwest coast. Two hundred of them are ultimately destroyed but not before they engulf a field hospital, causing many American deaths—but it is over. The entire cruddy island belongs to the Marine Corps. Even so, Iwo Jima's incredibly rugged and rippled topography, a virtual geologic labyrinth, still holds many hidden Japanese. Refusing surrender, 1,600 are hunted down and dispatched well into May. The gory arithmetic attests to the intensity of the Iwo battleground and the tenacious skill with which the Japanese chewed up the twenty-four USMC rifle battalions.* All told, the marines suffer almost 6,000 killed and 17,372 wounded, the total figure equating to one casualty for every Japanese slain.

Was marine command reckless in its commitment to an impatient frontal assault? Was the navy brass derelict in shelling the beaches for only three days rather than the requested ten? Embittered marines never forgive them for what they perceive to be a gross lack of support. Only the valor of marine combat troops and the gallant leadership of their non-coms and battlefield officers overcome rear echelon deficiencies in judgment. Of eighty Medals of Honor earned by USMC during World War II, twenty-two are won on Iwo Jima. In the final analysis, it is only through the Corps' indomitable fighting character that the island is taken. Perseverance driven by guts, fueled by *espirit de corps*, sees it through this costliest of marine victories. Admiral Nimitz pays magnificent tribute with his splendid accolade, "Uncommon valor was a common virtue."

DATE: DECEMBER, 1944

LOCATION: WESTERN EUROPEAN FRONT

Snow, freezing temperatures and a Wehrmacht staggering from hammer blows on two fronts mark the bitter European winter of 1944-45. A last ditch gamble commencing December 16 punches a large salient into the American line around the Ardennes. Its flesh and steel juggernaut slams

Author's Note: re Iwo Jima: Excerpted from Avery's West Point Military History, *pp 235:* The average casualty figure for the battalions was 687 killed, died and wounded. The 3rd Battalion/9th Marines suffered the least casualties–508; the 1st Battalion/26th Marines suffered the most—1,025. A line battalion normally had between 750 and 1,000 men injured. *Replacement casualties caused 1/26's figures to exceed its unit strength.*

toward the Meuse. Calm heads overcome consternation and panic, viewing the overextended thrust as an opportunity to destroy a huge portion of the German krieg machine. Early Nazi gains by three armies are soon stonewalled by heroic stands achieved by individuals and individual units of combat engineers, paratroopers, and infantry. Counterattacking Yank-armored infantry, supported with massive air cover, turn the ugly tide. Reacting swiftly, the dogged allies deflate the ominous wart, slaughtering and capturing many thousands comprising the now reeling panzer-infantry force. Their momentum crumbles, attrited to a retreating stampede. Enormous resources have been squandered, irreplaceable men and munitions which should have been husbanded to defend the enemy's last great natural barrier, the formidable River Rhine. In effect, Hitler's grandiose master stroke has gifted the western powers with a superb chance to demolish the Vaterland's final piston…which they do with great precision.

Fighting is especially brutal. By mid-January, the Americans and British have won a smashing victory. The Battle of the Bulge costs the Germans about 100,000 personnel casualties and upwards of 800 panzers. The now unstoppable Americans sustain 81,000 casualties and a number of tanks equal to the Jerries. The Brits lose 1,400 men while holding up their end. Eisenhower, Bradley, Hodges, and Patton are elated. Equally so are Montgomery and Horrocks commanding the English, Scots, Welsh, Canadians and other feisty commonwealth troops. The US First and Third Armies and British XXX Corps—victors of the Bulge, of countless junctions, bridgeheads, crossroads, cities and villages within the fuming Belgium-Luxembourg perimeter: Bastogne, St. Vith, Houffalize, Ortheuville, Malmedy, Laroche—will now roll to the great river.

January witnesses another significant success. Troops of US 7th Army acting in concert with the French 1st Army commence operations aimed at liquidating a small protuberance dubbed the Colmar Pocket. Lying within the Vosges Mountains in southern France, close to the German border, it holds a reduced sum of the Wehrmacht 17th Army. Again the combat is close and fierce. After roughly four weeks, the battered enemy withdraws across the Rhine, collapsing the pocket, enduring 36,000 casualties. The allied figure is approximately half that.

And throughout the grand breadth of Western Europe, beaten soldiers of the Reich are hammered across the frigid river, historic obstacle to invasion. By now boys in their mid-teens and wrinkled men have been integrated into the trenches. Hitler, ever insane, over-maddened by drugs, demands the impossible. A ruthless paranoia prevails, triggered by assassination attempts. Loyal and plotting generals are purged indiscriminately, along with "defeatists." His military judgment is impaired to stupidity, retarded to directives of "no retreat," regardless of circumstance. The suffering armies, underfed and outgunned, are termed "cowards."

Yet he is ever hopeful of a miracle, even with the Soviets advancing in great leaps across the Polish frontier. The relentless Russians pound away with a particularly cruel vengeance, payback for years of exterminative atrocities. Virtually all Germans view the eastern hordes as barbarians intent on raping grandmothers and daughters, on pillaging every vestige of culture. Therefore the Wehrmacht continues to fight with great motivation, despite shortages of rations and bullets. Manpower is dwindled to the point where some units, though represented by push-pins on the Fuhrerbunker map, are non-existent or understrengthed to ineffectiveness. Yet Adolf Hitler orders the phantom units about, refusing to recognize their dissolution. Like a teutonic spirit diffused through Wagnerian opera, Hitler insists the nation romantically fight on to extinction. He believes in divine intervention, mystical and inter-cosmic, will reward the German people for their patient fidelity. Only by suffering catastrophic tragedy will sweet rescue befall them. Consequently, his megalomania demands the country, and indeed the super race itself, be plunged into national mutilation. Berlin, Hamburg, Munich, Nuremberg, Frankfurt, Stuttgart, Koln and Dresden—stubbled and flamed to a molten maelstrom. Only a legacy of scorched residue will satisfy his demented logic.

March 7 presents the allies with an incredible stroke of good fortune. After meticulous German efforts to establish the Rhine as a defensive bulwark, they fail to blow the Ludendorff Bridge at Remagen. Onrushing soldiers of the 9th Armored Division capture the span intact. Several days later, Luftwaffe remnants destroy it but not before the US Army has punched lightning-quick divisions across the river. They fan out, seizing long stretches of river bank, enabling engineers to construct several pontoon bridges.

Before an enraged Hitler and the general staff can react, Fortress Germania is breached. Like the first crack in a crumbling dike, armor and self-propelled artillery pour deeply into the gouge, exploiting every success. Mechanized infantry swarm up and down the Rhine, overrunning German positions, rolling up the flanks. A Nazi counterattack by the Wehrmacht 7th Army is crushed. The Rhine defense buckles and folds like a punctured accordion. With the last great buffer surmounted, the Anglo-Americans poise to deliver the death blow. Three powerful Army groups, the 21st, 12th, and 6th, running from north to south, commanded respectively by Montgomery, Bradley and Devers, push hard into the ancient kingdoms and duchies of Saxony, Westphalia, Hesse, Baden-Wuerttemberg, and the Bavarian hinterland.

By early April, the western Allies are destroying the Ruhr pocket, perhaps the last dwindling resource of the Reich's once powerful industrial might. Beaten and weary, 325,000 prisoners are captured. In Italy, Mark Clark's 15th Army Group puts the Apennines behind them intruding the great Po plain. Forcing the river, they soon engage the vast Alpine redoubt, ultimately to penetrate the passes and valleys of Germany's annexed ally, Austria.

After a shattering siege which utterly reduces Berlin to smoldering mortar, the vindictive Red Army enters the crippled city. This, the last battle, is of immense scale. Marshal Zhukov's troops brutally slam through dregs of resistance. Uniformed German boys, some barely in their teens, take on tanks in blind response to Hitler's summoning. Regiments of Siberians drive through the rubble, gunning and grenading last stands of home guardsmen. The toll is awesome for combatants and civilians. By sunset May 2, the last bullets are fired.

An eerie aftermath of carnage and desolation replaces the thunder of weeks past. Hungry Berliners look to survive a demolished city devoid of food. Hitler and his wife of a few days have committed suicide, April 30. Among his last comments is a bitter castigation of the German people for having failed him in his battle against Bolshevism.

The instrument of unconditional surrender is signed the seventh of May by Germany's Admiral Friedeburg and General Jodl, military representatives of the politically bankrupt Reich. All hostilities are to end the next day at 2301 hours. May 9 witnesses final ratification of the surrender in Berlin. Another signing follows. Victory in Europe, "V-E Day," ends in quiet relief and somber celebration.

All resources, certainly America's manpower and arsenal, are turned to the Pacific and the unraveling yet deadly web of the rising sun.

311

CHAPTER XXVII
OKINAWA

DATE: WEDNESDAY, 18 APRIL 1945

TIME: 0845 HOURS

LOCATION: OKINAWA

"Luzak, get on down to Yontan Airfield and see if you can scrounge up a half dozen walkie-talkies. We've been shorted since day one. Same old crap. I guaranteed the X.O. that your larcenous soul would wheedle us a few." The speaker, Colonel Alan Shapley, commanding the 4th Marine Regiment, smiled a half squint at the hard-faced master gunnery sergeant. "See, S-4 claims there's not a spare radio left on the whole damn island, but you and I know better. Go wherever you've got to go, do whatever you must. Just get those radios!" Experience taught that master gunnies of the Old Breed have a particular capacity for locating difficult-to-come-by equipment. Men like Luzak could find a ruby in a scrotum if challenged.

"Aye, skipper." He was pleased to be leaving the immediate battle zone even for a few hours. The entire 6th Marine Division had been pushing north without respite since landing on Okinawa, Easter Sunday, April 1. His olive-drab utilities of herringbone twill, HBT, stunk with the malodor of masculine neglect, no more or less gamey than those around him. Still he found little solace in smelling as poorly as everyone else.

Readjusting the cloth camouflage cover surrounding his helmet, Tony Luzak set it atop the graying buzzsaw haircut and exited Shapley's tented command post. *Maybe I can grab a quick shower at Yontan. Those airdales always manage to rig up some kind of field shower.* As for the walkie-talkie negotiation, officially a Portable Radio Transmitter-Receiver, there was little doubt he could deal for them. But first he'd require some *wampum*, as Salty termed such media of exchange. Hidden within his shirt bulged a tropical-issue, rubberized canvas holster nestling a long-barreled 8mm semi-automatic Type 14 pistol/1925 model. Wampum! The souvenir had been lifted from a Japanese second lieutenant following the regiment's capture of Mount Yaetake, April 8. War prizes, especially pistols, commanded top dollar among support units and swabbies.

If the Philippines, and Luzon in particular, represented the *decisive battle* in the inscrutable mind of Japan's high command, then Okinawa would be *the final battle,* although no one knew it at the time. Operation Iceberg, the assault of Okinawa, purported to be the last step stone. From its coral beaches the empire's heart lay open, vulnerable to American invasion. Consequently, every available fighting ship and aircraft, including 1,900 Kamikazes, would be expended on behalf of Nippon, focused on the waters and skies around Okinawa.

The Ryuku chain of 140 islands is strung from Japan's southern home island of Kyushu, similar to how the Antilles stream into the Caribbean departing Florida and Cuba. For about 790 nautical miles, the Ryukus extend in a graceful, symmetrical arc like a samurai blade slicing the Pacific swells. Snaking in the shimmering East China Sea near the archipelago's midpoint reposes Okinawa, principal land mass of the chain, some sixty squiggly miles in vertical length. Bowing west at Okinawa's thickest width, the Motobu Peninsula protrudes for eighteen miles, pointing across a skinny channel to the lesser isle of Ie Shima. Below Motobu at Okinawa's narrow-most neck sits the two-mile-wide Ishikawa Isthmus, pinching the island's waist. An irregular coastline, defying simple analogy like tadpole or pork chop, corkscrews and serpentines in an exaggerated series of crooked coves and spits, indented estuaries, and craggy promontories. The land dips and undulates, especially the southern portion, affording the defender optimum concealment and substantial barriers to attack.

In total, the island's tidy rolling farms and parasol pines, its repetitive folds of horizontal ridges and hillsides of distinctive burial tombs, cover almost 470 square miles of the emperor's domain. On April Fools Day, four amphibious divisions, two each Army and Marine, splashed ashore, intent on ripping it from the emperor's embrace. Another infantry division, the 77th, seized a small island group, Kerama Retto, before it would storm Ie Shima, slaying 7,000 enemy in the process. By late April, the 77th would join the 1st and 6th Marine Divisions, along with the 7th and 96th US Infantry Divisions on Okinawa.

Offshore, the 2nd Marine and 27th Infantry Divisions bobbed in floating reserve. Ultimately the 27th and one regiment of 2nd MarDiv would enter the fracas. Protecting Hirohito's real estate stood General Ushijima's 32nd Army comprised of 77,000 Japanese troops and 20,000 Boeitai of the Okinawan Home Guard, bolstered by another 10-15,000 conscripts available for duty. Depending on who administered the head count, a force somewhere between 97,000 and 112,000 lurked the island's environs.

Luzak hitched a ride aboard an empty deuce-and-a-half rolling south to Yontan. The driver breathed easy, infinitely more relaxed after hauling volatile ammo to the 4th Marines. Too much heat or a seeing-eye bullet could blow the vehicle and trailer to cinders. The break in tension loosened his tongue, revealing a snatch of trivial information unique to him and testimony to the proficient War Department's ability to source war material across the varied breadth of American industry.

Both windows were cranked down and the cab's canvas roof rolled free, permitting a swirl of welcome ventilation. Bouncing along at 15 mph, Private Eugene Roper informed that this particular truck was not a Reo, Mack, or Dodge like most of his unit's transports, but a Curtiss Wright. "Can you believe that," he cackled, "a Curtiss fuckin' Wright! Hell, I thought they only made airplanes." True, Curtiss' principal contribution to the allied arsenal had been the P-40 Warhawk, but then again, General Motors was manufacturing Wildcats and Avengers under its Eastern Aircraft arm. Them that can, do!

Tony nodded, content to let Roper do the gabbing. But just to make sure, his eye lazily rolled toward the stamped copper plate riveted to the dusty dashboard. Beneath the vehicle specifications were stated its parentage and place of birth: CURTISSWRIGHT, SOUTH BEND, INDIANA. Luzak was interested, but not enough to marvel aloud. He tacitly grunted his awareness and gazed at the files of burdened infantrymen striding up both sides of the truck route, heading north to the rumblings of gunfire. And to the south even more detonations shook the spring air as soldiers and marines pressed hard against the formidable ridges approaching the Shuri line. Artillery duels marked much of that sector's action.

"And to beat it all," Roper rambled, "my Garand is a Smith-Corona! Every swingin' dick in Motor-T carries a Remington, Winchester, Marlin, or some other regular type gun-maker. But old Roper here has got himself a Smith-fuckin-Corona!" He howled aloud. "I'll bet I'm the only mother's son in the entire Marine Corps with an airplane for a truck and a goddamn typewriter for a rifle!"

Even a seen-it-all old salt like Master Gunnery Sergeant Luzak had to check this one out. He lifted Roper's M1 and spied the receiver where the manufacturer's name and serial number are punched. "Well, I'll be dipped in liquid shit if you ain't right, Roper. When they build the Marine Corps Hall of Fame in Quantico, I'll be one surprised war dog if your accomplishment isn't recognized on a silver fuckin' plaque!" Half mock, part jest, all hyperbole, veteran sergeants possess satirical expertise capable of deflating anyone's balloon. Grumpy sarcasm seems to grow in direct relation to each additional rocker sewn to the wearer's sleeve. By the day a sergeant's stripes peak at three up and four below, his ornery commentary, regardless of subject, will humble the most argumentative of barracks philosophers. Luzak had become skillfully versed in this art, honing it from Latin America to Shanghai, Manila, Brisbane, The Canal, Guam, and a host of backwater stations and ports domestic and abroad.

"Yessir, master gunny. That's me, a hall of fuckin' famer!" He swerved to avoid an oblong shell hole and lurched onto Yontan's littered access road, laughing as he spun the wheel. Perimeter guards waved them through and soon they rolled past rows of powerful USMC Hellcats of VMF-533(N) and VMF-542(N). The N stood for night fighter. Equipped with sophisticated APS-6 radar pods, Marine night fighters didn't have to make visual contact with targets to shoot them out of a moonless sky or soupy fog. Pilots of the rising sun spun into the choppy Pacific, never having seen their predatory adversary. Like raptors of the night, the two squadrons helped prevent enemy bomb runs on U.S. land installations and ships of the fleet prowling offshore. The newer Hellcat models featured a 2,200 horsepower brute of a radial engine, sporting eighteen cylinders. As the truck skirted the field, ground crews of VMF-542(N) worked on the burly cats, mechanics tinkering and fine-tuning under the hood, armorers cleaning and adjusting each's two 20mm cannons and quartet of dependable .50 caliber Brownings. At 366 mph, the Grumman Hellcat night fighter F6F-5N, soaring in the ink of night with bat-like accuracy, scared the kimonos off of Jap bomber crews. It goes without saying that one-way Kamikaze pilots flew in a hypnotic state beyond fear, unfazed by the night fighters. Their shadows disintegrated to a transparent pale the very same day they signed up for the outfit.

"Pull over here," Luzak instructed. Roper pumped the brake and pushed down on the clutch, allowing the gearshift to slide into neutral. Before the tires had crunched to a stop, Tony stepped out of the cab, signaling a young non-com supervising a ring of greasy mechanics. Wiping an oil-stained rag across his palms, Sergeant Lou Pinto approached the vehicle warily. Japanese infiltrators, some clad in American uniforms, had been known to strap explosives to their bodies and rush parked aircraft, detonating themselves while hugging the engine cowling... effective but messy, kind of foot-propelled kamikazes. Understandably, ground crews had become a bit skittish.

Bronze-skinned and sweating big beads, Pinto peeked at the driver to satisfy any leeriness yet harbored in a suspicious mind. Too many trusting mechanics had "bought the farm" stumbling on a shadowed figure thought to be friendly. VMF-542(N) had shown up at Yontan airstrip the very first day of Operation Iceberg, arriving directly after it was captured along with Kadena Field, farther south. The squadron had been flying out of Ulithi in the western Carolines before being summoned to Okinawa; so the veteran night fighters were no strangers to the unkind climate of the Ryukus. "What's the problem?" Pinto asked.

"Sergeant, where's the best damn supply area for radio communications equipment, and who's the senior NCO?" Luzak got right to the issue.

"We've only got one here at Yontan. Stay on this excuse for a road about three hundred yards until you reach the control tower. Actually it's more of a shack. Hang a right. There'll be four corrugated tin buildings beyond a wire fence. Go in the smallest structure and ask for Master Sergeant Guthrie. He's the supply honcho around these parts."

"Much obliged," Tony said. "And keep 'em flying."

"Semper fi."

In less than five minutes Tony had found his man and stated his business. "This is Marine Aviation, Luzak. We've no use for walkie-talkies, except for maybe them security Marines strung around the field." Jake Guthrie, twenty pounds overweight and wearing the cleanest HBT's on Okinawa, threw up his arms to emphasize the point. "Besides, if I had them, what makes you think I'd part with them? The Fourth Marines ain't exactly on flight status, if you know what I mean. Our inventory is for our Marine Air Wing exclusively!"

"Shit, I know that Guthrie. But I also know that if anyone is brilliant enough to get his hands on walkie-talkies, it's you. You got a rep!" (Until five minutes earlier, Tony had never heard of him.)

"Quit blowing smoke up my ass, Luzak. It's dryin' out my goddamn liver." Guthrie's bloodshot eyes rolled in a calculating glint, the art of the deal formulating in his conniving soul. "Even if I could get hold of a few, by breaking my sweet ass, why would it possibly be in my interest?"

Reeling him in like a fat trout, Luzak shook out a couple of Chesterfields. Jake took one and slipped the wrinkled cigarette between a pair of moist lips. Tony snapped a flame from his timeworn lighter bearing the embossed Chinese Dragon. "What will it take?"

By the time their horse-trading had cemented the transaction, Tony had "contracted" for a full dozen walkie-talkies in return for the Jap pistol—generously throwing in the form-fit holster, both as a sweetener and in exchange for a hot shower. Belly flags, helmets, bayonets, the usual crap were fairly easy to come by, but pistols and samurai swords weren't as common, exacting a high price in the clandestine craft of military requisition. More like barter than black marketing, it provided a system that by-passed the laborious, official distribution of needed items, shortcutting the bureaucracy and reams of paperwork… in triplicate!

The chubby master sergeant expeditiously disappeared, promising to return in a couple of hours. In all probability he was off somewhere dickering with a counterpart in communications supply, possibly someone who owed him a favor. More than likely, Guthrie was swapping excess inventory to another squadron in need. And so the network thrived, circuitously avoiding echelons of formal requisition forms and receipts.

While Tony luxuriated in the crude officers' shower, its construction negotiated from SeaBee entrepreneurs, he listened to the explosive thunder echoing from the south. He couldn't help but dwell on Captain Woodrow Luzak gutting it out with the Army's 96th Infantry Division. The 96th, or "Deadeyes," as they christened themselves, had been slugging the Nips since day one—"L-Day," the planners termed it. Solar-warmed water soothed his grimy skin. Thick streams cascaded from his scalp and gushed down the solid torso as he scrubbed neck and crotch in a soapless scour. It carried him back to Guadalcanal and salt water dunks that helped heal a body beaten by too many months in the jungled cesspool of the cruel Solomons. Something as simple, as basic as water, revitalized and extended therapeutic comfort beyond content.

A tinge of guilt played through his conscience as he considered the battalions of GI Joes and jarheads heaped in filth, duking it out with Ushijima's legions. But he quickly dismissed it, expunging the thought, shaking his dripping head violently to punctuate the effort.

Five days earlier, troops all over the island had been informed of Franklin Delano Roosevelt's death. Some men wept, others sat dumbstruck, while a few cursed or spat. In truth, most were so young they didn't know how to react. Few even bothered inquiring as to the identity of the succeeding president. Senator Harry Truman had been sworn in to his Vice Presidential term when men of the Tenth Army were at sea or scattered throughout remote atolls of the Pacific theater. For most of the young combatants, FDR had been the only president they could recall. His inspirational leadership had rallied their families through the ugly teeth of depression, and as commander-in-chief, imparted noble purpose to youthful lives wrapped in military khaki. After but eighty-three days in office, Truman inherited the awesome reins of government. He would grip them well.

"Sarge," a voice interrupted his musing. "Time to get out ricky-tick. You're pushing your luck. Them pilots don't cotton to NCOs using their shower stall, and there's a couple of 'em headin' this way."

Refreshed, Master Gunnery Sergeant Anton Luzak returned to Guthrie's supply shack minutes before a dented jeep from VMF-533(N) jerked to a dust-raising halt. Its driver, and sole passenger, wore the stenciled stripes of gunnery sergeant. Something familiar, not necessarily favorable, struck a note in Tony's brain, But he couldn't place the man's face, at least not yet. With a swaggering gait the newcomer entered the building and called out to a corporal processing a shipment of aviation parts. "Got an order I need filled on the hop." He held out a sheet of paper. "Make it happen!"

The pushy voice when married to the cocky face brought it home for Luzak. *Wilson? Walton? No, that's not it. Williams! Yeah, Williams. The same son-of-a- bitch who made that 'mud marine' crack back at Henderson Field on The Canal. Christ, that was over two-and-a-half years ago.* Tony kept his distance, not wishing to reveal himself even though it was doubtful Williams would recognize him.

Up the road, a three-quarter-ton truck, minus canvas, chugged toward the little complex of metal buildings, streaming a tail of coral dust. As it drew closer Tony could make out the moon face of Jake Guthrie set behind the dirty windshield. He pulled off the road surface to where the senior man stood with his TSMG slung over his square shoulder. Hopping out, he waved Luzak around to the rear and dropped the tailgate. A small wooden crate banded in flat baling wire and a smaller cardboard carton sat on the painted metal bed. "It's all here, twelve radios and a bonus box of batteries," Guthrie puffed. A prideful smile cracked his face. "Now, how about that pistol."

Luzak unbuttoned the utility shirt and slid out the holstered weapon jammed under his belt. Handing it over to Guthrie, he reached in a side pocket and withdrew a steel-blue rectangle. "A bonus magazine because you're so beautiful."

Guthrie took it and emitted a short chuckle. "How you gettin' back to your outfit?"

"I've got a jeep right over here. Give me a hand toting this shit over there." They lugged the crate and box to the vehicle and Luzak slid behind the wheel. Starting the engine, he gunned it a few times and jammed the floor shift into first gear. "It's been a slice of paradise doing business with you, Jake."

"Hey, this jeep belongs to V-M-F five-thirty-three N," he realized aloud.

"Yeah, there's a prick named Williams inside. When he asks, tell him an old 'mud marine' from The Canal borrowed it, and it'll be a frosty fuckin' day in Pensacola before he gets it back."

Guthrie laughed. In fact he howled. "Yeah, I know the smart-ass prick. And he's got it comin." He giggled again as he waved goodbye with the pistol.

"Adios." Luzak popped the clutch and roared off, purposely spewing a cloudy rooster tail. *Yeah, things have a way of getting even… although sometimes it takes over two-and-a-half years for payback.* Tony permitted himself a broad grin. He threw his head back and spit a wad straight up. It caught the wind and joined the dust stream. *Yeah, things have a way of getting even. Damn, I love the Marine Corps. Sure beats sellin' insurance in Cleveland.*

DATE: THURSDAY, 10 MAY 1945

TIME: 1230 HOURS

LOCATION: OKINAWA

Conical Hill lay directly in the path of the 96th Infantry Division's 383rd Infantry Regiment. Tomorrow its scrappy riflemen would jump off following a sunrise artillery pasting. Earlier they had blasted their way up the Maeda Escarpment, supported by flame-throwing Shermans, or "Zippos," as the fire-spitters were affectionately dubbed. And before that, they charged the Kakazu pocket, Tombstone Ridge, and Nishibaru Ridge, losing too many good men in the assaults. Southern Okinawa, characterized by a repetitive sequence of cross-island dorsals, had been reduced to a plodding killing ground, slow and deliberate, every square meter paid for in blood currency. Tomorrow would initiate another vicious chapter in the American push against General Ushijima's resistant Shuri Line.

Beyond Conical loomed Dick Hill, Sugar Hill, King Hill, Oboe Hill, Hen Hill, etcetera, all bisecting the battered island. The other Army and USMC divisions on line were up against a similar geographic pattern, tunneled and bunkered. Interlocking Nambu fire and registered mortar batteries marked every American advance. And when they got close enough, grenades and small-arms weaponry exacted a terrible toll. Overlapping the entire battlefield, Nipponese heavy artillery pounded away. Enemy counterattacks, usually after midnight, afforded zero rest for the fatigued assault regiments. And as always, suicidal banzais threatened to overwhelm even the most prepared. Psychological pressure became increasingly telling. Accordingly, casualties of the neuro-disorder variety multiplied as shell-shocked troops were subjected to horrid extremes week after week after bloody week.

At sea, angry waves of Kamikazes forced the issue. Most were obliterated by a formidable screen of Navy and Marine fighters, yet a handful slithered through, as did a number of bombers. Aboard the beleaguered fleet, anti-aircraft gunners cranked out a deadly hail of pom-pom flak and 50 cals. Still they came on like swarms of killer bees protecting the imperial hive. The sky hung thick with thousands of blackened ack ack clouds. Unflinching, the single-minded pilots zoomed through the suspended dark fuzz into arcs of Navy machine gun tracers. Like neon streaks, hot lead zipped over the East China Sea, seeking out the emperor's sky chariots. Incredibly, the Japanese would lose 7,800 aircraft over Okinawa and its insular waters. In their death dives a relative few, defying stacked odds, managed to plow through, slamming into vessels of the fleet. Thirty-four ships and small craft would be delivered to the ocean cellar… another 368 damaged, some severely beyond repair. By final count 4,900 blue jackets would perish and almost an equal number wounded, burned and riddled. American airplane losses will reach

763. It would be a gross understatement to say the sea and air war entwining Operation Iceberg was monumental. More like the colossal struggle of titans, its proportions rivaled those of mythic encounters. Irrespective of its ferocity, Okinawa, mercifully, was destined to be the World War's final pitched battle. But until it concluded, casualties soared.

For Woody Luzak, the upcoming assault of Conical Hill was just another position to be taken, one more cruddy hill. His heart swelled with thoughts of homecoming. How he longed for Swifty's embrace, for the touch of her sweet lips. He had celebrated Irene's second birthday midway round the globe, toasting her photograph with an aluminum canteen cup half full of C-Ration lemonade, the kind made from soluble yellow powder. Tepid and gritty, the undissolved crystals left a tangy residue on his lips, barely palatable. Brother Tony, he knew, was somewhere nearby. Having secured the island's northern half, 6th MarDiv had been relocated May 1 to Okinawa's principal front to help crack the Shuri redoubt. Five U.S. divisions, the Army's 7th, 96th, and 77th, in tandem with The Corps' 1st and 6th, clawed and scrapped, banging away at the tenacious Japanese. One division, at least, always rotated in reserve, using the "downtime" for rest and refit. The 27th had been pulled north, charged with maintaining security.

Soon spring rains would descend, a deluge like none had ever experienced. Visibility and traction would deteriorate to a sorrowful pittance. Mud, a trapping gruel of loose coral and topsoil, would collapse foxholes and protective pits, washing out paths, converting roads to canals. Tent pegs will float like wine corks, their canvas tarps whipped across the scarred landscape. Airfields would become virtually inoperable. But prior to the great flood, Conical Hill beckoned the Deadeyes.

Woody ran a toothbrush across the Garand peep sight which lay flat across his lap. He had long since disposed of the dinky carbine issued to officers of his stature. "Donate it to an ambulance crew," he sarcastically informed the battalion armorer. U.S. Rifle, Caliber 30 M1, in his mind, was the basic infantry weapon winning the close-in war. Most everyone agreed. Since initial familiarization at Aberdeen back in '41, his admiration for the rifle had grown to even a more lofty plateau, having witnessed its battlefield utilization, the ultimate test. Its proven superiority substantiated every claim he had ever advanced during bouts at Quantico. It amused him now that the Marine Corps thought of the Garand as theirs, its combat riflemen assuming the weapon to be the result of Quantico's foresight and ingenuity. Indeed the Japanese, whose weapons technology virtually ceased after Pearl Harbor, now recognized the inferiority of their primitive Arisaka, dwarfed by the Garand's firepower, range, and accuracy. Last month the dormant imperial bureaucracy got around to adopting a copycat version, identified as the Type 5, firing 7.7mm ammunition. But it was too late. The war had slipped away. Even with earlier acceptance it is doubtful that Japan's devastated industrial capacity could have produced the Type 5 in meaningful numbers. Prototypes of the weapon would end up in military museums labeled "experimental," curiosities for gunsmiths and historians.

On May 11, the 383rd Infantry kicked off its assault of Conical Hill. After vicious fighting, they cleaned out the Japanese defenders, both sides suffering heavy casualties. As was their practice, the enemy launched a violent counterattack on the thirteenth. Again, the combat proved particularly brutal. Despite the furious thrusts of Nipponese pledged to recapture the hill, the regiment held its costly won lump of cratered earth. Desperate units of fatalistic soldiers charged blindly into American guns, many welcoming the emptiness of death rather than another hour holed up in tremored bunkers. By May 15, Tenth Army declared Conical Hill secure. *On to the next crummy ridge!* Woody Luzak endured the battle. An inch here, an unsuspecting step there, one lucky, or unlucky mortar round could have made the difference between survival and a medic's statistic.

Post-combat exhaustion fell heavy on the men of his battalion and Luzak was no exception. GIs rolled into scratched out depressions and lapsed into a drug-like sleep, too beat to chink open a can of C-Ration stew, too fagged to take a whizz. Precious rest would come easy, unless of course the damned Japs laid in a few salvos. Individual replacements would come forward to fill out their depleted ranks, some to die before squad members ever learned their names. Tonight though, the doggies would sleep tight. In four days they'd have to assault King Hill.

DATE: MONDAY, 4 JUNE 1945

TIME: 0700 HOURS

LOCATION: OKINAWA

Six days past U.S. forces cracked the principal lines of Japanese resistance, symbolically signaled by capture of the ancient citadel Shuri Castle. Rubbled and smoking, its shattered walls admitted white-skinned invaders for the first time in their long history. As a partial consequence Ushijima accelerated withdrawal of his weakened but yet potent 32nd Army. As far as the overall U.S. land commander, Lieutenant General Simon Bolivar Buckner, was concerned, the pullback was both unexpected and gratifying. Actually enemy forward elements began giving up ground as early as May 22. Sensing a new momentum, American infantry and armor surged to fill the semi-vacuum.

Stubbornly, the Japanese fell back, fighting off pressing Shermans in the process, killing 153 of the steel monsters over the course of the great Okinawan battleground. By June 4, the Nipponese army had been tamped to the sack's bottom, occupying a jagged perimeter nine miles above the island's southern tip. The combined Army-Marine force relentlessly menaced the line, providing little opportunity for the gasping enemy to catch his breath. A major obstacle, however, threatened to impede Tenth Army's progress—the Oroku Peninsula, a phallic bulge jutting northwest, would have to be liquidated so that frontal assault troops wouldn't have to worry about enemy pressure on their rear flank. To secure the Oroku, the 4th Marines were tapped to storm the seething promontory via shore-to-shore amphibious assault across the narrow Kokuba estuary. LVTs, Landing Vehicle Tracked, would constitute the primary mode of travel, and 29th Marines would follow the 4th's lead over the exposed channel. Meanwhile, 6th MarDiv's other regiment, the 22nd Marines, would seal off the peninsula's base, converging to trap thousands of Japanese inside the bucket.

As the initial shock wave of roaring LVTs spun through the shallow Kokuba, it was met with light fire, mostly small arms. Grinding tracks bit into the flat sandbar spitting up clods of compacted earth. Jostled like dominoes, its cargo of marine riflemen poised in anticipation. A single amtrac chewed across the wet slime to a stretch of finer granulated sand. With a clanging jolt, the lumbering amphibian abruptly stopped, its conscientious gunner peppering the tree line with long, rippling bursts.

Tony Luzak gripped the lever controlling the hand operated ramp and let it fly. "Hit the beach!" he screamed as the rear-mounted ramp banged open. Tommy gun in hand, he raced out of the compartment and u-turned left to head inland. A split instant after he wheeled, a 7.7mm round skipped off the starboard bulkhead entering his skull just below the left eye. The sharp ping of jacketed lead on steel still reverberated as he pitched forward, ears deaf to the echoed hum. Nose down in coral grit, his brain ceased to function. Within minutes a corpsman rolled the motionless body and inspected the telling hole. He had seen too many dead these past few weeks not to recognize a fatal gunshot. *It's Luzak! Christ, I figured he was indestructible.*

He lay there for a while, the warm sum lapping his unflinching face, noble and handsome. As the tired expression goes, he never knew what hit him. No pain, no sensation, only instant darkness, his lights out for eternity. Master Gunnery Sergeant Anton Luzak, leatherneck of the fleet, China Marine, Navy Cross recipient, procurer of walkie-talkies, stalwart warrior of the Old Breed, was gone. With a lifetime of adventure and heroism enough to dazzle a scriptwriter, Tony had joined the phantoms of Corregidor and Bataan.

Full-blown and irresistible, June 5 saw the coming of a typhoon which tossed the great American armada like so many bathtub toys. It also swamped combatants struggling in the Oroku cauldron and along the collapsing Japanese front. Still the opposition, though futile, was as fierce as it had been two months earlier. The 7th of June saw dead and wounded Marines of the 4th and 29th regiments being evacuated back across the Kokuba River to the captive capital city of Naha. In a dilapidated municipal building serving as divisional morgue, Graves and Registration (G & R) marines functionally processed a flux of corpses rowed along the floor. One, segregated from the others, rested stiffly on a makeshift table, once an interior door. A shelter half-covered the face and shoulders, canvas point tucked under the webbed belt preventing it from slipping.

Slowly entering the littered hall, a haggard officer searched for someone in charge. Finally he settled on a Protestant chaplain gripping a King James Bible. "I'm Captain Luzak, here to view my brother."

"Captain Luzak, I'm Major Olsen. We've been expecting you."

"Yes, how do you do, sir," his voice whispered. "Colonel Shapley found out I was serving cross-island and was considerate enough to relay the news via my regimental command." He removed the grimy helmet, its cloth cover caked with the residue of battle. Woody reached out to shake the Marine padre's hand. They weakly squeezed palms, the captain preoccupied with an anonymous body elevated above the rest, boon-dockers pointed straight up. Instinctively he moved towards it. No one had to tell him it was Tony's bier. In the morgue's eerie gloom, diffused light streamed through a blown-out window, cutting through the dusty air. A sanctified quality pervaded the clutter. G&R men sidled about but their movement was undisturbing, voices subdued, like monks moving through a monastery.

"Yes, that's him," Olsen confirmed, picking up the stare. Woody said nothing, numbed by his brother's stillness and the presence of so many dead. Stepping to Tony, he lifted the tent cloth and lapped it in folds atop the waist, never taking his sad eyes off the face. Examining the square chin and tight lips, he reverently ran his hand over the strong nose and allowed his fingers to lay flat against the forehead partially covering the closed lids. Woody's lips moved in silent prayer, his pupils fixed on the purple puncture discoloring the socket. *Painless,* he thought. His memory sped through a medley of things past, boyhood conversations, surprise gifts from Shanghai, brandy and pigs ears in a Guadalcanal crate. Teary clouds welled and dribbled down his stubbled cheeks, falling on Tony's breast pocket, prompting the faded USMC stencil to appear brighter, the anchor and globe more vivid.

Major Olsen unbuttoned Tony's pocket flap and extracted a small, drawstring leather bag. "He was wearing this about his neck. I thought you might want it before the Graves people pack it with his other personal effects."

Silently the captain took the bag, rolling its soft chamois feel between his calloused fingers. Working open the closure, he allowed its contents to tumble onto his brother's chest. A Navy Cross, soiled with grit, the metal tarnished a dull green, dominated the mini-collection. Two polished stones of different sizes, one brown utility button, what appeared to be gut sutures, a small pearl, a lock of yellow-ribboned hair—Woody recognized the latter immediately. The golden brown curl belonged to Irene. An identical memoir, same yellow ribboning, had been mailed to him by Swifty. Evidently she had sent Tony a similar keepsake even though they had never met… and he had carried it close to his heart. Inconpicuous among the lot lay a shriveled leather clipping no larger than a chessboard piece, its arcane significance lost forever. And finally, the discolored gilt of a second lieutenant's bar faintly winked its presence.

"Do you wish to hang on to these, uh, contents?"

"No thank you, chaplain. But please make note to bury him with it all." He returned the little trove to the sack and drew the string tightly, replacing it in the pocket. "Was there anything else?"

"I'm not sure."

Respectfully as possible, Woody ran his hands inside the trouser pockets, searching for something his brother might want him to have, a keepsake to stimulate fraternal memory. Smooth and square, he felt its solid presence clinging to a crumpled pack of butts. Sandwiched between the cellophane wrapper and Chesterfield label, a silver cigarette lighter sporting a fierce Chinese dragon peered out at the solemn captain. His thumb glided across the beast's engraved head, and caressed the threatening face as if to say, you belong to me now. "I'll take this," he told the Major.

"I'm sure no one will object." Chaplain Olsen offered a sympathetic smile. "In a corps of heroes, your brother stood among the finest. Constant these men who sacrifice. Many the brave. Valiant the few."

Woody stared into the face one last time and bent to kiss the streaked forehead. He pressed his lips firm to the taut skin, holding it for three or four seconds, his eyes squeezed tightly in heavy grief. Replacing his helmet he wheeled to see every live eye in the morgue viewing his act of brotherhood. He nodded to them all, straightened his back and strode out the shambled doorway.

Ten days of savage combat squashed the Oroku purse, with over 4,000 Japanese slaughtered. On it went, Kunishi Ridge, Mezado Ridge, hillocks and depressions without names. On June 18, Lieutenant General Simon Bolivar Buckner, commander of the Tenth Army, final victory within his grasp, risked front-area mayhem to observe the freshly arrived 8th Marines (detached from 2nd MarDiv in the Marianas). He wished to be present for their early morning jump-off.

Compressed into a small enclave, the remnant enemy army yet possessed lethal capacity. Inevitable destruction awaited the hard-pressed defenders, growing numbers of whom began surrendering rather than succumb to fatalistic banzai or suicide. Most elected, however, to make a last stand. Waiting with subordinates at the regimental o.p., Buckner was about to confer with aides when a Japanese howitzer shell slammed into the earth off to their front. Flying shrapnel never touched him—but a jagged chunk of Ryuku coral blasted into the general's chest, denying him the champion laurel of final victory. His demise warranted swift promotion of the island's next-ranking officer. Lieutenant General Roy Geiger, USMC, would run the Tenth Army show for the succeeding five days.

On June 21, he declared Okinawa secured although several army battalions were yet administering the coup-de-grace in their active sector. Ushijima, his annihilated force existing only on war ministry maps, realized his ride with destiny was finished. He had overseen the extinction of 107,538 lives of the eradicated 32nd Army. Time-honored tradition demanded his being. Kneeling on a bluff overlooking the East China Sea, mid-day, June 22, true to his samurai code, Ushijima exacted the age-old ritual of hari-kiri. Number 107,539. Perhaps another 35,000 Okinawan civilians also perished in the brutal nightmare, gobbled up in the three months of non-stop savagery. No one is quite sure. The usual "mopping up" continued through June's end. Unnecessarily, the army's General Joseph Stilwell replaced Geiger at the finale, for reasons unexplained, though it smacked of inter-service one-upmanship.

At best estimate, Tenth Army casualty statistics were calculated as follows:

	US Army	USMC	TOTAL
KIA & MIA	4,052	3,561	7,613
WIA	15,348	16,459	31,807
Total Casualties	19,400	20,020	39,420

Additionally, Tenth Army suffered 26,221 non-battle casualties, most of them termed neuro-psychiatric. The latter represents the medical corps nomenclature for shell shock. Enemy gunners had massed a vast amount of artillery and mortar fire on American positions for most of the conflict. This continuous pounding crippled the minds of many, regardless how deep their burrows. Hardened troops, some veterans of other campaigns, unwillingly succumbed to emotional breakdown.

When U.S. ground casualties were lumped with the Navy's horrific losses, its gruesome total helped rationalize August's atomic bombings of Hiroshima and Nagasaki. In Washington, War Department statisticians computed a guesstimate of over one million American fatalities and wounded—should U.S. forces invade the home islands. The tenacious defense of Okinawa left no doubt that Operation Downfall, the storming of Japan, could up the butcher's bill to a seven digit figure. Nipponese military and civilian casualties might be triple that. So the decision was made.

Mushrooms of death enveloped two ill-fated cities, compelling the stunned emperor to sue for peace. By August 15, all hostilities ceased, and September 2 witnessed formal surrender in Tokyo Bay, aboard the battleship *Missouri*.

EPILOGUE

DATE: SATURDAY, 16 JUNE 1945

TIME: 1200 HOURS

LOCATION: LINDEN, NEW JERSEY

Dragging on a Pall Mall, sipping coffee, and lounging spread-legged in the noon sun, she watched the skinny Western Union messenger pedal his balloon tire bike up the slate sidewalk. Reading house numbers off posts and doors, he stopped pumping and lifted both knees free, resting them against the shiny handle bars, allowing the bicycle to coast. When he reached her front walkway, the red-headed youth, about fourteen years old, steered the red Schwinn up to the painted, wooden stairs. Stella, barefoot, wearing a sleeveless, orange print house dress, figured something was wrong. It wasn't so much a premonition as conditioned experience. Folks generally received telegrams in emergencies, notifications of the negative sort. She twisted uncomfortably in her gut, sensing the worst. *It's Tony. Must be. If Woody was in trouble, they'd inform Nancy, not me. Oh God, I hope he's only wounded, resting in a hospital. Maybe in Hawaii.*

Dismounting, he smoothly stepped down on the kickstand and let it rest. "Mrs. Stella Romanek?" he asked, the voice high-pitched and squeaky.

"Yes, I'm Mrs. Romanek."

"Telegram, ma'm. You'll have to sign for it. Company policy."

"Sure, sonny." Her tone sounded weak. Lips trembling, she scribbled her signature across the receipt. Red stood unmoving after she handed back the form and pencil stub, the look obvious. A gratuity was on his mind.

"Just a minute." She rose from her seat and entered the little house, screen door slamming hard. Hung on the heavy inside door, a small white pennant bordered in red, displaying two stacked blue stars, vibrated with the

329

impact. In about half a minute she came outside and handed him a dime, the going rate in 1945. Again, the door banged loudly.

"Thank you, ma'm." The silver coin disappeared into his knicker pocket. He expertly tucked the pencil behind a pointy ear. Red kicked up the stand, deftly swung a leg over the crossbar and hop-stepped the two-wheeler through a tight turn. Leisurely he went, whistling the Marine Hymn off-key and strident.

Stella flicked the butt towards the trim lawn and sat weightily, her well-rounded derrière plopping on the top stair, loose-fitting dress hiked knee high. Fumbling open the windowed envelope, she inhaled a deep, nervous breath and read slowly.

WESTERN UNION

NO 5 WA CK 75 GOVT WUX WASH DC JUN 16/1945
MRS STELLA ROMANEK 47 WENTON LANE/LINDEN NJ
DEEPLY REGRET TO INFORM YOU THAT YOUR BROTHER
MASTER GUNNERY SERGEANT ANTON LUZAK USMC WAS
KILLED IN ACTION IN THE PERFORMANCE OF HIS DUTY
AND IN THE SERVICE OF HIS COUNTRY. TO PREVENT
POSSIBLE AID TO OUR ENEMIES PLEASE DO NOT
DIVULGE THE NAME OF HIS SHIP OR STATION. PRESENT
SITUATION NECESSITATES INTERMENT TEMPORARILY
IN THE LOCATION WHERE DEATH OCCURRED, AND
YOU WILL BE NOTIFIED ACCORDINGLY. PLEASE ACCEPT
MY HEARTFELT SYMPATHY. LETTER FOLLOWS.

A VANDEGRIFT LIEUT GENERAL USMC COMMANDANT
US MARINE CORPS AM

Footnoted in tiny letters, a preprinted message from Western Union gratuitously mocked the gravity of Vandegrift's morbid revelation. *The company will appreciate suggestions from its patrons concerning its service.*

DATE: FRIDAY, 19 OCTOBER 1945

TIME: 1515 HOURS

LOCATION: CHICAGO, ILLINOIS

Tawny and shimmering, the bittersweet liquid rolled about the last melting ice cube. Reflecting the dim bar bulb, it sparkled like a wet diamond. He jiggled the dregs, causing the drink to swirl and slosh along the tumbler wall. His eyes became fixed on the action as melancholy remembrances drifted. After Corregidor, the Five-O-Three had been deployed to the southern Philippines, entering heavy combat on Negros. The unit was rumored to be departing the Orient via slow moving troopship late November, scheduled to disembark at Los Angeles around Christmas time. A parade and regimental review would follow at Camp Anza before the RCT was officially inactivated. But he wouldn't be there. For sure, he would not miss the steamy confines of sea transport—only two smells pervade troopship sleeping compartments, seasick vomit and ammonia, the latter used to purge the former.

Phil had hitched a ride aboard a B-29 en route to California a week ago, accumulating enough points to earn an early release. The point system took into account days spent in combat and awards, paramount among other lesser considerations.

Impressive strips of ribbons coupled with two theater participations and three campaigns more than satisfied his request for a quick trip stateside. He belted down the remaining half inch of Manhattan, chewing a hollow cube in the process. It was time to honor a pledge made eight months past. Phil Primo had been parked on Clancy's stool, a few city blocks from his destination, for an hour, using the time to fortify his thoughts, to recall events. He signaled the thin man polishing high ball glasses behind the bar. "How much do I owe you?" he asked, pulling out a five-spot.

"No charge," Clancy said. "On the house."

"It's not necessary," Phil softly demurred.

"I want to do it. Lost a nephew near Saint Lo." His slender jaw quivered as he lifted the empty tumbler and wiped down the bar, purposely avoiding contact with his patron's eyes. "Good luck to you."

"Much obliged." The stool squeaked as Phil rose. He reached for the oak and beveled glass door, half turning to the barman. "And I'm sorry about your nephew." He was about to add something like, *we lost a lot of good men,* but choked on the effort. Probably just as well, some sentiments had become superfluous beyond the trite, no matter how well intended the source. God knows, Phil had earned the right.

Tenements in big cities all look the same, grimy brick with raised stoops. Inside the hall, he checked the built-in mail box. *Callahan 3B.* Returning from school, a boy and girl, from the look of them probably brother and sister, entered the building. Clutching an armful of text books, the stuff of weekend homework, the eleven-year-old lad was awed by the husky paratrooper, bigger than life, the stuff of Warner-Pathe newsreels. Slate-blue eyes examined every aspect of the uniform. "Mister, you looking for Callahan?"

"Yes, I am."

"Two flights up. 3B. There's a gold star next to the door."

"Thanks."

The girl, a year younger, wearing the navy blue jumper of St. Margaret's School, whispered to her brother. He pushed her away. "My sister says to tell you he got killed."

"If you mean Nick Callahan, yes I know that. I'm here to see his mom."

"Oh, did you know him?" The inquisitive innocence of children makes it easier to answer their queries, more so than some nosy adults, forward and insensitive.

"Yes, he was my very good friend."

"We said prayers for him at school," the little girl piped in, wishing to add something. Her shyness had disappeared.

"That was very kind of you," Primo's voice cracked. "He would have been real happy so many nice kids cared to think about him."

The pair took the stairs two at a time, noisily racing along the second floor. They opened an apartment door and she yelled back, "Bye!"

"Bye," he whispered, audible only to himself.

The plump, gray-haired woman looked to be in her seventies, though Phil knew her to be around fifty-four from conversations he had with her son. Washed out, with sad, sunken eyes she asked, "Yes?"

"Mrs. Callahan?"

"Yes, I am she." A soft brogue accented her speech. She smoothed creases along the black wool skirt and gray cardigan.

"I'm Phil Primo, a friend of Nick." He clutched the airborne patched overseas cap, not realizing his jittery fingers were wringing it.

"Oh, the football player from Holy Cross. Nicholas often wrote about you, and always spoke well of your friendship." She opened the door broadly gesturing him to enter. "Please come in, Phil. I don't often get company except for the other children."

The furnishings were old and dull, but tidy. A framed photograph of Nick graced a small table, sharing space with an alabaster statue of the Virgin Mary. Dried Easter palms decorated the ensemble, reminiscent of so many shrine-like settings he had seen in Catholic and Orthodox homes back in Ansonia. He paused to register the smiling portrait. "He smiled a lot."

"Yes, he did." She held out a hand, encouraging Phil to be seated on a dark green, wing back chair. "Nick graduated from DePaul right here in Chicago." Her conversation was nervous. "It's a fine Catholic institution, as is Holy Cross, I'm sure. Mr. Callahan says Holy Cross has a fine football team. Of course he's partial to Notre Dame… the fighting Irish, you know. No offense." She smiled warmly and sat on the small sofa, smoothing a lace doily.

"None taken." He returned the smile, soft and caring. "I wanted to see you because your Nick was so special to me. In many ways he was like my kid brother."

"He was always the kid brother, Nicholas was the youngest of my brood."

"Yes, I know. He loved his family very much." The emotion was getting to the fullback. Better he get to the business of his call. "Mrs. Callahan, I was with Nick at the moment of his… " He couldn't get the words out. "… at the end. I held his hand as he passed on."

"That's good to know… I mean that he wasn't alone." She wiped a teary cheek. "Did he suffer much, Phil?"

"I don't believe so. No, no pain, I'm sure of it. He was relaxed, at peace. And I watched as a priest administered the last rites. The day was warm, but not steamy like it gets in the tropics most times. A little breeze was in the air, rolling off the water, brushing back Nick's hair. I remember it well. It will be with me forever." They shared a minute of silence, each in their own memories of Nicholas Callahan.

"I'm so pleased you came to see me, Phil." She reached out to hold both his rough hands. "Mothers try to visualize their children in times of joy and sorrow when they're away from home. Father Joyce calls it empathy. Sometimes our minds invent what we cannot see. After we received notification of

Nicholas' death, I always feared the worst… you know, I mean about him having to suffer. It's very comforting to be assured his death was serene."

"Yes, it was. It certainly was." Primo withdrew a white envelope and opened the tucked flap. "During those last moments Nick clutched this." He removed the worn scapular, pressing it gently into her hand. "Nick wanted you to know he wore it throughout it all. I promised to deliver it to you with his love. It was his final wish." The captain cleared the dryness from his throat brought on by the tender moment. "His last thoughts were of you."

A little cry escaped her throat. She held the cloth to lips and cheeks, kissing it many times, the salt of her tears mingling with Nick's dried sweat, perspired many months past on distant shores and in jungle depths.

Phil Primo kissed her as would his own mother and silently eased from the dim parlor. The shades were low, permitting but a few shadowed rays to dapple the carpet. Perhaps a piece of Nick's soul clung to the scapular, engendering a precious communion between mother and son. Frayed and pilled, the cloth represented a sort of spiritual homecoming. Mrs. Callahan continued to caress the flannel scrap, cooing softly as he slipped out the door.

DATE: THURSDAY, 20 DECEMBER 1945

TIME: 1900 HOURS

LOCATION: BRISBANE, AUSTRALIA

Whitfield-Pacific's newest and youngest vice president trotted up the gaily-flowered walkway, his gait almost a prance. How he enjoyed coming home to his little family. *Life is wonderful,* he thought. The sun shone low and brilliant, the waning ribbons of spring upon him. Post-war economy boomed as did his confidence. To date, Delane's contribution to W-P could generously be termed marginal—negligible might be more accurate. However, this morning had been especially rewarding. Word arrived that an American firm with whom he'd been dickering had committed for a substantial quantity of Merino wool.

The lead had originated with General Gordon Maxwell who had a friend, a former Marine, overseeing purchasing and shipping for a major New England mill. A deal like this would absolve him from pangs of nepotism.

Veteran and contemporary employees alike, though well meaning, invariably introduced him as "Jock's son-in-law," which annoyed him. It inferred a suggestion of tolerated incompetence. But it represented a tiny annoyance in a splendid opportunity.

Yes, things were moving well, the gods of fortune smiling beneficently on his path to happiness. Thanks to a few pulled strings also engineered by Maxwell, he had taken his military separation in Australia, to his parents' chagrin. He planned to visit them in February during a stateside business trip. Two months at Whitfield-Pacific had schooled him in the salesman's art of smoothing ruffled feathers. Mother and Father would require considerable preening.

"Is that you, Andy?" a voice called out from the kitchen.

"It sure is, gorgeous."

Outfitted in coffee slacks and buff yellow blouse, she entered the bright hallway, throwing arms around his neck. He wrapped his around Marla's slender waist. They smooched for an extended minute, hardly a perfunctory peck. Sensing a surge of passion building, she eased him away with a "later."

"Okay," he teased, "but don't forget."

"If I do, I'm absolutely certain you'll remind me." She playfully tapped a finger to his nose for emphasis.

"Anthony asleep?"

"Just put him down. He's been a holy terror all day."

"Must be genetic." Delane comically screwed up his mouth and forced a wide eyed look.

"Your side or mine?" She giggled, responding to his funny face.

"Yours, of course. After all, his insane Uncle Evan is a Whitfield! At least he was last time I checked."

"You make a bloody good argument, Yank."

"I love you," he said.

"I told you… later!" Marla flashed a seductive smile, the kind that turns husbands into obedient lap dogs.

Together they walked to the kitchen. "Any mail?" he asked.

"Almost forgot. A package arrived from your mom and dad. Probably a Christmas gift. I didn't open it because it's addressed to you… but I was tempted." About half the size of a shoe box, wrapped in plain brown paper, stickered "Air Mail/Par Avion," it sat atop the refrigerator. He recognized his mom's penmanship. Marla handed him the kitchen scissors and he quickly clipped the coarse twine, ripped off the wrapping paper, and opened the carton. Inside rested another box, colorful Filipino postage stamps filling most of the face. Taped to the surface a brief note met his eyes.

Dear Andy,

This package arrived for you on December 4—evidently the sender was unaware of your Australian address. Hope all is going well for you and family. Pass on our love to Marla and give Anthony plenty of hugs and kisses from Grandma and Gramps. The pictures Marla sent are wonderful. We miss you very much.

Love

Mom & Dad

Snipping again, he undid the second box. A nest of excelsior wood shavings cushioned a rotund cloth pouch. No note or return address accompanied the gift. By design, the sender chose to remain anonymous. Delane recognized its content immediately. A compass banded in filigreed silver, the workmanship exceptionally fine, rested in Andy's palm. The image of Rizal's face flashed through his mind. Weak-kneed, he dropped to a kitchen chair, gripping the graceful instrument, running fingertips along the glass face. He was speechless, touched by the memories it projected.

"What is it, Andy?" Marla moved close to him, sensing his change in mood.

"Snoozing upstairs…Anthony Whitfield Delane will grow up to be a fine man. Of that I'm confident. Hopefully he'll be as noble as the gentleman who carried this piece. No doubt he will understand the legacy of Whitfield and Delane. And someday this compass will be his, to remind him of Antonio Rizal, whose name he also bears."

ABOUT THE AUTHOR

Leonard A. "Len" Ferraguzzi, author, adman, entrepreneur, soldier, runner, historian, was reared primarily in Yonkers, NY, with a lot of growing up in Connecticut.

Following a stint in the US Army, he attended NYU, earning a Bachelor of Arts in History.

Along with his wife, Olga, he settled in Redding, CT, where they raised their family. Len currently lives in Florida.

52637579R00191

Made in the USA
Charleston, SC
23 February 2016